THE ★ GENERAL

THE ★ G

ENERAL

Patrick A. Davis

G. P. PUTNAM'S SONS
NEW YORK

G. P. Putnam's Sons
Publishers Since 1838
a member of
Penguin Putnam Inc.
200 Madison Avenue
New York, NY 10016

Library of Congress Cataloging-in-Publication Data

Davis, Patrick A.
    The general / Patrick A. Davis.
        p.   cm.
    ISBN 0-399-14411-0 (acid-free)
    I.   Title.
    PS3554.A937617G4   1998   97–49151 / CIP
    813'.54—dc21

Printed in the United States of America

10   9   8   7   6   5   4   3   2   1

This book is printed on acid-free paper. ∞

BOOK DESIGN BY RENATO STANISIC

To my parents, Bill and Betty Davis,
and my wife, Helen Davis,
whose faith in this book never wavered

Acknowledgments

My deepest appreciation to Dave Markl, my Air Force Academy classmate and fellow U-2 pilot, who didn't laugh when I said I wanted to be a writer; and to Eric Rush, Anton Wischik, Doug McInnes, and the rest of the gang from Sequim, Washington, who read, edited, and most of all, encouraged me to persevere.

A special thanks to my agent, Howard Pelham, the fine southern gentleman who has become both teacher and friend.

My gratitude to my editor, Christine Pepe, who patiently nurtured this novel throughout the publication process, and to the rest of the Putnam family for their faith in a new author.

My thanks also to Captain Doug Anderson and the staff of the Dallas/Fort Worth Flight Office of American Airlines for their support and understanding.

PROLOGUE

Thursday

I nodded to the rigid Marine sergeant standing by the door as I turned off the Pentagon's Eisenhower Hallway into the Office of the Secretary of Defense.

"Sir!" barked the Marine, his lips moving only barely, if at all.

Three good-size desks barely registered in the oversized reception area. The Secretary's executive officers, an Army brigadier general and a Navy captain, sat behind two of them. Both had phones stuck to their ears. A pleasant-looking woman in her thirties sat at the third desk. She looked up and smiled. I walked over and set my briefcase on the floor.

Before I could say anything, she glanced at the ID badge clipped to my lapel and asked, "May I help you, Colonel Jensen?"

I glanced at the nameplate on her desk. "I need to see Secretary Baines, Ms. Donner. The matter is urgent."

She was already shaking her head before I finished. Lowly Air Force lieutenant colonels don't stroll in and expect to be granted an audience with the Secretary.

"I'm sorry, Colonel. Secretary Baines's schedule is quite full." She looked toward the two officers. "Perhaps if you talked to—"

"No," I said sharply. "I must see the Secretary. Please, give him my name—Lieutenant Colonel Jensen, of the Air Force Office of Special Investigations."

Her mouth tightened. Out of the corner of my eye I saw the brigadier general cradle the phone and begin to rise. "Colonel," he growled, "what the—"

I didn't listen to the rest. Grabbing my briefcase, I walked rapidly past the general's desk toward a set of double doors.

"Sergeant!" bellowed the general.

The general grabbed my arm just as I opened the doors.

Secretary of Defense Robert Baines looked up from an enormous desk. He stared at me, frowning, his glasses on the end of his nose.

The general pulled at my arm. The Marine arrived and pointed his M-16 at my chest.

I'd had a lot of people point guns at me lately.

"Charlie!" boomed Secretary Baines, breaking into a slow grin. "What the hell are you up to now? Testing my security?"

The brigadier loosened his grip. "You know this man, sir?"

"Call off the dogs, General," Baines said, waving his hand. "Come in, Charlie."

I gave the general a smug look. He glared. I shut the door.

Baines came from behind the desk with an outstretched hand. "Christ, Charlie. How long's it been?"

"Seven years, Mr. Secretary."

I wanted to say "General." I still thought of him as Brigadier General Baines, the ex–fighter pilot I'd worked for when he'd been the head of the Air Force Office of Special Investigations. As we shook, I noticed his grip was still firm. And beneath his suit, he still had the athletic build, indicating he still found time to visit the gym.

"You look good, Charlie. Still have your hair, I see."

"You look good too, sir."

"Liar." He ran a hand over his thinning scalp. "Mine's been falling out by the handful ever since I took this damn job."

Baines nodded to a chair and took his seat behind the desk. He gave me a once-over with those slate-gray eyes I remembered so well. His face turned serious.

"How long were you my exec, Charlie?"

"Two years, sir."

Baines nodded. "Two years. Never known you to be impulsive."

I didn't say anything. I knew he wasn't referring to my barging into his office.

"You're in a lot of trouble, you know."

"You've heard, then, sir?"

Baines snorted, "Not like you've been exactly subtle." He shook his head. "You should have backed off."

I took a breath. Maybe I'd made a mistake coming here. "You know what happened at Cao Dinh?"

A nod. "I've seen the file."

"The file is a lie, sir."

Baines folded his hands. "Take my advice, Charlie. Let it go."

"General Watkins was murdered—"

"That's finished, Charlie."

"I know the truth, sir." I reached for my briefcase.

Baines's face turned hard. "Goddammit! You listening? No one wants to know the truth! We can't afford to know the truth!"

I slid a photograph across the desk.

"What's this?"

"The truth, sir."

Baines's eyes went down. He turned pale. "Is this . . . ?"

I nodded.

"My God!" Baines sat back heavily. "Where'd you get this?"

"A long story, sir."

Baines punched his intercom. "Lois, call Senator Burns. Cancel our lunch. And hold my calls." He looked at me. "Goddammit, Charlie! You just handed me a bucket of shit!"

"I know, sir."

Baines rose and walked to the portable black-lacquer bar in the corner, the same one he had when I'd worked for him. The bar was a trophy he'd collected flying F-4s out of Takli Air Base during the Vietnam War.

"Want a drink, Charlie?"

"Too early, sir."

"Better say yes. We're going to be here awhile."

"A scotch, then."

He made two drinks, gave me one, and returned to his desk. "I want to know everything, Charlie. Start at the beginning and leave nothing out."

I began with the phone call.

1

Monday

WE'D JUST FINISHED DINNER AT HOME AND I WAS HELPING MY WIFE, JEAN, WITH THE DISHES, HALF LISTENING TO THE EVENING NEWS from the portable TV on the fridge, when the phone rang. Tony, my fifteen-year-old, took the call in the living room. "For you, Dad!" he yelled.

My boss, Brigadier General Romer, Commander of the Air Force Office of Special Investigations, was on the line. That surprised me, since General Romer was supposed to be en route to Brussels for a NATO conference on terrorism.

"Hope I didn't interrupt dinner, Charlie," General Romer said.

"Just finished, sir."

"How are Jean and the kids?"

"They're fine, sir."

I braced myself. I knew the news was bad when General Romer engaged in small talk.

"Good. Look, my flight leaves in eight minutes, so I'll be brief. General Watkins was just found dead in his quarters at Fort Myer. Get your team over there ASAP."

I stiffened. General Watkins was the Air Force Chief of Staff, a member of the Joint Chiefs. "My God, sir! How—"

"Preliminary reports indicate a homicide."

"Jesus!"

Jean was watching me from the sink, shaking her head. Not again, her eyes said.

"I already talked to General Ferris at CID. I want you in charge of the investigation. As commander of the P-Directorate, this thing is right up your alley, but Ferris balked. Tippett's going to be primary. You watch him, Charlie. We can't mess this one up."

"Sir, Colonel Tippett is one of the best. He'll do fine."

"*Was* one of the best, Charlie. Look, I know you two are buddies. But you know damn well he's been slipping. The word is the guy's a drunk. Am I right?"

I was stunned. Romer wasn't someone normally tuned in to office gossip. "Look, sir, Colonel Tippett might have a drink every—"

"Yeah, I thought so. Watch Tippett, Charlie. Make sure he keeps that damned temper in check. We can't afford to have him pissing off any of the four-stars."

Me ride shotgun on Tippett? Fat chance. "I'll do my best, sir."

"You do that. . . . Damn, they're making the final boarding call. My office has the number where I'll be staying in Brussels. I want to know of any problems. Good luck, Charlie. You'll need it."

The phone went dead.

Jean started to say something. I held up a finger and punched the preset for the P-Directorate duty officer. Jean rolled her eyes in exasperation.

The P didn't stand for anything in particular, just one of those confusing military designations like D day. The P-Directorate had been created a year before to handle the OSI's high-profile and most demanding cases. We didn't worry about the routine stuff most OSI investigators were stuck with: the kid shoplifting a baseball mitt at a BX, the airman smoking a little weed in the barracks, or my personal favorite, the male fighter pilot who liked to sneak into his jet at night wearing panties and a bra.

"P-Directorate. Lieutenant Rickers."

Rickers was at the duty desk in the P-Directorate offices in a renovated BX building at Bolling Air Force Base. I told him to initiate a recall for the Response Team, staying on the phone as he ran the drill. Jean kept giving me disapproving looks as she finished stacking the dishes in the dishwasher. I sighed. The sudden call-out was what bothered Jean. After eighteen years of marriage, she still wasn't used to me running off at all hours.

My daughter Stacy was dancing that night in the annual teen talent show at the community center. The winner would get a five-grand education grant. I'd promised to attend. Now I'd miss her performance.

Stacy had been studying ballet since she was five, and she was quite good. A senior in high school, she had recently auditioned for Juilliard. We were still awaiting word on whether she'd been accepted for the following year.

"Everyone is notified, sir," Lieutenant Rickers said three minutes later.

"Thank you."

Jean was wiping her hands with a towel as I hung up. "You'll have to tell Stacy, Charles."

She always called me Charles when she was annoyed.

"I know, honey."

Jean hung the towel over the sink. "She'll be so disappointed, Charles."

At six-four and 210 pounds, I'm almost a foot taller and a hundred pounds heavier than Jean. I bent down, brushed blond strands away from her forehead, and planted a kiss on the tip of her pixie nose. "I love you."

"Hmm." After a moment, she smiled. "Get out of here, you big ape."

I grinned. Those three words were magic. I went upstairs to change, stopping by Stacy's room first. She was sitting on the floor in a blue spandex bodysuit, legs splayed in a painful-looking split. She looked up with a nervous smile, and I marveled again at how much Stacy resembled her mother. They both had long honey-blond hair, high cheekbones, and clear, green eyes. The main difference was their height: Stacy stood five-nine, with long fluid lines honed from her years of dedication to ballet.

"Hi, Dad."

I told her about the call. Her face fell. I, of course, felt terrible.

"I love you, pumpkin. I'd be there if I could."

"It's okay, Dad." She stared at the floor.

I never understood why those three words seemed to work only on Jean. I gave Stacy a bright smile. "Hey, you want to go look at cars this weekend?"

Her face immediately lit up. She'd been bugging me for a used car for six months, and I'd finally told her okay if she paid half. She had worked the summer as a checker at a nearby Giant grocery store, but she was still a thousand short for the red Ford Probe she wanted.

"You mean it?"

I nodded. "Knock 'em dead tonight, honey."

I went to my room and laid out a suit. In the OSI, we worked in civilian clothes because we found wearing our uniforms tended to hinder investigations. Enlisted men often felt intimidated if they knew the man questioning them was an officer, and officers under investigation often proved difficult if they knew the investigator grilling them was an enlisted man.

Frowning, I returned my suit to the closet and reached for my Air Force uniform. More than likely, the crime scene would be crawling with general officers. Experience told me they would want to know exactly whom they were talking to.

As I dressed, I realized that missing Stacy's dance recital was probably going to cost me about four thousand bucks.

Wetting a comb, I ran it through my hair, still mostly black except for flecks of gray just beginning to appear over the temples. A few years back, I might have been tempted to color it. But now, at forty-two with two teenage kids, somehow prolonging my youth didn't seem worth the effort.

I slid my 9mm pistol into my hip holster. As I left the room, I heard Stacy on the phone. She was describing the red Probe to someone.

Rush hour was winding down as I pulled onto I-95 northbound. I lived in Burke, Virginia, and the drive to Fort Myer, a few miles west of the Pentagon in Arlington, would take maybe twenty minutes. Settling back, I tried to recall what I knew about the dead man.

General Raymond Watkins, like most Air Force generals, was a pilot. Unlike most, he was also an ex-POW. He'd been the Air Force Chief of Staff for maybe six months, and had a reputation of being a real hard-nose type. I remembered Watkins had fired damn near everybody from the old chief's staff when he took over. I'd heard that Watkins thought his predecessor had run a loose ship. He figured the old staff would never adjust to his style. He'd also relieved three- and four-star generals from their posts during his first month. One three-star he'd canned was a long-time friend and ex-roommate from the Air Force Academy, which spoke volumes about Watkins.

A man like Watkins made enemies.

The publicity concerned me. The Washington press corps would scour General Watkins's death for any hint of scandal. But at least we didn't have the problems civilian cops had with leaks. We would be able to keep a lid on the story until we finished securing the crime scene.

I still held some hope that the prelim report was wrong and this would turn into a suicide. Sure would make life easier.

Truthfully, I was glad my office wasn't going to be the primary on the case. According to jurisdictional guidelines, where the crime occurred determined who ran the investigation. Since Fort Myer was an Army Post, the Army Criminal Investigations Division had the lead and the OSI would assist, which is why Tippett would call the shots. Contrary to what General Romer thought, as far as I was concerned Tippett was still the best.

Colonel Warren Tippett and I went back ten years. We'd worked dozens of cases together, and we got along like water and oil, always on each other's nerves. We disagreed on everything from the Redskins' chances each season to which service played the biggest role in ending the Gulf War. Tippett was ex–Special Forces, fiercely proud that he was one of the few colonels who'd never graduated from high school. He'd grown up dirt-poor, the oldest of something like ten kids. He had enlisted at age seventeen to get off his daddy's hog farm. He became an officer the hard way, going to night school between tours in Vietnam to earn a degree. I remembered the promotion party his wife, Dorothy, had given him four years earlier, when he'd pinned on the silver eagles of a full colonel. After everyone left, Tippett and I retired to his study with a bottle of Hennessy.

"I ever tell you what they called me at boot camp, Charlie?"

"No."

He leaned forward. "Pig fucker, Charlie. They called me a goddamn pig fucker." He took a large swallow, then looked at one of the silver eagles pinned to his shoulder. "I showed the bastards, Charlie."

I remembered thinking I finally understood Tippett.

Tippett gave me a crooked grin. "I'm gonna make fuckin' general someday, Charlie. Me, the pig fucker."

I nodded and smiled. Tippett was indeed on the fast track. His promotion to colonel had come a year earlier than normal. He was the commander of the Army's prestigious Washington, D.C., Criminal Investigations Division unit. I raised my glass in a toast. I knew nothing would stop him from getting a star.

I was wrong.

2

TIPPETT'S DIVORCE CAME A YEAR AGO.

JEAN CLUED ME IN TO THE POSSIBILITY. SHE SAID DOROTHY FELT Tippett was no longer interested in making the marriage work. At the time Tippett was working sixteen-hour days, and Dorothy wanted him to spend less time at work and more time with her and their two daughters.

I tried to tell Tippett he worked too hard. I suggested he take Dorothy on a cruise, offering to keep the girls while they were away. He didn't listen. Maybe he couldn't help being a hog farmer in pursuit of a star.

Tippett didn't contest anything in the divorce. After giving everything to Dorothy, he moved to a Crystal City high-rise a mile from the Pentagon. He quit coming by the house, and always seemed busy when I called.

Recently there have been rumors Tippett's been hitting the bottle hard. I heard he was showing up at work with booze on his breath. He also had a couple of cases tossed by the JAG because of procedural discrepancies in the investigation. Then I learned he'd been chewed out and almost fired by General Ferris, his boss. Out of concern for a friend and possibly to give him a chance to unload, I went by his apartment.

He was drinking.

He mentioned he'd been by to see his daughters and learned Dorothy was getting married again. He didn't say how much that affected him, but I could tell. He made himself another strong drink and told me something else. He told me General Ferris had given him a substandard rating on his annual performance report.

The implication was obvious. A substandard rating was the kiss of death. There would be no general's star for Tippett.

I told him I was sorry.

"Fuck them, Charlie!" he said savagely, the look in his eyes unnerving me. "Fuck Ferris and fuck the Army!"

He staggered into his bedroom, drink in hand, and shut the door. I waited fifteen minutes before I knocked. He didn't answer. I went home.

That episode was three weeks old now. I'd called him twice since and left messages. He didn't return the calls.

"Tippett just needs a good woman," Jean had told me repeatedly. "Set him up with one of our recently divorced neighbors," she advised.

Maybe I would. Despite our frequent disagreements, I still considered Tippett a close friend, even if the dumb bastard didn't know it.

★★★★

Fort Myer's Wright Gate was closed when I arrived, manned by two nervous-looking military policemen. I flashed my ID. The gate was quickly reopened and I was saluted through.

Most of the service chiefs lived in the six antebellum hilltop homes on the north end of Fort Myer. Appropriately, the homes looked down on the Iwo Jima Memorial to the north and Arlington National Cemetery to the east. I'd always thought that housing the service chiefs so close together was dumb. One car bomb could open up a lot of vacancies for four-star generals.

Driving through Fort Myer was like getting a quick lesson in military history. I cruised up Marshall past Stewart and Sherman to the top of the hill and turned right on Grant.

General Watkins's residence was second on the left. Vehicles with flashing lights lined the street, so I went around back and parked by the tennis courts, across from the four-car garage General Watkins shared with the house next door. A red Lexus was parked in the driveway. I cut across the manicured lawn to the front.

The house had one of those big, wraparound screen porches meant for sipping mint juleps and watching sunsets. I spotted two of my men by the wooden steps. They were surrounded by a half-dozen MPs and a few of Tippett's CID guys. Staff Sergeant Marsetti saw me and tapped Captain Furness. Marsetti and Furness were my criminologists. They wore suits with their badges clipped to a pocket.

Both were career men and well-trained, dependable investigators. Sergeant Marsetti was a handsome, dark-skinned Italian. Quite a ladies' man in a very correct sort of way. Captain Furness had an incisive mind. He brushed away the chaff and got to the heart of the matter. I valued both men highly. Like the other members of the five-man Response Team, I'd known them for years.

They nodded as I came up.

"Colonel Tippett's inside, sir," Furness said.

"Dr. Owens show up?"

Major Terry Owens was an M.E. out of the Armed Forces Institute of Pathology at Walter Reed.

"Inside, sir."

I nodded. Furness and Marsetti wouldn't go to work until Doc Owens finished and Tippett was done poking around. Then the evidence collection would be parceled out between Tippett's and my teams.

"How about Jonesy?"

Jonesy was Chief Master Sergeant Marion T. Jones the Third. Jonesy had been in the OSI twenty-six years and was my best investigator. I'd never heard anyone call him Marion.

"Checking the grounds, sir," Marsetti said. "And Captain Webster was here earlier. But Colonel Tippett sent him off someplace. Dunno where."

"Where's the body?"

"The study, on the second floor." Furness made a face. "It's a mess, they say."

"A mess?"

"So they say."

I had a bad feeling as I entered the house.

✯✯✯✯

I stepped off the second-floor landing into the doorway of the study and ran my eyes over the room. I saw one hell of a mess.

The room was designed and furnished to project the feeling of masculine elegance. The paneling was dark, and there were floor-to-ceiling bookshelves. The carpet was Air Force blue and very deep.

Books from the shelves to my left were tossed in a heap in the middle of the floor; the shelves to my right were untouched. Drawers from two file cabinets were overturned, their contents in a pile. A floor safe next to a computer printer stood open; files that had probably been inside were strewn in front. A desktop computer lay beside the safe. The monitor had been smashed.

This was no suicide.

I nodded to the CID man and the two sergeants in hospital whites who stood just inside the doorway. I'd never seen the CID man before. The two med techs belonged to Doc Owens. Two men crouched behind a large desk before the bay windows. I walked over to them.

One man looked up as I approached and quickly rose. He was short and thick, with a barrel chest that strained his jacket. Beneath a clean-shaven scalp, deep-set black eyes narrowed over a slightly off-center nose. His weathered face looked unusually flushed. I wondered if he'd been drinking before he'd received the call.

"About damn time you got here, Charlie," Tippett snapped. "And what's with the soldier suit? Trying to impress the big boys?"

"Jean sends you her love, Tip," I said dryly. I glanced down at the body. I was expecting to see the familiar chiseled face of the fifty-seven-year-old general. My stomach lurched. "Oh, Lord!"

"Yeah, some fucker really went to work on your boy with a knife," Tippett said.

I swallowed, trying to hide my horror as Doc Owens ran a latex-gloved finger inside the corpse's mouth. In my twenty years in the OSI, I'd seen people blown up, shot, strangled. But none of that came close to what I looked upon now.

General Watkins lay on his back. Eyelids, nose, and ears had been cut away, giving him a bloody, hideous jack-o'-lantern stare. His shirt was split, exposing a chest on which dime-size circles of skin had been peeled off. I thought of a bloody checkerboard.

Dr. Owens rose. He was small and soft-looking, and wore black-rimmed glasses that were too small for his round face. He took a couple of slow, deep breaths and shook his head.

"Colonel," he said to me.

I nodded, unable to take my eyes from the corpse.

"Whaddya got, Doc?" Tippett asked. As he spoke, he removed a packet of Red Man tobacco from his trousers pocket.

"The knife was unusually sharp," Owens said. "Could have been a long razor, or a scalpel. The cuts were made by someone who knew what he was doing. Very clean, almost surgical, removing just the epidermal layer to expose the nerve endings."

"Pretty obvious the guy was going for pain," mumbled Tippett, jamming a wad of tobacco into his mouth.

"Yeah," Owens said, giving Tippett a brief look of disgust. "Which is why the last cuts are so odd."

"Odd?" Tippett asked.

"The ones on the face." Owens pointed to these. "Bleeding was minimal. Seepage really."

"Watkins was dead when those were made?" I asked, finding my voice.

Owens nodded. "Problem is, I don't see a fatal wound."

"No stab wounds?" I asked.

Owens shook his head.

"So you've got no cause of death?" Tippett asked.

"A man his age and the excruciating pain he sustained, I'd guess cardiac arrest," Owens replied. "But I'll have to wait until I get him to the lab. I do know one thing . . ." His eyes shifted between Tippett and me. "You're dealing with a real sicko."

Tippett hesitated. "Maybe." He turned to the CID man by the door. "Hey, Lieutenant Dolenz, run down to the kitchen. Find me a paper cup or something."

"Yes, sir," Dolenz said, scooting out.

"How long's he been dead, Doc?" I asked.

"Body's near room temperature. Judging by the lividity, a couple of hours. I'll give you something specific later."

"I want the autopsy done tonight, Doc," Tippett said.

Owens let out a breath. "Just let me know when I can begin prepping the body for transport," he said, joining his men.

"Who found him, Tip?" I asked.

Tippett didn't reply. He crouched, chewing thoughtfully on the wad in his mouth, studying the corpse.

I went around the desk and squatted beside Tippett, careful to avoid the bloodstains in the carpet.

"Who found him?" I repeated.

"A Mrs. Gonzalez."

"Who's Mrs. Gonzalez?"

"Housekeeper." He pointed to one of Watkins's wrists. "See that?"

"Rope burns," I said. "On his feet, too."

"Somebody trussed him up good and tight so he could take his sweet time."

"You find any rope?"

"Not yet. Don't think we will. My guess is the killer brought the rope with him."

I nodded, knowing we were dealing with someone who was careful, smart, someone who had left nothing behind that could be remotely linked to him.

"Press is going to go nuts over this, Charlie," Tippett said.

"Yeah."

I was looking at the tiny welts. They appeared to wrap around the torso, from the upper chest to the waist. The horror sank in as I realized the killer had cinched something tight around the skin to cause bumps, then methodically sliced them off. I shivered, imagining the pain.

"You've never seen this before, huh?" Tippett asked.

I looked up, shocked. "Hell, no. Have you?"

Tippett paused. "Yeah. A long time ago."

He didn't elaborate, which was one of his most irritating quirks. He had a habit of drifting into a zone, rarely voicing what was on his mind until he'd thought things through about a hundred times. Even though I knew he wasn't conscious of this, I was still bugged. But over the years I'd learned he'd tell me eventually.

Lieutenant Dolenz appeared with a Dixie cup and cellular phone. He held them out to Tippett. "Captain Webster's on the line, sir."

Tippett and I rose. Tippett took both items, first spitting into the cup, and then putting the phone to his ear.

"Tippett. Yeah. Security should have a key. Just see if anything looks like it's been disturbed. And no one gets in. I don't care how many stars." He handed the phone back to Dolenz, then glanced to me. "I sent your boy Webster over to check out General Watkins's office."

"Fine."

Like most of the military brass, the service chiefs had a suite of offices on the Pentagon's E-ring. The E-ring was a perk for rank since, as the outermost ring, the offices afforded outside views.

Someone beyond the door announced the arrival of the photogs.

"Get their butts up here, ASAP," Tippett told Dolenz.

The lieutenant hurried out.

I considered the room's disarray. "When the techs finish, we'd better have a team search for whatever the killer was looking for."

"Yeah. Be a waste of time, though."

My eyes fell to the untouched books on the shelves to my right. I knew what Tippett was getting at. The killer hadn't finished the search for a reason. Probably because he found what he was looking for.

"Might get lucky."

Tippett shook his head. "Nothing in the rest of the house has been disturbed." He nodded to the corpse. "Watkins talked before he died, Charlie."

I glanced at Watkins's pain-etched face.

Tippett was right, of course.

★★★★

"So how'd the killer make the little cuts?" I asked Tippett. We were standing on the landing outside the room, watching Dolenz escort the two photographers into the study. One carried a 35mm Nikon; the other, a video camera.

"Used a fishnet," Tippett said.

"A fishnet," I repeated slowly. Wrapped tight, a fishnet would make the checkerboard bumps. "How do you know, Tip?"

But Tippett didn't answer. Turning to Dolenz, he said, "When the photogs are finished, give the green light to the criminologists and the techs. Tell Doc Owens he can have the body then, too."

I suddenly realized something odd. A four-star general, a member of the Joint Chiefs of Staff, was dead and no brass was poking around. I grabbed Tippett by the arm. "You did brief the big boys down the street?"

"Nobody in. All the generals have been in a meeting in the Tank all night. I got men interviewing the families."

The Tank was the Joint Chiefs' conference room in the Pentagon. "Did you contact the JCS, give them a heads-up?"

Tippett fired tobacco juice into the cup, shaking his head. "Relax, Charlie. I left a message with the watch officer about thirty minutes ago." He checked his watch. "Five bucks says they show in the next fifteen minutes."

"No bet. Wonder why General Watkins wasn't at the meeting?"

Tippett shrugged.

I was going to press him again on how he knew about the fishnet, but at that moment an MP ran up the stairs. He eyed us and came over. "Sir, the Wright Gate says they're on the way," he told Tippett.

"Who?" Tippett asked.

"The generals, sir."

Tippett spit his wad of tobacco into the Dixie cup, gave the cup to the MP, and headed for the stairs. The MP looked at me, shaking his head.

"You owe me five bucks, Charlie," Tippett said.

3

ACTUALLY, THE MP WAS WRONG. THERE WAS ONLY ONE GENERAL AND A FOUR-STAR ADMIRAL.

Tippett and I stood on the porch, watching through the screen as the Chairman of the Joint Chiefs, Air Force General Clayton Holmes, and the vice chairman, Admiral Henry Williams, emerged from a black staff car. Cars pulled up to the other homes, dropping off other members of the Joint Chiefs. At least they weren't going to gang up on us.

General Holmes led the way up the walk, limping noticeably on his left leg, Admiral Williams a couple of paces behind. Holmes was a gi-ant of a man, carrying at least two hundred and fifty pounds on a six-six frame. He had a regal-looking full head of close-cropped gray hair, accented by prominent cheeks that tapered to a square, determined jaw. In his Air Force uniform, with the four stars glittering on each shoulder and the six rows of fruit salad on his chest, he looked every bit the re-vered American soldier, which the polls showed he was. My eyes fell on the ribbon at the very top, the baby-blue one with the thirteen white stars. The Medal of Honor. I thought of the big box-office movie made a few years back, which showed how Holmes had earned that Medal of Honor.

Like General Watkins, Holmes had been a POW. Holmes and five others had escaped from a small prison near the Laotian border. Holmes and a second man had been the only ones to make it to the American lines; the others were either killed or captured. In the movie, the second man breaks his ankle and Holmes carries him on his back through the jungle for something like ten days—on the gimpy leg, no less, a gift from his North Vietnamese captors.

The Gulf War further enhanced General Holmes's reputation. He'd been Chairman of the Joint Chiefs when Iraq invaded Kuwait. He performed brilliantly and received the lion's share of credit for orchestrating the air war that led to the campaign's astonishing success.

I recalled also that the general was supposed to be wealthy, really big-time wealthy, from his family's oil business. Great wealth had heightened his legend, since he could have chosen the soft life.

"Holmes retires in a few months," I murmured. "A lot of people think he's going to run for president."

"Great," Tippett growled. "Just what we fucking need. Another politician." Tippett started forward. "Let's get this over with." We went down the steps.

After exchanging salutes, Holmes considered us for a moment from behind gold-rimmed glasses. "What can you tell me, Colonel?"

He was looking at me when he spoke, probably because of my Air Force uniform. "I only just arrived, sir." I glanced at Tippett. "Colonel Tippett is handling the case."

"Not much, sir," Tippett said. "Too early. We're just beginning the investigation of the crime scene."

"So you have no suspects?"

"No." Tippett let out a deep breath. "Too early for that, too, sir."

"But you're sure it's a homicide?"

"Oh, yes, sir. We have a murder, all right."

"I'd like to see the body," Holmes said. His tone indicated the statement was a command.

Tippett hesitated. He hated anyone waltzing into a crime scene, and he had never been intimidated by rank. For a moment, I thought he was going to protest.

The admiral, a heavyset man with a ruddy face and big ears, grunted sharply. "Colonel, I suggest—"

"Easy, Hank," said Holmes. To Tippett, he said, "I understand your caution, Colonel. But General Watkins and I were very close. We were both POWs and—"

Tippett abruptly turned and led the way into the house.

★★★★

"Take five, guys," Tippett said as we entered the study.

Everyone stepped by to let us pass. A few looked awed at the sight of General Holmes. Doc Owens was standing over the body, watching his men tape plastic bags over Watkins's hands and feet. Owens murmured something. His men stood and moved back.

General Holmes walked around the desk slowly. Admiral Williams followed.

"Careful of the blood, General," Owens said.

Tippett and I hung back a few paces. Lieutenant Dolenz came over, face flushed with excitement. He whispered something to Tippett about missing disks. I caught most of it.

"You sure?" Tippett asked.

Dolenz's head bobbed up and down.

"Good boy," Tippett said.

Finally, I thought, feeling a little excited myself.

General Holmes stared at Watkins for a full thirty seconds, showing no reaction. Admiral Williams, on the other hand, immediately turned pale and stepped quickly back. I heard him say "damn" a couple of times as he wiped perspiration from his face.

"Maybe that squid bastard will puke," Tippett whispered.

Holmes turned to us, his face still blank. Tippett and I walked over to him.

"Who knows about this?" Holmes asked.

Tippett furrowed his brow. "No one, other than the investigation teams, your staff, the generals' families, and Mrs. Gonzalez and Major Swanson."

"Swanson? General Watkins's aide?"

"Major Swanson was called by Mrs. Gonzalez after she discovered the body, sir," Tippett said.

"That's all?"

"Yes, sir."

Holmes lowered his voice. "I want you to keep this quiet. I'll let you know when you can release the story."

I glanced at Tippett. We both knew what the general was really saying. He wanted time to brief the power brokers on Capitol Hill and the White House. He wanted to come up with a story to offset the inevitable torrent of speculation about the brutal murder of a member of the Joint Chiefs of Staff.

"Yes, sir," Tippett said. "But the FBI will know something has happened. We use their forensics lab to conduct crime-scene analysis."

"I'll call Director Farnsworth to ensure there are no leaks." Holmes's eyes drifted around the room. "What was the killer looking for?"

"Information, I'd guess," Tippett said. "On something the general was working on."

Holmes's eyebrows arched a quarter inch. "Information? Such as?"

"I don't know, sir, but that seems logical because of the disks."

Holmes was looking confused and annoyed. "What the hell are you getting at, Colonel?"

Tippett casually pointed to the computer on the floor. "There are no disks for that thing in here, sir." He glanced at Holmes. "There should be."

Holmes and Admiral Williams eyed the mess strewn on the floor. There were papers, files, pencils, and photos everywhere. But no disks.

"Another thing, sir." Tippett walked to the computer. Reaching into a pocket, he removed latex gloves and pulled them on. The metal cover on the hard drive was slightly askew and had obviously been loosened. Tippett knelt and raised the cover, exposing the interior. "Someone went to the trouble of removing the hard drive, sir." He glanced at Admiral Williams, then General Holmes, eyes questioning.

The room became quiet.

"I see," Holmes said slowly. "Well done, Colonel." Holmes glanced at me. "I want a daily brief on your progress."

"Yes, sir."

The two four-stars headed for the door. "General Holmes," Tippett said to their backs.

Both men stopped and turned. "Yes?" Holmes asked.

"I'll need to talk to you, sir, and the rest of the Joint Chiefs. And the staffs."

"Tomorrow, Colonel," Holmes said coolly. "My office, 1500 hours." He left, Admiral Williams on his heels.

"So you think Holmes and Williams knew what Watkins was working on?" I asked Tippett.

"Don't you?"

"Sure. Might not tell us, though, depending on the security classification."

Tippett shook his head. "No. They have to give us something. This is too big."

I didn't reply. But I thought Tippett was wrong. They were four-star generals and this was the military. They didn't have to say a damn thing.

I went over to a phone on a desk. "Anyone check this out?" I hollered.

Furness answered. "Not yet, sir."

The phone had a speaker button. I punched the button with the tip of a pen and pushed the redial. The phone flashed through a series of beeps and began to ring. A woman answered. She had a thick, nasal accent.

"Hello. Little Saigon Tearoom. May I help you, please?"

I frowned, my eyes going to Tippett. He looked surprised.

"Where are you located?" I asked.

She told me.

"You want a reservation, sir?"

"No."

Tippett stepped near and said something into the phone in a language I didn't understand. The woman replied. Tippett said something else and then nodded to me. I punched the speaker button and hung up.

"Think the general likes Vietnamese food?" Tippett asked.

"How should I know?"

"Maybe we should ask Major Swanson." Then he winked.

★★★★

"Was that Vietnamese you were speaking?" I asked as we reached the stairwell. I knew Tippett had learned Vietnamese when he'd been a Special Forces liaison with the South Vietnamese Army during the war.

"Yeah. Little rusty. But I think I understood what she was saying."

"Who?"

"Miss Vinh."

"So the last call General Watkins made before he died was to a Vietnamese restaurant. Don't you think that's strange?" I asked.

He looked at me, perplexed. "Not at all."

"You knew what was programmed on redial?" I asked.

"No, but I expected a Vietnamese connection to come up. I just didn't expect to find it so soon."

"Why?"

We went down the stairs.

"Because of the mutilation, Charlie. Particularly on the face and the use of a fishnet to skin Watkins. That was an old trick of the Vietcong, their variation of the Chinese 'death by a thousand cuts.' When they captured our guys, the Cong tied them to trees and stripped them. Then they wrapped fishnet around their bodies, forcing the skin to come through. Get their fucking jollies by scaling them like goddamn fish, slicing off pieces of skin a quarter inch at a time. I've heard guys scream for hours, begging to die. But we couldn't get to them. Their version of psychological warfare. Twice, when the Cong pulled out, I found boys still alive, ears and nose and dicks jammed down their throats. Those gook bastards wouldn't even kill them."

We'd reached the first floor. I stopped, feeling sick. "What did you do?"

"About the boys?"

I nodded.

Tippett stared at me for a long time. "What the hell do you think?" he said softly.

As Tippett talked with one of his men, I stepped outside for a few minutes.

I needed air.

4

I RETURNED TO THE FOYER. TIPPETT WAS STILL TALKING TO ONE OF HIS MEN. THE NIGHT AIR HAD MADE ME FEEL BETTER. I PEERED INTO the formal living room. The chamber was spacious, with polished wood floors accented by an enormous carpet depicting a blue dragon breathing fire. The furnishings consisted of a white leather couch, two armchairs with matching ottomans, a recliner, and a love seat, all spaced around a black-lacquer coffee table. The walls were adorned with Asian paintings, mostly bamboo stalks with birds, or scenes of women in Japanese kimonos.

My pulse quickened as I focused on the female major sitting on the couch. She talked softly to a black man at her side. I smiled. Jonesy was already a step ahead of everyone else.

"Watkins's vehicles look clean," Tippett said, walking up. "Tow trucks are on the way."

I didn't reply.

"Major Talia Swanson. Hell of a looker, eh?"

I nodded. Even in her unflattering Air Force uniform, Major Swanson was indeed a looker. Her blond hair was cut stylishly short, revealing tanned, flawless skin and the high cheekbones of a classic Nordic beauty. Her eyes were large and blue, and fixed on Jonesy as she chewed worriedly on her lower lip. She nodded at something he said, then glanced at us and smiled sadly.

"Where is the maid, Mrs. Gonzalez?" I asked,

"Doc Owens had her taken to the hospital. She's in severe shock. I talked to her briefly but couldn't get much out of her."

At that moment, Jonesy noticed us and quickly came over.

When I had taken command of the P-Directorate, the first thing I did was make Master Sergeant Marion T. Jones the chief of investigations, a position normally reserved for the second-highest-ranking officer. No one in the unit complained. They knew Jonesy was good. The guy had a master's in criminology from Maryland, and more investigative experience than everyone else put together. But the OSI brass didn't like it.

"Goddammit, Charlie, he's an enlisted man," General Romer had said.

I stood my ground. In the next six months, Jonesy busted a ring of Air Force mechanics smuggling drugs on military jets coming into Andrews AFB from Panama. Next, he ferreted out a lieutenant colonel in the Pentagon who'd been using dummy defense contracting accounts to embezzle thousands of dollars.

General Romer never complained about Jonesy again.

"Find out anything?" I asked Jonesy.

He ran a hand over his close-cropped graying hair as he referred to a notepad. He was tall, thin to the point of gaunt, with long arms and legs that gave him a slightly disjointed appearance. He had a friendly, unassuming face that matched his quiet, efficient demeanor. The E.F. Hutton television commercial of a few years back characterized his style. He didn't talk much, but when he did, people listened.

"Not much, sir," he said. "Major Swanson says she got a call from Mrs. Gonzalez at around 1915 on her cellular phone. Said Mrs. Gonzalez was hysterical. Kept repeating Watkins's name. So Major Swanson drove right over."

"Were the MPs notified then?" I asked.

Jonesy shook his head. "Apparently Major Swanson was only a few blocks away. She was on her way here for a 1930 meeting with the general. She says she decided she'd better see what had happened first before raising an alarm." He paused. "Mrs. Gonzalez doesn't speak English very well, and the major couldn't make heads or tails of what she was saying."

I nodded.

"Major Swanson had a meeting tonight with the general?" Tippett asked.

"Yes, sir. General Watkins called her at the office at 1700. Said she was to show up here at 1930."

"Swanson say where Watkins was calling from?" Tippett asked.

"No, sir."

Tippett looked at the major. "She know what the general wanted?"

"Major Swanson says the general was in the habit of calling her up in the evenings to come over and prepare correspondence to get out the next day."

Major Swanson was staring at us, squeezing the flight cap in her hands. I could see puffiness around her eyes.

"I'll just bet he was," Tippett said dryly.

"Watkins was a widower, wasn't he?" I asked.

"Wife passed away last year," replied Tippett.

"So the general lived alone?"

Jonesy shook his head. "According to Major Swanson, Mrs. Gonzalez usually stayed here five days a week—Monday through Friday. Her bedroom is on the second floor. This week she asked for an extra couple of days off to visit a sick sister. She wasn't supposed to return until sometime tomorrow." He flipped a page on the notepad. "Then there's a Mrs. Greer. A cook. Only works part-time. If the general's entertaining."

"Any relatives? Children in the area?" I asked.

"The general has a daughter," Jonesy said. "She attends a school in Paris. Studying fashion or art. Major Swanson says the daughter visited a few months back. And you know about the general's wife passing away." Jonesy closed the notepad.

"Got the phone numbers and addresses of the daughter and the cook?" Tippett asked.

"Yes, sir. From Major Swanson."

"Give Lieutenant Dolenz a copy."

"Find anything outside?" I asked.

Jonesy shook his head. "Windows were secure. Side and back doors locked. No sign of forced entry anywhere, sir."

"Was the general in the habit of locking the doors when he was in?" I asked.

"No, sir," Jonesy said.

"So someone could have walked in."

"Or been let in, sir," Jonesy said.

Tippett headed for Swanson.

"Thanks," I told Jonesy.

✯✯✯✯

I sat on the love seat across from Major Swanson. Tippett joined her on the couch.

Major Swanson spoke softly, pausing often to suck on her lower lip. She told us she'd been working for the general for almost two years. She'd been his aide-de-camp at Hickam Air Force Base, Hawaii, where he'd been the Commander, Pacific Air Force. She'd jumped at the chance to accompany him to Washington.

"Most people thought General Watkins was difficult to work for, but . . ." she swallowed hard, "but I liked it. He was very good to me."

"You arrived at 1923?" Tippett asked.

She nodded. "I rang the bell. There was no answer. I found Mrs. Gonzalez in here. She was crying, saying things. Unbelievable things . . ."

I asked, "Was the door unlocked?"

She nodded. "When either Mrs. Gonzalez or the general is home, the front door is never locked. But I could have let myself in. I have a key."

"What did you do next?" Tippett asked.

"I . . . I went to the study." She leaned back against the couch, staring at her hands clasped together in her lap. "It was horrible."

"Did Mrs. Gonzalez accompany you?" I asked.

Major Swanson shook her head. Her mouth trembled.

Tippett and I said nothing for a few moments. Then, gently, I asked, "When was the last time you saw the general?" I almost added, "alive."

"Around . . . around 1400 hours." Her eyes misted. "At the office. He left for a meeting."

"What meeting?"

"I don't know."

My eyebrows went up on that one. Aides almost always had their general's schedule memorized. This was one of their primary duties. Make sure the constellations got to where they were supposed to go.

"Does anyone know where he went?" I asked.

"Sergeant Randolph does, I'm sure. His driver." She picked up the plain black handbag at her feet. "I have his number."

"Thank you," I said. As she pulled out one of those little electronic organizers that looked like a calculator, I asked, "Was the meeting planned?"

She punched an entry into the organizer. "No. I think something just came up." She handed the organizer to me.

"Why do you think that?" I asked, putting the organizer on the coffee table. I removed a notepad from my shirt pocket.

She began tapping her right foot. "The meeting wasn't on his schedule, and . . . and, well, he'd been preoccupied for the past few days."

Tippett leaned closer. "Preoccupied? Why?"

"Working on something. He didn't say. But he'd canceled meetings, appointments."

"Including tonight's meeting in the Tank?"

She nodded. "But not until shortly before he left the office. That's why I think the meeting he went to must have been unplanned."

"Would you know if he was working on a classified project?" I asked.

She sounded tired. "Colonel, almost everything we work on is classified."

"So you're saying you would know? Even highly sensitive items?"

"That's our job, Colonel. We all have Top Secret, compartmentalized clearances. We prepared General Watkins's briefings and papers."

I handed her back her organizer. "We?"

"The staff. Colonel Jowers and Colonel Ryerson, the execs, Mrs. Moffitt, the secretary, Major Laura Parker, and the admin people. And myself."

"Odd that General Watkins kept what he was working on from the staff," I said.

She nodded. Her voice cracked. "Especially me. I'd been with him the longest. Since before his wife died. He'd tell me things he didn't tell the others. Not just about work. Personal things." Her eyes welled. I fished into my pocket for my handkerchief.

"Thanks," she said, taking it.

"Did the general like Vietnamese food?" I asked.

Swanson was dabbing her eyes. She stopped, her head popping up, almost as if the question startled her.

"Just tell us the name of a restaurant he frequented," Tippett said quickly.

I frowned. Tippett almost sounded as if he was giving Major Swanson an order.

Swanson's eyes lingered on Tippett for a moment. "There is a place he went sometimes. The Canton Café. In Bethesda."

"That's Chinese," I said. "We want to know about a place called the Little Saigon Tearoom."

Her eyes went to Tippett, then back to me. "I've never heard him mention such a place."

"Never?" I asked. "Think hard."

"Uh, Charlie." Tippett was pointing at my notepad. "Why don't you check with the driver?"

I hesitated.

"He might know something useful."

I shrugged. "Sure, Tip."

When I reached the foyer, I looked back. Tippett was huddled close, saying something to Swanson. What, I asked myself, had he not wanted me to hear?

I watched them for a moment.

★★★★

Sergeant Randolph answered on the second ring. I could hear a baby crying in the background. He sounded young, and very tired. After I identified myself, he immediately became wary. I understood. Most people in the Air Force looked upon the OSI as the bad guys, the ones who get their rocks off busting people.

After telling him why I'd called, I gave him time to collect himself. He took almost thirty seconds. He now sounded nervous, almost scared. "What do you want with me, sir?"

The baby was crying more loudly. A woman called out, "Johnny, we're out of Pampers."

"Honey, I'm—" Sergeant Randolph covered the phone. He came back a few moments later.

"How old?" I asked.

"Sir?"

"The baby."

"Uh, six months, sir."

"Your first?"

"Yes, sir. Name's Rachel."

"Sounds like she's got some strong lungs."

I could almost hear him relax. "Oh, yes, sir. Don't know how she does it. All that noise, being so small and all."

The baby let out a shriek.

"Johnny!" the woman called.

"Sounds like you need to go, so I'll make this quick, Sergeant. When you picked up the general this afternoon at the Pentagon, where did you go?"

"Why, his quarters, sir. I dropped him off at around 1420."

"Then where did you take him?"

"No place, sir. The general told me he wouldn't need me the rest of the day. I left."

I paused. This didn't make sense. "Was anyone waiting at his quarters?"

"Not that I saw, sir. But I didn't go inside."

"Any cars parked along the street you didn't recognize?"

"I . . . I don't remember any. But I wasn't really looking."

"You saw nothing unusual?"

"No, sir."

"Have you ever taken the general to a Vietnamese restaurant called the Little Saigon Tearoom?"

"No, sir."

"Have you ever heard the general mention the Little Saigon Tearoom?"

"No, sir."

"Thank you, Sergeant. Call me if anything comes to mind." I gave him my office number and hung up.

★★★★

As I reentered the foyer, Jonesy was just coming in the front door. He had a clipboard in his hand. "Talked to the MPs at the Wright Gate," he said.

Fort Myer had three gates, but the Wright Gate was the closest to the general's residence. "That their log?"

"Yes, sir." Jonesy handed the clipboard to me.

As I took it, I asked, "You check with the guards on duty at the other gates?"

"Sent two MPs to pick up the logs."

I nodded as I looked over the entries for the day. There were two pages, almost forty names. Coupled with the logs from the other gates, a rundown on every name would take days.

"Probably be a waste of time checking the names out, sir," Jonesy said.

I knew what Jonesy was getting at. Fort Myer was an open post during the day. The guards checked IDs for people coming in only after sunset.

"Still gotta run the drill, Jonesy. Now, the names here are those who don't have military IDs, right?"

"Not quite, sir. People without IDs can come on post without being logged in as long as someone in the car has an ID. Doesn't even have to be the driver."

I shook my head. Such lax security requirements on an installation where the highest-ranking members of the military resided boggled my mind. I handed the clipboard back. "See if you can get the Provost Marshal to check these out, and any other visitors on the other logs."

Jonesy said, "The MPs did say something mighty curious, sir. They said the general came back around 1415 today, give or take a few minutes."

"I know. I just got off the phone with the driver."

"Here's the funny part, sir. About fifteen minutes later, they saw the general leave in his Caddy. Alone. Wearing civvies."

"They sure about this?"

Jonesy nodded. "Said he returned just before 1700. Alone."

We went to brief Tippett.

★★★★

As we walked back into the living room, Tippett's man who had inspected the general's vehicles was giving what appeared to be car keys to Major Swanson. He wore a worshipful look and a nervous, almost timid smile.

"I parked your car out back along the street to the left," the man said to Swanson. "A real nice car, ma'am. Real nice."

Major Swanson appeared a bit unnerved by the compliment. "Thank you. I . . . I haven't had it very long."

"I set the parking brake. So don't forget to release it before you drive."

"No, I won't."

He gave her a final smile and left.

I motioned to Tippett. He came over. "What's going on?" I asked.

"Had to move her car from the driveway so the tow trucks could haul off the general's vehicles."

"That's her Lexus?" I asked, surprised.

Tippett nodded. "Rich and beautiful. Hardly fair, is it?"

"Uh-huh. You know her from someplace?"

"Me? No. Why?"

I shrugged. "Just wondered what that was all about earlier. You and her."

"What do you mean, Charlie?"

"The look she was giving you. The way she acted when I mentioned the restaurant. You didn't notice? And the way you two were talking after I left."

He waved a hand in dismissal. "You're seeing things, Charlie. Now, what have you got?"

I told him. Afterward, I said, "Think I'll drive on out to that restaurant, see if maybe General Watkins went out there today."

Tippett shook his head. "You said the driver hasn't ever heard General Watkins mention it, right?"

"Yes, but—"

"And neither had Major Swanson. I'm thinking the restaurant is going to be a dead end."

"Dammit, Tip, you said yourself you were looking for a Vietnamese connection."

His face tightened for a moment. "Okay, we'll check the place out, but later. First, I need you to do me a favor."

"Now what?" I asked.

5

IVE MINUTES LATER, I DROVE OUT OF FORT MYER FOR THE TEN-MINUTE RIDE TO THE PENTAGON. I LOOKED OVER TO MY PASSENGER AND GAVE Major Swanson a sympathetic smile. "You sure you're up to this?"

She nodded.

"Your first name's Talia, right?"

Another nod. A hesitant smile.

We drove in silence for a few minutes. I came up to Columbia Pike and made a left, heading east. "I'm a little curious, Talia. About the decor in the house, considering General Watkins's POW experience."

She looked confused for a moment. "You mean the Asian stuff?"

I nodded.

"The general liked the Orient. He respected the people. Their work ethic, their values." She gave her eyes a last dab, then dropped her hand down, the Kleenex balled inside. "He didn't lump them all together. We traveled all over the Pacific when he was the Commander of PACAF. He had a real understanding of the differences between the Chinese, Japanese, Koreans . . ."

"What about the Vietnamese?"

She hesitated. "He never said much about them." She looked at me. "He never talked about his experience as a prisoner."

"Ever?"

"No. He even refused to attend the POW reunions."

"Did you have a feel for what he thought of the Vietnamese?"

She thought. "I don't think he liked them."

"Why?"

"I assumed he didn't like them because of what he went through. And when he came back last week, he seemed angry. Upset."

"Came back? From where?"

Major Swanson looked uncomfortable. "I'm not sure I can say. It's . . . it's classified."

"Talia—"

"I'm sorry, but . . ." She looked out the window.

We were going by the Naval Annex. I spoke quietly, but firmly. "You and I both know what the regs say about compartmentalized information. True, I don't have the clearance now, but I can get it. And if what you know is important, all you're doing is delaying the investigation and helping the animal who killed the general. Is that what you want to do?"

She stared out the window for a moment. Giving a slow shake of her head, she said, "No, of course not." She looked at me. "My problem is . . . this . . . this is very classified. Strictly need-to-know."

"I will find out eventually," I repeated.

Talia sat back in the seat. "General Watkins flew to Hanoi."

"Jesus!" I said.

"His secretive behavior began with a request from the White House two months ago," Talia explained. "To counter the President's pending recognition of Vietnam, the Republican Congress was threatening to pass legislation declaring any financial dealings between the U.S. and Vietnam as illegal. Included in the bill was also a measure to withhold funding for the proposed embassy in Vietnam. The vote was supposed to be held sometime in October. The vote tally was going to be close and messy, with possible constitutional implications. The White House wanted both General Holmes and General Watkins to testify. They knew if two members of the Joint Chiefs who were ex-POWs came out in support of the administration's recognition of Vietnam, Congressmen sitting on the fence might be persuaded to change their votes. General Watkins had first rejected the proposal. The White House hounded him. In fact, the President called General Watkins personally. Finally the general relented, but only if the Vietnamese could satisfy him that all POWs had been accounted for."

We were passing the Pentagon's enormous south parking lot, heading around the loop toward the River Entrance. The world's largest office building loomed dark and foreboding against the night sky.

"What happened then?" I asked.

"The White House contacted us. The Vietnamese agreed to allow General Watkins to go over for a week. Look anywhere, talk to anybody."

"Who went with General Watkins?"

"An interpreter."

"No one else?"

"The White House wanted to keep the visit under wraps. They told us that they would only approve the general and an interpreter."

"Who was the interpreter?"

"A Dr. Theodore Masonis."

"A civilian?"

"He's a professor of Asian Studies from Duke University. Mr. Birelli recommended him."

My eyebrows went up. "Colonel John Birelli? The guy who used to run the POW/MIA office in the Pentagon?"

"Yes."

We arrived at the Pentagon's River Entrance, the one generally used by brass. I continued to the annex parking lot and pulled into a spot reserved for general officers.

"So what did General Watkins decide?" I asked as we walked along the sidewalk.

"About testifying?"

"Yes."

"He told the White House no. He said the Vietnamese hadn't allowed him the freedom to check all the sites on his list."

"How long ago was this, when he told the White House?"

"The day he returned. Two weeks ago. August eighteenth."

"Could that be what had preoccupied him? Something to do with the trip?"

Swanson hesitated. "Possibly. I know he was getting a lot of pressure from the White House to change his mind. I think he may have been considering it."

We reached the entrance. I opened one of the glass doors, and she preceded me in.

"Did he tell you he might testify?"

"No, but I heard him on the phone telling someone he might."

"Who was that?"

"General Holmes, I think."

"Had Holmes decided to testify?"

"I don't know."

Talia showed her ID to a bored guard at the security checkpoint and was waved through a metal detector. I flashed my badge. The guard nodded. I walked around the detector.

Even at this hour, the corridors hummed with life, the reason most enlightened military members detested duty at the "puzzle palace." The fun just never stopped.

"This way," Talia said.

She led me down a hallway to a beautiful polished wood staircase, which took us to the fourth floor.

★★★★

We stepped into a hallway of dark paneling and soft blue wallpaper. Paintings of previous Air Force Chiefs of Staff lined the walls. A wooden door to the left said simply "Chief of Staff" in brass lettering. A young man in a suit stood guard in front.

"Have you been here before?" Talia asked as we approached the door.

"Walked by a couple times. Never been inside."

The young man stiffened, started to open his mouth. Recognizing me, he relaxed.

"Hello, Sergeant Mathews," I said. Mathews was one of Tippett's investigators.

"Hello, sir. Captain Webster's inside." He gave Talia a smile, opened the door, then stepped aside.

"Any problems?"

"A few questions, sir. No one tried to enter."

I nodded. Talia and I went in.

More paneling and paintings in the reception area. A number of desks for General Watkins's staff and the expected assortment of file cabinets and computers. Talia led me through a set of double doors into General Watkins's private office. We found Captain Webster sitting behind the general's mahogany desk, rummaging through an open drawer. He looked up, then popped to his feet.

I introduced Talia, then asked, "Find anything?"

Webster, a muscular, handsome man in his late twenties, was looking at Talia with more than a passing interest. "Uh, no, sir." He waved a hand at the safelike steel file cabinets against the far wall. "Most everything is locked up, sir. I'll need a list of combos." He gave Talia an expectant look.

But Talia shook her head. "I know them, of course, but most of the information is classified Top Secret or higher. Operational and contingency plans, next-generation weapons. Colonel, I'm not sure . . ."

I sighed. "They all have the clearances, Talia. I promise you, we won't remove any files. You can watch if you like." I nodded to the cabinets. "Please."

She had everything open in a couple of minutes.

"Go ahead," I told Webster.

"Try not to mix up the files, Captain," Talia said.

Webster popped a salute, grinning. "Yes, ma'am."

She then pointed to the computer on a stand to the left of the general's desk. "Want me to search his computer now?"

I nodded, watching Webster open one of the cabinet drawers. Talia sat down behind the desk. Swiveling around, she pulled the cover from the monitor and flipped on the power. "What am I looking for?"

"I don't know."

She glanced up at me.

"Something worth killing for," I said.

She hesitated, then began clicking the mouse.

The hard drive immediately began whirring at a furious pace.

"My God!" she cried.

"What?" I said, coming up behind her.

Talia frantically clicked the mouse. I stared down at the screen. A random pattern of numbers and symbols was literally flying across, left to right, line by line. In seconds the screen filled, began scrolling.

Talia clicked. "It's not responding."

"What did you do?" I asked.

"Just typed in the general's password."

"Do a reboot," Webster said. He came over, a stack of files in his hands.

Talia punched the Control, Alt, Delete keys. The numbers continued to scroll across.

"Turn it off," I said.

She did. A second later, she flipped the power back on.

The numbers continued to fly by. Then the screen flared and went black.

We stared in stunned silence.

"Damn, never seen that before," Webster said. He looked around, then dropped the files on the desk.

"I don't understand," Talia said. "I've logged on lots of times. I set up the computer for the general."

"You sure about the password?" I asked.

She nodded. "Six-Pack. His call sign when he was shot down over Vietnam. But even if he'd changed the password, all that would happen is I couldn't log on."

"Try another reboot," I said.

She did. This time the screen remained blank, even though the power light was illuminated. She switched off the computer.

"Maybe the hard disk is fried," Webster said.

I stiffened. The comment had jogged my memory. The same thing had happened the year before in an investigation Jonesy had run.

"How many computers do you have in the outer offices?" I asked.

"Uh, seven, including mine."

"Come on," I said, already to the door.

★★★★

I knew what was going to happen, but I had Talia check anyway. She sat at her desk in the reception area and tried her own computer. She typed T-O-M-H-A-N-K-S. and punched the button.

The numbers danced across the screen.

"I'll be damned," Webster murmured.

Talia slumped back in her chair. "I just don't understand, unless . . ." Her eyes widened. "A virus?"

"Yes," I said. "A very convenient virus."

I reached for her phone.

6

I CALLED THE CID CELLULAR. LIEUTENANT DOLENZ ANSWERED. NO, HE DIDN'T KNOW WHERE COLONEL TIPPETT WAS. MAYBE DOWN THE street to talk with the generals' families. Yes, he would have Colonel Tippett call the moment he returned. Sergeant Jones? Yes, sir. He's here someplace.

I explained the situation to Jonesy and hung up.

"Now what?" Talia asked, swiping back a few strands of hair from her eyes. Her face looked tired but still beautiful. She pointed to the two computers on the executive officers' desks. "Want me to check those, Colonel?"

I shook my head. "They're infected also. Who was the last one to leave the office this evening?"

Talia frowned. "We didn't have anything hot, so Major Parker and I walked out together a little after five. Amanda left maybe ten minutes before that. Colonel Jowers was already gone."

I'd been trying to keep track. "That leaves Colonel Ryerson. He was still here?"

"Working on a talking paper for the general. On Bosnia, I think." She blinked. "Oh, surely you don't think he would . . ."

"No, but I'll need to talk to him tonight. His number?"

Talia read it from a staff roster under the Plexiglas on her desk. "Virginia number?"

"Yes."

I dialed. Colonel Ryerson wanted to come immediately. I told him he'd just be in the way, but I would appreciate a meeting with the staff at ten-thirty the next day. He reluctantly agreed. He told me he'd left at 1845, give or take. Yes, he'd been the last one. Of course, he'd locked the door. He wanted to talk to Talia.

I handed her the phone. Webster and I returned to Watkins's office. I went through each drawer twice. Webster made a quick check of the file cabinets.

Talia walked in as we were finishing up, my handkerchief balled in her fist. She looked as if she'd been crying.

"Did the general keep disks in this office?" I asked. I was sitting at the desk.

She nodded and came toward me. "In the bottom drawer. On the right."

I shook my head.

She stopped. "They're gone?"

"Yes."

"Maybe he took them downstairs."

I frowned. "Downstairs?"

"Into the Joint Chiefs of Staff area. He has another office there."

"Let's go!"

★★★★

Talia and I went down the wooden staircase. The staff for the Joint Chiefs operated out of a highly secure labyrinth of offices on the second floor.

As we walked down a hallway toward a guard sitting behind a glass booth, Talia said, "This isn't much of an office. But since General Watkins spent so much time down here, he wanted some place where he could go to make phone calls, maybe do some paperwork between briefings. He had us set up this office."

"Good evening, Major." The guard smiled. "Back already?"

Talia said, "You know how it is, Willie. Sometimes I think I need to join a union." She held out her entry badge. Willie chuckled, not bothering to look at it.

Since I didn't have a JCS entry badge, I had to show Willie my military and OSI IDs and sign a log, after which he gave me a plastic visitor's badge. Talia led the way through the glass doors into a long corridor. More paintings. I recognized faces: Grant, Pershing, MacArthur, Marshall.

"That's the National Military Command Center over there. General Watkins's office is here."

The door was locked. Talia had a key. We walked into a small room. None of the expected frills for a four-star here. Just a desk, a couple of comfortable chairs, a phone, and a computer and printer.

I went to the desk and began going through the drawers.

"Try the third one down," Talia said.

I did. Another flip-top disk container. Empty. I slowly closed the drawer.

Talia powered up the computer. We had our answer in fifteen seconds. I shook my head as the numbers flew by.

"Turn it off."

The screen went dark.

"Now what?" she asked.

We went upstairs in silence. I was thinking hard, wondering how someone could have gotten through JCS security. The phone on General Watkins's desk was ringing as we walked in. Webster answered and held the instrument out to me. Tippett was on the line.

"Hungry, Charlie?" he asked.

★★★★

Jonesy and two CID men arrived at 2136. The CID men would remove the computers from this office and the one in the JCS and take them, along with any floppy disks, to the basement of the Pentagon, where the Department of Defense's massive computer system was housed.

Major Maria Gutiérrez, commander of the computer security branch, was an old friend. If anyone could retrieve information from the general's computers, she could. Jonesy and Webster would search through all the office files, a job that would probably take all night, if not longer.

I offered to drive Talia back to Fort Myer to pick up her car, but she declined.

"I'd like to stay," she said. "Sergeant Jones and Captain Webster might need help interpreting what they find."

I called Jean. The answering machine picked up, and I told it I would be home late.

Talia told me the JCS security officer had his office off the main corridor near the entrance. Back down the stairs again. I knocked at the door marked "Security," then walked in. There were three desks in the anteroom, unmanned. I could hear music. I headed for the partially closed door at the back. I found the duty officer, an overweight, tired-looking Army major, behind his desk, feet up, munching on a candy bar and reading a newspaper. A portable radio on a bookshelf played a country song.

I cleared my throat.

When the major looked up, his eyes widened as he stared at my uniform. The newspaper and the candy bar hit the desk, and he struggled to his feet. "Colonel. What can I . . . ?"

"How many people have JCS entry badges?"

He licked a bit of chocolate from his lip. "Sir, I'm not sure I can—"

"General Watkins was murdered tonight," I growled. I shoved my badge in his face.

He swallowed and peered into the computer on his desk. It took him thirty seconds. "Three hundred and seventy-six, sir."

"I'll be back to pick up a printout," I said.

Tippett was waiting on the curb when I pulled up in front of Watkins's residence.

He didn't look happy.

★★★★

"Deaf, dumb, and fucking blind," Tippett groused, climbing into the car. He had another Dixie cup in his hand. "A four-star gets whacked, and no one sees a damn thing! Unbelievable!"

I nodded down the street in the direction of the other homes as I pulled away from the curb. "They weren't any help, I take it?"

"Nah. Hard to believe," he said. "MPs on patrol said they drove by half a dozen times between 1700 and 1900. Nothing. So far, we haven't found any physical evidence to link to the killer. The son of a bitch must have been invisible."

"Maybe we'll turn something up at the restaurant."

Tippett shrugged. "Maybe."

"Don't you wonder why General Watkins would go to a restaurant on Fourteenth Street, of all places?" I asked.

"Maybe he had something else on his mind besides dinner."

"What's that supposed to mean?"

"Guy was a widower. You figure it out."

I shook my head. Tippett was referring to the fact that portions of Fourteenth Street were considered the red-light district.

"Restaurant's address is well north of the hooker hangouts," I said.

"So now you think the killer is someone in the JCS, eh?"

"Makes sense, Tip. That's why the Fort Myer gate guards didn't notice him if he passed through tonight. He must have had a military ID. Hell, he might even have been in uniform. How else can you explain how he got into Watkins's office in the JCS area? You know the security there. Only way someone gets in is with an entry badge, or else shows a military ID, gets vouched for, and is logged in."

"How long did you say the general's main office was unoccupied?"

"About two hours. The exec left at 1845. Webster showed at 2033."

"How about Watkins's office in JCS?"

"Hard to say. Apparently, Watkins didn't use it regularly."

Tippett thought for a moment. "So you're saying the killer waits for Watkins when he returns home. Takes maybe an hour to chop him up. Then drives to the Pentagon, hits Watkins's office upstairs to screw with the computers, then goes down into the JCS, taking a chance that the guard will remember him coming through the JCS checkpoint. Does all this hoping like hell the body isn't found and an alarm raised in the meantime."

We were coming to a red light. I tapped the brakes. "Timing works out," I snapped.

"You said both offices were locked, right?"

I nodded.

"No signs of forced entry?"

"No. But that doesn't mean anything. The general must have had a set of keys."

Tippett reached for the phone. Thirty seconds later, he hung up. "Lieutenant Dolenz says they've turned up a coupla sets of car keys in the bedroom. Thinks they were probably spares."

"That's all? No office or house keys?"

"None so far. Still looking, though."

"They won't find them."

"Probably not," Tippett agreed. "You check the JCS log?"

"Seven people signed in between 1800 and 2110. Four civilians, a Navy captain, and two Army majors—"

A car horn blared. The light was green. I punched the gas.

"But if the killer had a JCS entry badge, he wouldn't be on the log. And I'm betting our guy had a badge. He wouldn't put his name on any log."

Tippett stared thoughtfully out the window. I recognized the look. He was in his zone. We were crossing the Key Bridge into Georgetown, and traffic was picking up. I left him alone and concentrated on my driving.

I drove east on M Street, past rows of upscale bars and restaurants. The sidewalks were crowded with the city's young and beautiful. Traffic was bumper to bumper.

Tippett came alive again. "Say, didn't you work on a computer-tampering case in the puzzle palace two years back?"

"Jonesy handled it. Turned out to be some high school kid, a summer intern in one of the Navy offices. Kid was a damn genius. Came up with a homemade virus. He was running around uploading his virus into any computer he could find. Nailed about a hundred before we stopped him."

"You're sure this was a different virus?"

"Oh, yeah. The kid designed his to blank out the screen and print 'Fuck you' in three-inch letters."

Tippett chuckled. "Gotta admit, that's damn funny."

"A riot."

I gave him a long look. I thought I could smell a faint odor of alcohol. I knew the dumb son of a bitch had sneaked a drink. . . .

Tippett grinned. "Look, Charlie, I think it'd be a helluva thing if you were right. Could even be we've got a homicidal general on the loose. Serve the fucking brass right. The press would love it. Imagine the headlines."

"But you don't buy it?"

Tippett took a deep breath and slowly exhaled. "Hell, anything's possible. I think you're right about the thing being connected to the general's trip to Vietnam. And yeah, somebody in the JCS could be involved. But your scenario . . ." Tippett shook his head. "You make the killer rush around, take risks. Doesn't fit. This guy is the careful type, a planner. We know he was in no hurry to finish off Watkins."

"Maybe the killer had an accomplice in the JCS."

Tippett ran a hand over his smooth scalp. Under the flickering streetlights his face turned hard. "All I know is the killer's got to be a soldier. A vet. Someone who's killed like this before."

Tippett was confirming my suspicion. Such a murder would have been a natural response in a dirty, vicious war in which you've seen your buddies butchered. The Cong weren't the only ones to master brutal ways of killing.

"So you no longer think the killer is a Vietnamese?"

"I didn't say that," Tippett snapped. "I said a vet. I didn't say whose side he fought on."

I started to argue and stopped. But I couldn't see how a Vietnamese could get past the MPs and into Watkins's residence without being noticed. Much less get into the Pentagon or the JCS.

Tippett looked over. "Hell, maybe you're right, Charlie. Maybe one guy could have killed General Watkins and then gone back to his office afterwards. If that's the case, though, you can bet he's assigned to the JCS. How many guys are on the list again?"

"Three hundred and seventy-six."

A low whistle. "Well, maybe we can narrow that down a little." Tippett checked his watch. "Better hurry. The place closes at 2300." He leaned back and shut his eyes.

I shook my head.

No doubt about it. I smelled alcohol.

7

TIP, SOMETHING'S WRONG."

TIPPETT OPENED HIS EYES, SAT UP AND BLINKED A FEW TIMES. Flashing lights from four squad cars blocked the right lane in front of a building with a neon sign. We were too far away to make out the name.

"You think that could be the restaurant?" Tippett asked.

"Yeah." I'd been watching the building numbers.

Traffic in the left lane crept along. A uniformed cop on the curb by the building impatiently waved a flashlight, trying to get the drivers to pick up the pace. A few seconds later, we could make out the sign.

"Fuck," Tippett said, sagging back.

"The Little Saigon Tearoom," I murmured, reading the greenish glow.

Tippett rolled down his window as I came to a stop next to the cop. Car horns blared from behind. The cop hollered, "Move it, mister. Nothing to see."

Tippett hopped out. "Hey!" the cop shouted, coming over. He shined his flashlight on Tippett. When Tippett flashed his badge, the cop relaxed. More horns. I pulled away. In the rearview mirror, the cop was talking to Tippett, pointing back to some men on the sidewalk. I found a parking spot in an alley about three blocks away. I wondered if I'd have my tires when I returned.

I walked fast, past rows of seedy tenement houses, boarded-up shops, and a bar with a flashing sign that said "Bubba's." A couple of black guys staggered out. One hollered, "Hey, gen'rul, where da fuckin' war?" The other laughed. I quickened my pace. "Hey, fuck you, soldier boy!" the first one yelled. More laughter.

I kept walking.

As I approached within a block of the restaurant, the neighborhood changed. I passed two grocery stores, a dry cleaner's, some well-kept row houses, and a restaurant. All had Vietnamese names. The police had set up a yellow-tape barricade on the sidewalk in front of the Little Saigon Tearoom. There were perhaps a dozen people looking on, mostly black and Hispanic. I was surprised there weren't more.

A cop positioned at the barricade motioned me over. I reached for my ID. He waved it off. "Go on in, Colonel Jensen." He pointed to the restaurant. "You'll find your friend inside."

I ducked under the tape, nodded to two uniformed cops by the door, and went in.

The Little Saigon Tearoom was small, with five booths and a half-dozen cheap Formica tables. The wood floor was polished to a shine. The place had a flowery, pleasant smell. A variety of rice-paper water-colors accented the jade-green walls. Two carved screens of black wood occupied two corners. The lighting was subdued.

Tippett stood by a set of swinging double doors at the back, talking quietly with a lanky Asian in a dark suit. At a table to my left, two burly black detectives were talking to a pretty Asian girl in her twenties.

"Charlie!" Tippett called.

I joined Tippett and the lanky Asian.

"This is Lieutenant Harry Lee, Charlie," Tippett said. "D.C. Metro Homicide. Asian Gang Task Force."

"Colonel Jensen," Lieutenant Lee said.

We shook hands. His grip was firm. He looked maybe thirty-five. His voice was surprisingly deep, with just the hint of a New England accent.

"Colonel Tippett filled me in on your situation."

I stared at Tippett, who shrugged.

"Don't worry," Lee said quickly, flashing a grin. "Colonel Tippett emphasized the need for discretion. The last thing I need is a bunch of talking heads from the press giving me a hard time."

"Thanks, Lieutenant," I said. I looked around. "So what's up?"

"Restaurant was getting ready to close," Lee said. "One of the cooks takes a tray of food to the owner, who lives in an apartment upstairs. Found the guy dead."

"Murdered?" I asked.

"Yes."

"How was he killed?"

"An ear-to-ear slice job. Looks like one cut. Very clean. Very professional. Still waiting for the M.E. to come and make it official."

I swallowed. "Any other marks or cuts?"

"No. But I only gave the body a quick once-over."

"Who's she?" I asked, nodding to the girl.

"The hostess on the phone. A Miss Vinh. Her brother was the cook who found the body. She speaks some English. What I've learned I got from her. Doesn't appear to know anything about the murder, though. We've got the cook in the kitchen. He's a young kid, maybe twenty. He's real shook."

"Any other witnesses?"

"A couple of busboys. Girl says they took off before we showed. Probably illegals. We're trying to round them up. I'm guessing they headed over to Chinatown on Seventh. I'm sure there are others. This place does a good business. But they won't come forward. Notice how there isn't much of a crowd outside?"

I nodded.

"See any Asians?"

"Come to think of it, no."

"That's pretty standard. If this happened in any other neighborhood, the crowd would be packed three-deep. But this is a Vietnamese neighborhood. Vietnamese don't want anything to do with the police. Holdover perception from their homeland, where the cops are worse than the criminals. Makes finding witnesses damn tough."

"Can we see the body, Lieutenant?" I asked.

"We were about to go up, Colonel. But I can only give you a few minutes. Forensics should be here soon. They won't like finding you snooping around. But, hey, I was in the service. Navy. You guys ever been on a ship?"

Tippett and I shook our heads.

"Sucks. No women, no booze. Now I guess they got girls. Shoulda done it earlier." He winked.

"You mentioned something about forensics arriving soon?" Tippett said.

"Right." Lieutenant Lee pushed open the swinging door. "After you."

I walked through.

★★★★

A slight, scared-looking boy with a mass of black hair sat at a small table in front of a screen door at the rear of the narrow kitchen. He stared at the floor, rocking back and forth, hands clenched in his lap. A husky female detective hovered nearby.

The boy looked up. First there was confusion in his eyes, then something else. Fear? He leapt to his feet, yelling in Vietnamese and gesturing.

"Shit!" the female detective said, and dropped her notepad.

Lieutenant Lee rushed past me, grabbed the boy's shoulder, and spoke in a firm voice. The boy jerked away and let out a torrent of Vietnamese. Lee raised his voice. I was surprised he was speaking English. The boy shook his head, his replies urgent, jumbled.

Tippett stepped forward. He spoke sharply in Vietnamese. The boy looked up, stunned into silence. Lieutenant Lee and the detective stepped aside, relief on their faces. Tippett said something else. The boy's eyes darted to me. *He's terrified*, I thought. A grunted command from Tippett. The boy nodded and slowly sat down. Tippett continued talking, quieter now.

"Well, I'll be." The female detective smiled. "Good thing he was around."

I went over to Lee. "You don't speak Vietnamese?" I kept my eye on Tippett and the boy.

"Hell, no," Lee said. "Understand a little Korean, but I was born and raised in Boston. I've called for a Vietnamese officer to question him, but he's working a drive-by uptown. Be a couple hours till we get the kid's story."

The boy was talking softly, still looking very afraid. Tippett was nodding, throwing out an occasional word. I said to Lee, "There's only one Vietnamese cop in your department?"

"Four, actually. One per shift, with some overlap. We need more, but the city's got budget problems. The department figures we're doing okay as long as one of us Asian types is on the scene."

Tippett said something. The boy shook his head, said something back. He wouldn't look at Tippett. I said to Lee, "Even if you can't communicate?"

"Colonel," he said, "we do what we can."

"He'll be fine," Tippett said, coming over a few moments later.

"What set him off?" I asked.

Tippett pointed to my uniform. "That."

I frowned, confused.

"The soldier thing," Lee said. "Yeah, I should have thought about that. The only thing that scares the Vietnamese more than a cop is a soldier."

"We were the good guys in the war, Lieutenant," I said dryly.

"You can't be serious, Colonel," Lee said, glancing at the now-docile boy. "A lot of these younger Vietnamese were raised in the indoctrination camps or slave farms where their parents had been sent after the war. Brutal stuff, from what I hear. To that kid, anyone in a uniform is a bad guy."

I was about to respond when Tippett said, "He did mention something interesting, Lieutenant."

"What?" Lee asked.

Tippett pointed to the screen door. "He saw a man walk by shortly before he went upstairs to see the owner."

Lee motioned the female detective over. "Description?"

She pulled out a notepad.

Tippett spoke quickly. "Very tall, well over six feet, medium build, perhaps late forties to early fifties, dark suit, and—"

"Colonel, could you slow down a sec?" the detective asked. She wrote furiously for a few more seconds. "Okay."

"He was Caucasian," Tippett said.

I stiffened. "The kid's sure?"

Tippett nodded.

"Anything distinguishing about the guy?" Lee asked.

Tippett smiled. "One thing. The hair. Short. White."

"White," Lee said. "You mean like gray?"

"No," Tippett said. "He's certain. White."

Kid was damned observant, I thought. For some reason, that surprised me.

"Hell, that's something." Lee smiled at Tippett. "Thanks, Colonel. Now all we have to do is find some guy that looks like Donahue."

"I'd like to see the body now, Lieutenant," Tippett said.

Lee pushed open the screen door. "After you."

★★★★

A uniformed cop stood by the wooden stairs attached to the rear of the building.

"Hello," I said to the cop.

He looked surprised. "Evening, sir."

As I climbed the stairs, I looked at the darkened alley below. The only light around came from a single bulb over the screen door. If the kid hadn't looked out when he did, the man would have disappeared into the shadows of the alley. We'd been lucky.

"Remember, don't touch anything," Lee called from behind.

8

THE BODY LAY FACEUP ON THE FLOOR OF A TINY SITTING ROOM, A SKINNY LITTLE MAN WITH A LABORER'S WEATHERED FACE. HE LOOKED OUT OF place in a dark blue three-piece suit. Blood had stained the shirt and jacket and soaked the cheap throw rug he was lying on. Wire-rimmed glasses lay to the side, maybe three feet away, lenses intact.

I knelt for a closer look. The cut along the throat was very clean. No visible tears in the skin. Then I noticed the bruise on the right side of the forehead.

Tippett grunted. "Could be the same knife."

"Looks like he might have been knocked out first," I said.

"Explains the position of the glasses."

"Yeah. Nice suit," I said. "What did this guy do in the restaurant? Act as maître d'?"

"He usually cooked," Tippett said.

"He cooked? Wonder why he put on a suit, unless—" I stopped. "Damn," I said softly.

"What?" Tippett asked.

I looked up, excited. "He was meeting someone. Someone important."

Tippett gave me a thoughtful look. "You're probably right, Charlie."

Probably, hell, I thought.

The sitting room was part of a larger room, which included a dining area and a kitchen. The furnishings were modest: a threadbare couch, a tattered recliner, a cheap wooden dining table with two chairs. The uniformed cop I'd talked to downstairs stood by the front door and watched us closely. Tippett turned and walked down a short hallway where Lieutenant Lee had disappeared.

I studied the body for another minute. Particularly the right hand. Black smudges on the thumb and forefinger. With a nod to the cop, I headed toward the back.

There were two bedrooms on either side of a bathroom. I found Tippett and Lieutenant Lee in the first bedroom. The room was tiny and cluttered. There was a single iron bed against a wall and two green footlockers stacked in a corner. A battered rolltop desk and a file cabinet took up the wall space by the door. An old manual typewriter sat on the desk, a few sheets of typing paper nearby. What amazed me were the photographs on the wall. Dozens of them, neatly framed. Most were black-and-white and faded. Lee was copying something from a framed document that hung above the desk.

He closed his notepad. "That should help us get some background."

"What is it?"

"A certificate of naturalization for Mr. Yuen Ki Tho."

Tippett seemed to have zeroed in on one of the larger pictures.

I went to the desk. In addition to the typewriter, there was a small bottle of Wite-Out and a jar of pens and pencils. I peered down into the typewriter and frowned. There was no ribbon, and the trash can was empty, too.

Tippett was still staring at the large photo. As I came over, he turned. "Not much here, Charlie. Let's go."

"In a minute, Tip."

"Suit yourself." He left the room.

I glanced at the photo Tippett had been studying. The years hadn't been kind to Mr. Tho. But the resemblance was unmistakable. "Damn," I murmured, looking closer.

"What?" Lee asked. "That Mr. Tho was a soldier in the war? Hell, half the Vietnamese who came over were soldiers. Big deal."

The man was in his twenties. He stood proudly as he saluted a senior officer. Behind him, similarly dressed young men stood at attention. A flag waved in the background.

"Look at the flag, Lieutenant."

Lee leaned closer and froze. "You mean . . ."

"Our Mr. Tho was a North Vietnamese officer," I said. "A major, actually."

"Well, I'll be. Good catch, Colonel."

I wondered how Tippett could have missed that flag.

"You better get out here, Lieutenant!" a voice called.

★★★★

Through the open front door, we saw the uniformed cop standing on the short landing, peering over the wooden railing into the alley. Tippett stood next to him.

Lee reached them first. "What's going on?" he demanded.

"I'm not sure, sir, but I heard some yelling and thought I heard running."

"Sounded like the yells came from out there, Lieutenant," Tippett said, pointing into the alley.

We were silent, everyone listening. I thought I heard the distant sound of footsteps on pavement. I heard the voices more clearly, a woman's and a man's.

Lee took the stairs two at a time. Before he entered the darkened alley, he took out a pistol from an inside holster and disappeared into the alley, weapon drawn.

I heard him yelling at someone. Someone responded. The female detective?

Then came the sound of clanging metal, like a trash-can lid hitting the pavement. "Goddammit!" Lee roared. "Didn't somebody bring a flashlight?"

An inaudible reply.

Lee: "Anybody see him?"

Two faint replies.

Lee again: "Aw, for the love of . . . I fucking can't believe this!"

Tippett glanced at me, eyes questioning.

We headed for the alley.

★★★★

The smell of rotting garbage hung like putrid fog in the humid air. Something skittered past to the right. In front, where the alley ended, we could see filtering light emanating from a cross street. Then figures appeared, running. They disappeared around the corner.

I heard Tippett stumble. "Screw this," he growled. "Let's head back."

"We've come this far."

Tippett grunted something unintelligible, but we kept walking.

We were turning down the cross street when Tippett said, "Look at that."

Ahead I saw the familiar "M" by a stairwell on the corner. "A Metro station," I said.

Then Lee appeared in the stairwell and walked quickly toward us. "Five bucks they lost him, Charlie."

"No bet."

Lee approached. He stared at us and shook his head in disgust.

Tippett gave me a knowing look.

We headed back.

★★★★

Ten minutes later, the three detectives sat around one of the tables in the restaurant. Lee paced in circles around them. The young Asian girl was still in the booth, back rigid, looking scared. Tippett and I hung back by the kitchen door.

"Come on, Rita," Lee moaned. "How could you let this happen?"

Rita, her shoulders slumped, face dejected, shook her head. Refusing to look at Lee, she said, "The boy started crying, Lieutenant.

Wouldn't stop. I thought maybe if I got his sister he might calm down. I only left him alone in the kitchen for two minutes."

"That's right, Lieutenant," a male detective said. "Rita was out here not more than two minutes tops."

Lee glared.

The detective's eyes quickly found something interesting on the wall.

Lee's voice was barely controlled. "Rita, you left the kid by an open door, and you knew he was scared."

"Yes, sir. I . . ." She took a deep breath. "I just blew it, okay, Lieutenant?"

The front door opened, and a cop entered the restaurant. "Lieutenant, forensics and the M.E. just showed."

"About damn time," Lee said. He gave Rita a hard look and went to the door.

"They won't find him unless he wants to be found," Tippett murmured to me.

"He can't get far," I said. "The police are checking the Metro stops, and Lee has patrol cars canvassing the neighborhood."

"You're assuming he got to the Metro."

"You don't think he did?"

"Think about it. Vietnamese are tight, Charlie. War made them that way. Anyone in this neighborhood'll take the kid in and hide him from the police. Hell, they've done it for years, from the Japanese, the French, the Americans. Not to mention their own government." He waved a hand. "He could easily have slipped into one of those row houses, the ones with the back doors in the alley."

"The cops'll find him, eventually."

"Can't search them—not without probable cause—and no one's going to give him up. No, the cops won't find him until he's ready."

I looked at the girl in the booth. "His sister would know his friends. Worth a shot."

Tippett nodded. "Come on." We walked toward the detectives, who were rising from the table.

Rita was shaking her head. She muttered, "Son of a bitch, like I did it on purpose."

"Excuse me," Tippett said.

Rita gave him a frosty look and stalked off toward the kitchen.

"Don't mind her, Colonel," one of the male detectives said. He was the taller of the two, the one who'd stuck up for Rita. "What can we do for you?"

Tippett nodded to the sister. "Have you asked her where her brother might have gone?"

"Sure. She says she doesn't know."

"And you believe her?" I asked.

He grinned. "Hell, no. But . . ." He shrugged.

Tippett asked, "Did she mention if Mr. Tho had any visitors today? Specifically, around three P.M."

"Yeah, Colonel." He turned to the other male detective. "Lester, what time did the old guy show?"

Lester fished out a notepad and flipped a couple of pages. "Around three-fifteen. Miss Vihn said he was old, about sixty. Caucasian. Short hair, medium height, stocky. Wearing a blue sports coat. The dead guy, Tho, was waiting for him. They went upstairs. Old guy stayed maybe thirty, forty minutes." He paused and looked closer at the page. "Yeah, here it is. Old guy left, carrying an envelope. One of those big brown ones."

"I see. Thank you." Tippett looked at the girl. "Do you mind? I have a few questions."

The first detective waved a hand. "Knock yourself out."

The girl cowered against the back of the booth when Tippett approached. He smiled, speaking Vietnamese. She flashed a tentative smile and said something back. Tippett sat.

I went outside to talk to Lieutenant Lee, who was briefing the forensics team.

"There is a high probability the murder of Tho is linked to that of General Watkins," I told him when he was finished. "I think maybe the same man murdered both."

"Because of the M.O.?"

I nodded.

Lee thought that over. "But you have no idea why?"

"Something from the war, but at this point, it's only a guess."

"Then you think General Watkins was the man the girl saw here this afternoon?"

"Description fits, and he was seen leaving Fort Myer thirty minutes before the arrival of the visitor. I'll send over a photo of the general. You can show it to the girl."

A blue and white squad car cruised up the street. A cop stuck his head out the window.

"Hey, Lieutenant!" he yelled. "We don't see the kid anywhere. Want us to keep looking?"

"Hell, yes!" Lee roared.

The head ducked quickly inside and the car rolled down the street.

"Stupid shit," Lee muttered. "Look, I've got to go inside, Colonel." He took out his wallet and gave me his card. "Keep me posted."

"Sure." I gave him one of my cards after jotting down Tippett's home and office numbers on the back.

Tippett came out a few minutes later. "Very bright girl. Came over last year. She's taking English classes. Wants to go to college. Become a nurse."

"So where did she say her brother went?"

He shook his head. "Used all my charm, Charlie. I must be losing it. If she knows, she wasn't about to tell me."

"She knows."

"Probably."

We ducked under the tape barricade and began walking. To our left, cars still crawled by, though not as many as earlier. Someone honked, then hollered an obscenity at the cops.

"Now we know where General Watkins went this afternoon," I said.

"Yeah, the girl said Mr. Tho appeared very respectful. She knew the visitor must be an important man."

Which explained the suit, I thought. "Tip, did you notice the stains on Tho's fingers?"

Tippett nodded. "Ink. He must have changed a ribbon in the typewriter recently."

"But there was no ribbon in the trash and no ribbon in the machine."

"You saw that, huh? Then you probably noticed there was no trace of what he was typing on the desk."

"Maybe the cops will turn up something."

"Not a chance. This guy's too smart, too careful. He's killed two men for something Tho knew, and done a helluva job removing any documentation. Anything Tho had in the apartment is long gone."

"You make this guy sound like he's some kind of superman," I said. "He'll make some mistakes."

"Hasn't so far, Charlie."

"Sure he has, Tip. He let himself be seen, and there's the phone call."

"Phone call?"

"The one on the redial. The one that led us here. He should have checked and removed it. Then there is the photo back there." I let the statement hang, watching him.

We walked five paces before Tippett said, "What photo is that?"

"For chrissakes, Tip! The one that shows Mr. Tho was a North Vietnamese major! The one that you were looking at!"

"I don't know what you're talking about, Charlie."

I stopped and grabbed his arm.

He spun around, his face angry.

"Tip, what the hell is wrong with you?" I snarled.

Tippett's jaw clamped tight.

"Is it the booze? And don't lie to me! I know you're hitting the bottle on the job. Dammit, Tip, you're already in enough hot water!"

"Fuck you, Charlie!" Tippett spit. He looked as mad as I'd ever seen him. I thought he might punch me.

Instead, he walked away.

9

TWO BLOCKS LATER, TIPPETT STOPPED BY A STREETLIGHT AND I CAUGHT UP.

He turned and gave me a friendly smile. "Sorry about that back there, Charlie."

I glared at him.

"Yeah, I know. I drink too much. But I'm gonna get me some help. Get in one of those programs."

"Uh-huh."

"The thing with the picture. Hell, I just missed it. I've got a lot on my mind. This is my last case, you know."

"What?"

Tippett faced the street and watched a few cars drive by. "Gonna hang it up. I put in my papers last month. Retire in twelve days. After twenty-seven years and three months."

I couldn't find my voice for a second. "This is straight?" I asked when I did.

Tippett's expression was both serious and a little sad. "I was going to tell you earlier, but the time never seemed quite right."

"Why, Tip? Dorothy?"

He shrugged. "I'd be lying if I said no. But it isn't just Dorothy. It's a lot of things." He looked at me. "You know I'm not going to make general?"

"I know, Tip."

He shook his head. "I've been fucking up some. Got a letter of reprimand for slapping a dope-dealing corporal that mouthed off. You mighta heard. Some other things, mostly small. I just don't care anymore, Charlie." He began walking, and I fell into step.

His voice remained quiet, but there was an edge to it. "General Ferris was going to relieve me. You believe that? All the stuff I've done for the Army and that bastard, and it don't count for squat. So I made him a deal. Told him I'd retire instead." He paused. "I couldn't have handled being relieved."

"What're you going to do?"

"Who knows? Can't afford much. Dorothy gets half my retirement. Twenty-seven years of putting my ass on the line for Uncle Sam and I don't have a pot to piss in. Doesn't seem fair."

"You could get a job as a security consultant."

Tippett snorted. "Baby-sit a bunch of snot-nosed security guards? No way. Not this boy. No shit jobs for me."

We crossed a street.

"Tell you the truth, I've really been thinking about Costa Rica. Heard it's nice. Cheap to live. Maybe get a place on the beach. Always wanted a place on the beach."

Tippett had mentioned Costa Rica a few times before. "Be hard to see the kids," I said.

"Yeah, but they'll both be in college in a couple of years." A moment later, he said, "Not that I ever saw them much anyway. 'Course, you know that. Hell, I never took Dorothy and the kids on a vacation. Not once. Never even thought of it. Too busy bucking for rank." He took a deep breath. "You can want something too much, Charlie, and end up losing what you have."

"You did your best, Tip."

He gave me a sad smile. "Charlie, you're a damn liar."

"Yeah, Tip, I know."

I shook my head. I'd never have expected Tippett to just bow out. The Army had been his life.

I pointed. "Car's over there."

As we turned into the darkened alley, Tippett stopped. "I'd really like to finish this case, Charlie. That would mean a lot."

I sighed. "You stay off the booze and I won't say anything to General Ferris."

He smiled. "We'll work together like in the old days, Charlie. You and me. Mutt and Jeff. On a tough one."

"Sure, Tip."

"Maybe I'll come by for dinner. Been a while since I had Jean's pot roast."

"That'd be nice, Tip."

I felt for Tippett. I couldn't help myself. Though I'd always questioned his dedication to achieving promotion, he'd served his country well in the process. Besides that, if the difference in personal style was swept away, we were friends, maybe the only friendship he ever accomplished.

Frankly, I was scared for him. Now that the rudder of his life, that devotion to the dream of rising to general, was gone, Tippett would pay a terrible price, the extent of which I knew he had no idea. With no purpose, he wouldn't last six months in Costa Rica before he either put a gun to his head or returned home to look for some sort of acceptance that wouldn't be there for him.

Should I have voiced my fears? I don't think Tippett would have listened even if I had.

He would never come to dinner, either.

★★★★

We said little on the drive back to Fort Myer. I had the feeling Tippett thought he'd said too much already.

I placed a call to Watkins's office. Jonesy answered.

"Don't bother with going through all the files," I said. "Just concentrate on the ones having to do with Vietnam."

"Anything specific, sir?"

"No. Webster there?"

"Stepped out to the john. Sir, Colonel Ryerson is here."

"Ryerson?"

"General Watkins's exec. You called him earlier."

I remembered. "Guess he couldn't stay away. Is he causing any problems?"

"No, sir, he's been very helpful in going over the files."

"Okay. Tell Webster to go to the JCS security office. They should have photos on file of everyone authorized a JCS entry badge. Have him run a check. Look for anyone with white hair." I repeated the description the kid had given Tippett.

"Got it, sir. Who is this guy?"

"Maybe the killer." Then I explained.

"Close hold, sir?"

There was caution in Jonesy's voice; Talia and Colonel Ryerson were probably nearby. Jonesy was asking if he should tell them we had a description. I understood Jonesy's concern. Since they worked closely with the JCS, there was the chance they might let the information slip. "Close hold," I said, and hung up.

Tippett was leaning back in his seat, eyes closed. "Too bad our star witness took off," he murmured. "Could've had this thing wrapped up by morning."

I watched him for a moment. I could still smell the booze.

"Yeah," I said. "Too bad."

★★★★

I dropped Tippett off at General Watkins's residence. As I pulled away, I noticed Tippett's car at the curb. The front windows were down. On impulse, I double-parked alongside. A couple of MPs watched me from the house. I waved.

I crawled into his car and found a bottle beneath the passenger seat. Returning the bottle to its hiding place, I eased myself from his car and climbed back into my own.

My boss, General Romer, had been right. I'd have to watch Tippett.

★★★★

After parking at the Pentagon, I pulled out my notepad and wrote down three questions, something I often did to help me think.

What did Mr. Tho know?

What was in the envelope Mr. Tho gave to General Watkins?

Who was the Donahue look-alike?

Then I added a fourth.

Why was the Vietnamese boy so afraid?

I stared at the last. I could still see the terror in his eyes.

I didn't care what Tippett and Lieutenant Lee had said. No way that much fear came from seeing me in uniform.

★★★★

When I went inside, I stopped by the JCS security office. Webster sat alone at one of the desks in the anteroom, whistling as he sorted through stacks of what looked like five-by-seven cards. *Youth*, I thought. I felt exhausted, while Webster bubbled with energy. I heard music filtering from the major's office. This time the door was shut tight.

Webster grinned. "Hey, Colonel. We should nail this guy down pretty quick. Not many guys matching the description."

"How many so far?"

He picked up two cards. "Got a slight problem, though," he said, handing them over. "They're generals. An Air Force two-star and an Army one-star."

The cards had a passport-size photo taped to the top left corner, along with the person's name, rank, office symbol, and authorization code, all neatly typed. Both men had almost-white hair.

Webster looked amused. "Still want me to pick out the flag officers, sir?"

"You bet."

He grinned. "Gonna cause some fireworks when the big boys

find out they're suspects." He gave an exaggerated shake of his head. "Might want to strap on some Kevlar when you break them the news, sir."

"Thanks for your concern, Captain."

Webster grinned again. "Anytime, sir." He tapped a file on the corner of the desk. "Got that printout of everyone authorized a badge."

"Hold on to it. How much longer until you're finished?"

"Maybe an hour."

"I'll be in Watkins's office for the next few minutes."

Webster was again whistling as I left.

★★★★

Sergeant Mathews wasn't guarding the door to General Watkins's office anymore. In the reception room, I noticed all the computers were gone. On a back table, a fresh pot of coffee warmed on a coffeemaker. Blue coffee mugs with the Air Force seal hung on a rack over the table. I poured myself a mug and sipped gratefully. I found Jonesy and Talia sitting at the general's desk, each hunched over an open file. Next to them stood a short, fleshy colonel with salt-and-pepper hair, sorting through his own short stack of files.

Spotting me, Colonel Ryerson quickly introduced himself. He had a surprisingly firm grip. "What a terrible thing to happen," he said. "General Watkins was a great man. A great soldier. And soldiers shouldn't die like that."

I nodded sympathetically. "We'll do all we can to—"

"And what's this about our computers? Someone screwed with them?"

"A virus."

"Connected to the death?"

"We're not sure."

"How could a virus get into our computers?"

"I don't know."

Ryerson shook his head. "The whole thing is unbelievable. Just unbelievable."

I looked at Jonesy. "CID guys already take the computers downstairs?"

Jonesy nodded. "About half an hour ago. I told them to go back to Fort Myer. Sergeant Mathews too. After your call, I figured I didn't need them, sir."

"And General Watkins's computer in JCS?" I asked.

"I dropped that one off personally."

I tossed my hat onto the desk and sipped my coffee. "How many more files do you have to go over?"

Talia sat back in her chair and picked up a half-full mug, identical to mine except that her name was written on the side in gold script. "This is the last, Colonel," she said. "Everything was catalogued, so we pulled all the ones with Vietnam references. So far, they appear routine. A copy of a contingency plan to invade Vietnam, a country study, the semiannual intelligence papers on the military and political situation, a study of their tactical air capabilities. I'm going over the five-year threat analysis. Sergeant Jones has the latest projections for Vietnam's defense expenditures." She took a sip, adding to the lipstick smear on the rim.

I sagged into a chair. "That's it?"

Colonel Ryerson was again sorting through the files on the desk. "We don't track much on Vietnam in this office," he said without looking up.

"Anything new? In the last, say, couple of months."

"No, sir," Talia said. "Threat analysis is the most recent. It's three months old."

"What about the general's trip to Hanoi?" I asked. "You must have something on file?"

Talia shook her head. "The office pretty much stayed out of that. The White House arranged the travel and visas and the intel briefing. Remember, this was supposed to be very hush-hush, sir. None of us knew any of the specifics."

I looked to Ryerson to see if he wanted to add anything, but he'd set down the files and was now at a file cabinet. He looked perplexed.

"Not even an after-action report?" I asked.

"No," Talia said. "At least none I'm aware of."

Ryerson had the cabinet open. He was pawing through a drawer. Then he spun around, his round face showing agitation.

"There's a file missing," he said.

10

I PUT THE FILE IN HERE MYSELF, THIS AFTERNOON," RYERSON EXPLAINED. "THE GENERAL GAVE IT TO AMANDA, THE SECRETARY, TO MAKE A LIST of names he'd marked."

Talia was on her feet in a flash. She went to the file cabinet and began her own search.

"Slow down, Colonel," I said. "What file? What names?"

"MIAs. The file on MIAs. Remember, Talia?"

Talia nodded. "I'd forgotten about that file." She looked for a few more seconds and slid the drawer shut. "It's gone. Maybe General Watkins took it home with him."

Ryerson shook his head emphatically. "I put the file in here after he left for the day!"

"And this was a file of all the MIAs?" I asked.

"Yes," Ryerson replied.

"With only certain names marked?"

"Yes." Ryerson's brow was furrowed.

"What names?"

"I don't know. Just some names."

I looked at Talia. She shook her head.

"And he wanted them typed into a list for—" I stopped, because Ryerson was walking to the door.

Talia gave me a *who knows?* look and hurried after Ryerson. Jonesy and I followed.

We found Ryerson rummaging at another file cabinet by the secretary's desk. He said, "Amanda doesn't trust computers. Never has and never will. So she always makes a paper copy of everything. Ah hah!" He removed a piece of paper. When he turned, he had a satisfied smile.

"That's the list the secretary made from the original file?" I asked.

Ryerson nodded and gave me the paper. Jonesy and Talia crowded around.

The heading at the top said simply "MIA Listing for General Watkins." Then came names, in alphabetical order, numbered one to twenty-three. By each name were entries under four headings: Date, Category, Location, and Source.

"The date is the day the men disappeared," Ryerson said.

"What's the significance of the category?" I asked.

"DIA's code on whether North Vietnam could know the status of the MIA," Talia answered. "The category numbers go from one to five. A one indicates North Vietnam had to know the missing man's status."

"You mean if they confirmed he was a prisoner?" I asked.

"Yeah," Ryerson said. "And a two means there is a strong possibility North Vietnam should know someone's status, and so on, to five, which indicates there is little likelihood the North Vietnamese would have any information."

"Which would be what, some guy goes down over the Gulf of Tonkin and his body isn't recovered?"

"Something like that," Ryerson said. "I'm not sure what DIA uses as specific guidelines. Are you, Talia?"

Talia shook her head.

Jonesy said, "What about the initials under Source? They're different. See Cleland. Then look at Cutler."

I looked at the list. Cleland, Roland A., Captain, U.S. Air Force. February, 17, 1967. Category 1. Then lat and long coordinates. Under Source, the letters JB. I went down the page. Cutler, Terrance. NMI, Commander, U.S. Navy . . . My eyes went to the Source column. The letters DIA.

I said, "DIA is obviously the Defense Intelligence Agency. How about JB?" I looked up. Ryerson and Talia were shaking their heads.

"Know why General Watkins might have been interested in these particular names?"

Another head shake from Talia. Ryerson shrugged. "Might have to do with his trip to Hanoi."

"We're going to keep this," I told Ryerson. I handed the list to Jonesy.

"No problem," Ryerson said. "You think this may have something to do with the murder?"

"I'm not sure." I checked my watch. "Look, it's late. Maybe we'd better call it a night."

"I'll wait for Captain Webster, then lock up," Jonesy said.

Ryerson reached for his flight cap, which was tucked into his belt. "Well, if that's all . . ."

"You've been of tremendous help, Colonel," I said.

With a nod, Ryerson started for the door. He stopped, looking suddenly uncomfortable. "You know, there's a rather ominous implication about that file."

"Yes?" I said.

"Well, the missing file was in the cabinet, which is normally kept locked when in use. Only the staff has the combination."

"Isn't it possible General Watkins may have . . . may have given the killer the combination?" Talia said quickly.

I stared at her for a moment. "Yes, that's possible."

Ryerson took a second to catch on. Then he nodded. "I understand," he said softly. "Well, good night."

As Ryerson walked out, I said to Talia, "Come on. You've had a rough day. Let's get those files put away and I'll give you a ride to your car."

Talia seemed preoccupied.

"Major?" I said.

Her eyes focused. "Um, sure. Okay."

Talia gathered her purse and hat. "Oh, I almost forgot." She opened her purse and fumbled around. "I picked these up today for the general. I . . . I was going to drop them off when . . ." She bit her lip, then pulled out a thick yellow packet.

I read the name on the side. Kodak.

When she gave me the packet, her hand trembled. "Pictures from the general's trip to Hanoi. I . . . I don't think I can look at them."

She walked out.

"That's a little strange," Jonesy murmured.

I began spreading the pictures out on the desk as Jonesy stared at the doorway through which Talia had departed. He had a preoccupied look in his eyes now.

"What's strange?"

Jonesy didn't reply for a moment. Then he said, "Oh, just thinking, sir. I find it a little odd Major Swanson didn't know the file was missing. I saw her digging around in that drawer earlier tonight."

I shrugged. "She's had a rough day. I'm sure it was just an oversight." I laid out the last picture, which made thirty-six.

"Yeah. Maybe."

"Take a look," I said.

Most of the pictures were of the general with a variety of Vietnamese, both soldiers and official-looking men I took to be government types. The Vietnamese were smiling. General Watkins always looked grim.

I studied the first six pictures. The general standing outside a large stone building; the general in a tiny, barred room; the general walking in a walled-in courtyard; the general outside a barbed-wire compound; the general in a large concrete room.

"All prisons," Jonesy said. "The general was looking for MIAs, all right."

I nodded.

"Who took the pictures?"

I scanned the photos. The general was the only westerner I saw. "Probably the interpreter. Some professor."

"This guy?" Jonesy pointed to a picture showing the general and a tall, heavyset man in plain khakis and a straw hat.

"Probably," I said.

"Big guy. Looks like one of those safari hunters." Then he swore, and Jonesy almost never swore.

I caught on a split second later. Because of the hat, I'd almost missed it. I felt my pulse quicken.

Jonesy said, "Christ, sir. You think—"

"Talia!" I yelled. "Come in here!"

★★★★

"Yes, that's Professor Masonis," Talia said, carefully looking at the photo. She was sitting at the desk, with Jonesy and I huddling over her.

"You're sure?"

She gave me a long, questioning look, then nodded. "He spent a couple weeks over the last month and a half meeting with the general about the trip to Hanoi."

"He'd come here, to the office?"

Talia nodded. "He'd show up every other week or so, stay for a few days."

"What do you know about him?"

She gave me an uncertain look. "Not much, other than he's supposed to be a real expert on Vietnam. The general liked him. Professor Masonis seemed nice, pleasant. Good sense of humor. And he's single."

Jonesy coughed softly.

Talia gave him a dirty look. "He doesn't wear a wedding ring, Sergeant." She put her hands on her hips. "Come on, Colonel Jensen. What gives?"

"Bear with me, Talia. You don't know anything else about him? For instance, what he and the general talked about?"

"No, I had dinner with him at the general's residence one night. He didn't talk about himself much, but he was very charming. He likes golf. He and the general talked golf for hours. I almost got the feeling they were avoiding mentioning anything about the trip." She suddenly pushed away from the desk and went over to a bookshelf near the door. She returned, carrying two hardcover books. "These might help."

The first one was titled *Why America Lost: A Critical Analysis of the Vietnam War.* The second was titled *The Shame of America's MIAs.* Both were written by Dr. Theodore Masonis.

"The general read those," Talia said. "Thought they were quite good."

I flipped one of the books open to the back jacket. Masonis's picture showed a sturdy, chiseled face, intelligent eyes.

But I wasn't interested in his face.

I stared at his hair. A full head of hair. Neatly cropped white hair.

The bio was short. Dr. Masonis was a professor of Asian Studies at Duke University. This information was followed by a laudatory listing of his academic credentials. Next came a list of five other books he'd written. But the line that got my attention was the last one.

"Son of a bitch," I said.

"What's that, sir?" Jonesy said.

I slowly closed the book. "Masonis won a Silver Star in Vietnam."

Jonesy's eyebrows went up.

"So what?" Talia asked.

"Better check him out first thing in the morning," I told Jonesy.

"Sir, you want to tell me what you are talking about?" Talia said.

"First thing," Jonesy said.

"Sir?"

I turned and found myself looking into two very angry blue eyes.

I told her.

★★★★

Talia led us into the admin room on the other side of the reception area. Inside the room were four desks, two copying machines, two laser printers, a fax machine, and the usual assortment of bookshelves and file cabinets. Apparently, the office of the Air Force Chief of Staff generated a lot of paperwork. Talia went to one of the file cabinets, opened it, and produced a green binder.

"Sometimes the general and Dr. Masonis went into the JCS," Talia said. "Usually to his office down there. I think they just wanted a little more privacy. Gets real hectic up here. But I know Dr. Masonis turned in his temporary entry badge, Colonel." She flipped open the binder, thumbing through pages. "He wouldn't have been able to get in without an escort if he went in today." She stopped, frowning. "I don't understand this."

"What?"

"We collected his first entry badge, but—"

"First badge? There was another one issued?"

Talia nodded, a little dazed. "It must have been while I was at lunch."

I looked over her shoulder at the last entry: *Dr. Theodore L. Masonis*, printed in a neat hand. A signature, an unrecognizable scrawl, was in the authorization block. I checked the date.

"Christ. That's today. Or yesterday now. That means . . ."

"He was here, sir," Talia murmured. "That's the general's signature, authorizing it."

"Looks like we may have our killer," Jonesy said.

"You're mistaken," Talia said a little too quickly. "He . . . he couldn't have killed the general."

I frowned, surprised at her reaction. "Why not?"

Talia looked away. "He seemed so . . . well . . . so nice."

So did Ted Bundy, I thought.

★★★★

Talia had Dr. Masonis's North Carolina number on file in her little electronic organizer. I called. Calling seemed the quickest way to rule Masonis out as a suspect. There wouldn't have been time for him to kill Tho and return to North Carolina. The phone rang. I really didn't have anything prepared to say. But then, I didn't think he'd answer. After the fourth ring, there was a click. A recorded voice came on. Deep, garrulous. "Hi. You've got Ted Masonis. Sorry—"

I hung up.

I glanced at my watch. After two in the morning. Tracking Masonis down would have to wait till morning.

Talia looked exhausted. Over her protests, I told her I was taking her home. I called the CID cellular. Lieutenant Dolenz answered. Tippett had gone to see Doc Owens at Walter Reed. Dolenz promised to have someone drop off Talia's car at her apartment in Falls Church.

I checked in with Webster on the way out. He was two-thirds finished. Nine possibles. He grinned when I said I was driving Talia home.

Talia was quiet, almost reflective, during the ride. She lived in one of those town-house developments. Without traffic, the drive took twenty minutes. As she climbed out, she turned, looking troubled. "Colonel, I meant it. I don't think Dr. Masonis is capable of killing. I can't explain, but . . . well, I think you're wrong." She jumped out before I could muster a response. I watched as she walked away.

I sat there shaking my head. Why would she come so strongly to the good doctor's defense, having known him so casually and for such a short time? Could she and Masonis . . . ? I didn't want to finish the thought.

★★★★

When I walked into my living room, I immediately knew I was in trouble. My wife, Jean, was sitting on the living-room couch in her bathrobe, hands folded, legs crossed, eyes fixed in a critical stare.

I gave her a tentative smile. "Hi, honey. What're you doing up?"

"She sounds too young for you, Charles. I put her at, say, twenty-seven, blond, big tits, IQ of a turnip."

"Honey, who're you talking about?"

Jean smiled sweetly. In one of those fake southern belle accents, she said, "Why, the poor young thing who just called and woke up the house. She insisted she just had to talk to Colonel Jensen. Would I have him call the moment he came home, please?"

I joined Jean on the couch, taking her hand. I was encouraged when she didn't yank it away. "Honey, I have no idea what you're talking about."

She considered me for a moment. "Hmm. The name Talia ring any bells? She mentioned you had just left her place."

I jumped up. "Oh, Christ. She's General Watkins's aide. I just gave her a ride home. She's had a tough time today."

"I'll bet."

"Jean, she found his body."

"Oh! God, Charlie, I was just kidding."

"Did she say what she wanted?"

Jean shook her head.

I fished out my notepad and reached for the phone on the end table.

Talia answered on the first ring. "I was hoping you'd call."

"What's up?"

She paused. "I had a message on my machine. He wants to ask me out."

"Who?"

There was a long silence. "Dr. Masonis."

11

M Y MIND TOOK A FEW SECONDS TO KICK INTO GEAR. THEN I FELT ANGRY. I PUT AN EDGE INTO MY VOICE WHEN I SPOKE. "OKAY, TALIA, tell me everything. And this time don't leave anything out. Got it?"

Talia swore there was nothing between them . . . yet. They had only talked casually, mostly at the office, and of course at the dinner. She sensed he was interested in her. And to be frank, she found him rather fascinating. But there was no time, and it would have been awkward with the general around. However, after the general and Masonis returned from Hanoi, she'd had a call. Masonis wanted to know if she would consider having dinner the next time he was in D.C. She'd said yes.

"And that's it?" I asked, still annoyed.

"Yes. I haven't heard from him since that call, which was over two weeks ago."

"Did he leave a number? Say where he's staying?"

"No. He said he'd call back tomorrow."

"Don't go to work, then. I want you to be there when he calls. I'll let Colonel Ryerson know you won't be in."

"Okay."

"And I'll arrange for Captain Webster and a team to come by. He'll set things so we can trace the call."

There was no response.

"Talia?"

"I'm here. I was just thinking it doesn't make much sense. I mean, if he's the killer."

"I don't follow you."

"Asking me out. I mean, who kills two people, then calls up a girl and asks her for a date?"

I couldn't think of a response, nor could I think of a reason for what she'd said to make me angry, but I was. "Just make sure all your doors and windows are locked tonight," I growled. "Captain Webster will be by with a team in the morning."

"Uh . . . okay, sir."

I hung up.

★★★★

"Hi. This is Jim Rockford," said the answering machine in a surprisingly good James Garner imitation. "Ha, ha. Not really. You've reached Johnny Webster . . ."

I left a message at the beep, then called Lieutenant Lee. The detective who answered gave me a mobile number. I called, was told to wait a minute. Lee finally came on the line.

He said they still hadn't found the boy.

I told him about Dr. Masonis and the call on Talia's machine. I also told him I'd drop off one of the book jackets tomorrow morning, along with a picture of General Watkins.

Lee said he'd send a car over immediately.

I groaned. Then I leaned back on the couch and closed my eyes. Dammit, Talia had a point, I thought. Hard to believe Masonis would call her if he was the killer. But if he thought he'd gotten away with it . . .

"Honey."

I opened my eyes.

Jean patted her lap. I put my head there. She massaged my temples. "Everything okay?"

I looked up into her eyes. "Now it is. How'd Stacy do?"

"Good. Danced wonderfully. Only two little mistakes. You'd have been proud, Charlie."

I smiled. "Always am. So you going to tell me how she placed?"

"Second. That cute little Margaret Han played a dazzling Chopin number on the violin. She deserved to win."

"How'd Stacy take it?"

Jean ran her fingers through my hair. "Stacy said, 'Mom, I'm glad Margaret got first.' I asked her why. She said, 'Because she was better than me, Mom.' How do you like that, Charlie?"

I squeezed her hand. "We've got good kids, Jean."

She smiled tenderly. "We do, don't we?"

I closed my eyes. Jean rubbed my head for a few more minutes, then kissed me lightly on the lips. "Is she pretty? The girl that called?

I looked up into her eyes again, giving her a mischievous grin. "You're not jealous?"

"Of course not. Just curious."

I laughed. "Because if you are, I think that'd be great. My wife, getting a little jealous after all these years. Shows I still have it."

"Men!" She shoved my head off her lap. "I'm going to bed."

I chuckled, and lay back down on the couch. I was almost asleep when the doorbell rang. Rita, the detective, looked as sour as usual. I gave her Masonis's book.

I stumbled into bed about four and drifted off thinking about Tippett and that bottle.

Damn him.

12

Tuesday

SOMEONE WAS SHAKING ME. "CHARLIE. CHARLIE." SHAKING HARDER. "CHARLIE."

I groaned, feeling drugged.

"Charlie!"

I opened my eyes. Sunlight streamed through the blinds. Jean stood above me.

"Finally. I thought you were dead." She pointed to the phone on the nightstand. "Sergeant Jones."

I sat up. I'd set the alarm for nine. "What time is it?"

"Almost nine. Bacon and eggs, or cereal?"

"Uh, cereal, honey." I picked up the phone and croaked, "What's up?"

Jonesy's monotone voice said, "Colonel Jensen?"

"It's me, Jonesy. Still half asleep."

"Think you better turn on the tube, sir. Channel Five. WTTG. They're carrying the press conference on General Watkins's murder."

"Shit."

I looked around for the remote, which, as usual, was nowhere to be found. "Hang on, Jonesy." I jumped up and flipped on the portable TV on the dresser and flicked to the proper channel.

General Clayton Holmes, Chairman of the Joint Chiefs, stood at a podium in the Pentagon pressroom, his medals and ribbons glistening under the lights. He looked regal, intimidating.

"At this time," he was saying, "I can't provide specifics on the investigation into this brutal murder, but I can say that all the resources at our disposal are directed to finding the person responsible. Rest assured . . ."

I picked up the phone. "You at the office?"

"Yes, sir."

"Know if Webster got the message about Major Swanson?"

"He just picked up the equipment and left with Jurgens and Peters. And Major Gutiérrez called from the Pentagon. She wants you to stop by ASAP."

"I'll meet you at her office at 1130."

"Roger, sir. I went over that list of MIA names. Found something interesting."

"Go on."

"All were category one. Means they were verified as POWs by the North Vietnamese."

"Uh-huh."

"What's really interesting is the lat and long readouts. I plotted them. All the men disappeared just north of the DMZ, within about ten miles of each other. Most were shot down."

"What are you getting at, Jonesy?"

"Maybe they were interned together. You know, the same compound. And if they were, and none of them ever came back . . ."

I ran a hand over my face. Jonesy's implication was ominous.

"Better fax me the list, Jonesy. I'll check with DIA. And change of plans. Meet me at General Watkins's office." I hung up.

I tried to concentrate on the TV, but I kept thinking about what Jonesy had implied.

But why would the North Vietnamese have killed so many of their valuable bargaining chips? That didn't make sense.

A thought hit me.

I remembered the rumor that sprang up after the POWs came back. The one that said the North Vietnamese had wanted a way to ensure the ten billion dollars which Nixon had promised would be paid when the war was over.

No, killing POWs didn't make sense.

But if some had been kept alive . . .

"Jesus!"

★★★★

I fully expected Holmes to talk for perhaps ten minutes, answer a few questions, maybe have the Secretary of the Air Force say a few words, then turn things over to the Pentagon press secretary. That's the way these things usually occurred. Heavy hitters were there only to emphasize the significance of an event.

But twenty minutes later, Holmes was still talking. He'd turned the press conference into a eulogy, recounting in great detail Watkins's career and their mutual experience as POWs. What I found fascinating was the transformation of Holmes the longer he spoke. It was so subtle I almost missed it. His face gradually softened, his voice wavered. Then came the pauses, longer and more frequent. Finally, in a dramatic moment, he suddenly stepped back from the lectern. The camera closed in. You could see the pain now, the reddening eyes, the tremble of the lips.

Then a tear ran down his left cheek.

A single tear, by God, which he slowly reached up and wiped away.

"Give me a break," I grunted at the TV.

This couldn't be the same man who had looked at Watkins's mutilated body with such stoic calmness. Then a thought occurred to me. Tomorrow, Holmes's anguished face was going to be front page all over the country. The networks would run excerpts on the evening news. The old warrior would be seen as human, caring. If Holmes had his eye on the White House, as I had heard, that would mean votes. A lot of votes.

"You sly bastard," I murmured.

Holmes took a deep breath and stepped forward. He looked directly into the camera and spoke with feeling. "When I looked at his mutilated body, I remember thinking that a man who survived so often in situations which had claimed so many others shouldn't die in such a cruel fashion. I was also struck that General Watkins was cut down before he could pass on one more legacy, something which showed the true measure of this great American." Holmes paused. "Last month, General Watkins made a trip to Hanoi, a trip to the source of his suffering. He was torn on whether to support the President's recent executive order to normalize relations with Vietnam. He had to know, first and foremost, if the Vietnamese had indeed been forthright in their accounting of America's MIAs."

I watched the screen in disbelief. Holmes was going to use the opportunity to slam the President's policy.

Holmes's eyes panned the audience, then returned to the camera. "Yesterday, General Watkins came to me and said that he had decided to support the President's decision toward official recognition of Vietnam. General Watkins was finally convinced that Vietnam had never kept back any live Americans. 'You can't hold grudges forever,' he said."

Holmes took a moment to gather himself, heightening the anticipation. His voice stirred with emotion. "If General Watkins can forgive, so can I. I officially announce my support for the United States' policy to recognize Vietnam."

There was stunned silence. Then came a barrage of questions. Two men in military uniforms appeared on stage and escorted Holmes off. More shouts. The Pentagon press secretary took the podium, demanded order. More questions . . .

But I wasn't listening. I was wondering why General Watkins had changed his mind.

And had someone killed him because he did?

★★★★

I was in my study when the phone rang. I slipped Jonesy's fax into my suit jacket, a gray pin-striped number. "Honey!" Jean called from downstairs. "Can you pick up?"

"Colonel Jensen?" a man asked when I had put the phone to my ear.

"Yes."

"Thank God! I called your office. You're running the investigation into General Watkins's death?"

"Actually, I'm assisting. The Army CID—"

"But General Watkins was Air Force."

"I'm sure you don't want to discuss jurisdictional guidelines. What can I do for you?"

"I think we need to talk."

"Look, who are you?"

"John Birelli."

"The colonel who used to head DIA's POW/MIA office."

"Yes, but I'm retired. I now run the MIA association. Did you catch Channel Five? General Holmes's press conference?"

"Yes."

"He's lying."

"What?"

"General Holmes is lying about General Watkins. The general wasn't going to agree to recognition of Vietnam. Never!"

"What do you mean? If you have any information . . ."

"Tell me, did you find pictures in General Watkins's quarters? POW pictures?"

"Pictures of POWs?"

"Believe me, you'd know if you found them. I figured as much. Look, I don't have much time. I've got to leave for the Capitol. Are you free this evening? Say, 1900?"

"Yeah, but . . ."

"I've really got to run. You have a pen?"

"What about these pictures you mentioned?"

"Not over the phone. You want the address or not?"

"Hold on. Okay, I'm ready."

"It's near Manassas."

After I copied down the directions, I wrote *John Birelli*. Then I froze. John Birelli . . . J.B.

The same initials under the Source heading on General Watkins's MIA list.

13

THERE WERE A LOT OF GOOD THINGS ABOUT LIVING NEAR WASHINGTON, D.C., BUT I THINK I WOULD HAVE TRADED THEM ALL FOR A PLACE where traffic actually moved. Because of a jackknifed eighteen-wheeler, it took me an hour to fight my way up I-395 to the Pentagon, a ride that usually takes about thirty-five minutes. But I had time to think about Colonel John Birelli's call. I honestly believed the man had to be mistaken. Sure, General Holmes had used the press conference to enhance his political capital. But so what? He was a Medal of Honor winner and a four-star general with an eye on making a run at the presidency. Besides, why would he lie about Watkins's position on Vietnam? Holmes didn't have anything riding on the Vietnam-recognition issue. He could have said Watkins was against the President's policy and still come out ahead.

But Birelli's phone call did give credence to Talia's account that Watkins had been against recognition, at least initially. Assuming they were both right, then Watkins must have changed his position in the last few days.

I thought of the twenty-three names on the MIA list. Was there a connection between them and Watkins's death?

And what the hell were these POW pictures Birelli mentioned?

As I pulled into the Pentagon's south parking lot, I was already feeling the faint poundings of a headache.

★★★★

You have to understand the logic behind the hub-and-spoke layout of the Pentagon in order to navigate its corridors. Five concentric hallways or rings, designated from A to E, expand outward from the center. Ten perpendicular corridors, the spokes, intersect these, and are numbered 1 to 10. With an office number, you can immediately tell the precise location. For example, room 4C322 is on the fourth floor, C-ring, off of corridor number 3.

At about ten o'clock, I walked into the Special Office for POW and MIA Affairs, deep inside the Defense Intelligence Agency's maze of secured offices on the second floor. I'd called before I left the house and the chief of the department, Colonel Randy Butcher, was expecting me. His secretary waved me in.

I'd never met Army Colonel Randy Butcher, but I'd caught him on TV a few times. He was the government's chief spokesman on MIA issues. A squat, heavyset man with Popeye forearms and a quarter-inch flattop haircut, he rose from behind his cluttered desk wearing a big, friendly smile. "So what can I do for the Air Force OSI, Colonel?" He pointed to a chair.

I sat and reached into my jacket. "Appreciate the time, Colonel. You hear about the murder of General Watkins?"

Butcher's face turned somber. "Bad business. You running the investigation?"

I nodded, laying Jonesy's fax on the desk. I slid it over. "I'm curious about these names General Watkins selected from the MIA roster in his office. Wonder what you can tell me about them."

Butcher took the list. He looked up after a few moments. "They're MIAs from Cao Dinh."

"Cao Dinh?"

"A POW camp. You want some coffee?"

I nodded. "Black."

Butcher punched the intercom. "Jeri. Get me the file on General Watkins's request from last week. And two coffees, black."

I sat up. "So all these names were POWs from this one camp?"

He stared at the fax. "I think there's a few extra here. We passed on something like eighteen or nineteen names." He leaned back. "You ever heard of Cao Dinh?"

I shook my head. The door opened. The secretary came in, carrying a small tray with the coffees, a file under her arm.

After she left, Butcher leaned back, mug in hand. He flipped open the file, which had a red Top Secret cover. "Yeah. General Watkins sent a request to us to ID all POWs we could confirm at Cao Dinh. We came up with eighteen. I don't know where Watkins got the rest." He sipped. "Cao Dinh was a POW camp about four miles north of the DMZ, near the Laotian border. Built back in 1966. The camp was used primarily as a staging base for POWs who were later transferred to Hanoi. In 1971, a marine recon team captured two soldiers who turned out to be guards at Cao Dinh. That's when we first learned of the camp."

"These guards, did they provide the names of the POWs?"

Butcher nodded. He spoke slowly, as if choosing each word. "Some, but not all. Plans were made to try and make a raid to free the prisoners. But a few months later, we discovered the camp was no longer in operation. We assumed the North Vietnamese had gotten nervous, maybe over the missing guards. Anyway, we thought they moved the POWs to Hanoi."

"Did they?"

A pause. "No."

I expected him to elaborate. He didn't.

"Then where were the POWs sent?" I asked.

"I can't say."

"Can't, or won't?"

Butcher's jaw tightened. "Can't." He set the mug down. "We haven't been able to confirm that those POWs were sent to any of the other camps."

My eyebrows went up. "You're saying no one ever saw these men after they were at Cao Dinh? What do you think happened?"

"Hard to say," he answered cautiously.

"You don't think they might have been kept back intentionally by the Vietnamese?"

"Hell, no! Don't tell me you think there were live POWs left behind?"

"I've heard the rumors, of course."

"Look, the official list says there are 2,231 MIAs. You know what that really means? Just one damn thing. There are 2,231 bodies that haven't been recovered. That's all. It doesn't mean they're alive."

This was obviously an argument in which Butcher specialized. I said nothing.

Butcher stared at me for a moment. "You're an Air Force guy. Say you're flying along in a fighter, okay?"

"Okay."

"You're in an F-4. Flying over Vietnam. You look out just in time to see your wingman get blown all to hell by a SAM. Plane literally disintegrates before your eyes. No chutes. Two of your buddies gone. What do you report when you land back home?"

"I . . . well, that they were shot down."

He leaned forward. "Do you say they're dead?"

"Sure."

He shook his head. "Not the way it was done in a lot of fighter units. Because of the benefits for the families."

"Benefits?"

"Sure. If you report your buddies in the F-4 as KIA, their families get a lump-sum death benefit from Uncle Sam, period. But you say maybe you think there was a chute, and presto, the guys' wives and kids keep on getting their pay, all military privileges, housing . . . for years. And the pay keeps going up, because MIAs are automatically promoted up through colonel. We're talking a difference of hundreds of thousands of dollars. To a lot of guys, saying a buddy might be alive was their way of looking out for his family."

"Even if the family took false hope?"

"Better than having them suffer financial hardship."

"But surely that doesn't explain the, what . . . two thousand–plus names on the MIA list?"

"No, most of those are there because of how we define an MIA. The definition generally boils down to if there's no body, he goes on the list." He paused, shaking his head. "Even if we know he's dead."

"Why don't you change the rules so you can change the MIAs to KIAs?"

Butcher snorted. "Hell, we tried. Back in 1977, we began calling guys we knew were dead KIA-BNR . . . 'killed in action and body not recovered.' We were able to get a number of the names off the list. In 1979, the MIA families won a lawsuit. Got Congress involved. Anybody we hadn't got around to listing as KIA-BNR went back on the list, along with some others. The sad thing is we knew almost all of them were dead. But what can you do? Those were our orders."

"But what about all the sightings? The photos . . ."

"Horseshit. We've checked out over fifteen thousand reports of MIAs since 1975. You know how many have turned up anything?"

"No."

"Zero. There's a whole POW/MIA industry in Thailand, Laos, Cambodia, and Vietnam. People who make dog tags, manufacture photos, letters, anything they think they can use to get money from the families or from rich guys like Perot. You remember the photo that came out in 1991? Made a big splash? Showed a guy who was supposed to be a POW, Captain Don Carr?"

I nodded vaguely.

"Turns out the picture was of some German national named Günther Dietrich. The picture had been taken at a bird farm in Thailand. We tracked down this Dietrich, and he admitted the photo was his. When we put the word out that the whole thing was a hoax, it was the same old shit. People accused us of engaging in a cover-up." He shrugged. "The problem with the MIA situation is people want live POWs, and they aren't going to be swayed by the fact that there just aren't any."

"So you can confirm everyone on the MIA list is dead, no doubt at all?"

"Damn near. You know how many of those names we have questions about? Where there isn't strong evidence they died?"

I shook my head.

"Thirteen."

My eyebrows went up.

"Thirteen," he said again. "And all but nine of those we are pretty certain were willing defectors to North Vietnam. Like Bobby Garwood."

"Then the men at Cao Dinh?"

"Dead."

"But how?" I jabbed at the list. "You obviously don't think they were kept behind. Seems implausible that not even one of these men returned unless . . . Hell, I'll ask you straight out. Were these men executed?"

A long pause.

"Look, Colonel." Butcher tapped a finger against his mug, his mood somber. "I've probably already given you more than I should. The prisoners at Cao Dinh are dead. The specifics are classified. I'm sorry."

"I can't accept that." I looked him in the eye. "I don't think you understand, Colonel. I think there is a link between General Watkins's trip to Vietnam and his death. That connection may be Cao Dinh. If you want me to go above your head to get authorization, I will."

"Don't be a damn fool! The record is Eyes Only."

"Eyes Only? I can still—"

"The President's Eyes Only, Colonel."

"Oh." I sat back, my bravado gone.

"Yeah, if I tell you, I go to Leavenworth. And my ass is too cute for prison." He made the comment without a smile.

I shook my head in frustration. This thing was beginning to stink. "General Watkins? Did he mention to you why he wanted information on Cao Dinh?"

"No, and I wasn't about to ask. I didn't know he was going to Vietnam until General Holmes said so in the press conference this morning."

I leaned forward. "If the truth came out about Cao Dinh, would Congress block the President's executive order to normalize relations with Vietnam?"

Butcher placed his elbows on the table, pressing his fingers together, brow furrowed. "I can't answer that, Colonel." He checked his watch.

I took the hint, picked up the list, and refolded it. "Thanks for the coffee." At the door, I said, "Oh, one more thing, Colonel. What is your opinion of John Birelli?"

"Birelli," Butcher spat. "He's a cock-sucking opportunist."

"Wasn't he your predecessor?"

"Yeah."

"I see."

I left, my headache suddenly worse.

14

I KNOCKED ON THE DOOR TO WATKINS'S OFFICE, BUT THERE WAS NO RE-SPONSE. I OPENED THE DOOR. THE USUAL OFFICE SOUNDS: SOFT CON-versation, phones jingling.

"The SECAF wants the recommendations on the POM now?" roared Colonel Ryerson from behind his desk. He wore an incredulous look. "You've got to be kidding, Laura. Don't they know the general's dead, for chrissakes!"

I stood in the doorway, trying to figure out whom Ryerson was talking to about the POM, which was a fancy acronym for the Air Force budget. Then I saw the large, rather plain-looking female major at Talia's desk. She had a hand cupped over a phone, and she sounded frustrated as she answered Ryerson. "Of course, sir, but the SECAF needs to finalize the budget numbers."

"Murdered!" Ryerson spit out the word.

"But, sir, the House Armed Services Committee is meeting tomorrow, and the Secretary . . ."

Ryerson snapped the pencil in his hand, slamming the pieces on his desk. "He's dead, Laura. Tell them that. Tell them we have no computers, and therefore no goddamn report. Tell them General Tupper is running the Air Force. Tell them to leave us the hell alone."

I shook my head in amazement. Ryerson wasn't the calm, quiet man of last night.

Laura sighed, nodded, and began talking into the phone.

I stepped inside and closed the door.

Phones continued to ring incessantly in the background. People darted about, arms filled with papers or folders. A lanky colonel with bushy eyebrows walked by, head down, scribbling furiously on a pad. He went to a file cabinet and yanked it open. An elegant, elderly woman sat at a desk, a phone on her shoulder, talking softly, dabbing her eyes with a Kleenex. A wooden nameplate by her elbow read "Mrs. Amanda Moffitt."

I coughed.

Ryerson noticed and waved me over. "As you can tell, Colonel, the shit has definitely hit the fan. How long are you going to need Talia? We sure could use her."

"I'm not sure. A day or two."

"Yeah? Okay."

I tried to look sympathetic. "Look, if I've come at a bad time . . ."

"Hell, no. Your investigation has priority. The Air Force certainly won't disappear if we don't answer the phones. Oh, checked with the rest of the staff. No one removed that file on the POWs."

"Thanks. I only have a few questions."

"Sure, everyone's been briefed. They'll cooperate, but I doubt you'll get much. Most of them are still in shock."

"I understand. I'll make this as quick and painless as possible." Out of the corner of my eye, I saw Jonesy enter. He came over.

"Sorry I'm late, sir," he said.

Ryerson nodded to Jonesy, then asked me, "So who do you need?"

"The key staff for now." I read him the list of names Talia had mentioned the night before. "And anyone else you care to add."

"No. Those names are good." He lowered his voice. "But I might reconsider Mrs. Moffitt."

"She's the general's secretary, isn't she?"

"Yeah, but she's getting along in years and she's very emotional.

Might be a good idea to wait until she's had a little time to get over the shock."

I thought about that for a moment. "I'll have to insist. I'll be discreet, don't worry."

He nodded. "Give me a sec to notify the admin people to cover the phones. We'll use the conference room, okay? Hey, Hugh!" He went over to the other colonel.

Jonesy and I walked toward the back, where I remembered the conference room was.

★★★★

We sat around the conference table, Jonesy and I at one end, Colonel Ryerson and Colonel Jowers down one side, and Mrs. Amanda Moffitt and Major Laura Parker, the chief of admin, down the other.

After expressing my condolences, I said, "Now, I talked to Colonel Ryerson and Major Swanson last night—"

"Where is Talia?" Colonel Jowers grunted suspiciously. The knitted bushy brows on his angular face gave him a fierce look.

"I told her not to come in. We need her help concerning a matter—"

"I'll just bet," Jowers said. He made it sound like an accusation.

"Hugh . . ." Ryerson said, his voice rising in warning.

"What's the real story?" Jowers asked. "The princess too overcome with grief?"

"That's enough, Hugh," Ryerson said, more urgently.

"Because her meal ticket is gone? That it? No more free rides!"

"Dammit, Hugh!"

But Jowers was focused on me, talking fast. "You know she's on the lieutenant colonel's list? Two years early. And she was two years early to major. Four damn years ahead of her peers. For what? Smiling? Looking pretty? Hell . . ."

"Shut up, Hugh!" Ryerson said.

"Colonel Jowers!" Mrs. Moffitt was staring at Colonel Jowers, looking horrified. "I'm ashamed at you. Major Swanson had a shock. She found . . . the . . ." Mrs. Moffitt put a hand to her mouth and shook her head.

Colonel Jowers blinked, his face softening. "I'm sorry, Amanda." He sat back slowly and folded his arms.

Major Laura Parker reached out and patted Mrs. Moffitt's hand. Then she looked at me, started to open her mouth, then closed it again.

I said, "Something on your mind, Major Parker?"

She hesitated, then shook her head.

"Anyone else?" I looked around the room.

"Let's just get this over with," Jowers said.

★★★★

I went through the questions. The responses verified what Talia had told me. Colonel Jowers and Colonel Ryerson did most of the talking, but that was to be expected. General Watkins had been preoccupied, secretive. No one knew exactly what he had been working on the past few days. No one knew why the general had been interested in the MIA names. They knew about the trip to Vietnam and Masonis's participation, but no details.

"Ask Talia," Jowers growled.

"I did. She has no idea what General Watkins was working on."

Jowers snorted. "Is that right?"

I frowned. "Are you saying Major Swanson did know?"

Jowers leaned back. He seemed amused. "All I'm saying is if Talia didn't know, that would be a first. Hell, she knew more about the old man's affairs than he did." He looked at the others. "Am I right?"

Heads nodded. Even Mrs. Moffitt's.

Jowers grinned. "Maybe you just better ask Talia again."

I said, "But you did notice General Watkins was angry upon his return from Vietnam?"

"I understand the Vietnamese wouldn't let him check some of the camps," Ryerson answered.

"Do you know which ones?"

"No."

Everyone shook their heads.

"How about the Vietnam-recognition issue? How did General Watkins feel about that?"

"He was dead set against it," Jowers snapped. Ryerson nodded his head vigorously in agreement.

"Then you don't know why he changed his position?"

Jowers frowned. "I honestly can't believe he would have. He compared recognition to selling out."

"Sure did," Ryerson said. "I agree with Hugh. Darn hard to believe General Watkins changed his mind." He paused. "But I guess he did."

"Yes, it would seem so. What did you think of Dr. Masonis?"

"Seemed capable, pleasant," Ryerson said.

"Good guy," Jowers said. "Boss liked him. Why?"

I ignored the question. "Mrs. Moffitt, your impression?"

Mrs. Moffitt looked surprised to be asked a question. "Oh, well, a very nice man. Well-mannered."

Again Laura seemed to be on the verge of saying something, but she remained silent.

I flipped the notepad closed. "Who was here when Masonis came into the office yesterday?"

"Masonis was here?" Jowers asked.

"Around noon, Colonel," Mrs. Moffitt said. "General Watkins and Dr. Masonis spoke for a while. Dr. Masonis left around one, I think."

"I was at lunch," Laura said. "But when I came back, the general told me he'd authorized Dr. Masonis another JCS entry badge."

"I remember the general mentioning that," Ryerson said.

"Anyone know why Dr. Masonis was here?" I asked.

Negative responses all around.

"How about the virus, then? Any idea how it could have been introduced into your computers?"

More head shakes.

"Our policy is to virus-scan any disk before uploading it," Ryerson said. "So I don't understand how it could have been introduced. Everything was fine when I left yesterday evening."

"You said last night you locked the office."

Ryerson nodded.

"Who has keys?"

"The general, of course, had a set." Ryerson looked around the table. "And us. The essential staff."

"Let's not forget Talia, shall we?" Jowers said dryly.

"And everyone here has keys to the general's office in the JCS?"

"Except for Mrs. Moffitt," Ryerson said.

"Okay." I glanced at Jonesy, my eyes telling him I was finished.

Jonesy folded his hands on the table. "One question. Over the past week, did General Watkins say anything, do anything which seemed out of character or unusual?"

Faces frowned. Then a smattering of negative responses.

Jonesy said, "Now, take your time. This could be anything. Even something seemingly insignificant?"

The nod Mrs. Moffitt gave was almost imperceptible.

Jonesy caught it. "Mrs. Moffitt?"

"It's nothing, I suppose." She looked at the others, almost embarrassed.

Jonesy said, "Ma'am, let us decide that."

"Maybe I'm just being a little sensitive, but he's never done that before. And I was just trying to help."

"Yes?" Jonesy leaned forward.

Mrs. Moffitt took a breath, looking right at him. Her lip quivered. "The general yelled at me."

Jonesy frowned. I frowned. Everyone else looked confused.

Then Mrs. Moffitt explained, "General Watkins was always very polite, you see. A gentleman. That's why I was surprised. It was two days ago. In the morning. I'd gone into the general's office to take him his coffee. He was on the phone. A fax came through on his machine. I went over to pick it up like I often did." She paused, looking at me. "He almost knocked me aside when he snatched it out of my hand." She swallowed.

"And he yelled at me. Told me never to do that again." Her voice cracked a little and her eyes misted.

"But you saw the fax," Jonesy said.

A nod.

"What was it?" I asked.

"Some . . . some kind of financial statement. I didn't see the numbers."

"Yes?"

"But there was a name across the top."

"Yes?" I waited. She just stared at me.

I said, "Mrs. Moffitt . . ."

She shook her head. "I . . . I can't remember exactly. I only saw it for a moment."

I could see she was getting flustered. Gently, I said, "But you do recall something?"

A timid nod.

"What?"

"Like . . . dinosaur."

"Dinosaur?"

"Like the sound . . . in the beginning. Dine something."

"Two words?"

She frowned. "One, I think."

I wrote in my notepad. "Anything else?"

A head shake. "I'm sorry." She rubbed a bony hand over her brow. "Maybe it will come to me later."

"I'm sure it will," I said. I gave her a smile.

★★★★

None of the others knew anything about the fax. I went around the room, asking a few more questions, trying to find out if General Watkins mentioned anything even remotely connected to Vietnam.

"Don't know," Jowers said. His bushy brows narrowed. "So you think maybe the general was murdered because of his trip, huh?"

"I can't comment on the investigation," I said.

Jowers sat up. "But that's where you're headed, right?"

Before I could reply, Ryerson sighed. "Hugh, shut up."

"Hey, just curious."

"You can all go," I said.

Jonesy wrote something in his notepad and slid it over so I could read it.

I nodded.

"Major Parker, one moment . . ."

★★★★

Major Parker fidgeted with her hands, chewing her lip, as she looked at Jonesy.

Jonesy slowly walked around to the side of the table, watching her. "Then there is nothing you wanted to say, Major? Nothing at all?"

"No. I've told you everything."

"Concerning Major Swanson? The comment Colonel Jowers made? About Major Swanson's grief?" Jonesy leaned over the table, hands spread. He kept his voice casual, almost friendly. "You started to say something earlier. I just want to know what was on your mind."

She looked to the table, clasping her hands tight. "I just . . . I didn't want you to get the wrong impression. About Colonel Jowers."

Jonesy said nothing, but he continued to look at her.

"I mean I think we all feel like he does about Talia. But Colonel Jowers . . . well, he says things. You always know what's on his mind. Gets him into trouble sometimes." She glanced at me. "Look, sir, I don't want to spread gossip."

"Please, Major, let us be the judge of what's gossip."

She sighed. "Talia is very beautiful. She affects men. They do things for her. Maybe if I was in her situation, I'd do the same thing. But she . . . well, she uses them. You know, to get ahead."

"Why is Colonel Jowers so angry with Major Swanson?" Jonesy asked. "Is there a specific reason?"

"I don't know about specific. I think he just resents the way Talia moved in on the general after his wife died. I mean that literally. She practically lives at his place. You know they have dinner three, four times a week?"

I shook my head.

"That's not right. She even pays his bills, grocery shops, does his laundry!"

"Are you saying they are having an affair?" Jonesy asked.

Laura looked horrified. "Not General Watkins. No, no. This was more like a father-daughter thing."

"Maybe she really cares for him?" Jonesy said.

Laura looked at him as if he were crazy. "You don't know Talia very well."

"Then she didn't care for him?"

Laura leaned forward, placing her elbows on the table. She looked right at Jonesy. "Talia never cared for anyone but herself in her life."

Her voice more than her words was what surprised me. No hate, no bitterness. Just a statement of fact. Jonesy was looking at me. Questions? I shook my head.

"You can go, Major," Jonesy told her.

As Laura walked to the door, I said, "Could you ask Colonel Jowers to come in?"

She spun around.

"Relax, Major." I smiled reassuringly. "Your name won't even come up."

She gave me a long look and walked out.

★★★★

Colonel Jowers closed the door hard. "Christ, what now?"

Jonesy waved a hand to a chair.

As Jowers sat, Jonesy said, "Why don't you like Major Swanson, Colonel?"

"Did Laura . . . ?"

"You haven't exactly been very complimentary, Colonel," Jonesy said dryly.

Jowers shrugged. "Right. Sure. Hell, I don't make a secret out of it. I can't stand the bloodsucker."

Jonesy's eyebrows went up. "Bloodsucker?"

"Bloodsucker," Jowers said. He repeated much of what Laura had said, his voice becoming louder and more bitter with every word. By the end, he was almost shouting.

"The Lexus!" Jowers jabbed a finger at Jonesy. "You ask her! Ask Talia where she got the Lexus! Ask her!"

"You tell me, sir."

"Watkins! She talked the general into buying her the damn thing. Can you believe it? Makes me sick."

"You're sure?"

"Damn straight. I took the call. From the dealer. Three months back. Fifty-three thousand bucks."

Jonesy said, "Maybe Major Swanson really cares for the general, Colonel?"

Jowers's eyes widened in disbelief.

Then he laughed . . . and laughed.

★★★★

I watched Jowers leave.

"Like a daughter," Jonesy said. He was looking at me. "Isn't that how you said Major Swanson described her relationship with General Watkins?"

"Exact words."

"Makes the jealousy in the office understandable."

"Sometimes being beautiful can be a burden." I stared at my notepad and slowly circled a word.

Glancing down, Jonesy read, "Dinosaur." He shook his head.

I wrote something else.

Jonesy looked up. "You don't think General Watkins changed his mind about Vietnamese recognition?"

I tucked my notepad into a pocket and didn't answer.

"Dr. Owens called the office," Jonesy said. "That's why I was late.

Stopped by to talk to him about the autopsy. He was a little put out we didn't drop by last night, since he gave it a rush job."

"Tippett went over last night."

Jonesy shook his head.

"No Tippett," he said. "Nobody."

I felt a wave of frustration. What the hell was wrong with Tippett?

"Heart attack," Jonesy said.

"That the official cause of death?"

Jonesy nodded. "Time of death somewhere between eighteen and nineteen hundred."

"Sir!" A sergeant poked his head in the door. "There's a phone call."

15

THE PENTAGON'S EFFICIENT DESIGN CHANGES DRAMATICALLY WHEN YOU REACH THE BASEMENT. THE UNMARKED CORRIDORS ARE MAZES OF GRAY. The ongoing renovation project made things worse. Hallways were blocked, offices relocated, wooden shoring jammed everywhere. I often felt like a rat in a B. F. Skinner experiment when I went down there, always getting lost. On this occasion, I wandered around for five minutes until I found the one landmark I recognized, the purple water fountain. The computer security center was two hallways down, on the right.

The sign on the steel door said "Pentagon Information Technology Services, Security." I punched the intercom, and a voice answered. I identified myself and pushed in at the sound of the buzzer.

The room was colorless and open, with maybe a dozen computer stations. Most were occupied by fresh-faced second and first lieutenants furiously clicking away.

A female Army captain sitting at a desk by the door rose. "Major Gutiérrez will be here shortly, sir. I understand a Sergeant Jones is coming?"

"He's going to be delayed."

The phone call had been from Army personnel, responding to a request Jonesy had made earlier on Masonis. He stayed to receive the incoming fax.

"Um, would you care for coffee, sir?"

"No, thank you."

I watched the young faces at the consoles. It could be argued that they had the most important job in the Pentagon. They were the hacker-scanners, charged with protecting the DOD computer system, which contained the entire military budget and force structure allocations. In round-the-clock shifts, they monitored the various databases, both classified and unclassified, looking for any signs someone was attempting unauthorized access into the system.

"You've got a lot more personnel in here than I remember," I said.

"We've doubled the number of scanners in the past seven months, and we still can't keep up."

"What's the daily average now of people trying to break in?"

"Thirty-two," said an authoritative voice. "Hi, Colonel. Jonesy coming?"

"In a bit."

I smiled warmly at the Air Force major coming toward us. A graduate of MIT, Maria Gutiérrez looked like anything but one of the military's premier computer minds. Trim and petite, she had large expressive eyes and a button nose that made her cute rather than pretty. She wore her long dark hair pinned back above the collar, as prescribed by Air Force regulations. She laughed easily and often. We'd met four years before when our sons played on the same Little League team; Maria's husband, Frank, had been the coach. Our families still socialized together. Over the past few years, she'd been the OSI's unofficial computer consultant. We had our own computer techs, but none that could match Maria. The last time she'd worked for us was the virus incident with the teenage intern.

Maria returned the smile. "We think we'll be up over fifty a day by next year, and no end in sight. But hey, you didn't come here to talk about my troubles, right, Colonel?"

I grinned. I liked Maria. "But you love it," I said.

She winked. "Sure, sir. But let's keep that a secret, huh? The minute the personnel weenies upstairs find out I love my job, they'll ship me out."

"Mum's the word. So what did you find out?"

Her face turned serious. "C'mon back. I'll show you."

★★★★

We entered some kind of high-tech maintenance room. There were a couple of slab tables in the middle, surrounded by shelves brimming with various computer parts. Two oscilloscopes were parked along a wall. A heavyset, curly-haired female second lieutenant sat in a corner at a separate computer station, clicking away on a keyboard.

The nine computers the CID guys brought down were on the tables, each marked with a name taped on top. Maria pointed. "I analyzed General Watkins's computers first. Then Major Swanson's." She ran a hand down the line. "Then I checked out the rest. You guys were right. All the hard drives were infected with a virus."

"Then everything on them is shot?"

She smiled. "Not quite. On the last six belonging to the staff, I was able to bypass the virus, retrieve the information, and clean it up. Got all the stuff on floppies. Good thing you didn't initiate the trigger on those."

"Trigger?"

"The command to activate the virus. Sometimes it's a date or time, maybe a sequence of keystrokes. In this case it was designed to kick in when you typed in a password."

I felt like slapping myself. "Then because we logged on, the information on General Watkins's and Major Swanson's computers is gone?"

Maria nodded. "Probably. But don't be too hard on yourself. You couldn't have known. I'm pretty certain this virus was hidden in the boot segment and designed to attack through the operating system. Basically, when you entered the password, the virus told the operating system to overwrite everything on the hard disk with random numbers, eventually frying it."

"You said probably."

"Sometimes bits and pieces are recoverable. Viruses are like any other program. They have to be told when and what to target. Files or programs not on their hit list can often be recovered. And time is also a factor, depending on how long the virus was allowed to run. When I get a chance, I'll take a look and see what I can recover. But the hard drives on both of Watkins's computers are pretty shot. I can't promise anything."

"How much time would it take to destroy the data?"

"Hard to say. This virus is pretty quick. Computers this size, maybe, oh, five to ten minutes."

"But we didn't power up the computers for more than a minute or two."

Maria looked surprised. "That's all?"

I nodded.

"Strange." Maria's eyes drifted past me. She was frowning deeply. "Doesn't make sense, not with the damage we've found."

"What doesn't?" I asked.

Maria didn't seem to hear. But a couple of seconds later, she asked, "Could whoever loaded the virus have known General Watkins's password?"

The question caught me off guard. After I thought about it, I told Maria the killer could have gotten the password from General Watkins.

"That explains it," Maria said. Seeing my puzzled look, she continued, "General Watkins's computers have significantly more data loss than Major Swanson's, and much more than I would expect after just being run for a minute or two. That tells me that someone almost certainly used Watkins's password to trigger the virus on his computers, probably right after uploading it. Guess they didn't want to take any chances. They wanted to make sure any information Watkins had was destroyed."

"So when we logged on . . . ?"

"Everything was already pretty much gone." She gave me a quick smile. "Look on the bright side. You're off the hook."

The news didn't make me feel any better. "How long would it have taken to upload the virus?"

"Were these hooked up to modems?"

I shook my head. "Only a couple of the admin computers. Major

Swanson said they were careful that any computers containing classified information were not hooked up."

"So someone infected them manually off a floppy. Say five minutes or so. Certainly no more."

"Could the virus be uploaded without knowing a computer's password?"

"Sure. Remember, the virus is installed in the operating system, which doesn't require a password to access."

"Any idea where someone would have gotten a virus like this?"

Maria looked amused. "Yes."

"And?"

"That's why I was able to bypass the virus so easily. I'd seen it before. Knew how it worked. Of course, it could be a different strain. Hackers are always modifying existing viruses. Or sometimes, viruses are designed to modify themselves." She glanced at the lieutenant. "We've isolated the virus and transferred it to that IBM for analysis. Cindy's checking it out now. We should know if it's a match shortly."

"A match to what?"

"Oh, to the one in our files."

I stared. "You have a copy of this virus here?"

"Sure."

"Major!"

The lieutenant turned toward us. "I think it's finished replicating."

We went over.

The screen was filled with symbols that I didn't understand.

"You confirmed it was hidden in the boot segment, Cindy?" Maria asked.

Cindy nodded.

"Go ahead and clear the screen, then trigger it."

Cindy began typing.

Maria explained, "When a virus is first introduced into a system, it replicates itself onto any acceptable host programs, usually ones where there's enough memory where it can hide without being detected. When that process is done, the virus sits, waiting for the trigger."

"Aren't you worried it will damage this computer?"

"No. This thing has been designed specifically for virus analysis. Sort of like an electronic prison where the virus can go crazy. It's got a second, isolated hard disk which prevents the virus from spreading."

"Ready." Cindy punched Enter.

The hard drive whirred, and the numbers flew.

"Reminds me of the Brazilian Bug," Cindy said. "Except this one displays numbers instead of insects as it digests the software. Jeez, it's fast." She typed in a command. The numbers froze. She typed in something else. The display changed to symbols and numbers.

Maria explained, "We've got software that gives us snapshots of the virus as it attacks the operating system. Sorta like freeze-framing on a videotape." She stared at the symbols. "Okay, Cindy."

They continued this process for the next ten minutes.

"I've seen enough. Thanks, Cindy. When you're done, install the program into Conan and make a copy. Let's go, Colonel. I need some coffee."

We went out into the hallway.

I asked, "Conan?"

She smiled. "After Conan the Barbarian. It's a computer setup with a utilities program which lets us rip apart the virus into the assembler language."

"Cute. So what's the verdict?"

She frowned. "On the program?"

I nodded.

"Oh, it's identical to ours."

★★★★

We sat in her office with the door closed. I rubbed my temple, watching Maria sip coffee. I'd declined any, opting instead for the aspirin she'd had in her desk.

"Charlie, you look like hell." Since we were old friends, behind closed doors we always used first names.

"Thanks," I said dryly. "And you're not helping. You were saying

you didn't create this virus? That it came to you from Fort Leavenworth?"

Maria nodded. "Someone infected the Army Training and Doctrine
Command computers. We sent a couple people out to clean things up.
What a mess that was. Took TRADOC almost two months to get their
system operational after we debugged it."

"You always make copies of the viruses you find?"

"Whenever we can. Helps us stay ahead of the hackers."

"So how could someone have gotten a copy?"

"Lots of ways. This virus was created by a Serbian terrorist group in
Germany to attack the NATO computer network. They were trying to
cripple NATO's capability to support the Bosnian Moslems."

"A virus could do that much damage?"

"If it infects enough systems, certainly. Think about it. All intelligence and targeting information relies on computers, the fighter jets are
controlled by communication systems that are computer driven, not to
mention the radar controllers which would be blind without their traffic
computers. And it goes on. Supplies, troop movements, the phone system. NATO, like any large organization, operates on the quick and secure
transfer of information. Anything that shuts down that link effectively
shuts down NATO."

"So how did the virus make it to Leavenworth?"

"We think it was inadvertently brought over by a German exchange
officer attending the Command and General Staff College through a
floppy he didn't know was infected. He introduced it into the war-gaming
computer. From there it spread into the TRADOC system."

"So whoever sabotaged General Watkins's computers could have
gotten it from someone at Leavenworth, or maybe even been stationed
at Leavenworth?"

"That's possible. No telling how many people got their stuff
infected. But there are plenty of other ways. Bulletin boards, the
Internet. And there are a lot of hacker clubs where this stuff gets passed
around."

"Any way someone could have gotten a copy of this thing from you?"

She peered at me from over the rim of her mug. "Sure." She nodded to a safe in the corner. "All our virus disks are in there."

"And who has the combination?"

She set the mug down slowly. She looked amused again. "Me."

"Who else?"

"Just me." Then she rose, went over to the safe. She returned moments later and tossed a floppy on the desk.

"That's it? Just one disk?"

"Most viruses don't take a lot of memory. They're replicators. That's why they can hide so easily." She returned to her seat, gave me a smile. "So, Mr. Policeman, am I a suspect?"

I sighed. "Anyone ask you for a copy?"

"No."

"Did you ever make any copies, or give anyone access to these since you had them?"

"No."

I rubbed my face. "Shit."

I was about to leave when Maria's phone rang.

"Jonesy is here," Maria said. "Go on out front. I'll get the disks with the info we retrieved so far and bring them out."

"Thanks, Maria."

16

JONESY RARELY LOOKED EXCITED, BUT HE DID NOW. HE STOOD BY THE CAPTAIN'S DESK, SHIFTING HIS WEIGHT BACK AND FORTH. HE SPRANG forward as I approached, a folder in his hand that I knew contained Masonis's RIP, a computerized personnel summary sheet taken from Masonis's Army records.

He spoke quickly, keeping his voice low. "Masonis's RIP looks real interesting, sir. He was Special Forces. Had two tours in 'Nam in the early seventies. Deep recon specialist with a Special Forces battalion. Checked with a buddy of mine who's a retired SF type. Said a lot of those guys in that unit were involved in the Phoenix program."

"Phoenix? That's the CIA program, right?"

"Yes, sir. Declassified maybe ten years back. They were the guys who went deep into the North to assassinate or capture leaders in the North Vietnamese or Vietcong units."

"Have you confirmed this?"

"Got a request into the Army for a list of Phoenix personnel. Should get it later today. But if this guy was Phoenix . . ."

"He's our man," I said. "Good work, Jonesy."

The phone at the desk rang. The captain picked up.

I saw Maria coming toward us, carrying a box. "Here you go, Colonel."

I took it.

"Colonel Jensen, Colonel Tippett's on the line for you," the captain at the desk said.

★★★★

I began to feel sick as Tippett talked. "God. How? When?"

"Don't know," Tippett said. "Lieutenant Lee just called. Look, I'm leaving my apartment. I'll pick you up at the River Entrance."

Tippett's place at Crystal City was less than a five-minute drive. "On my way." I hung up slowly.

Maria stared at me. "What's wrong with you?"

I shook my head. "Can't say. But thanks for the help, Maria."

She started to open her mouth, then shut it. She squeezed my arm. "Sure. Anytime . . . Colonel."

Jonesy and I left.

★★★★

We stopped in the hallway. Jonesy was looking at me, eyebrows raised.

I told him about the call, that the Vietnamese girl, Miss Vinh, had just been found dead. Then I said, "Drop those disks off at Major Swanson's and have her and Webster make a search."

He gave me a doubtful look.

"Swanson was the closest person to the general. If anyone knows anything pertinent, she does."

A pause. Then a nod.

"And, Jonesy, maybe you'd better tell Major Swanson what happened to the girl. I want her to know what kind of a son of a bitch this Masonis is."

"Yes, sir." He was frowning now.

"She likes him, Jonesy."

"Sir?"

"Major Swanson. I think she's got a thing for Masonis."

"Oh?"

"And get back in touch with Army personnel. See if you can dig up Masonis's old performance reports. Better yet, see if you can get his entire file sent out. Maybe Masonis has some kind of history of excessive violence."

"Okay, sir."

"And have the FBI run a check of his financial records, bank statements, investments, etc."

"Already requested, sir."

"Did you run him through the NCIC?" The NCIC was the FBI's National Crime Information Computer.

"Not even a parking ticket, sir."

"Anything I've forgotten?"

"Can't think of anything."

I went to meet Tippett.

★★★★

I watched Tippett as he drove. I felt saddened and helpless, and profoundly disappointed. He'd tried to conceal that he'd been drinking, of course. His hair was still wet from a recent shower, and he'd changed his suit and put on a generous amount of cologne. But he couldn't hide the flushed and bloated face, the overly loud voice, the nervous twitches.

Tippett found time to look at me amid the bumper-to-bumper traffic. "What's wrong, Charlie?"

"Jonesy talked to Doc Owens," I said quietly.

"Yeah?"

"Doc says you never went by last night."

"Things got a little hectic at Watkins's place."

"Tip, I called. You weren't there."

He glanced at me again. "What the hell is this, Charlie?"

"Where were you?"

Tippett snorted. "Oh, I get it. You think maybe I scooted over to some bar. Had a few belts."

"I didn't say that."

"But that's what you're thinking, right? Thanks for the vote of confidence, buddy."

I shook my head. "Tip, look at yourself. You look like you haven't slept in a week. You can barely hold the wheel without shaking. You've been making mistakes."

He spun around. "Get off my back, Charlie. I'm fine!"

"Tip! Look out!"

Tippett jammed on the brakes. The tires squealed. I was thrown against the shoulder strap. We stopped just inches from slamming into a Mercedes.

Neither one of us spoke for a few moments.

Without looking at me, he said, "You're going to talk to General Ferris, aren't you, Charlie?"

"Get some help, Tip. Maybe AA. They're good."

Tippett hunched over the wheel. We were moving again.

"I'll go with you, Tip. Help you any way I can."

Tippett stared straight ahead.

I let my hand drop below the seat. I leaned forward a bit and felt for the bottle.

"It's gone, Charlie."

My head snapped up. Tippett was still staring at the road.

"I saw you last night," he said quietly, not bothering to look over.

I sat back, feeling suddenly ashamed.

We rode the rest of the way in silence.

17

T|HE CARS QUEUING UP FOR A LOOK WERE BACKED UP A HALF-MILE.
TIPPETT PULLED IN FRONT OF AN AMBULANCE BY THE ENTRANCE TO
the large rooming house on Twelfth Street, maybe four blocks from the
restaurant. Unlike the night before, there was a substantial crowd on the
sidewalk pressed against the yellow-tape perimeter, shouting, jostling. A
half-dozen haggard-looking cops manned the interior. Two more stood
on the curb, keeping a path clear into the rooming house. Then I saw the
cameras.

"Dammit," I said, shaking my head.

Tippett killed the engine. "Come on, let's get this over with."

A uniformed cop jumped out of a squad car and ran over. He was the
same one who'd been at the apartment the night before.

"Hello, Colonel," he said.

I nodded, my face grim. I read his name tag. "Okay to leave the car
here, Officer Davis?" I asked.

"Sure. Okay. I'll make sure no one screws with it."

"Thanks."

"Hey!" One of the cops on the curb bolted toward two figures darting
into the street toward us, a stunning girl with short blond hair and a guy

with a ponytail and a TV camera. The girl waved. "Hey, Colonel! Over here!"

My eyes shot up in surprise.

"Aw, shit!" Tippett said.

"Better get going, sir," Officer Davis said.

The cop was blocking the path of the reporters. Ponytail pointed the camera at us. The female was arguing with the cop. She worked for Channel 7. Though I recognized her, I couldn't remember her name.

"Hey, guys, how about answering a couple of questions?" she yelled at Tippett and me. "Come on, Colonel. Give me a break. Why's the military here?"

We stepped onto the sidewalk. Shouts came from the crowd. Cameras clicked. A tattered awning hung over the entrance to the rooming house. Faded letters read "The Jubilee."

"Fucking beautiful," Tippett muttered. "Annie had to be here."

"Second floor," said a cop in the perimeter, jabbing with his thumb.

We went up the steps. "You know her?" I asked Tippett.

"Interviewed me for the Bosler homicide last year."

We went inside.

The rooming house had been a hotel at one time, built around the turn of the century. There was an unmanned reception desk in the foyer, the wood cracked, the varnish faded. A chain dangled above the foyer, where a chandelier had once hung. There was a sitting area with a worn vinyl couch, a chair, and a chipped coffee table with an overflowing ashtray. As we walked up the creaking stairway, I noticed the smell. Strong, like something rotten.

"*Nuoc mam,*" Tippett grunted. He must have noticed my blank look, because he added, "Vietnamese staple. Sauce made from fermented fish."

"Smells like shit."

He shrugged. "Tastes pretty good, actually."

We reached the landing. The hallway teed right to left, rooms on either side. A few doors away, an elderly Asian man in a gray suit was talking to a female detective whose face was lined with fatigue.

"Hello, Rita," I said. "Surprised you're still on duty."

"Yeah? Tell that to the lieutenant." She and the Asian gentleman stepped aside.

I heard Lieutenant Lee swear from a room just ahead.

★★★★

Three men were going over the room. Lee stood by the door, a cellular phone against his ear, his face contorted. "Yeah, Bernie. That's right. I want five more men. I don't give a shit. You tell the captain when he gets back from jerking off just what I told you. This thing is big. Press is already here. When they figure out the connection, all hell is gonna break loose. Yeah. Fine. I'll be waiting." He looked up. "Man, what a day. I'd just gotten to sleep when I got the call. Sometimes this job really sucks."

"Hello, Lieutenant," Tippett said.

I nodded at Lee, then looked around. The room was larger than I had expected. Big enough for two single beds, a desk with an electric burner, makeshift shelves with books—mostly in what I took for Vietnamese, with a couple of English primers. Men's clothing hung from a broom handle rigged in the corner. On a dresser were women's undergarments, neatly folded. And a few photos. A small refrigerator sat on the floor, a few canned goods stacked next to it. Everything was neat and tidy.

Then I heard voices coming from the bathroom. Someone swore. A young man came out, went over to a black bag, and removed a long thermometer used to check a body's temperature rectally.

"She's in there?" Tippett asked.

"Yeah," Lee said. "And it's not pretty. Hey, Doc!" He eased his head into the bathroom. A moment later, he turned to the young man. "Hang on a minute." To us he said, "One at a time. I want you to check out the marks on her body. See if they match the ones you saw on General Watkins."

Tippett went first. He came back a minute later, face grim. I walked in. The M.E., a thin black man with a mustache, stood by the tub. He nodded to me.

She lay nude in the tub, faceup, legs together, hands folded, head cocked to the side, revealing a thin cut mark along her neck. There was little blood. Like Watkins, there were welts on her chest and stomach. Unlike Watkins, only a few had been sliced off. Then I noticed the nipples, and the bile rose in my throat.

I turned to go, then realized the M.E. was holding a plastic Baggie. Something in it, pinkish, in the shape of a shiitake mushroom, but thinner. I swallowed. "Is that—"

The M.E. held up the bag. "Her nipples. He must have run the shower. Found them in the drain."

I went out fast.

★★★★

"Charlie, you look like you're going to puke."

I ignored Tippett, saying nothing.

Lee gave me a sympathetic look. "Rough, huh? Come on. Let's get out of here. I've got to have a smoke." He led us down to the foyer, to the sitting area. Lee took the sofa. I joined him. Tippett sat on the chair. We could see the crowd through the window.

Lee lit up, inhaling deeply. He stared at us for a moment, then looked outside. "Man, she is one hot lady."

I asked, "Who?"

"That girl reporter. Annie McDaniel from Channel Seven. Got a helluva body." He sighed. "But she can be a real pain in the ass. She's smart. Tough. Probably the best crime reporter in the city. Rumor is she's got sources in every precinct in town." He flicked an ash into the ashtray and leaned back, his eyes shifting between Tippett and me. "You know she was here when I arrived? One of the uniforms told me she and her sidekick pulled up fifteen minutes after the call went out."

"We saw her when we came in," I said.

"What's your point, Lieutenant?" asked Tippett.

"The point, Colonel, is Annie doesn't show for your run-of-the-mill chickenshit homicide. She handles the big stuff. The multiple murders, the ones with scandals, or where some high roller is involved. Annie would never grace us with her presence over the murder of some poor immigrant girl unless, of course, Annie knows something."

"Are you suggesting she knows about the link to General Watkins?" I asked.

Lee blew a series of perfect smoke rings. "No, I haven't mentioned our conversation to anyone yet. Someone in the department probably told her the murder of Tho and the girl might be linked. But once I turn in my report confirming the connection, she'll know for sure."

"Hell, she might figure that out on her own," Tippett said. He glanced at Lee. "She recognized me."

"Not good," Lee said. "Annie's smart."

"So when are you going to pass the information on?" I asked.

"In the morning," Lee said. "My captain's on my ass for the report." He carefully ground out the cigarette, looked up, and grinned. "So that gives us, say, until tomorrow night till all hell breaks loose."

"If we're lucky." Tippett grunted.

Lee sat back and folded his arms. "Now, how about you guys telling me everything you know about this Dr. Masonis."

I looked to Tippett. He gazed out the window.

I told Lee about Masonis.

★★★★

After I finished, Lee consulted his notepad. "Masonis arrived last Thursday at National on an American Airlines flight. Rented a blue Tempo from Avis. I had all hotels in the area checked. Nothing, but he's probably using an alias." He flipped the notepad shut. "Got an APB out, and I've notified the Durham PD in case he shows back home."

"You put out the word Masonis is ex–Special Forces?" Tippett said. "He could be real dangerous."

"Taken care of, Colonel."

"Now, about the girl," Tippett said. "What the hell happened? Weren't you watching her?"

There was a flash of anger in Lee's eyes. "Sure. We knew she was our best link to her brother. We had people watching this place, front and back."

"You tap her phone?"

"She doesn't have one. Which is why we thought she'd try to slip out and contact her brother."

"She could have used a neighbor's phone."

Lee shrugged. "I suppose."

"Were those her brother's clothes upstairs?" I asked.

"Yeah, they lived together. The brother came over from Vietnam three months ago."

I looked around. "What's the story with this place? Cater only to Vietnamese?"

"Mostly, but there are Chinese, Thais, Koreans. Owned by some guy who was a general in the South Vietnamese Army. Supposedly came over to the U.S. after the war with a ton of money. Owns about four of these places around the city, plus a number of restaurants and dry cleaners. Most of those are in Chinatown."

"That the old man upstairs?" Tippet asked.

"Him? No, that guy is . . . or was, the sister's English instructor. They had a lesson today. He found her."

"So how did your people miss the killer?" Tippett asked.

Lee shook his head. "Can't figure that out. I had two men parked across the street. A couple more watching the entrance to the alleys. They swear they didn't see anybody matching the killer's description go in."

Tippett snorted. "But they weren't really looking for him, were they, Lieutenant? I mean, they were just supposed to keep an eye on the girl, or watch for the brother if he showed."

"Look, Colonel!" Lee snapped. "I checked with the surveillance teams. No Caucasian males came in. One guy left around three A.M. through the front door. But he didn't match Masonis's description. Masonis is supposed to be six-three. This guy was short, stocky, and bald."

"They could still have missed him in the dark," Tippett said. "Especially if they were asleep."

"Colonel," Lee said slowly, an edge in his voice, "if my boys said they didn't see the son of a bitch, they didn't see him."

"You consider that maybe this guy was an accomplice?" Tippett fired back. "Your men get a good look at the white male?"

Lee hesitated. "No, but we might get a line on him when we question the neighbors. Maybe he lives here, or has a girl stashed. Lot of rich guys keep their broads here."

Something bothered me. "How did the killer know?" I asked.

They both looked at me.

"How the hell did the killer know about the girl and the brother?"

Both Tippett and Lee looked blank.

"Look," I said, "the only way this scenario fits is the killer must have known the brother was a witness. Knows he has to shut the kid up. Somehow he finds out where the kid lives, comes to the apartment. Girl's there instead, and he kills her after making her tell him where her brother is. That how you guys see it?"

A vague nod from Tippett.

"Something like that," Lee said. "Only, the killer may not have known the girl and the brother lived together. He might have come here because he knew the girl would know where the kid was."

"Yeah, okay," I said. "But the part that's bothering me is there's only one way the killer could have known the kid saw him. That was if he'd noticed the kid looking at him when he left Tho's apartment."

"Yeah," Lee said.

"Then why didn't the killer take care of the kid then?"

"Someone could have been in the kitchen with him, Charlie," Tippett said.

"So? He could have waited until the kid was alone. Remember, at that time, no one knew Tho was upstairs, dead. The killer had time. And we know this guy is a methodical son of a bitch. Why leave a witness to give a description for the police?"

Lee nodded. "Could be he didn't know there was a witness when he left."

"Which means he found out later," added Tippett. "So there must be a leak." He looked right at Lee.

"With all due respect, fuck you, Colonel," Lee said. "If you think my guys—"

Tippett's face darkened. "You said yourself your department leaks like a goddamn sieve."

"Knock it off, Tip," I said.

"No, Charlie. If—"

"Tip!"

Tippett clamped his jaw shut and glared at me.

"We got bigger things to worry about," I said to him. "Like whether or not the girl, Miss Vinh, knew where her brother was hiding. 'Cause if she did . . ."

"So does the killer." Lee shook his head. "Well, all I can do is question the neighbors. Maybe they saw something."

"Lieutenant!"

I turned. An excited Rita was coming down the stairs, the old man on her heels.

"Lieutenant! You better hear this."

18

THE OLD MAN SPOKE IN BOOK-PROPER ENGLISH TO LEE, IGNORING TIPPETT AND ME. I UNDERSTOOD. EVEN THOUGH LEE WAS NOT VIETnamese, he was still an Asian. "Lieutenant, on your word of honor, I want assurance that the boy is not wanted for a crime."

Lee looked exasperated. "No, like I said, we only want him for questioning. As a witness. I give you my word."

"You think he knows the man who killed . . ." The old man paused, closing his eyes for a moment. "Miss Vinh was a very able student. I shall miss her."

Lee asked, "Did Miss Vinh know where her brother is hiding?"

The old man gave Lee a long look and nodded.

"And where is that?"

The old man just looked at Lee.

"Sir, you must know the boy is in danger," I said.

The old man acted as if he hadn't heard. I was about to repeat myself when he looked at me. "You will not harm him?"

"No."

"If I tell you, I must insist I be allowed to accompany you."

"Fine," Lee said.

"Your word, Lieutenant?"

"Yes. Now, let's have it."

"There is a boat . . ."

★★★★

I sat in the back with the old man and Tippett drove. We were behind a squad car that contained Lee. The flashers and siren were going full blast but not helping much. The D.C. traffic crawled along, bumper to bumper.

Tippett swore.

I ignored him as I listened to the old man's story. He sat straight up, knees together, bony hands clasped in his lap.

"He was very frightened, Colonel," he was saying. "We gave him tea, and he told us about Mr. Tho. Very sad."

"And your town house is just a few doors down from the restaurant?" I said.

A nod.

"Didn't you hear us in the alley?"

He looked me in the eye. "Of course, Colonel."

"Then you knew young Mr. Vinh saw the murderer?"

The old man looked surprised. "No."

I blinked. "What?"

"No," the old man said again. "He said no such thing."

"But you said he was frightened."

"Of you, Colonel. Or rather, the police. He said you would blame him for the killing."

"How the hell—"

Tippett cleared his throat. I looked at his face in the rearview mirror.

"I might have to take some of the blame for that, Charlie. To get him to talk, I told him he'd be a suspect until we found someone else."

"Dammit, Tip, you knew the kid was scared."

"Hey," Tippett snapped. "It worked, didn't it? The kid confessed to seeing the killer."

The old man was giving the back of Tippett's polished scalp a look of disgust. I didn't blame him.

"And your son took Mr. Vinh to his houseboat?" I asked.

The old man took his eyes off Tippett and nodded. "I thought it was the wisest thing. I knew you would be searching our neighborhood."

"Did you talk to Miss Vinh, let her know about her brother?"

The old man nodded. "I telephoned another of my students in the building. She contacted Miss Vinh and brought her to the phone."

"Where is your son?"

"At work. He is employed by the Prudential Securities firm. You would be surprised, Colonel, at how many Vietnamese have money they want to invest. My son is very successful. He bought the boat for his clients." He gave me a thin smile. "He is learning to be American."

Tippett's cellular rang. He answered, then glanced back. "Lee says the Prince George's County Sheriff's Department is at the marina. They want to know if there are any firearms in the houseboat."

"No guns," the old man said with surprising feeling. "You tell him, no guns."

Tippett relayed the message.

I watched the old man. He was obviously agitated. "You were a soldier in the war?" I asked softly.

The old man looked out the window. "I am only a teacher."

I could feel the car pick up speed. We'd finally reached I-395.

★★★★

"Shouldn't be much longer now," Tippett said twenty minutes later.

I nodded, staring out at the homes lining the winding two-lane that led to the Tantallon Country Club. A few minutes later, we turned left into a subdivision and went down a hill. Off to the left, an expanse of water flickered through the trees.

"Show time," Tippett said with a grunt.

Ahead I saw a sheriff's radio car parked along a dirt shoulder. Lee's car slowed and pulled in behind. To the left, a flotilla of boats, power and sail, bobbed gently against extended piers. A sign alongside the road read "Fort Washington Marina."

"Looks like we walk from here," Tippett said, pulling in behind Lee as a couple of deputy sheriffs sauntered up to his car.

"You're not sure he's in there, then?" Lee asked the deputies as we got out.

"Didn't want to get too close and spook the guy," the deputy replied.

"But ain't no one left yet, Lieutenant," the other officer added.

Lee peered over the bluff toward the boats. "Which one is it?"

The first deputy pointed. "See where all them houseboats are? 'Bout halfway down the line. The baby-blue one with the white roof. Name's, uh . . ."

"American Dream," the old man said. To me, he added, "My son is very proud of being an American."

"Two of our boys are watching from inside the marina office," the first deputy continued. "They've got a good view of the houseboat from there." He pointed to a large building across the wide parking lot. A sheriff's car was parked to the rear of the building. The deputy unclipped a walkie-talkie from his belt and keyed it. "Steve, Chuck, you guys up?"

"Yup," a voice crackled.

"That D.C. lieutenant is here. See anything yet?"

"Nope."

Lee reached into his car for binoculars. He focused on the houseboat. After a moment, he said, "I'm going on down."

"Might be better if I go," Tippett said. "I can talk with him."

The old man said, "Lieutenant, let me accompany you. He knows me. He trusts me."

Lee thought for a moment. "We'll all go."

"Lieutenant, the kid's scared as it is," I said. "Be better if only you or Tippett go with the old man. Might not seem as threatening."

"I speak Vietnamese, Lieutenant," Tippett repeated.

"All right," Lee agreed. To the deputies he said, "Tell your boys we're going in. Tell them I want them to stay out of sight." He looked at Tippett. "We'll go down in your car, since it's unmarked. Colonel Jensen and I will wait while you and the old man go in."

As the four of us headed for the car, I pulled Tippett aside. "Be nice to the kid, Tip."

Tippett smiled. "You know me, Charlie."

★★★★

From the backseat, Lee and I watched Tippett and the old man walk down the dock. Lee raised the binoculars. After a moment, he said, "Want to take a look?"

The houseboat was divided into two sections. Up front, I could see the wheelhouse. Behind was the living compartment, sided in wood to a height of maybe three feet, then windowed all the way around. Two large outboards hung off the back. I studied the interior, but I saw no movement.

"He might not be in there," I said.

"Know in a minute," Lee replied.

Tippett and the old man approached the houseboat.

Lee took the binoculars. "Looks like they're calling to him. Don't see anybody. Going on board. On board now. Still nobody. Colonel Tippett is opening the back door."

I could see that much. Tippett and the old man disappeared inside.

"They're walking around. Hey. Maybe he's there. Looks like they just sat down."

A minute later, Lee said, "Someone is standing. Sat down again."

Another minute passed.

"What the hell are they doing?" Lee muttered.

We had the windows open. It was hot, muggy. Perspiration slid down my neck.

A little later, I asked, "Anything?"

Lee dropped the binoculars to his lap. He wiped his damp brow with the back of his hand.

"Nada. He must be in there, though, or else they'd be out by now."

A family passed in front, heading toward the houseboats. The man was lean, tanned, about forty; the wife, also tanned, cute figure, maybe ten years younger, two young boys in tow. They climbed onto a house-boat two berths from the one we were watching.

I murmured, "Must be nice."

"Yeah," Lee said. He raised the binoculars.

Another minute passed. Then two, three.

"This is nuts," Lee said. "Kid's got to be in there. Come on." He reached for the door.

We were walking up to the houseboat, maybe twenty yards away. Lee turned to me to say something, but he never got the chance. At that moment we were knocked flat as the houseboat exploded.

19

MY EARS RANG FROM THE CONCUSSION, AND I TASTED BLOOD. I HEARD MYSELF GROANING AS I STRUGGLED TO MY FEET.

The air was filled with smoke. Debris floated lazily through the air, hitting the pier and splashing in the water. I focused where the houseboat had been. At first I could see only flames. My eyes burned, and I blinked rapidly to clear my vision. The entire compartment above the deck was now only bits of burning wood.

Tippett!

Then I heard screams.

The other houseboats were burning. Figures staggered out. Some were on fire.

I started to run, tripped, almost fell. A moan. I looked down and saw Lee. He was lying facedown. He moaned again and tried to push himself up.

I pulled him to his feet. Blood streamed down his face.

"Go on back!" I hollered, and ran toward the flames.

A man leapt onto the dock, his shirt on fire. He screamed. Before I could reach him, he jumped into the water.

"I'll handle him!" a voice yelled. I turned to see Lee. He dove in.

I reached the remains of the houseboat Tippett and the old man had gone into. The craft was sinking sternfirst from the weight of the two outboards still attached. The shattered deck burned furiously, debris still floating down into the fire. The dock planking had splintered and portions were burning. I covered my face with my hands and sprinted through.

The air was acrid, heavy with smoke and the smell of fuel. Then I heard the screams again.

A man and a woman lay on the dock. I dragged them to their feet and pushed them away from the flames. They weren't the family I'd seen earlier. The woman cried out again. Her extended hands were blistered and raw looking.

"Get out of here!" I yelled. "As soon as the fire reaches the fuel tanks in the boats, this whole area could go up."

The man nodded.

"That way!" I pointed toward the far end of the dock, which was connected by a crosswalk to the other walkways. "You have to go that way."

He nodded again, and guided the woman unsteadily away.

I reached the houseboat where I'd seen the family.

The forward half was in flames.

I heard a smothered cry.

I yelled, waited a moment, and then leapt aboard.

Smoke burned my lungs and eyes. A woman screamed. I followed the sound and reached the compartment.

She was lying just inside the rear door, bleeding profusely from a foot-long wooden splinter embedded in her thigh. She was cradling one of her boys to her chest. He lay still.

She cried out hysterically, "My son! He's dead!"

"Miss . . ."

"He's dead . . . dead!" she wailed.

I gripped her shoulder hard. "Stop it!"

She looked surprised.

"Where is your husband and your other son?"

"He . . . Garrett is up front with Ricky. . . . Oh God, they're dead! They're dead!"

The flames were shooting twenty feet in the air, covering the bow. I didn't even bother to look.

I cradled the woman and the boy and carried them to the dock.

She kept murmuring, "They're dead, they're dead."

I was staggering down the walkway when one of the deputies said, "I got them, sir."

I let go.

★★★★

I was talking to Jean over the car's cellular.

"You're sure you're all right, Charlie?" she asked for the fourth time.

"Yeah, I'm fine, honey."

"Poor Tip. You're sure he's dead, Charlie?"

"I'm afraid there's no doubt. You think you should call Dorothy? I wouldn't want her to hear about this on the news, and there's no telling how long the Army will take to get to her."

"I'll . . . I'll go on over. I hope she's home. Maybe I should call. But I don't want to tell her over the phone. I . . . she . . ." Jean fell silent.

"Jean?"

"I'm here. I was thinking what if it had been you?"

"It wasn't. Look, honey, I don't know when I'll be home. I'll try and call you at Dorothy's. You going to be all right?"

"Sure. Guess I better go. And, Charlie, I love you."

"I love you, too."

★★★★

Lee and I leaned against the car in the parking lot and watched as the firemen put out the last of the flames. I counted eight houseboats destroyed, maybe four or five others damaged. All around us were fire trucks, ambulances, and police cars. EMTs from the Prince George's County Fire Department were tending to the dozen or so injured. The woman and the little boy had been taken away. An EMT told me the boy had a severe concussion but should make it.

That was something.

Lee turned to me, wet hair matted above a tired, strained face. He had stripped off his wet jacket. One of the EMTs had put a bandage over his left eye. "I'm sorry about Colonel Tippett," he said.

I licked my split lip and said nothing.

"He saved my life. I should have been in there. Feels kinda funny."

I looked where the houseboat had been. Only bits of floating debris remained. "Think there will be anything to bury, Lieutenant?"

"Probably not." Lee paused. "He married?"

"Divorced. Two kids."

"That's rough."

We watched in silence for a few more minutes. Firemen were beginning to board some of the burned-out boats. I wondered how many more bodies they'd find.

Lee pointed out over the water. "See that?"

I looked. Just a dot. Soon I heard the beat of the prop blades.

As the Bell helicopter came over the parking lot, I saw the logo.

"Channel Seven," Lee said. "That's Annie McDaniel."

The helicopter touched down on the aft portion of the parking area, maybe forty yards away. Some deputies ran out from barricades, waving their arms, screaming soundlessly into the chattering of the blades. Annie McDaniel and the ponytailed man jumped out. Annie wore a navy-blue suit. The wind whipped her skirt above her thighs.

"She is so fine," Lee said longingly.

I gave him a look of irritation and pushed away from the car.

"Where are you going?"

My face was grim. "To give her an interview." I began walking.

Lee joined me. "I thought you wanted to keep the publicity to a minimum."

I didn't reply.

The deputies were trying to force Annie McDaniel and her cameraman back behind the barricades.

"Let them through," I said.

The deputies looked at Lee. They knew I had no real authority here. Lee nodded.

Annie grinned broadly and hurried forward, the cameraman on her heels. She was pretty, but it was her body you noticed. Her tailored jacket swelled from the fullness of her breasts, tapering to a thin waist. Her legs were tanned and firm. But there was a hardness to her face, mostly in her eyes and the almost arrogant set of her jaw when she questioned someone. Which is probably why I'd always assumed she was a bitch.

Before she could say anything, I demanded, "If I give you an interview, can you guarantee coverage on all the networks?"

She stopped, flustered. "Uh . . . depends. If it's a big enough story, yes. Now, what are you, CID?"

"OSI. Lieutenant Colonel Jensen. We're talking at least ten murders now, including General Watkins. That enough to guarantee coverage?"

"So they are connected. I knew it." Annie grinned triumphantly. "Sure. You want to go national. No problem, Colonel. No problem at all."

"I want you to arrange for transcripts of the interview to be sent out to the *Post* and *Times* in time for tomorrow's editions. Along with a photograph of the suspect, which we'll provide."

"Okay. As long as I can get the story out on TV tonight, I don't care who else gets it."

"I'm not going to answer questions. I'll state what I know about the case. Then I'll stop."

Annie shook her head. "Look, I've got to do an interview."

"No deal." I turned around.

I felt a hand on my arm.

"Hey," Annie said. "Okay, Colonel. We do it your way." She glanced at Lee. "How about you, Lieutenant? For old times. Maybe you'd like—"

"No," Lee said. "This is Colonel Jensen's show."

Annie gave a little pout. "C'mon, Lieutenant. All I need is a statement on what happened here. Was it a bomb?"

"You know the drill, Annie," Lee said. "This isn't my jurisdiction. The sheriff's office will be releasing a statement."

Annie shrugged. "If you change your mind . . ."

"Where should I stand?" I asked.

But Annie had turned to the cameraman, saying something I didn't catch.

The cameraman tugged on his ponytail. "Annie, we should get the ambulances and the emergency crews."

"The boats too," Annie said. She began walking to her left, toward the edge of the parking lot. She stopped, pointing. "Frankie, how about over there? Pan first over the ambulances and the victims. Get close-ups. Then to the left." She began walking again. "Take a wide shot. Make sure you get both the boats and the firemen. That'll be the opening. Then move in tight. I want to see faces."

"Yeah, perfect. Man, this is going to be good," Frankie said.

Annie held the mike out to me.

"Rolling," said Frankie.

I began talking. I looked like hell. My clothing was covered with soot and ash. My lip felt the size of a basketball. I'd removed my jacket and combed my hair. That helped some, but not much. General Holmes was going to be pissed that I didn't clear this with him first. But I didn't give a damn.

I wanted Masonis.

So I told Annie about Dr. Theodore Masonis. I told her he was a suspect in the killing of General Watkins, Mr. Tho, and the girl, Miss Vinh. And possibly was involved in the explosion of the houseboat. I told her all about Tippett, and the old man, and the boy.

"Anyone seeing Masonis should immediately call the police," I said. Then I nodded and stepped back. I waited for Annie to say "Cut" or something.

Instead, Annie gave me a cool look. "Now, Colonel, you've told us what you think this Dr. Masonis has done. But you haven't told us why. Or really provided any specifics on the investigation. Could you elaborate?" She jabbed the mike in my face.

I said nothing. The camera was pointed at me. I tried not to look angry.

She smiled sweetly. "Colonel, for instance how . . ."

Then Frankie yelled, "Hey!"

I looked over.

Lee was pulling the camera out of Frankie's hands.

"Interview's finished," I snapped. "You gave me your word."

Annie smiled. "Hey, can't blame a girl for trying. The deal is still on. Now, where do I get a picture of this Dr. Masonis?"

"I've got copies at the office," Lee said. "I'll send some over."

"Great!" Annie was already looking back over her shoulder. "Frankie, better see if we can get statements from the victims." She winked at Lee and me. "Ta ta, boys."

"I was right," I said as Annie and Frankie walked away.

"Huh?" Lee said.

"Annie is one hard woman."

"Yeah, but what a looker."

★★★★

I tried to ignore the feeling of guilt as I searched Tippett's car, but I didn't want the bottle to be found, nor did I find it. I felt a sense of relief. Tippett hadn't lied.

"What was that all about?" Lee asked when I returned to his car.

"Nothing." I shrugged.

He studied me a moment. Then he said, "Looks like they found another body."

I followed his eyes. A fireman on one of the boats a few berths from the one that had exploded was peering over the side, waving and calling out he'd found something. He leaned over and hauled something out of the water.

Lee was wrong. It wasn't another body.

It was a leg.

I don't know what I was thinking. Certainly I wouldn't be able to identify the leg as belonging to Tippett. But I had to check it out anyway.

As we approached, two firemen in the boat carefully picked up a tarp-covered bundle and laid it on the dock.

"Mind if we take a look?" I asked.

One of the firemen glanced up, his face heavily lined with fatigue. He shrugged. "Not much to see."

I knelt down and unwrapped the tarp. Lee crouched beside me.

White bone gleamed up where the leg had been torn away just below the knee. I swallowed when I noticed the leather tie-down shoe still attached to the foot. I quickly wrapped the tarp over the leg.

Lee murmured, "Black low-quarter shoe. Military style."

I nodded.

"Wasn't Tippett wearing black low-quarters?"

I nodded again. "C'mon." We headed back to the car.

$$\star\star\star\star$$

Thirty minutes later, the firemen had finished searching the last of the houseboats. They'd found six bodies, which now lay zipped in white bags in a roped-off perimeter on the asphalt. In the distance, a launch with police markings puttered toward the dock, divers visible on deck.

From the car, I watched Lee step away from one of the body bags. He walked over.

"Looks like two males and three females. Hard to tell exactly on the last one 'cause of the burns."

"Any of the males have missing legs?"

Lee shook his head.

"Any children?" I asked quietly.

"Yeah. One."

I didn't want to look. I'd seen enough death for one day. Lee stared past me. "Looks like we got some more company."

I turned. Two unmarked sedans were coming down the road. They stopped at the police checkpoint, now congested with a throng of newspeople. Most of the fire trucks and ambulances had departed minutes earlier, and the parking lot was almost empty. The sedans pulled in and parked a few yards away.

Jonesy emerged from one sedan. Two grim-faced members of the CID climbed out of the other.

"I'll be in touch," I told Lee. I started to turn away, when I felt Lee's hand on my shoulder.

"We'll get him, Charlie," Lee said softly. "We'll get the son of a bitch."

"Sure . . . Harry." I gave him a half-smile, waved to Jonesy, and began walking to the cars.

Even though I told them there might not be any remains, I wanted the CID men to wait until the divers finished. If by some miracle Tippett's body was recovered, I wanted to be notified immediately.

For Dorothy and the kids.

"Let's go, Jonesy," I said. I tossed one of the CID men Tippett's car keys and climbed into Jonesy's car and closed my eyes.

"The Pentagon, Jonesy," I murmured.

★★★★

When I opened my eyes, we were on Indian Head Highway, northbound.

Jonesy looked over. "You going to be okay, sir?"

"Yeah." I struggled to sit up.

"The Phoenix listing from Army personnel came in."

"And?"

"Masonis was on it."

I stared out the window, feeling something close to hate. "Any word from Webster?"

Jonesy shook his head. "Not as of about an hour ago. But Major Gutiérrez left a message at the office. Says she might have something."

I reached for the car phone. "How about Masonis's performance evaluations?"

"Army personnel is working it. They're stored someplace in St. Louis. I asked for them to be faxed to the office. Should get them tonight or tomorrow morning."

"They couldn't just FedEx the entire personnel file?"

"Faxing is easier. All the old files have been transferred to computers."

I punched in Maria's number. The female captain answered. Maria wasn't in but should be back in an hour. I left a message that I'd stop by around 1630 hours.

Feeling exhausted, I leaned back and closed my eyes.

Jonesy coughed softly. "Sir?"

"What?" I murmured.

"I wonder about that explosion," he said.

"What about it?"

"I was wondering why Masonis blew up the boat. Seems like over-kill when he could have used a knife or a gun on the kid. Doesn't make much sense, sir."

I didn't reply.

"And what's his motive? Political? Money?"

"FBI get back with the check into Masonis's finances?" I asked.

"Not yet. You think it's money, then?"

I sighed. "I wish I knew, Jonesy."

20

COLONEL JENSEN!"

I CAME OUT OF THE FOG. JONESY WAS LOOKING AT ME.

"We're here . . . at the Pentagon."

I glanced around. He was right.

I probably should have gone home and changed my soiled suit first, but I was past caring. Anyway, the time was almost 1500 hours.

"Meet me at Maria's office after the meeting with General Holmes," I told Jonesy. "And check with the FBI again. I want the information on Masonis's finances."

"Yes, sir."

The guard at the Pentagon entrance frowned in disapproval as I showed him my ID. I almost told him to go to hell. At the men's room near the A-ring, I washed up as best I could.

The staff of the Chairman of the Joint Chiefs gave me disparaging looks as I walked in. Then I mentioned my name.

Three minutes later, I was escorted into the JCS secure area. Two right turns and a left and I was ushered into a private conference room.

"Sit at the far end of the table," the Army colonel told me.

I sat and watched the walls for twenty minutes.

Then the door opened and I popped to attention.

The Chairman, General Holmes, entered first, followed by General Streeter, the Commandant of the Marine Corps; Admiral Benson, the Chief of Naval Operations; General Worthen, the Army Chief of Staff; Admiral Williams, the Vice Chairman of the Joint Chiefs; and General Tupper, the Deputy Air Force Chief of Staff. Under the lights, the constellation of forty-eight silver stars on their shoulders was nearly blinding.

Normally, I would have been awed, but not today.

They took their places. Holmes sat opposite me at the end of the table. Six pairs of eyes stared at me. "Sit down, Colonel," growled Holmes.

Then the door opened again and the Army colonel I'd talked to earlier entered, went over to Holmes, and whispered something. Holmes nodded, and the colonel walked out. Five seconds later, a distinguished-looking man in a dark suit entered. He nodded to Holmes and took a chair along the paneled wall without speaking. He had an erect, almost military carriage. The chiefs paid him only scant attention, but I had the feeling they knew him.

Holmes looked angry as he addressed me. "I've been told you were on television a few minutes ago. A special report on the case. Care to explain, Colonel, why you chose to go public without first briefing me and your superiors, as you were ordered to do?"

"Sir," I said slowly, "I made a judgment call. I didn't see a problem, considering you released the story earlier at your press conference. Neither I nor the police have any idea where Dr. Masonis is. Getting his likeness out into the public increases our chances of apprehending him."

"Probably a wise decision," Holmes said dryly, "since so far you've been less than sterling in your performance."

General Tupper, the Deputy Air Force Chief of Staff, cleared his throat. He had wavy brown hair and smooth features that made him look much too young for the four stars he wore. "Come now, General Holmes, you're jumping to conclusions. Colonel Jensen hasn't been at this for twenty-four hours." To me he said, "I understand the lead investigator, Colonel Tippett, was killed in the explosion. My condolences."

I gave a slight nod. I didn't know much about General Tupper except that he was an ex-astronaut and had been commander of U.S. Space

Command before being appointed to the Air Force's number-two position. I realized his comments didn't necessarily mean he agreed with me. Maybe he was defending me out of service loyalty. No matter, I was glad he'd spoken up.

But Holmes wasn't. He glared at Tupper.

Tupper didn't look back.

General Holmes said to me, "Perhaps you might give us the particulars you've already provided the press and the public." His voice dripped acid.

I spoke carefully, highlighting what I'd learned. The chiefs listened with few interruptions . . . until I mentioned Cao Dinh.

At the mention of Cao Dinh the man in the suit leaned forward. His eyes seemed to look through me. I tried to ignore him.

"We discovered from the list of the twenty-three names in General Watkins's office that all had been POWs reportedly interned at a camp called Cao Dinh," I continued. "None of the prisoners on the list were released after the war. I think General Watkins went to Vietnam to find out what really happened to these men. I think he tried to search Cao Dinh and I think he was rebuffed by the Vietnamese. When he returned from Vietnam, he came into contact with Mr. Tho, who I suspect provided him with information concerning Cao Dinh. Someone, probably Masonis, learned of this and killed both men."

I folded my hands on the table to signify I was finished. For a few moments, no one spoke.

Then the room erupted in questions.

"What was Dr. Masonis's motive for murder?"

"What's so important about Cao Dinh?"

"Who were the prisoners?"

"What did this Mr. Tho give General Watkins?"

"Quiet!" Holmes barked, his face a grim mask.

The questions ceased immediately.

Holmes gave me a look of disgust. "Colonel, do you even know what you're talking about?"

"Sir, I . . ."

"Concerning Cao Dinh. Have you seen the report on what happened to the prisoners?"

I hesitated. "No, sir. I tried. I understand it's Eyes Only."

"You're damn right." Holmes waved a hand around the room. "Not even the men here are aware of the particulars."

"What are they, General?" asked General Worthen, the Army Chief.

"Yes, sir," General Streeter, the Marine Commandant, said. "If the North Vietnamese executed prisoners wholesale, I sure as hell want to know."

"It's our duty to know," General Tupper said quietly.

I noticed that Admiral Williams, the Vice Chairman, said nothing. Which reinforced my earlier judgment that he was a Holmes pawn.

Holmes panned the room with a stony stare. Then his eyes went to the man in the suit. The nod was barely perceptible.

Who the hell is this guy? I thought.

"This is never to be mentioned again, understood?" Holmes said. Nods around the table.

"Cao Dinh," Holmes continued, "has indeed been kept quiet. But not because of something the North Vietnamese did, as Colonel Jensen is intimating. Rather, the silence is because of what we, the United States, did." He leaned forward in his seat. "Gentlemen, on July 27, 1971, a U.S. Air Force F-4 out of Takli dropped napalm on Cao Dinh."

The room fell into a shocked silence.

"My God," the Vice Chairman, Admiral Williams, murmured. "This has been confirmed? We fried our own men?"

"Yes," Holmes said. "The camp was wiped out." He gave me a disparaging look. "So you see, Colonel, your theory about General Watkins's professed concern for Cao Dinh amounts to nothing. Unless you want to argue that General Watkins was seeking to humiliate the U.S. by bringing this sad event to light."

I shook my head. "But, sir . . ."

"And I might remind you that General Watkins personally told me he fully supported Vietnamese recognition. Which again dispels your inferences of some kind of Vietnamese atrocity."

"Sir, the existence of the list indicates General Watkins was interested in Cao Dinh."

"Do you have the list with you?"

I nodded. I removed it from my jacket and walked it to him on the other side of the table. I remained standing as Holmes read through the list.

He looked up and addressed me as if I were a child. "Colonel, do you know where these names came from?"

"I assume from defectors, or other prisoners perhaps."

The Marine Commandant cleared his throat sharply. "General Holmes, what was the name of the prison camp you escaped from?"

I knew, even before Holmes replied.

"Cao Dinh," Holmes said. "I provided our intelligence with the names. Eighteen of them, the ones who were there when I left. The others I don't recognize. But from the dates, they could have been interned after I'd escaped."

I felt overwhelmed with both confusion and anger as Holmes thrust the list at me. I turned to walk back to my seat.

"Colonel!" Holmes barked.

I about-faced. "Yes, sir."

"I hope you've done a better job of building a case against Dr. Masonis. Tell me, do you have anything linking him to any of the murders?"

"We . . . I had a witness, General. But he was killed today."

"Then you have nothing implicating Dr. Masonis?"

"Not at this time, sir."

"Do you have anything showing why Dr. Masonis should want to kill General Watkins? Anything in his past? A motive? Anything at all, Colonel?"

"He had the training, sir, and as far as I can tell, the opportunity. He was in a position to know about Cao Dinh and he had access to General Watkins's office, and he seems to be in hiding."

"Then you're saying you have nothing concrete. All you've got is innuendo and suspicion. And on that, you have publicized to the world that

Dr. Masonis is responsible. What if you're wrong? You . . . *we* are going to look like grade-A jackasses, Colonel. Not to mention you've probably opened us up for a major lawsuit."

Our eyes met. I knew better than to answer.

"I'm going to recommend you be relieved, Colonel. You've shown me nothing. With the death of Colonel Tippett, I'm not sure if you're emotionally equipped to continue. You are dismissed."

I didn't move.

"Colonel, I said—"

"Two questions, General," I interrupted. "About General Watkins. Did he know the story about the POWs at Cao Dinh . . . that they had been killed by us? If he did, did he believe it?"

Holmes glared at me. For an instant, I thought I would be summarily dismissed. He surprised me.

"Yes on both counts, Colonel," Holmes said calmly.

I nodded and walked out. I knew I might have been mistaken about almost everything. Maybe Masonis wasn't the guy. Maybe Watkins had been killed for a reason I still had to figure out.

I *was* sure about one thing.

Holmes had just lied. But why?

21

COLONEL JENSEN!"

I WAS IN THE HALLWAY OUTSIDE THE CONFERENCE ROOM. I turned. "Yes, sir?"

General Tupper took my arm and guided me down the hallway. "I've got to get back, but . . . in here."

We went into a break room with vending machines. A captain and a sergeant were buying soft drinks. They greeted Tupper with nervous smiles and left.

Tupper shut the door. I was surprised to hear him click the lock.

He gave me an appraising look. "I want straight answers, understand? No bullshit, Colonel."

I found myself standing almost as if in a brace. "No, sir."

He waved a hand. "General Holmes had a point in there. Pretty damn stupid you going on TV."

Christ. "Yes, sir."

"Especially if you're mistaken."

"Yes, sir."

"But you don't think you're wrong, do you?"

I hesitated. "No, sir."

"After what General Holmes said, you still think Watkins was checking out Cao Dinh?"

I took a breath. "The MIA list indicates that, sir. General Watkins wouldn't have been working on it if he bought the story that we killed our own POWs."

"And you still think his death is related to Cao Dinh?"

"Yes, sir."

"Why?"

"I think something happened there, sir. Something that's being covered up."

"So you don't buy General Holmes's story about the F-4?"

"Sir, let me ask you. If you were the North Vietnamese and the U.S. had just napalmed their own men, what would you do?"

Tupper almost smiled. "I'd have gotten every reporter I could find, hauled them out to the site, and had pictures plastered in every goddamn paper in the world. Hell, I'd have even dragged Jane Fonda over if I could."

I nodded. "So would I, sir. Propaganda value would have been enormous."

"I'll be damned," Tupper said. "If you're right, then Holmes was feeding us a line." He shook his head. "Which means the North Vietnamese might have executed the prisoners. And if Watkins knew that and made it public, the whole Vietnam-recognition thing could have gone down the tubes."

"Which could cost billions to a lot of companies, sir, and be a major scandal if the administration is involved in a cover-up."

"Sounds like a motive to me, Colonel, except for one thing. Why's Holmes covering this up?"

"Sir?"

"He's a POW. He'd be the last person to want to cover up executions of prisoners, especially men he knew."

"I . . . I wish I knew, sir."

The door handle rattled.

"You're still working the case, Colonel," Tupper said.

"But General Holmes . . . ?"

Someone knocked. Then more rattling. A voice. "Anyone in there?"

Tupper's face turned hard. "Until the new Chief of Staff is appointed, I'm running the Air Force, and you are still in the Air Force. You're on the case."

Tupper was going out on a limb for me. I smiled my appreciation. "Thank you, sir."

He shrugged, pointing to the four stars on his shoulder. "One of the perks. I can afford to piss people off."

"Sir?"

He smiled. "I don't have to worry about promotions." He started to turn away, then stopped. "I wonder . . ." He gave me a thoughtful look. "You know, there was a rumor I heard about Holmes back during the war. If it was true, could be someone is using it to pressure Holmes."

"What rumor?"

Tupper looked uncomfortable. "If you check it out, you better be damn discreet."

I nodded.

Tupper took a deep breath. He'd arrived at Takli Air Base a year after Holmes had been captured. In the squadron he'd heard rumors that Holmes, with a wife back home, had supposedly fallen hard for a nurse at the base. Rumors were he'd knocked her up, and the nurse had suddenly been reassigned back to the States.

"Now, I can't confirm any of this," Tupper said.

I nodded. "But if someone uncovered that Holmes had an illegitimate child, and they threatened to go public . . ."

"Might explain Holmes's actions," Tupper said. "Remember, be discreet."

Pounding now. "I can hear you in there! Open up, dammit!" the voice shouted.

"One question, sir. The civilian in the briefing?"

"Civilian? Oh, Major General Bailey."

"A major general?"

"White House liaison from DOD." Tupper shook his head, a hint of disgust in his voice. "You must not be aware of the White House policy. President's staff doesn't like the military liaisons to wear uniforms around our commander in chief. Think it highlights the President's lack of military experience. Keep me posted." He opened the door and walked out past a backpedaling and chagrined Army colonel.

I stood in the hallway for a moment. Then I shook my head and started to walk away. Then a woman's voice called me.

Now what, I thought, and turned.

Mrs. Moffitt.

★★★★

She beamed at me, her face flushed, breathing hard.

"Thank God, I caught you," Mrs. Moffitt said. "I called your office. They said you were here. So I came over. Then Marcie said you had just left. I hurried . . ."

"Please, Mrs. Moffitt, slow down."

"But I know the name."

I frowned. "The name?"

"Because of the phone call."

"Phone call?"

"The man. Mr. Pinock. When he said it, I knew. That was the name on the fax that General Watkins received."

"The one he grabbed from you?" I said, finally understanding.

"Yes. And I have Mr. Pinock's number. I told him you'd call." She thrust a yellow Post-it note at me. "Dynatech," she proclaimed. "That's what it was. Dynatech Transports. Not dinosaur."

I smiled. "Thank you very much."

Her voice became motherly. "Now, you call him."

"I most certainly will."

She nodded in satisfaction.

I patted her hand. "You've been very helpful."

She blushed, turned, and walked away down the hall.

★★★★

Someone answered on the second ring. In the background, a printer clattered, people shouted. The female voice said, "Pinock Financial, Mr. Pinock's office."

I identified myself, and in a moment a gruff voice said, "Pinock."

"Lieutenant Colonel Jensen, Mr. Pinock."

"Ah, the man running the investigation into General Watkins's death, right?"

"Yes."

A pause. "I knew the general for a lot of years. Spent twenty in myself. Two hundred and thirty-six missions over 'Nam. F-4s. Ole Six-Pack was a helluva stick."

"He'll be missed," I said.

"Yeah. Anyway, look, I'm not sure if what I got is going to be any help. But General Watkins called me a few days back, said he wanted me to run a detailed analysis into a corporation. Said it was hot. So I had my people give it priority. Then I heard about the murder. I wasn't sure what I should do."

"You're doing the right thing, sir. Now, this corporation is Dynatech Transports?"

"Yeah."

"What was the general's particular interest?"

"Irregularities. Unexplained losses, questionable bookkeeping, investments, and ownership. Especially ownership."

"Who owns Dynatech?"

"Don't know yet. We're still trying to sort things out. So far we've worked our way through a maze of four corporations."

"How much longer until you're finished?"

"Maybe tonight or tomorrow. We're waiting on the results of a number of computer queries."

"Did General Watkins say why he was so interested?"

"Not to me."

"Could you call me the moment you're finished?" I asked. I gave him my number and hung up.

★★★★

As I walked out of the JCS area past the security guard, I first noticed the glare of a bright light, then Frankie, holding up a TV camera. Annie McDaniel was standing in silhouette, her back to me, talking into a microphone. A number of onlookers, civilians and military, were gathered to one side.

I quickly swung wide and picked up my pace.

Annie was speaking loudly, saying, ". . . been no additional comment from General Holmes or the members of the Joint Chiefs on the status of the investigation. Sources indicate . . ."

I glanced over. A few more seconds and I'd turn the corner. . . .

She saw me, and her eyes widened. "Shit!"

"Cut," Frankie said. "Annie, you can't say—"

"Colonel Jensen!" she yelled.

I ducked my head and kept walking.

The clatter of heels. "Colonel Jensen!"

I walked faster.

People in the hallway were staring. Someone snickered.

Aw, hell. I stopped and turned.

Annie and Frankie slowed to a walk, Annie's pretty face breaking into a big, almost predatory, grin. A young Army captain trailed behind, looking nervous.

Annie reached me first. She spoke between breaths. "Colonel Jensen, did you just brief General Holmes . . . ?"

I held up a hand. "No comment, Annie." Frankie began to raise the camera. I gave him a hard look. He lowered the camera. I glanced at the captain. "Who are you?"

The captain swallowed. "Captain Barstow, sir. Public Affairs."

"Off the record, okay?" Annie said. "I give you my word—"

"Yeah," I snapped. "And we know what that's worth." I turned and began walking.

Annie fell into step, Frankie and the captain following. "You're not still mad about that? C'mon, Colonel. That was nothing. I followed through on the rest."

"Annie, I'm busy. I've got nothing to say." I stopped by a stairwell. My eyes went to the captain. "Barstow, if these two follow me, I'm going to have your ass. Got that?"

Barstow looked sick. "Yes, sir. Absolutely, sir."

I opened the door.

"Colonel Jensen . . . ?"

I stepped into the stairwell.

"Any truth to the rumor that General Holmes has relieved you?"

I stepped back into the hallway. "How the hell did you know that?" As soon as I said it, I knew I had made a mistake.

Frankie wore a cocky smirk. Barstow looked puzzled.

Annie smiled sweetly, winked, and walked away. Frankie chuckled and followed. Captain Barstow stayed where he was, his head swiveling between Annie and me.

Charlie, you goddamn idiot, I thought.

★★★★

"Go on back to the maintenance room, sir," the captain at the desk said when I walked into the computer security center. "I'll buzz Major Gutiérrez, let her know you're here."

"Thank you." I forced a smile and walked past the lieutenants clicking away on their computers.

Jonesy waited for me outside the door of the maintenance room. He must have noticed my foul mood, because he asked, "Something wrong, sir?"

I shook my head.

He looked at me for a moment. "I checked with the FBI again."

"And?"

"Nothing yet."

I knew checking a person's financial records, usually through his tax returns, was no big deal for the Bureau. They could do it in minutes.

"Who'd you talk to?"

"Agent Weatherby."

The name didn't mean anything to me. "Give you a reason?"

"Says they're having trouble downloading the data. Something with the IRS computers."

"You believe him?"

"I called the IRS. Mrs. Baker. Worked with her on the embezzling case last year. The Air Force lieutenant colonel."

I nodded. I remembered.

"Anyway, she seemed surprised when I said I'd heard they were having computer problems. So I gave her Masonis's name. Said she'd fax us the info to the office, no problem."

"Maybe it's the Bureau's computers that are down," I said.

"Maybe," Jonesy said. But his expression told me he didn't believe that for a minute.

I told him about the conversation with Pinock.

"Dynatech," Jonesy said. "Never heard of it."

"Me neither," Then I mentioned what Tupper had said about Holmes possibly having an illegitimate child. Jonesy whistled and said he'd check it out.

At that moment, the door opened. "There you are," Maria said, placing her hands on her hips. "I thought you two got lost. So, are you coming in or not?"

22

"PRINT IT, CINDY," MARIA SAID.

MARIA STOOD BETWEEN JONESY AND ME AS WE WATCHED THE computer screen over Cindy's shoulder. Cindy was sorting through what had been salvaged from General Watkins's and Major Swanson's computers. Most of the documents displayed belonged to Major Swanson. I had skimmed those, but this particular document was the Officer Performance Rating General Watkins had apparently been writing on Colonel Jowers.

Jonesy and I together began reading the OPR.

A laser printer nearby whirred and went quiet. Maria moved to collect the short stack of papers deposited in the printer's tray.

Even before I was finished reading the Jowers OPR, I knew the colonel's career was over. To a civilian, the OPR would seem to say Colonel Jowers was an exceptional officer. But any Air Force officer could pick out the subtle words and phrase manipulations that made the evaluation so damning: the use of the word "satisfactory" instead of "outstanding"; "promote" instead of "promote now"; and worst of all, the use of the word "average"—even once would be bad, and the word had appeared four times.

Jonesy finished reading a moment later. I checked my watch. We'd been there almost an hour.

Maria brought the thick stack of documents to me. "These are all we could retrieve, Colonel. You might want to take a look. Some we printed before you arrived."

I nodded and accepted the documents.

Cindy, seeing that Jonesy and I were finished reading the OPR, punched a button. An alphabetized listing for General Watkins's word processing program appeared.

"Actually, we were lucky to get those," Maria said, referring to the documents she'd given me. "The virus replicated itself into ninety-plus percent of the files."

"I appreciate this, Maria," I said, still looking at Cindy's computer screen. "Damn!" I said in surprise when I saw the words "Cao Dinh."

"Cao Dinh," Jonesy said, reading the file name aloud.

"What're you talking about?" Maria said, peering past my shoulder.

"File about a third of the way down, ma'am," Cindy said.

I broke into a grin. This had been written two days earlier at 1637 hours. I almost couldn't believe it.

"What's Cao Dinh?" Maria asked.

I asked excitedly, "Were you able to retrieve that file?"

"I'm not sure," Maria said. She nodded to the papers. "It'd be in there."

"I don't think so, sir," Cindy said. "In fact, I know we didn't."

I went over to a slab table and quickly flipped through the papers. There were maybe thirty sheets. Letters mostly, to Watkins's acquaintances. A few additional performance reports on subordinates. One or two that almost looked like pages from memoirs. Toward the end of the stack, my hopes began to fade. I flipped over the last page. Maria and Jonesy were staring at me. I shook my head.

"There's no way to get the rest of the files?" I asked Maria.

"No."

Cindy shook her head.

"At least we know the general was working on Cao Dinh, sir," Jonesy said.

"What's Cao Dinh?" Maria asked again.

"You don't want to know," I told her.

"Okay, I can take a hint. You don't have to tell me what's going on."

"I will, someday."

"I won't hold my breath."

"Major, it's almost 1730," Cindy said, looking at her watch.

"Thanks. Come on. We'll watch in my office."

★★★★

"I wonder who wrote it," Jonesy murmured. We were standing side by side at urinals in the men's room around the corner from Maria's office.

"The Cao Dinh file?"

"No, sir. Colonel Jowers's OPR."

I frowned. Then I understood. It wouldn't be the first time a general had one of his staff draft an OPR. "You think Major Swanson wrote it?"

"Explain a lot of the resentment, especially if Colonel Jowers found out."

He flushed, providing an interesting punctuation mark to our unspoken thoughts.

★★★★

We sat around Maria's desk and watched the local news broadcast on Channel 7. Annie had been good as her word. The story was the lead, and it began with a live shot of Annie standing in front of the marina, explaining what had happened that afternoon. In the background were the houseboats, with investigators poking around. A moment or so later, the scene switched to Frankie's earlier video of the victims, the ambulances, the fire trucks, and the boats. Then Annie again.

I sipped a soft drink. Annie must have gone to the marina immediately after our confrontation. I wondered when she was going to announce her bombshell that I'd almost been relieved. I also wondered who the hell had told her.

Annie was saying, "This could be the largest murder case in recent memory. First, there was the brutal murder last night of General Watkins, who was found in his home on Fort Myer. General Watkins was the Air Force Chief of Staff . . ." As Annie provided voice-over, we saw a shot of the Fort Myer Wright Gate. Then a shot of the Little Saigon Tearoom as Annie discussed Tho's murder. The report of Miss Vinh's murder was backed with a clip of the rooming house, then of Tippett and me parking and walking inside, as Annie explained in a conspiratorial tone that we were military investigators. Then the screen returned to Annie, live at the marina.

"One of the military investigators you just saw was Lieutenant Colonel Charles Jensen of the Air Force Office of Special Investigation. As I mentioned, Colonel Jensen is apparently convinced that a Dr. Theodore Masonis, a professor of Asian Studies from Duke University and a noted author, is the prime suspect in these deaths. An unnamed source in the Washington, D.C., police department informed me that Lieutenant Harry Lee, the detective in charge of their investigation, is also pursuing the theory that Dr. Masonis is involved. But so far, this reporter has been unable to discover any possible motive for Dr. Masonis to have committed these crimes. If the police or the military know of a motive, they're not saying. Detective Lee declined an offer for an interview. Colonel Warren Tippett, of the Army Criminal Investigations Division, was the lead military investigator but, sadly, he perished in the explosion. I was fortunate to get Lieutenant Colonel Jensen of the Air Force Office of Special Investigations to grant me an exclusive interview, which this station aired earlier today. Here now is a replay of that interview. . . ."

And there I was. Annie showed my entire speech, except for the part where she'd tried to ask me questions.

Frankly, I was surprised she'd cut it.

Annie's report finished with Masonis's picture filling the screen. The shot was the one from his book jacket.

Annie signed off.

A beer commercial with the three guys fishing on a dock came on. Annie never mentioned that I was almost removed from the investigation. I didn't know what to think about that.

Maria, pale, looked over to me. "God, Charlie, I didn't know."

"Sorry. I should have said something." I had made a conscious decision not to tell her about Tippett's death. I guess I was hoping she'd have heard already.

I drained the soft drink and crumpled the can. The death toll in the explosion had been nine. Names hadn't been released. The boy in the houseboat I'd crawled into had been the only child killed. He'd just turned seven on Saturday. I felt my anger return.

"Maria, check CNN, please," I said.

Maria punched her remote.

We caught the tail end of Annie's report, then CNN's trailer, which described Masonis as a Vietnam veteran and one of the country's foremost experts on Vietnam. There wasn't time to wait for the network telecasts.

Maria walked us to the exit. "I liked Colonel Tippett, Charlie. He was gruff, but nice."

"You knew him?"

"I worked with him on the Leavenworth thing. He's the one who first called me to help him with the investigation into the virus proliferation there. He thought a lot of you."

I didn't say anything. We reached the door.

"Oh, you might check with his office. I'd forgotten. He might have a copy, you know."

"Copy?"

"Of the virus."

"Thanks."

She gripped my arm and looked into my eyes. "I hope you get the guy, Charlie."

"We will."

★★★★

Jonesy drove. En route, I called Talia's number. She answered cautiously, relieved I was the caller.

"I saw the news, sir. They said they haven't found three of the bodies."

"No."

"Is Colonel Tippett one of the missing?"

"Yes."

"I'm sorry."

"I take it Dr. Masonis has not called?"

"No." She sounded as if she wanted to say something else.

I waited. Finally I asked, "Did you check the disks?"

"Yes. Nothing on Vietnam or his trip."

"How about Cao Dinh?"

"What?"

I spelled it. "It's a prisoner-of-war camp," I said.

"I don't remember seeing anything like that."

"No reference to POWs at all?"

"No, sir. Jonesy told me these disks weren't from the general's computer."

"So . . ."

"Then there probably wouldn't be anything pertinent on them anyway."

"All right. You holding up okay?"

"Yes." Again, I had the feeling she wanted to say something.

I said, "May I speak to Captain Webster?"

"Sure."

Webster came on. He sounded subdued. I told him I'd be on Jonesy's cellular if anything broke.

Jonesy gave me a sideways glance. "You think there's any chance Masonis is still going to call Major Swanson?"

"Not unless he's crazy."

★★★★

Because of the HOV rush-hour restriction on I-66, we had to take Lee Highway which added at least twenty minutes. The traffic finally thinned to a manageable level west of Fairfax. I had tuned the radio to a jazz station to help me think, but the jazz didn't seem to work. I couldn't figure out why Annie hadn't mentioned General Holmes almost removing me from the case. Hell, I'd as much confirmed the action myself.

"Sir . . ."

Jonesy was staring into the rearview mirror. "We got company," he said.

23

Y OU SURE?" I ASKED, RESISTING THE URGE TO TURN AROUND.

"PRETTY SURE," JONESY SAID. "BROWN MINIVAN. WHITE MALE. Dark hair. Two cars behind now. Not very good at tailing, though. First noticed him when we pulled onto Highway 50. He almost ran some guy off the road, cutting in behind us. Stayed on our rear until just a few minutes ago, then must have decided he was too obvious and dropped back." Jonesy looked at me. "Every time I slow, he slows. Does the same thing when I speed up."

I leaned forward, my eyes on the passenger-side mirror. The van came into view. The driver appeared to be the only occupant. I had the impression he was young.

I dug out my notepad. "I'll get the plate."

"I already got it." Jonesy recited a number.

I wrote it down.

We turned south on Highway 28 toward the rolling hills of Manassas. The van followed.

"Pull over," I said.

Jonesy eased the car onto the shoulder.

The van slowed, then suddenly accelerated past. The driver hunched over the wheel and kept his eyes straight ahead. I didn't see him clearly because of the speed. We watched the van disappear around a bend.

Jonesy gave me a questioning look and waited for a gray car to roll by before pulling out.

★★★★

Five minutes later, we approached an intersection with a convenience store and a veterinary clinic. Ahead, the gray car pulled in beside a handful of vehicles in the parking lot. No van. We turned right. I read the address on the first house. "Should be maybe a mile farther. On the left."

Jonesy gave a low whistle as he looked around. "I thought this guy is a retired Army Colonel."

"He is."

Jonesy's reaction was understandable. All the homes were enormous, on what I guessed were five-acre lots, surrounded by brick-and-iron fences.

"Used to be horse farms here," I said.

"These places must go for a couple million easy."

"More like four or five."

"What the hell does this guy do, sir?"

"He runs the MIA Association."

"Yes, sir. I know that, but . . . well, damn. There can't be big money in that."

"No, I wouldn't think so. The next one, I think, with the white-brick fence."

We pulled up to an iron gate. A gold plaque read "The Birellis." Through the grillwork we saw a three-story mansion set back behind a manicured lawn. To the left was a tennis court. I climbed out and went to the intercom on the gatepost. A small sign said "Push for Admittance." Below that: "Invited Guests Only."

I pushed. In the circular driveway out front I saw a Mercedes and a Jaguar.

A metallic voice said, "May I help you?"

"Lieutenant Colonel Jensen for Colonel Birelli. I have an appointment."

"Very good, sir. Please come in. Park in front, please." There was the whirring sound of an electric motor. The gate swung open.

As I turned around, a car rolled by. The same gray one I'd seen earlier. I glanced down the road.

Damn.

I raised a hand to shield my eyes. I was looking into the sun and couldn't be sure. But the vehicle parked beside the road a half-mile back appeared to be a brown van.

I climbed into the car, and Jonesy drove through the gate.

★★★★

A black-jacketed Asian man with hair neatly slicked back stood on the portico as we drove up. He stepped down and opened my door. He spoke with a heavy, singsong accent that told me he wasn't the guy on the intercom.

"This way, please."

He led us down a stone path that snaked between the pool house and what had to be a five-car garage.

Jonesy looked around, slightly awed.

I couldn't believe places like this existed so close to D.C., but if you have enough money . . .

The crack of a shot was loud and clear. Another instantly followed.

"Sir?" Jonesy said, pulling up.

I was watching our escort, and he appeared unconcerned. I gestured Jonesy's attention to him.

We passed through a flower garden. A large water fountain bubbled off to the right, near a gazebo the size of a small house. A huge lawn opened up before us.

We heard two more shots.

Then I saw a man with a shotgun. Behind him stood a dark-haired woman with some kind of small box in her hand. The man crouched, grunted a command. Two clay pigeons flew out from behind a berm.

The man swung the gun up. Two rapid-fire reports. The pigeons exploded.

Our escort stopped and pointed toward the man, after which he turned and walked back along the path.

"Shit hot!" the man hollered, doing a little jig.

The woman clapped a hand against the box gleefully.

"Come on," I murmured to Jonesy, and we walked out across the lawn.

24

I'D NEVER MET U.S. ARMY COLONEL (RETIRED) JOHN BIRELLI, BUT HE'D BEEN IN THE PAPERS A LOT, AND I RECALLED HIS STORY.

During the mid-eighties, Birelli had been given command of the Defense Intelligence Agency's POW/MIA office. He had been chosen because he was a war hero with a Distinguished Service Cross and two Silver Stars from Vietnam, and because he had a reputation for being smooth, glib, and charming. The second criterion was by far the more important.

When Birelli took over, the DIA's POW/MIA office was being besieged by Congress, the families, MIA activists, and the press. The office was accused of being uncaring, unresponsive, bungling. Some of the more vicious charges linked the office to a major conspiracy to cover up the existence of live POWs still in Vietnam. The decision was made to bring in a PR man. Enter handsome, smiling Colonel John Birelli.

The move backfired.

The key to the animosity against the POW/MIA office was the families. The military thought if the families could be made happy, the criticism from the other sources, the various lobbying organizations and Congress, would wither away. Birelli's job was to ingratiate himself with the families, placate their concerns, dispel any notion of a cover-up or the existence of remaining prisoners.

Six months after assuming his post, Birelli called a press conference, announced he was resigning from the Army, and dropped his bombshell that, from the evidence that had come across his desk, he believed there was indeed a strong possibility of live prisoners in Vietnam. He also claimed the DIA bureaucracy was hampering his attempts to verify their existence.

Overnight, Birelli became a cause célèbre. To the families, activists, and some politicians, he evolved into something of a saint. The military considered court-martialing him. They might have had they not known the move would lead to a public-relations nightmare. They wisely allowed him to retire.

Birelli quickly capitalized on his newfound notoriety. He established the POW/MIA Association and became the MIA cause's most prominent fund-raiser and advocate. He organized highly publicized expeditions to Laos, Cambodia, and Vietnam. The fact that he never returned with any proof of live POWs didn't seem to matter to his supporters.

Birelli was a continual problem for the Pentagon, particularly the DIA. Unlike most activists, Birelli possessed credibility. The DIA couldn't dismiss his charges as baseless or uninformed. He'd been one of them. He knew the truth.

Colonel Butcher's loathing for Birelli characterized the opinion of most of the Pentagon leadership. To them, Birelli was an outlaw, a zealot, and an opportunist who preyed on building false hope in the MIA families to keep himself in the limelight.

Which made me curious. Why would General Watkins, of all people, have had anything to do with the man?

The gun barked. The smell of gunpowder filled the still air.

"John!" the woman called. She was looking at us. I could see the box in her hands now, a remote-control device to launch the clay pigeons.

Birelli was dressed casually in a shooter's vest over a polo shirt. He looked like his pictures: handsome, rugged features; dark hair, blow-dried back off his ears; salt-and-pepper mustache trimmed to the edge of his lip. He had to be fifty, but he looked years younger.

Grinning, Birelli cracked the shotgun and removed two shell casings and dropped them into a pouch on his hip. Hanging the shotgun over a muscular shoulder, he waited as Jonesy and I walked up.

"Colonel Jensen, glad you could make it."

"Nice shooting, Colonel Birelli."

"John," he said, sporting a relaxed smile.

We shook. His grip was firm. I introduced Jonesy. The woman joined us. She wore a blue sundress that projected a casual elegance. She looked no more than twenty-five, with large eyes, delicate features, and long black hair that fell over slender shoulders. A fragile, beautiful woman.

"My bride, Lisa, gentlemen," boomed Birelli, putting a tanned arm around her.

Lisa smiled. "Hello, Colonel, Sergeant." She had a strong British accent.

"Lisa grew up in London," Birelli said. "Everybody asks."

"You have quite a home, Mrs. Birelli," I said.

"Thank you. And please, call me Lisa." She smiled graciously. "I must confess I'm still not accustomed to it. It's rather pretentious for my taste."

Birelli laughed. "It's a bribe. My father-in-law paid me off with this place to take Lisa off his hands."

"John!" But she was still smiling.

He rubbed her shoulder playfully.

Lisa gave him a tolerant look. "Give me the gun, John. I'll return it to the study so you lads can play or frolic or whatever it is you want to do."

Birelli dutifully handed over the shotgun.

"Best damn thing that ever happened to me," Birelli said as we watched Lisa stroll back to the house. "Known her father for years. Used to be an ARVN colonel, big-time province chief. I helped get him and the family out in '75. Now he owns six factories in Malaysia. Hired me on as his vice president of marketing. Works my butt off. Ugly cuss, too. If you saw him, you'd swear Lisa couldn't be his daughter."

"She's very attractive," I said.

Birelli took a deep breath, then winked at Jonesy. "Only marry for two things, Sergeant. Money and looks."

"Then I'm oh-for-two, sir," Jonesy said, and laughed.

Birelli laughed too. "C'mon. Let's have a drink."

✯✯✯✯

We sat around a wrought-iron table on a raised patio behind the main house, overlooking the garden. Off my left shoulder, the sun hung low on the horizon. Crickets were just beginning their shrill symphony in the background. Jonesy and I sipped soft drinks, while Birelli gulped down a rum and Coke. He sighed contentedly, then raised the glass, rattling the ice.

The Asian man appeared and replaced Birelli's glass with a full one.

Birelli took a long pull. He set the glass down, looked at Jonesy and me, then shook his head. "Caught some of your little spiel with that good-looking reporter on TV. What do you go by, Charles?"

"I prefer Charlie."

"Okay, Charlie. Heard about Tippett. Ran into him a few times when I was in DIA. Wish I could say I was sorry. But I always thought he was an arrogant SOB."

I felt my temper rise. "You said something about General Holmes being a liar. And photographs. Get to it."

Birelli smiled easily through perfect teeth. "Relax, Charlie. What's your hurry? Let me get you something stronger. You too, Sergeant."

I didn't say anything. Jonesy said, "I'm fine."

Birelli shrugged. "So you really think Dr. Masonis killed Watkins, eh? And the others? Blew up the boat . . ."

"He's a suspect."

He smiled again. "You're goddamn nuts. Ted Masonis never killed those people."

I fought off my anger. "You know Dr. Masonis?"

"Very well. He came to me, what . . . three years ago. I helped him research his last two books. You read them?"

"No."

"Too bad. Should. They're good. Mentions me a few times." He took a large swallow. "Look, Charlie, I'm just trying to help you out. Ted Masonis isn't your man."

"How can you be so sure?"

"I know him. Besides, why would a successful guy like Masonis want to kill Watkins and the others? He's got no reason. He's just a hardworking academic type."

"He matches an eyewitness description. And the murders might be connected to General Watkins's trip to Vietnam, which Masonis participated in."

"Yeah. I know about the trip."

"From General Watkins?"

Birelli nodded. "The general asked me for a recommendation for someone to accompany him."

"Did you recommended Masonis, sir?" Jonesy asked.

"Guilty. Masonis was the most qualified guy I could think of. He spoke the language, was familiar with the MIA situation. Most importantly, wasn't government connected."

"Why was that important?" I asked.

"General Watkins wanted a civilian."

"Why?"

Birelli considered me for a moment. "He never came out and said."

"But you must have some idea?"

"I think he wanted someone he thought he could trust."

I removed the list of POW names from my jacket. "Then Watkins conferred with you about these?"

Birelli glanced at the list. "Yeah, he wanted to know if I had any information on the POWs at Cao Dinh."

"And you gave him these names, the ones marked with your initials?"

He nodded.

"Where you'd get them?"

"I had them on file. I've been researching Cao Dinh for years."

"How come the DIA doesn't have those extra names?"

He smiled. "I've got better sources, Charlie. And I check things out. DIA is a bureaucracy. They specialize in sitting on their asses." He leaned back, swirling his drink. "Want to hear the whole story?"

"Yes."

Birelli's eyes drifted over the garden. "General Watkins came here last month. He wanted to talk about Cao Dinh, find out what I knew. I told him the whole thing stunk. I never bought the story we bombed our own guys." He paused. "You know about that?"

I nodded.

He looked surprised. "The thing that got me suspicious was the way the story came out. In '75, the Vietnamese said the men died in captivity, no explanation. We kept bugging them for an accounting. Two years later, the Vietnamese come back with the horseshit about the napalm and the F-4. Even released pictures of what they say is Cao Dinh, all burned to hell."

"And our government didn't question it, sir?" Jonesy asked.

"No. And Sergeant Jones, knock off the 'sir' shit. I'm a civilian." Birelli was smiling. He seemed to smile a lot.

"Okay," Jonesy said.

Birelli leaned back, crossing his ankles. "Uncle Sam's reaction was understandable. By the late seventies, everyone was trying to forget the war, trying to keep the healing process on track. No one wanted anything which could energize the antiwar pukes again. Which is what could have happened if the story about Cao Dinh had got out."

I shook my head. "That seems like a stretch—"

"Maybe. But consider the political fallout if we had called the Vietnamese liars and they leaked the pictures to the world press. Hell, everyone knows we bombed about every inch of the country. Easy to believe we killed our own guys. We'd lose the propaganda war, look like assholes, get our own people riled up. So the White House slaps an Eyes Only classification and orders that any copies of the file be destroyed."

"What did the Vietnamese gain by withholding the information from the press in the first place? I'd have thought they'd have been champing at the bit to get the Cao Dinh story aired."

"That, Charlie," Birelli said slowly, "is the million-dollar question.

My guess? They killed the prisoners and can't risk anyone digging into Cao Dinh."

"So how'd you find out about Cao Dinh if the White House destroyed all the records?" I asked.

Birelli smiled. "You must know the drill, Charlie. DIA generated the Cao Dinh file for the White House."

I nodded. Birelli was telling me DIA had made and kept an unauthorized copy, just in case they needed a little leverage someday. This was a common practice in the intelligence community. After all, information was power.

"After I take over the DIA's POW/MIA office, I get briefed on the Cao Dinh file. Right away my gut tells me the story has to be bogus. Which means those poor bastards must have been killed off by the North Vietnamese. I mean, they were all at the camp, right? And none of them return. Except for that cocksucker General Holmes, of course, and Major Brady Hanson."

"Major Hanson?" Jonesy asked.

"The guy who came out with Holmes. Gooks really worked the poor bastard over. Messed up his head. He's been locked up in a loony bin, a place called Rolling Hills Sanitarium down near Danville, since '71. But that's another story." Birelli drained his glass, held it up. "Anyway, the North Vietnamese had to have a hell of a reason to kill off over twenty POWs. After all, POWs were their only real leverage, right? So I began digging. I put the word out through my connections. Nothing. Zip. Got statements from a few villagers in the area, but . . ."

He waited for the houseman to replace his drink before continuing. "The villagers confirmed a large fire at the camp. They said after that they never saw the prisoners again. But the interesting thing is, the villagers saw the guards leaving."

A moment passed before I understood the import of that statement.

"Christ," Jonesy said, seeing the significance immediately.

"Damn," I said as I began to understand.

"Yeah," Birelli said sarcastically. "Pretty selective napalm, eh, that kills only prisoners. Somehow the Pentagon brass finds out I'm checking out Cao Dinh. Next thing I know, I'm called onto the carpet by General Sorenson, the DIA three-star at the time. Orders me to scrap the investigation." He grinned. "Man, General Sorenson was really pissed. I think he was scared, too. I could tell he was getting pressure from the top."

"The White House?" I interrupted.

"Probably."

I told Birelli about Major General Bailey, the DOD White House liaison, attending my meeting with General Holmes and the military chiefs.

Birelli's face turned somber. "You watch yourself, Charlie. The political wonks know you're digging into this thing. You keep it up, you're gonna start getting pressure to back off. Things could get nasty for you. You hear what I'm saying?"

I swallowed. I was thinking of General Holmes's attempt to relieve me. "Yeah."

"Maybe even deadly."

"Are you suggesting our government could be behind General Watkins's death?"

"Possibility."

"What? Like maybe a CIA operation?"

"Just be careful, Charlie. People are going to be watching you. At the least, what you do will affect your career."

I almost mentioned the van.

Birelli sat back. " 'Course, you could always do what I did. Say to hell with a career." He grinned. "After General Sorenson ordered me to back off, I saluted him smartly and told him to kiss my ass. That's when I called the press conference and resigned."

"But you said your resignation was over live sightings."

"Sure, and that's true. I honestly do think the North Vietnamese kept prisoners. Not many, and those few might have stayed voluntarily, particularly if they were collaborators. My beef is I don't think the DIA does enough to check out all the reports of live sightings. But . . ."

"The real reason was Cao Dinh," I said.

Birelli nodded. There was a glow in his cheeks now. "You got it.

Because that's not just a fantasy, like hoping we'll find one half-dead prisoner still alive. Cao Dinh is a major, major scandal, maybe bigger than Watergate and Iran-Contra rolled into one. Think about it: POWs executed wholesale, and the U.S. government and five administrations all take part in a cover-up. Someone's got to get the truth out." He shook his head. "For the first few years, I didn't have much luck getting new information. Takes a long time to set up an information network, especially one halfway around the goddamn world. Anyway, last year I finally turned something up." He raised his glass in a toast and took a large swallow.

I placed my elbows on the table, edging closer.

"During my last trip over to Thailand, a friend told me about a guy in one of the refugee camps. Supposed to be some high-ranking North Vietnamese officer. Turned out he was only a colonel, but he'd worked for a general. Guy was coughing his brains out from TB. He said he'd accompanied this general to Geneva back in 1971 to pick up fifteen million dollars in cash. After they secured the money, the general wanted to celebrate. They went to some whorehouse, then out drinking. Guess the general got really crocked. That's when the colonel found out where the money came from." Birelli's face turned ugly. "From some goddamn American. The colonel said the general laughed and told him sometimes prisoners were worth more dead than alive."

Jonesy shook his head in disgust.

"You believed him?" I asked.

"I might not have, except that he gave me a date. July 8, 1971. Know what day the F-4 supposedly dropped that napalm, and when the villagers told me Cao Dinh burned? Less than a week before."

"A payment," Jonesy said. "You're saying the money was a payment to the North Vietnamese for killing the POWs."

"A distinct possibility."

"Why didn't you go public?" I asked.

"Couldn't. The colonel died a few weeks later. I still don't have anything concrete, anything irrefutable."

"So Watkins was going to check this out?"

Birelli swirled his finger in his glass. "Yeah. I talked to him after he came back from that worthless trip to Vietnam. He said the Vietnamese were all smiles until he started asking questions about Cao Dinh. Then they put up the wall. That's why I called you about Holmes. Watkins was plenty pissed when he returned. He never was going to support any recognition of Vietnam. Not in a million years. Not after what he found out from Mr. Tho."

"Mr. Tho . . ." Jonesy said.

"You mean the guy who was murdered?" I asked.

"Yeah, the same guy who got whacked."

I felt a little light-headed. "Then you know the connection between Tho and General Watkins?"

Birelli stared at me for a moment. "I should. After all, I found Tho."

He raised his glass and rattled the ice.

25

AS DUSK SETTLED, THE SKY TURNED A MIXTURE OF RED AND YELLOW. A DOG BARKED FROM A NEARBY YARD, AND MOSQUITOES BEGAN TO BUZZ annoyingly. Birelli killed half his drink in two swallows.

He let out a deep sigh, stretched back, the glass on his stomach. He talked fast, his speech a little slurred. "So after Watkins tells me he came up empty, I get pissed. I talk to Lisa's father. Told him I wanted five hundred grand to buy information on Cao Dinh. He put up the money. I passed the word to my contacts in Thailand, Vietnam, Laos, here. Big bucks for anyone who can prove what happened at Cao Dinh. Bingo. Tho calls."

I shook my head. "Lisa's father gave you half a million dollars?"

"Hell, he'd give ten times that much to kill recognition of Vietnam. He hates those bastards in Hanoi."

"With that kind of money, you must have gotten a lot of calls," Jonesy said. "How did you know Tho's was genuine?"

"Because I've known Tho for years. He's one of my sources. Very reliable. When he contacted me with his story, I was very curious. I'd known he was a North Vietnamese defector, but he always said he was a rear-echelon type, training cadre with a stint in supply." Birelli shrugged. "Not that I believed him, really."

I was getting impatient. "What's so important about Mr. Tho?"

Birelli gave me a long look. "He was the fucking ace in the hole, Charlie. The piece to the whole puzzle." Birelli sat up and, stumbling over his words, said, "Tho was the commander, the son of a bitch who gave the order."

Jonesy and I looked at each other.

"Don't you get it?" Birelli said. "Tho was the Cao Dinh camp commandant."

Jonesy made a sharp sucking sound.

"I'll have that drink," I said.

★★★★

I sipped a double scotch, neat. "Why didn't Tho come forward earlier?"

Birelli snorted. "He'd have been a dead man. Tho wasn't his real name. The Vietnamese government would have taken him out in a minute if they learned who he really was. Not to mention the U.S. government. Hell, he's a war criminal, but with half a million bucks, Tho figured he could disappear where no one would ever find him."

"You were going to give him all of it?"

"Not at first. Originally, the deal was for three hundred grand. Tho told Watkins and me what happened on the night they executed the POWs. We could tell his story was the real thing. The general wanted Tho to write everything down. We promised half for Tho's Cao Dinh account, written up. Then the rest for the real kicker."

"The real kicker?"

Birelli paused, his eyes going to Jonesy, then settling on me. His voice was absolutely cold. "Yeah. The fucking reason why the POWs were killed, including the name of the American bastard who paid to have them whacked." He paused. "Including what Tho called absolute proof of what he was saying. Said we'd be damn happy."

I leaned forward. "Who was the American?"

Birelli shook his head. "He didn't say."

I was incredulous. "What!"

"Hey," Birelli said. "Tho was calling the shots, playing everything very close. He said he'd notify us when he was ready. Then last week Tho pulls a fast one. I was in Singapore, scrounging up business for my father-in-law. Got a call from Watkins. He says Tho decides he wants two hundred grand more. I squawk, but Watkins talks me into okaying the extra bucks. Says Tho's info is worth it and then some."

"You said something about proof?" Jonesy said.

"Photographs," I said, remembering Birelli's earlier call. "That it? That the proof?"

Birelli took a breath, then nodded. "Tho said he had pictures which would verify what he was saying. Made by a propaganda team out of Hanoi."

Jonesy and I looked stunned. "The North Vietnamese actually documented their own atrocity?" I asked. "I find that hard to believe. Have you seen the pictures?"

Birelli shook his head.

"Then how do you know they even exist?"

Birelli looked me in the eye. "Because General Watkins told me he saw them, Charlie."

Birelli casually swatted a mosquito on his neck and wiped his hand on his pants. "I was at our L.A. office meeting with some investors when Watkins calls me. He said Tho wants to meet ASAP. Watkins went to pick up the information, including the pictures. After verifying everything, he called me back from Tho's place and I wired the money to an account in Panama. Man, was Watkins upset. Almost in a rage."

"About what?" I asked

"The stuff in the goddamn pictures! He told me to pay Tho, said Tho had earned the money."

"What did the photographs show?"

"He wouldn't tell me."

"What!"

"How about the identity of the American who had the POWs killed?" Jonesy asked.

Birelli shook his head. When he spoke, he sounded bitter. "General Watkins wouldn't tell me why the prisoners were murdered. And I asked, believe me. Best I didn't know, he said. I got damn angry. Hell, I put up the money."

I swore softly.

"Would Masonis have known about Tho?" Jonesy asked.

"I never told him."

"That's not the question," I said.

Birelli half-closed his eyes, a sloppy smile spreading slowly across his lips. "Okay, Charlie. How's this? I knew Ted was still doing research into Cao Dinh for the general. And that's all I knew."

"Then it follows that Watkins probably would have told Masonis about Tho."

A shrug.

Jonesy said, "But you knew Masonis was in town?"

"I think the general might have mentioned that. Yeah."

"Did the general happen to mention where Masonis was staying?" I asked.

Birelli's brow furrowed. He still had that silly smile on his lips. "Maybe, but I can't seem to recall. Too much booze, I guess."

"Goddammit, John! This is a murder investigation. If you know where Masonis is . . ."

Jonesy looked over my head and coughed sharply.

I turned. Lisa was standing behind me, wearing an apprehensive smile.

"Colonel Jensen," she said, "the phone in your car is ringing."

★★★★

We had to leave anyway, but I had one final question. While Jonesy ran out to the car, I asked, "You ever hear General Watkins or Mr. Tho mention a corporation named Dynatech Transports?"

Birelli shook his head. His eyes were glassy. "Never heard of it myself. Why?"

I shrugged. "I'm not sure. Name just came up as something General Watkins was checking out."

"Sorry," Birelli said.

Birelli and Lisa walked me around the path toward the front of the house.

As we approached the car, Birelli put his hand on my shoulder as though we'd been friends for years. "You run into anything you need help on, Charlie, you give me a call. I mean it. Anything at all. And back off of Masonis. He's not your man. Someone is just trying to make you think he is."

I smiled politely. "I'll try." But I was thinking Birelli had spun quite a tale notably absent of any proof. Could he have really been working with Masonis, setting up Watkins and Tho? I didn't think so, but . . .

I opened the car door and climbed inside.

Jonesy started the motor. "The phone quit ringing before I could pick up," he said.

"They'll call back."

Birelli and Lisa stood on the steps, arm in arm. They waved. I waved back.

"Think he knows where Masonis is?" I asked Jonesy.

"He knows."

"Yes, I suppose he does." Buckling up, I looked at Jonesy. "What do you think about the rest of his story?"

"Everything fits."

I frowned at something in his voice. "But you're not sure?"

"No, sir. Colonel Birelli tells a good story. But he never actually gave us any proof. We have to take his word for everything, especially on what Tho was going to say and about the existence of those photographs."

Jonesy slowed to a stop at the gate. There must have been one of those electronic eyes hidden nearby, because the gate opened automatically.

Jonesy said, "Seems like either way Tho was going to go, a lot of people would have a lot of reasons to keep him quiet."

I nodded. I'd been thinking the same thing.

"If, like Colonel Birelli says, Tho could confirm that POWs were executed, then this Vietnam recognition is in trouble, right?"

I nodded again. "And if Tho really intended to go the other way, and say we killed our own prisoners, the U.S. gets nailed for a cover-up."

"So Masonis could be working either for Uncle Sam, the Vietnamese government, or some crazy rich American who paid to have POWs murdered. Or maybe Masonis had his own agenda and acted on his own." Jonesy paused, then added, "There's always the possibility Masonis isn't the killer."

"And there's Dynatech," I said.

"You think maybe they've got money riding on Vietnam opening up?"

"A thought." I sighed. "It's a crock, Jonesy."

"It's a crock, all right."

I scanned the road. The sun was setting in a bloodred sky.

"No van," Jonesy said. "Maybe it wasn't him."

"Maybe not."

But I knew Jonesy didn't believe that, and neither did I.

☆☆☆☆

The phone rang as we turned at the intersection by the convenience store. I recognized the voice of Lieutenant Linda Martels, the P-Directorate duty officer. "Gee, sir, I've been trying to contact you for the last hour."

"What's up, Linda?"

"The Army personnel people called at 1810. Said they can't provide you with the performance evaluations on Dr. Masonis, sir."

"They say why?"

"Yes, sir. They said his records have been sealed."

"Sealed?"

"Yes, sir."

"Hang on, Linda." I cupped the phone. "Jonesy, you know anything about Masonis's personnel records being sealed?"

Jonesy looked puzzled. "Can't be, sir. They sent me his personnel RIP out of the computer this morning, so they weren't sealed then."

"Did you get a name, Linda?"

"Yes, sir. Staff Sergeant Vincent."

I looked at the clock on the dash. A little after seven P.M. "Do me a favor. Find out who the commander is. I'll need his home number."

"Take a while, sir, and I've got a few more messages."

"Go."

"Your wife called. Wants you to call her at Mrs. Tippett's. You have the number, sir?"

"Yes. Who else?"

"Lieutenant Lee's called twice in the last thirty minutes. Says it's urgent. He's at home. I have a number if you're ready, sir."

I copied the number. "That it?"

"One more thing, sir. We received the faxes Sergeant Jones wanted. The ones he's hot about. Financial records on Mr. Masonis. What do you want me to do with them?"

"From the IRS?"

"Yes, sir. And one from the FBI. Looks like they're the same thing. Sergeant Jones was real hot for them."

We weren't going to be anywhere near a fax machine. "Hang on to them."

"Okay, sir. I'll get back with you with that commander's number."

I hung up. "Maybe you're just too suspicious, Jonesy."

"What's that?"

"Sounds like the FBI computer really was down earlier." Then I told him about the faxes.

Jonesy didn't say anything.

★★★★

I called Jean at Dorothy Tippett's.

"Me, honey. How's Dorothy?"

Jean spoke just above a whisper. "Okay. The girls are here. The problem is the press has been calling. A few have stopped by. They're insufferable, Charlie. One reporter asked what she was going to do if the police can't find anything to bury. Can you come over tonight? I think she'll appreciate it."

"I want to, but . . ."

"I know. Too busy."

"Jean. That's not fair. I'm trying to find the SOB that killed him."

A pause. "I'm sorry, it's just . . ."

"I'll come by tomorrow. Stacy and Tony know?"

"Yes. They're here now." She paused. "Have they recovered the body? Dorothy asked."

I got mad at myself. "I'll check."

Another pause.

"I love you," I said.

"I love you, too."

" 'Bye."

✯✯✯✯

Lieutenant Lee answered immediately. In the background, I could hear rock music.

"Gimme a sec," Lee shouted. The music disappeared. Lee again. "Hey, Charlie. I was just leaving. You get the word?"

"What word?"

"Gotta hand it to you. Your little TV spot is paying off. About half a dozen calls so far. Couple are real interesting. One's from a neighbor of Masonis's."

"A neighbor?"

"Masonis is renting a furnished apartment in Falls Church. I'm on my way to check it out. But the one that's got me curious is the call from a Nurse Jacobs in Danville, Virginia. At someplace called the Rolling Hills Sanatorium. She said Masonis was there this afternoon around five P.M. He wanted to see a patient named Hanson."

I took a deep breath. "Brady Hanson?"

"I'm not sure about the first name. Why?"

"He's an ex-POW. Escaped back in 1971 with General Holmes." Then I gave him a quick overview of what Birelli had said about Cao Dinh.

"So you think all this is tied to some POW camp? Pretty wild."

"I don't know. Possibly. Keep it to yourself until we find out more. Where is Masonis now?"

"Nurse Jacobs told Masonis he would have to get permission from Hanson's mother before he could see Hanson. Masonis left."

"Did she know where he was going?"

"Yeah. She said Masonis was pretty angry at being turned away. He said something about going to see Hanson's mother. She lives here in the city in an apartment at the Watergate. I've sent a couple men over there."

"This Nurse Jacobs was sure it was Masonis?"

"Far as I know, yeah. I didn't talk to her. One of the detectives at the precinct handled her call and called me. Masonis gave some story about wanting to interview Hanson for a book."

I heard someone shout in the background.

"Look, I've got to run," Lee said.

"Give me Masonis's address. I'll meet you."

I wrote it down. Then I told him about the van and gave him the license number to run a check.

"I'll call it in."

Another shout.

"Gotta run, Charlie."

"Just one more thing, Harry. About Colonel Tippett's remains?"

Lee's voice got quiet. "Sorry, Charlie. Nothing definite. The divers found bits and pieces. The leg was the largest thing they found. M.E. is going to have to run DNA tests."

Which could take months, I thought. "Thanks." I hung up feeling a little sick wondering what I was going to tell Dorothy.

★★★★

I read Jonesy the address. We were on Highway 28 just south of Centerville. We could pick up I-66 in three miles and take it into Falls Church. I looked behind. No van.

"That apartment seems pretty close to Major Swanson's place," Jonesy said.

I glanced down at Masonis's address. Jonesy was right. Just two streets over from Talia's condo. I flipped the notepad closed. "Chances are he'll get picked up by the highway patrol."

"What's he driving, sir?"

"Tempo. Blue."

"Lot of them on the road. Cops can't stop them all."

"You think Masonis may try to contact Talia?"

"Not really, sir. Just thought it might be a good idea to at least give Captain Webster and Major Swanson a heads-up he could be coming to the city."

"I guess." I still thought it a waste of time.

26

THE NEXT TIME THE CAR PHONE RANG, IT WAS LIEUTENANT MARTELS WITH THE NUMBER I HAD REQUESTED. THEN I DIALED LIEUTENANT Colonel Frederick Marsden of the Army Reserve Personnel Center in St. Louis.

A child answered. I had to ask for daddy twice before Colonel Marsden came to the phone.

I explained who I was and inquired about the Masonis file.

Marsden swallowed. "Damnedest thing. Sergeant Vincent notified me. He'd never seen this happen to a file before, and quite frankly, neither had I."

"I'm not sure I follow."

"Classifying an unclassified record. Let me explain. Normally, when we upload records into the computer and they're still classified, we put in a code. Occasionally, as the determination is made to declassify records, we remove the codes. We've never classified a record that has been previously declassified. Like in this case of Masonis. What's the point?"

"I see."

"I mean his records have been declassified for ten years. But Sergeant Vincent tried to call the file up on the screen, and there was an

XSC by the name. That's the code for nonaccessible for security reasons. Even I couldn't get into it."

"But I understand portions of the file, the RIP, were retrieved only this morning."

"Yeah. That's what Sergeant Vincent said. Which is why I ran a query up to Army Personnel in the Pentagon. I thought there must be a mistake. No mistake. Someone up at headquarters restricted the file this afternoon."

"How can I get it removed?"

"You're in D.C., right?"

"Yes."

"Then you'll have to talk to someone there in the Pentagon. In Army personnel. The authorization code came from Lieutenant General Reiser's office. He's the Army personnel chief."

I couldn't believe it. "Could the directive have come from a higher office? I mean from someone above General Reiser?"

Marsden chuckled. "Sure, Colonel. This is the military. You know how the chain of command works."

"Thank you." I hung up.

"Sounds like someone doesn't want us checking into Masonis," Jonesy said.

I suddenly felt angry. Dammit, who the hell did they think they were? This was a murder investigation. And I had little doubt who was behind the order to seal Masonis's file.

"The White House?" Jonesy asked, as if he could read my thoughts.

"They have the power to have the records sealed, and they sent their liaison officer to the briefing with General Holmes. If Birelli is right, they can't afford to have Cao Dinh brought to light."

We drove for a moment in silence.

"Must be something damned important in those records," Jonesy said.

"Not much we can do about it, though."

We stopped at a light. Jonesy looked over, his voice suggestive. "You know, sir, those records are on computer."

"Yeah, so?"

Then I understood.

I reached for the phone. All she could do was say no.

★★★★

She answered on the third ring.

"Maria, Charlie. I need a favor." I explained.

When I finished, Maria responded immediately. "You're crazy, Charlie."

"I know."

"I'm supposed to protect the computer system. Jesus! You know what you're asking?"

"I wouldn't ask if there was another way."

"This is about General Watkins's murder, huh?"

"I swear."

"And you really need the information?"

"The information is vital."

She sighed. "Look, we're about to have dinner. Then I'm going to help Richie with his trig homework. I'll be at least two hours."

"That's fine, Maria. And there's one more thing."

A long silence during which I could almost see her rolling her eyes. "Now what?"

"You have a fax machine there at home?"

"Of course."

"There's something I need to see. I was wondering . . ." After she gave me her fax number, I said, "You are a jewel, Maria. Thanks."

"Uh-huh. And Charlie?"

"Yes?"

"You can be a real pain in the ass sometimes."

★★★★

Linda promised to get the faxes out immediately. Jonesy pulled up to a Burger King drive-through. Waiting for the order, I called Talia and relayed the news that Masonis might be coming to town.

I hung up, tapping the phone with a finger.

"What's up, sir?" Jonesy asked. He passed over the bag with the Whoppers and fries.

"I'm not sure. . . ."

"A diet Coke?" called out the voice.

I looked over to the drive-through window.

A teenage girl with dreadlocks was staring at Jonesy. "Was that a diet Coke, mister?"

Jonesy glanced up. "Yes. And a regular."

The girl frowned at the two large drinks in her hand. "Well . . . some-one sure messed up. I got two regular Cokes here." She gave Jonesy an expectant look.

"We ordered a diet Coke, miss," Jonesy said.

The girl let out an exasperated sigh and stepped back from the window.

"Regular is fine," I murmured.

Jonesy acted as if he didn't hear. The girl returned, sullen-faced. She passed over the drinks. As Jonesy placed them in the cup holder on the center console, he looked at me. "These kids have to learn right is right, sir."

As Jonesy pulled away from the window, I gave him a little smile and opened the paper bag.

"The call to Major Swanson," Jonesy said, checking traffic. "Some-thing bothering you about that, sir?"

"Nothing I can put my finger on. Maybe she sounded a little too excited at the news. About Masonis."

Jonesy shrugged as he pulled out. "She likes the guy, sir. Mine's the one without pickles."

I fished out a Whopper, inspected it under the reading light, and handed it over.

"Yeah, she likes him, all right," I said. Why did that bother me?

★★★★

The address was an older, stucco high-rise in the north part of Falls Church near Ellison Square, just down the street from a Giant grocery store and a strip mall. Jonesy drove slowly into the parking lot. The parking spaces for the tenants lined one curb and were numbered. The space for apartment 5E was empty. We parked around the corner.

I didn't see any police, but then, I didn't expect to. They wouldn't show themselves until Masonis appeared.

We walked up the sidewalk to the front. The double-glass entrance doors didn't have one of those security locks controlled by a buzzer, so we went inside. The lobby was empty except for a security guard sitting at a desk in the corner. He motioned us over.

He looked around, then whispered, "Colonel Jensen?"

I nodded.

"Lieutenant Lee mentioned you would show, sir. You know the apartment number?"

"Yes. Thank you."

Jonesy and I stepped into the elevator.

"Cop," Jonesy murmured.

I nodded, pushing the button for the fifth floor.

27

APARTMENT 5E WAS THE THIRD ONE ON THE RIGHT FROM THE ELEVA-
TOR. I LISTENED FOR A SECOND AND HEARD MUFFLED, ANGRY VOICES.
I glanced at Jonesy. He knocked.

The door flew open. "Fuck you, Harry!" someone shouted from
inside.

A short, fat man in a wrinkled tan suit glared at us. "Who the hell are
you?" he asked.

Lee appeared behind the fat man. "They're okay." Lee's smooth
face was frozen in a dark scowl. "I cleared it with Captain Wilson, Fred.
This is Lieutenant Colonel Jensen and Sergeant Jones of the Air Force
OSI."

Fred didn't budge. "Go to hell, Harry. You didn't clear it with me. As
for you two soldier boys . . ."

"Get your fat ass out of the way, Fred!" Lee snarled. "Or I tell
Captain Wilson you been hustling freebies from the hookers over on
Fourteenth. Like Jasmine, and Bitchy Bernice."

Fred spun around. "You fucking gook son of a bitch!"

Lee suddenly stepped forward until his face was an inch from Fred's.
He spoke just above a whisper. "Say that again and I'll shove your nuts
down your throat, you bigoted piece of shit."

Fred seemed to shrink under Lee's withering gaze. Abruptly, he pushed past Lee.

Lee shook his head as he moved aside. "Come on in, Charlie, Jonesy. Sorry about the scene."

We walked tentatively into a combination living and dining room that was filled with cheap oak veneer furniture. Fred slumped heavily on the couch and folded his arms, glaring at us. Another fat man who could have been his twin sat beside him, talking into a walkie-talkie. He acknowledged us with an indifferent nod and kept talking.

I said, "Look, Harry, if there's a problem—"

"No. No problem. Everything's fine. Close the door, Jonesy."

The door clicked shut.

As I looked around, I wondered if this was the right apartment. Other than the furnishings, there was absolutely nothing visible to indicate someone lived here: no magazines, newspapers, books, plants. I looked past the island into the kitchen. The bare countertops gleamed, without so much as a coffee cup on them.

Lee must have noticed my reaction. "Yeah, not much to see, is there? Masonis didn't spend much time here. Come on to the back."

"You got five minutes," Fred grunted thickly from the couch. "You hear, five minutes."

"Shut up, Fred," Lee said without looking over.

Fred rose to his feet.

But we were already in the bedroom.

More oak and veneer furnishings here, and an obligatory still-life flower painting on a wall. But at least there were signs of life. An unmade double bed, and a blue terry-cloth robe slung over the back of a chair.

Lee shut the door with more force than necessary.

"What's his problem?" I asked.

"Fred Lufkin is a prick, Charlie. No one in the Falls Church PD can stand the guy. He's particularly bad this time of year."

"Time of year?"

"After the results of the sergeant's exam are announced." Lee grinned. "Fred just busted for the seventh year in a row. Stupid shit, he's never going to pass. Anyway, he's pissed because I showed up. Fred hates sharing in a collar, especially a big one like Masonis."

"One of those," I said. I knew the type. The military, like any large organization, had its complement of men obsessed with looking good.

"Probably be a good idea not to hang around too long," Lee said.

"We won't. You find anything?"

Lee shook his head. "Nothing."

Jonesy went to the closet, flipped the light switch on the wall, and disappeared inside. I followed.

"I talked to Mrs. Anuncio, the neighbor who called," Lee said. "Lives next door. She said Masonis showed up about two months ago. Usually she'd see him maybe three, four days at a time, then he'd disappear. Says he's real nice, friendly. She says there's no way he could be a killer."

"Another Masonis fan," I grunted over my shoulder. "A lot of them around."

"What was that, Charlie?"

"Nothing."

I was looking past Jonesy at the items in the closet. Three pairs of slacks were neatly hung on hangers along with a couple of silk shirts and a very expensive pin-striped suit. I looked down. Sneakers and a pair of black wing tips. I stepped back out.

"You already check everything out?" I asked Lee.

Lee nodded.

I went into the bathroom. In the vanity mirror above the sink, I found a bottle of cologne and a packet of disposable razors. I ran a finger inside the tub. Clean. No hair in the drain. Even the rim of the commode looked scrubbed. I walked out.

Jonesy was inspecting the terry-cloth robe. Lee leaned against the door, arms folded, watching.

"Harry, did Masonis have maid service?" I asked.

"Monday, Wednesday, and Friday, according to Mrs. Anuncio."

"That explains it," I said.

"I know what you're thinking. Place is still too clean."

I nodded. "You find any papers, notebooks? A laptop computer, maybe?"

"Nope. Masonis probably took any of that stuff with him."

"Guy was a writer. Should be some stuff around."

"You think maybe someone came in, cleaned this place out?" Lee asked.

I shrugged. "I didn't find a toothbrush. Looks like Masonis must have been planning on staying the night somewhere."

Jonesy held up the terry-cloth robe. "Sir, Masonis looked like a pretty big guy in those pictures, right?"

"He's six-three," Lee said.

Jonesy removed his jacket. Lee and I watched as he donned the robe. He dropped his hands to his side.

"I'll be damned," Lee said.

The robe looked comical on Jonesy's six-foot frame. The sleeves ended at midforearm and the bottom fringe hung just below his groin.

"A woman's," I said.

There was a banging on the door. Lee rolled his eyes and stepped aside. The door opened and Fred poked his head in. He looked at Jonesy and shook his head.

"Get that shit off!" he grunted. "You look like a goddamn fairy!"

Jonesy's face tightened, but he began removing the robe.

"What's the matter, Fred?" Lee asked. "He looking good to you? Or maybe you want to put it on yourself."

Fred turned red, speechless for a moment, his heavy jowls shaking. "You fucking queer. Get the hell out of here! You . . . you . . . you . . . fuck!"

"How's your health, Fred?" Lee asked calmly.

"Go to hell!"

"You don't look so good, Fred."

"What the . . ."

"You hear about Bernice?"

Fred swallowed, anger giving way to confusion. He ran a tongue over his thick lips. "What about Bernice?" he asked suspiciously.

"Word's out on the street."

"What word?"

"Bernice has AIDS."

"You're lying."

"Hey, I'm just passing on what I heard."

Fred's mouth worked, but no sound came out. When he finally spoke, his voice was hoarse and barely above a whisper. "You're lying, you son of a bitch."

Lee shrugged. "If I were you, I'd get myself checked."

Fred looked pale. "You better not be shitting me."

Lee turned to me. "You ready?"

I nodded.

As the three of us walked out, Fred was furiously punching numbers into a cellular phone.

★★★★

The elevator doors opened and we stepped inside. I punched the button for the lobby.

"Lieutenant, this Bernice really have AIDS?" Jonesy asked.

"Oh, I don't know," Lee said, and smiled. "Rumors are always so unreliable."

28

WE LEFT THE APARTMENT BUILDING BY A SIDE DOOR THAT BROUGHT US OUT AROUND THE CORNER NEAR WHERE JONESY AND I HAD parked. Lee walked us to our car.

"What's the plan if Masonis shows?" I asked.

"Lufkin's got three teams. Two out front, one out back. First option if there are no civilians around is to take him when he gets out of his car. Backup is the apartment."

I nodded. "You going to stay?"

"Yeah. I'm not gonna let Freddie boy screw this up. Hey, I almost forgot." He reached into his jacket pocket. "Ran that plate." He flipped on a penlight and consulted a notepad. "Nineteen ninety-two Plymouth Voyager. Brown, two-tone. Registered to Potomac Properties, Inc." He looked up, smiling.

"Who is Potomac Properties?" I asked.

The penlight went out. "You mean you don't know?"

"Should I?"

Lee chuckled. "You're not gonna like it."

"Colonel," Jonesy grunted suddenly.

I looked over. Jonesy was stepping off the sidewalk and appeared to be looking at something across the street.

I frowned, watching the mall traffic cruise past.

Then I noticed the brown van, clearly visible from the headlights of a passing car. I watched as it pulled in next to a Dumpster.

Figures emerged from the van. They hesitated and then darted across the street. For an instant, they were caught in the glow of headlights.

I swore. Now I knew what Lee was trying to tell me.

"Oh shit, they're going into the building," Lee said. "Dammit, they could blow the whole stakeout." He took off running.

Jonesy and I walked toward the front of the building.

Lee caught them in the parking lot, maybe twenty feet from the door. I heard angry voices, and I expected more cops to swarm in, but they elected to allow Lee to handle it.

Jonesy and I kept walking. The group moved toward the light by the entrance. One figure turned, clearly visible now.

The face lit up in recognition as Jonesy and I approached.

"Hey, Colonel, how about telling this dumb cop about the First Amendment," Annie called.

Lee grabbed her by the arm. "Annie, get the hell out of here!"

"Now that's police harassment," Annie said, jerking her arm away. "And I got witnesses!"

Two cars pulled in. A man walking his dog looked over. "Take it inside," I growled. "Now!"

I followed as Lee ushered everyone inside.

★★★★

The cop posing as the security guard unlocked the closet-size guard's room at the far end of a hallway. An odor of urine and something else wafted out. Inside were four metal lockers, a wooden bench, a commode, and a sink. Light came from a single bare bulb dangling from the ceiling.

There were three of them: Annie, Frankie, and some skinny kid in his early twenties with dark hair and a nervous tic of a smile. Annie looked splendid in a pale yellow suit that matched her hair. As usual, Frankie carried his TV camera, but he made no move to use it. I suspected he thought Lee would have killed him if he had.

We were packed so tight inside the little room, everyone had to stand. Lee continued to glare at Annie. "You got it from Sergeant Sanders, didn't you?" he said to her as soon as I closed the door. "That big-mouthed son of a bitch tipped you off!"

Annie smiled sweetly. "Now, you know a good reporter never reveals her sources, Lieutenant."

"Did you know the police had the building under surveillance, then?" I asked.

"Sure."

I shook my head. "So what were you going to do? Go up to Masonis's apartment? Never mind that your presence could jeopardize the apprehension of a killer."

Annie gave me a look of disgust. "What? Are all you cop types sexist? The dumb broad reporter, right, Colonel? You really think I'm that stupid? That immoral? You make me sick."

"What were you going to do?"

Annie looked me in the eye. "Go to hell."

"I can have you hauled in for interfering with an investigation," Lee said.

"Do that, and I'll have you and your department served with a lawsuit so fast your head will spin. The press has rights too, you know. Or haven't you read the Constitution? Oh, I forgot. Our Founding Fathers used words with more than four letters."

"Aw, save it," Lee snapped.

"Annie . . . baby . . ." Frankie said soothingly, one hand fidgeting with his ponytail. "Remember what Jim said. No trouble on this one. Be cool. Just tell them what they want to know."

Annie gave Frankie a dirty look.

Frankie turned to me. "We were just going to slip in. Stay out of the way. No trouble for anybody. No one would know. Stay cool. That's what our producer told us to do, okay?"

"Jim has no balls," Annie said.

"Maybe you should listen to Frankie, Annie," I said.

Annie glared at me. She gave a resigned shrug. "Yeah? Well, okay." Her face relaxed. "Frankie's right," she said. "We were going to play this real low-key. One of the grips at the studio has an apartment in the building with a view out the front. Figured we'd hang out. If Masonis showed and was taken into custody, we'd be ready." She gave Lee a look of pure malevolence as she pointed at him. "No one would have even noticed us. Then Rambo here has to barge in." I thought she might jab Lee's chest with her finger, but she stopped short of that.

"You still should have cleared it with us, Annie," Lee insisted, but he was no longer angry.

"Yeah? Like you're gonna go along, huh? And that Neanderthal Lufkin. You must really think I'm an idiot, Lieutenant."

I was watching the kid. I noticed his eyes kept darting to Jonesy and me. The nervous tic in his upper lip was getting worse.

"Son," I said sharply.

His eyes got wide.

I gave him a long look. "What do you think, Jonesy?"

"Could be him, sir."

The kid's eyes went to Annie. He looked frightened.

I expected Annie to deny everything. Then I'd confront her with the license number.

But instead Annie said, "I had Jerry follow you from the Pentagon."

"No kidding," I said dryly.

"He said you spotted him."

"Yeah."

"And he almost lost you."

"I know." I looked at Jerry. "How did you find us again?"

Jerry swallowed. He looked at Annie. She nodded.

Jerry sounded relieved. "I thought you might come after me, you know. I got scared and pulled off on a dirt road. Then I drove around, thinking maybe I'd get lucky. I pulled up to the intersection, you know, the one at the store. I saw the car pulling out."

"No way," Jonesy said. "I was looking. You weren't anywhere around."

Jerry looked confused. "Oh, not your car. The other one."

Jonesy frowned. "What other one?"

"The gray one."

"Gray?" I asked.

Then I remembered.

★★★★

Jerry finished explaining about the gray car. I shook my head, angry at myself and Jonesy for not noticing. Jerry's sloppy attempt to follow us had been the perfect cover, causing us to focus solely on the van. Not to mention that the van had also shielded the car from our view much of the time.

"He stayed behind you the whole way?" I asked.

"Yeah, as far as I could tell," Jerry replied. "Every now and then he'd pop out, like to make sure you guys were still there. That's when I began thinking maybe he was keeping an eye on you, too. Made me kinda nervous."

"You definitely saw him when we left the Pentagon?" Jonesy asked.

"Oh, yeah. Followed us right out. The windows were real dark. That's why I know this was the same car. You don't see many of those, except maybe limos."

"Plate number?" Lee said.

Jerry shook his head. "I got it, but . . ." He looked at Annie.

"Won't do you any good," Annie said. "I had a friend run it."

"Sanders, I'll bet," Lee said.

Annie gave Lee a frosty look, then continued, "Plates are registered to a car belonging to a John Olson. Father John Olson. He seemed quite surprised to find out his plates were no longer on his car."

"Swapped or stolen?" Lee asked.

Annie said, "Swapped. I've got the numbers of the plates on Father Olson's car if you want. He has since reported the theft."

Lee nodded. "I'll check it out. Ten bucks says they're hot too."

"How long did you wait after you saw us drive into the gate?" I asked Jerry.

"I left pretty quick," he said. "On account of the car came back."

"The gray one?"

Jerry nodded. "Thought he might be coming for me. You know. Find out what I was doing. I took off."

"And this is a Mustang?" Lee asked.

I answered. "One of those five-point-oh muscle cars."

Lee wrote it down. "Not much to go on."

Annie had been leaning back against one of the lockers, watching Jonesy and me with interest. She pushed upright. "So you guys really have no idea who was in the car, huh?"

"No," I said.

"Not even a suspicion?"

"No."

"Couldn't be Masonis, not if he was seen in Danville, Virginia, at five this afternoon. That's a good three-and-a-half-hour drive."

"No."

"Could be an accomplice," Lee said.

"What's Colonel John Birelli got to do with this thing?" Annie asked.

"Nothing," I said. "We were just running down leads."

"You're lying, Colonel," she said coolly. "But that's okay. I'll find out eventually."

"Yes, Annie, I expect you will," I said.

"You know you owe me, Colonel."

I nodded to Jerry. "The information is duly appreciated, but you should not have had him follow me. Don't do it again."

A tiny smile appeared on Annie's face. "Not that, Colonel."

I needed a second to understand this was a not-so-subtle reminder about her not mentioning publicly that I'd almost been relieved. I said nothing.

Annie turned to Lee. "I've cooperated. Now it's your turn, Lieutenant. We're going upstairs."

"Masonis shows, you don't move until you get the word from me," Lee said.

Annie hesitated, then nodded.

"You like jelly donuts?" Lee said, reaching for the door.

"Why?" Annie asked.

"I like them," Frankie said.

Lee grinned at Annie. "I'm staying with you. Come on. I'll take you up. We can talk, get to know each other."

"Oh, brother," Annie said.

Lee winked at me and escorted Annie out.

★★★★

As Jonesy and I walked down the sidewalk to our car, I told him about Holmes wanting to remove me from the case. Jonesy listened without comment. At the car, he turned to me, his face barely discernible in the dark.

"I should have spotted the guy in the Mustang, sir."

"He was a pro, Jonesy."

"CIA?"

"I'm not sure. The type of car bothers me. I don't see a spook driving a muscle car. Stealing plates."

"A contract freelancer?"

"That's possible," I said. In sensitive situations where plausible deniability was essential, the CIA had been known to use individuals with no direct links to the Agency.

"First it was Masonis's personnel file being classified, then General Holmes tries to have you removed. Now the car . . ." Jonesy looked away.

"Like Birelli said, this is big, Jonesy. And it's going to get worse the more we dig. Look, if you want to pull out, it's okay. But I can't."

"Because of Colonel Tippett, sir?"

I nodded. "I owe him that much."

A car roared around the corner of the building, squealing into a parking spot a few spaces away. A man staggered out. He walked unsteadily toward the front.

We watched.

The man stumbled, stepped onto the curb, and swore loudly. He finally disappeared around the corner.

"Colonel, you think we'll find out the truth?" Jonesy was looking at me again.

"I'm not sure."

He took a deep breath. "I don't believe we will."

I didn't reply.

"You can't fight city hall," Jonesy said.

"No, probably not."

"We'll only find what they want us to find."

"Probably so."

"Really pisses me off, sir. They know we're nobody. They know they can do as they please."

"The arrogance of power, Jonesy."

"And there's not a damn thing we can do."

"We can try," I said softly.

"Yes, sir. I guess we can at that." He started toward the car, then stopped. "Oh, I'm in, sir. All the way."

"I know."

"Right is right," Jonesy said.

★★★★

I decided I'd better warn Birelli about Annie. I knew she would call and try to worm an interview out of him. Not that someone had to try very hard to get Birelli to show his face on camera.

I recognized the Asian man's voice.

"Lieutenant Colonel Jensen for Colonel Birelli," I said.

"He no here, sir."

"Please tell him to call me at—"

"No here. He go away."

I tried speaking more slowly. "Yes. I understand. When he comes back—"

"Long time. Go. You understand? Long time."

I frowned. "How long?"

"He say maybe one year."

One year? Christ. "And Mrs. Birelli?"

"Go."

"Where?"

"No say."

"I see. Thank you." I hung up slowly. Call for help anytime, Birelli had said. And I believed him. I shook my head. The gray car. Had to be. But Birelli wouldn't scare easily. He'd proved that in the past. So what changed his mind?

Then I knew.

Back then Birelli didn't have a beautiful young wife, a wonderful home, money. Back then Birelli didn't have something to lose.

"They got to him, Jonesy," I said.

29

MARIA WAS WAITING FOR US WHEN WE WALKED INTO THE DOOR OF THE COMPUTER SECURITY CENTER. SHE SMILED AT JONESY BUT GLARED at me. She led us to her office. She picked a folder off her desk and gave it to me without a word.

Jonesy smiled, amused at my chilly reception.

I opened the folder and confirmed it contained the faxes from the IRS and the FBI concerning Masonis's finances.

Maria went to her safe and began twirling the dial. "Lock the door."

Jonesy did.

I handed Jonesy the folder. "Anything we can do?" I asked Maria.

Maria didn't reply. She reached into the safe, fumbled around, and removed a binder holding pages of computer paper. She went to her desk and flipped the binder open. She ran a finger down a page. "Okay," she murmured. She lowered herself into her chair, spun around, and pulled the cover off the computer behind her desk. Jonesy and I sat across from her. Jonesy leaned back, opened the folder, and began reading.

"I really appreciate this," I said lamely.

Maria had the computer on. She hunched over the screen, her hands flying over the keyboard. "Just promise me one thing. You'll testify that you ordered me, okay?"

"What?"

She looked up with a wry smile. "At my court-martial."

"You can't get into the system without being caught?"

Maria looked back at the screen. "The Army Personnel Computer, right?"

"Yes."

She glanced down at the binder, then turned back to the computer. "I don't know yet." She clicked away. "Depends if they have a trapdoor open."

"Trapdoor?"

Maria went into a routine of typing a few lines, studying the display, then typing some more. "Yeah. Used to be real common in most large programs. Trapdoors act kind of like a maintenance hatch on an airplane. So programmers can get into it to modify the software, fix problems, without having to go through the hassle of getting the latest passwords for the various files. That's what's in the book here, instructions for various trapdoors. But supposedly the doors are all closed now. Ironic."

"What's ironic?"

"I'm the one who instructed all DOD agencies to close all the trapdoors. For security. But we've been finding some still open. Maybe we'll get lucky."

She punched in an entry and sat back, folding her arms. "Damn! Closed!"

I started to rise. "Thanks anyway—"

"Sit down, Charlie." She sounded tired.

I sat.

Maria looked at the screen, saying nothing.

"You can still get in?" I asked.

"Oh, yeah. Getting in is not the problem. Getting in without being detected is." She turned her chair around to the front. "I have two choices. I can get into the security system, disarm it, retrieve the information, and download it without anyone finding out. Only problem is, while the security system is down, any Tom, Dick, or Harry can also gain access." She gave me an expectant look.

I didn't know what to say.

"Or I can use my password, but there will be a trail. Someone would be able to tell I accessed the system."

"I will take responsibility, Maria," I said.

She gave me a thin smile. "You can't, Charlie. You don't have the authority." She took a deep breath. "Masonis better be the killer," she said, and began typing.

I knew she'd used her own password.

★★★★

Twenty minutes later, the printer in Maria's office went quiet. I retrieved the stack and handed half to Jonesy.

A minute later, Maria shut down the computer. She opened a desk drawer. "That what you want?"

"Yes. How did you bypass the security seal on it?"

She tossed me an empty brown portfolio, the kind with string around it. I caught it. "My password allows me access into any file, Charlie."

My eyebrows went up. "Even Black World programs?" Black World was the military code name for the most sensitive military technology under development.

"Sure. I'm responsible for computer security systemwide." She gave a tired smile. "Only, I usually use my power for good, not evil."

Jonesy chuckled.

Maria returned the binder to the safe and locked up.

I was flipping through the file.

"Go ahead and hang around," Maria said. "I'm going home."

"Thanks," I said.

"Sure. Hope it helps. And Charlie . . ."

"Yes?"

"Next time you think about calling me for help, don't. 'Night, Jonesy. You, I like."

She left.

★★★★

"Fifty-eight pages, sir," Jonesy said almost thirty minutes later.

"I've got about the same," I said. I read over the last few pages.

We switched stacks.

Masonis's personnel file was pretty standard: a chronological compilation of annual performance evaluations, records from the various military schools . . . Ranger, Airborne, Language . . . promotion recommendations, copies of orders, assignments, awards. He'd enlisted in 1968. He'd been sent to Vietnam in 1969, and again in 1971. Upon his return from his second tour, the Army sent him to the University of Tennessee to earn a degree. He received a commission upon graduation in 1974. Reading between the lines, he had indeed been involved in clandestine activities while in Vietnam, most likely the Phoenix program. He had left the Army in 1985 as a major. His performance up to that point had been exemplary and he consistently was rated exceptional. There was little doubt in my mind that Masonis had been well on his way to making full colonel, possibly even general. He'd been doing all the right things, been sent to all the right schools.

There was certainly nothing I saw that would indicate anything even approaching questionable or violent behavior.

A few pages from the end, I looked up. Jonesy had finished with his stack. He was again reading the folder with the faxes. I yawned but kept reading. A minute later, I finished.

"You see anything?" I asked.

Jonesy shook his head without looking up.

"Me neither. I don't get it. Why would anybody seal this file? There's nothing here. Guy appears to have been an exceptional officer."

"Unless we missed something, sir."

"Don't see how. Anything in Masonis's finances?"

"Not yet, no."

I stepped around Maria's desk and called Talia to tell her we were on the way. I glanced at Jonesy. "Ready to go?"

Jonesy didn't answer. He was staring at two fax pages on the desk that he'd placed side by side.

I shrugged, began gathering Masonis's personnel records into the portfolio, when Jonesy suddenly sat back. He looked worried. "We have a discrepancy, sir."

★★★★

Jonesy used a pencil to point to the entries on Masonis's financial records. He explained, "Up until 1991, both copies match. All Masonis's income comes from the university, books, and what I guess are honorariums for speeches. But look here, under 1991, in the fax from the FBI." He jabbed at a line on the left printout.

I read, "Duc Tho Trading Company, LTD. Fifty thousand dollars. Damn."

Jonesy's pencil went down chronologically, pausing at each identical fifty-thousand-dollar entry. There were five. A quarter of a million dollars.

"So Masonis was working for the Vietnamese?" I said.

"Look here, sir." The pencil went to the right printout, the one from the IRS. The point hovered over 1991, then eased down where a fifty-thousand-dollar entry should be. Except there was a problem.

"What the hell?" I asked.

"No entry." Jonesy's pencil ran down the paper. "No fifty-thousand-dollar entries at all on this sheet from the IRS."

I was confused, and scanned both printouts again.

"Someone altered his records," Jonesy said. "Notice the transmission times, sir. On the faxes." Jonesy held up the original cover sheets. "The FBI's fax is almost two hours after the one from IRS." He gave a thin smile. "And we know the IRS printout to be the source document."

"You were right all along," I said. "There wasn't a problem with the FBI computer. The FBI was stalling us to alter Masonis's records.

But why?" I stopped. "A motive. They altered the documents to give Masonis a motive."

"That would be my guess. The FBI is . . . encouraging suspicion of Masonis. The question is why?"

"Those bastards tampered with evidence."

Jonesy shrugged. "It's not like it's a surprise."

I frowned.

"Like I said, you can't fight city hall." He sounded sad.

As we gathered the portfolio and papers, I was thinking Jonesy was right, and I was scared.

✮✮✮✮

Jonesy drove. I stared absently at the street ahead, looking at nothing in particular. When we stopped for a light, Jonesy said, "I'm starting to think maybe Masonis isn't our guy, sir."

"Maybe not, but he's still our only suspect. And until we can rule him out . . ." I pointed. "The light's green."

"Could be hard to do, sir," Jonesy said, pulling away. "Considering all the help we're getting from the FBI. And don't forget, their lab boys are handling the forensics work." He sounded bitter.

"Yeah, I know." Jonesy had a point. Based on the altered fax, one couldn't have much faith now in what the FBI forensics report would reveal. I swore softly.

Jonesy stayed quiet for the next few minutes. But he kept looking over at me, which meant he was practically distraught.

"What's on your mind, Jonesy?"

"We've always been straight with each other, right, sir?"

"Always."

He paused. "I know you were close to Colonel Tippett."

"Relax, Jonesy. I'm not on a mission of vengeance. Okay? We clear Masonis, we clear him. I'm after the truth."

Jonesy appeared visibly relieved. "That's fine, sir."

I wasn't bothered. Jonesy had a right to know if I could set my emotions aside and be objective.

on the map light, I opened my notepad and made the following entries:

> *Assumption: General Watkins and Tho killed _____ Cao Dinh atrocity quiet.*
>
> *Who was behind killing of Watkins and Tho? 1) American government. 2) Vietnamese government. 3) Third party (business interests possibly). 4) Combination of above. 5) Masonis (possibly working for one of above).*
>
> *Who is pressuring FBI to fabricate evidence against Masonis? 1) White House. 2) Someone high-up acting on own or with any of above.*
>
> *Why pick Masonis to frame? 1) Masonis is guilty and evidence fabricated to expedite investigation before details on Cao Dinh revealed. 2) Masonis is innocent but convenient patsy to protect government involvement in killings.*

I closed the notepad. I still believed Masonis was the most logical choice as the killer. But the FBI's actions bothered me, and seemed to suggest the government was involved in the killings. The key was Cao Dinh. If I could find out what really happened there, everything else would fall into place.

Clicking off the light, I found myself thinking about the twenty-three names on the list. I wondered if they had been married, if they had children. I wondered if they were still mourned. When you thought of them as just names on a list, the men themselves and their families were easy to forget. But when you realized they were men . . .

We were approaching the dark expanse of Arlington National Cemetery.

How appropriate, I thought.

★★★★

We had just turned onto Broad Street in Falls Church when the car phone rang.

Captain Johnny Webster sounded as if he was out of breath. "He called, sir. I couldn't believe it. He actually called."

I knew he had to be talking about Masonis. "When?"

"Maybe two minutes ago."

"Did you get a trace?"

"He was using a cellular."

"Damn!"

"No, you see, we know where he is."

"How?"

"He told Talia, sir."

"He what?"

"A meeting, sir," Webster said. "He wants a meeting with her."

I gripped the phone hard. "When? Where?"

"ASAP, I guess. At some rest area off of I-95."

"Stay where you are. Jonesy and I will be there in five minutes." I hung up the phone and briefed Jonesy.

"I can't believe it," Jonesy said as the car picked up speed.

30

I WAS SURPRISED WHEN I WALKED INTO TALIA'S THREE-STORY BRICK TOWN HOUSE. I KNEW WHAT AN AIR FORCE MAJOR EARNED, AND I FELT AS THOUGH I'd walked onto the set of the latest James Bond movie.

Webster led the way, talking continuously, as if giving a tour. "We're set up back here, sir. Talia's upstairs, getting ready. I never thought he'd call in a million years, did you, sir? Check out this place. Nice, eh? Talia has great taste. Kitchen's over there. Dining room on the right. Some table. And the paintings. Talia says they're big bucks. She mentioned the artists. Nobody I'd heard of."

I wasn't really listening to Webster, but I was taking in the decor. Modern, you'd call it. All dramatic angles and contrast. Snow-white walls and carpet. An enormous chrome-and-glass dining table. A painting of a black triangle with a white ball in the center hung opposite a painting of a white triangle with a black ball in the middle.

The living room had subdued lighting, crystal figurines on glistening black pedestals, a wall unit the Jetsons would have been proud of purring out soft music. Jurgens and Peters, two of my technicians, rose from a black leather-and-chrome sofa that seemed to be suspended in midair. Above their heads, a series of three paintings depicted increasingly larger three-dimensional triangles balancing on what looked like a cracked egg.

I suppose that meant something profound. Jurgens and Peters nodded a greeting.

Webster kept talking, then suddenly went mute. My eyebrows went up. I realized everyone was looking behind me.

I turned.

Talia stood by the stairwell, dressed all in black, a large black handbag dangling over a shoulder. Her Air Force uniform certainly hadn't done her justice. A pullover shirt clung to her every curve, running seamlessly down from her full breasts into tight-fitting jeans. Her blond hair was combed straight back, highlighting the beautiful lines of her face. The effect proved devastating. Webster couldn't take his eyes off her, and neither could I.

She gave me a hint of a smile and glided into the room. I nodded a greeting. To Webster, I said, "You were saying about the call . . ."

"Uh, yes, sir." Webster looked at me reluctantly. "Mr. Masonis seemed very upset at General Watkins's death, sir. Almost like—"

Talia interrupted. "Colonel, I should be leaving."

"In a minute." I asked Webster, "You have the conversation on tape, right?"

"Yes, sir."

Talia looked irritated. She abruptly walked over to the sofa and sat, curling her long legs underneath, fingers drumming on the armrest.

"Go ahead and play the tape," I said.

Jurgens went to the glass coffee table where a metal case filled with electronic equipment lay open. A wire lead ran from the case to a telephone, which was also linked to a portable tape player. Jurgens punched the Play button.

A hiss.

Talia's voice, tentative: "Hello, Major Swanson."

"Talia? Ted."

A pause.

"Talia?" Masonis said again.

"Hi, Ted."

"Look, I'm not sure if I should be calling, but I just heard on the radio about General Watkins. I didn't know who else to call. I can't believe it, they're saying I'm a suspect. Jesus."

"You just heard?" Talia asked, surprised.

"You sound like you think I did it."

"No, but his death has been all over the news, Ted."

"I've been out of town most of the day. I was at the Rolling Hills Sanitarium. Haven't seen a TV since yesterday. Have you been talking to the cops? Stupid question. Christ, sure you have."

"Calm down, Ted."

"Yeah? How can I calm down." A harsh laugh. "Damn tough when you know you're being set up. Your boss told me this could be dangerous. Unbelievable."

"What? What's so dangerous, Ted?"

"Ah, it's kind of complicated. I'm going to have to turn myself in, I guess. But I need to get a lawyer first. Maybe talk to the press. Get my story out. Yeah, that's my only chance."

"Ted, can you come here, to my place?" Talia asked. "Maybe I can help you."

A long pause. "I'm not sure I should get you involved."

"Come on by, Ted. I'll help you."

"Yeah. Okay. If I make it. Cops must have a description of my car by now."

"I can meet you somewhere, then," Talia said.

"No. Aw, maybe you'd better. If I stay on the road, I'm sure to get spotted."

"Where, Ted? Where do you want to meet?"

"Hell, I don't know."

"Where are you now?"

"Just south of Quantico. There's a rest area about five, ten miles north of here."

"I know it."

"Good. Hey, I really appreciate this."

"I'll be there, Ted."

"Yeah, I know I can count on you."

The line went dead.

Jurgens hit the rewind.

I'd been watching Talia. Her lip had begun to quiver as soon as Masonis's voice had come on. Then came the rapid eye blinking, the hand wringing. After Masonis's last comment, she took a deep breath and gave a little shake of her head. I glanced at Jonesy. He was watching her too.

Obviously, Talia was very upset. Still, something about her reaction bothered me.

"Colonel Jensen."

Webster had a phone in his hand. "Sir, you want me to contact the state police?"

I hesitated. "No, we can handle it."

Webster looked at me as if I were crazy. So did Jurgens and Peters. I knew what they were thinking. We had no jurisdiction to apprehend Masonis. Procedures required I notify the local police.

"We don't want to spook him," I said. Even to me, the excuse sounded a little ridiculous.

Jonesy's head dipped in a sign of approval. Talia looked relieved.

I explained the plan.

Afterward, Talia rose, dug into her handbag, and offered me her car keys.

"He'll be expecting you to drive," I said.

31

I RODE WITH TALIA IN HER RED LEXUS, WHICH STILL SMELLED NEW. WEBSTER AND JONESY WERE FOLLOWING IN JONESY'S SEDAN, JURGENS AND Peters in a van.

As we turned off the beltway onto I-95 southbound, traffic slowed, then stopped. Up ahead, I could see flashing lights.

"Looks like an accident," I said.

Talia nodded absently, not bothering to look at me.

I leaned back and began tapping a finger against my watch. Of all the luck . . .

Ten minutes later, we slowly began moving toward the lights. "Finally," I murmured. We came up on the accident scene. Two cars with crumpled quarter-panels sat in the middle two lanes in a haphazard V, bracketed by two state patrol cruisers. One cop set out flares in a perimeter while another waved traffic past. A third cop was talking to two men in business suits, obviously the drivers.

I frowned, thinking it curious.

Both drivers appeared to be Asians.

"Doesn't seem too serious," I said as we drove by.

Talia kept her eyes straight ahead and said nothing. The Lexus picked up speed as the traffic fanned out. I watched her for a few minutes. I couldn't see her face well, but her body language—the sagging shoulders, the death grip on the steering wheel, the constant swallowing—turned my earlier suspicion into a certainty.

Major Laura Parker had been wrong. Talia could care for somebody.

Maybe I should be angry, but I wasn't. It was hard to be angry at someone that beautiful.

I said softly, "You and Masonis were more than just casual friends, weren't you?"

Talia's head snapped around. "What do you mean?"

"You don't hide your feelings well. Besides, a man in trouble doesn't call someone he's only dated once. Unless maybe you are a lawyer."

She said nothing.

"Then, of course, there's Masonis's choice of renting an apartment two blocks from your condo. And the robe we found. Blue terry cloth. A woman's robe."

She visibly started. "I don't know what you're talking about."

"No?" I leaned back, watching, waiting. She wouldn't look at me. But I could see the cracks in her armor slowly appear. A tongue ran over her lips. She swallowed more often. Then an occasional furtive sideways glance. She wanted me to say something.

But I just kept looking at her.

"Damn you." She turned to me. "Damn you, Colonel."

"It was your robe, then?"

A nod.

"How long have you been seeing him? The truth this time."

"Two . . . two months."

"Why the charade? It's got to be more than you were afraid General Watkins wouldn't approve."

Talia shook her head. "It was the general."

"Come, now. Why should—"

"I'm married, okay? Is that what you wanted to hear, Colonel?"

"I see," I said softly. The response surprised me. She wore no ring.

"It's not what you think. My husband is stationed in Hawaii. Things haven't been going well for years. We've been stationed apart more than we've been together. You know how it is with the military. We're talking divorce, but—" She must have realized she sounded as if she was making excuses, because she abruptly clamped her mouth shut, eyes returning to the road.

When Talia spoke a minute later, her voice sounded almost affectionate. "You had to know General Watkins. He was so proper. To him, marriage was sacred . . . a duty. He really loved Barbara . . . his wife." She paused, a tiny smile coming to her lips. "You know, they knew each other less than a month before they got married. It's true. Almost like a movie. The general met Barbara at the hospital when he was recuperating after his release; she was his nurse. General Watkins said it was the craziest thing he ever did. But I guess it wasn't so crazy. They had one of the few truly happy marriages I've seen. Close to twenty-five years."

Her sincerity sounded genuine. I guess I wanted to believe that her coworkers' portrayals of her were just the result of petty jealousies. Anyway, I felt better. "Twenty-five years is a long time," I said.

She nodded. "I think the general thought every marriage should be like that. And when Barbara died, well, he never got over it." She gave a little shrug. "He knew Brent and I were having problems. He would counsel me, urge me to keep trying, even offered to have Brent assigned to D.C. so we could be together, work things out. I think he believed that we would get back together." She shook her head. "No, Colonel, he would have been horrified, and I think hurt, to find me having an affair." She turned. Oncoming headlights illuminated her face. She looked sad. "I couldn't disappoint him."

We drove in silence for another minute.

Then Talia said, "And I couldn't have handled the office gossip." She paused. "You spoke with Colonel Jowers? The others?"

I nodded.

"They must have had some very interesting things to say about me, I'll bet." She sounded bitter. "They bring up this car?"

I nodded again.

"They would." She pounded a hand on the wheel. "Look, I never wanted this damn thing. I . . . was as surprised as anyone when the general had it delivered. I tried to turn it down. But he insisted. I mean really insisted. Said it was too late, he'd bought it. Besides, it made him happy. He was . . . he said I was like his family. . . ." She choked out the last word.

"I understand you made lieutenant colonel on the last promotion board. Congratulations."

A faint smile. "Thanks."

The road hummed.

I became aware of her perfume. Subtle. Something stirred in me. I stared at her in the darkness. I felt a desire to reach out and touch her. Then I remembered what Major Laura Parker had said. Talia affects men . . . uses men . . . I looked out the window until the feeling disappeared.

I said, "I need the truth now."

"Of course."

I looked at her. "You lied to me twice."

"Yes—"

"In a murder investigation."

"I know—"

"You could be in a lot of trouble."

"I tried to tell you earlier."

"On the phone?"

She nodded.

"Do you love him?"

"I don't know."

"But you care for him?"

"Yes. Very much."

Sincere, I thought again. "Feeling the way you do about Masonis, why did you call me last night and tell me about his message on your machine?"

"I . . . I almost didn't. I was so confused. I didn't think Ted could be the killer, yet . . . I also knew I didn't really know him that well. He didn't talk about himself much. And you said you had a witness." She shrugged. "I hated myself afterwards. Calling you."

"But even then, you didn't feel the need to tell me you two were . . . close?"

She gave a harsh laugh. "You mean lovers, don't you, Colonel? I was . . . I don't know . . . scared, I suppose. I knew what your conclusion would be, knowing we were intimate."

I didn't say anything. She wasn't looking for a response.

Talia said, "You'd have to at least consider that I was involved in General Watkins's death, wouldn't you? After all, I'm his aide, and my lover is your prime suspect."

"Yes," I admitted. "But you still should have told me."

"Why?" she asked sharply. "So you could confirm your own suspicions that Ted must be the killer? Maybe fantasized that he and I had some kind of conspiracy going? Absurd. While the real killer—"

She was getting herself worked up, looking at me more than the road. "Calm down, Talia," I said.

"Sure. Calm down—"

The car surged as she punched the gas pedal. I looked outside, saw we were coming up fast on the car ahead. "Talia—"

She whipped into the left lane. I glanced at the speedometer. Eighty-five. I looked behind. Jonesy was still there, but the van was dropping back.

"Dammit, Talia. Slow down."

After a two-count, she eased up on the gas, slipping back into the right lane. The van began catching up. Talia looked straight ahead, ignoring me. We rode in an awkward silence for the next few minutes.

"I'm sorry, sir."

"You're upset," I said. "It's understandable."

"No, it isn't. It's just tonight. Ted trusts me. I feel like . . . like . . ."

"Judas."

She nodded.

"Look, would it help if I said I'm inclined to think he may not have murdered anyone?"

She looked over. "But the witness—"

"A scared boy," I said. "Who only gave us a general description, not a positive ID. And there are other things that don't fit. Doctor Masonis's military record is exceptional . . . no history of irrational behavior, excessive violence. He's now apparently a very successful academic and author. Everyone we've talked to seems to vouch for the man's character. He's got no apparent motive. Then there's Jonesy."

"Jonesy?"

I smiled. "Jonesy seems to have decided Dr. Masonis is innocent."

"You put a lot of faith in Sergeant Jones, don't you?"

"He's rarely wrong about these things. It's a gift I wish I had."

"Is that why you didn't call the police, then? Because you think Ted is innocent?"

"His innocence has nothing to do with my decision."

"No? Then why—"

"The phone call. Your boyfriend is scared. He as much as said he knows why General Watkins, Tippett, and the others were killed. Knows he's probably next. And there are powerful interests who may not want what he has to say revealed. I'm not about to turn Masonis over to anyone until I find out what the hell he knows."

"You still think it's got something to do with that POW camp the general wanted to see—"

"Heads up." I pointed. "To the left. I think those lights are what we want."

32

WE HAD TO DRIVE TO THE NEXT EXIT AND DOUBLE BACK NORTH-BOUND A FEW MILES. AS WE TOOK THE REST AREA EXIT, I SAID, "Pull over."

Talia rolled to a stop on the shoulder. Jonesy and Webster drove past. The van with Jurgens and Peters pulled in behind us.

A minute later, Talia's cellular rang.

Jonesy said, "Two cars by the rest rooms. A third one way down at the east end. Pretty dark. Can't tell the color too well, but Webster says it could be blue."

"Jurgens and Peters are on the way," I told Jonesy. I rolled down the window and motioned the van forward. They pulled out.

I gave Talia a few last-minute instructions, then climbed into the backseat. She seemed nervous, but that was to be expected.

Five minutes later, I said, "Okay."

Talia drove down the road.

The rest area was quite large, with separate parking for cars and trucks. We went to the right at the Y, following the signs for cars.

"I don't see him," Talia said as we rounded a curve. She slowed to a stop.

I was crouching in the back. I peeked out. The parking area was illuminated by three light poles near the rest rooms. There were two cars in front, a pickup truck, the van, then Jonesy's car.

"There." I pointed. In the shadows at the far end, the silhouette of a car.

Talia drove forward. I heard her click on the high beams. She breathed a sigh of relief. "It's blue."

"Remember. Not too close." I didn't want Masonis to be able to jump back into his car if he spotted me. A car chase was the last thing I needed. I unclipped my pistol from my waist holster.

She slowed to a stop, the engine running.

"You see him?" I asked.

"Yes."

"Is he getting out?"

"No."

"What's he doing?"

"Just sitting there, I think."

I peeked. There were three parking spaces between the two cars. I could make out a form in the front seat. "What's he waiting for?"

"Maybe he's afraid to come out. Maybe he suspects something because I didn't pull in next to him."

"He'll get out." But I thought she might be right. I decided to give Masonis another thirty seconds before my men moved in.

I heard the click of the door.

"Talia?" I poked my head up.

But she had climbed out, leaving the door open.

Goddammit! That stupid . . . Talia was walking toward Masonis's car. Damn! If he drove away now . . . !

I punched the redial on the cellular, watching Talia. I couldn't see well in the dark, but her voice came in clear through the open door. The phone rang.

"Ted?" Talia called. "Ted?" I thought I heard a sharp intake of breath. She was opening the car door. "Ted . . ."

Jonesy answered.

And then Talia screamed.

★★★★

"Scramble!" I hollered, dropping the phone.

I came out low, fast, banging my knee on the door. My first thought was that Masonis had tried to hurt Talia. Talia was backing away from the open driver's-side door, looking at her hands, still screaming.

"Talia!" I rushed forward, gun drawn. I took her by the arm.

She made a coughing sound, tried to pull away. "Oh, God! He's dead!"

I yanked her to the side, gun trained on the driver's door. "Are you hurt?"

"Dead . . . he's dead. . . ."

"Easy, now." I took a step forward and looked into the car. There wasn't much light. But there was enough.

Talia was shaking, words tumbling out. "Blood! On my hands! I touched him!" She held out her hands.

"Easy now, easy," I said again, guiding her to her Lexus. I put her in the backseat, took out a handkerchief, and wiped her hands.

Jonesy's sedan and the van appeared moments later, skidding to a stop, boxing in Masonis's car. I waved my arms into the headlights as the men clambered out. Jonesy and Webster had pistols out; Peters and Jurgens were unarmed.

Jonesy hollered, "Boss, you okay?"

"I'm fine. Just relax, everyone."

Illuminated by the lights of the vehicles, the body was clearly visible. Webster took a couple of steps forward. "What the hell?"

"Masonis is dead," I told him.

"How?"

"Shot in the head." I could see people climbing out of the vehicles at the other end of the lot. Some began walking toward us. "Jurgens, Peters, see if anyone saw anything. Check with the truckers, too. Make sure no one comes over here."

Jurgens and Peters trotted away.

I looked in on Talia in the backseat of her car. She had calmed down, but she still wiped her hands with my handkerchief from time to time. Webster jogged over, his face knotted in worry. I had him escort Talia to the rest room to get cleaned up.

"You haven't called the highway patrol, have you, sir?" Jonesy asked.

I shook my head. "Let's take a quick look first."

Jonesy nodded, then disappeared into his car. He returned carrying a flashlight and two sets of latex gloves. We donned the gloves and crossed to the Tempo.

Even under the glare of two sets of headlights, the Tempo's front end was still in partial shadow. As we approached, Jonesy carefully splayed the flashlight beam on the ground by the driver's door. Blood and bits of a wet-looking doughlike substance glimmered from the asphalt. Footprints were visible.

"Talia and I stepped here."

"No glass," Jonesy murmured. He illuminated the door. "Window's down. Odds are someone heard a shot."

I nodded. "Warm night. Blood hasn't even started to dry. He hasn't been dead long."

Jonesy raised the flashlight.

Masonis was slumped against the seat, his face cocked toward us, his body strapped into the shoulder harness. His white hair was still neatly combed, but where his left ear should have been, there was a ragged hole the size of a half-dollar. Blood had soaked into his white shirt, matting it to his skin.

Jonesy and I moved closer, stepping carefully.

"Entry wound looks like a medium caliber. Nine millimeter or maybe a thirty-eight," Jonesy said. "Hollow point, judging by the damage. Wanted to make sure, I guess."

"Check down by the seat. If it's suicide, there should be a gun."

The beam dropped. Something glimmered. "What's that?" I asked.

Jonesy leaned across the seat, a hand on the dash. "Here, hold this, sir."

I took the flashlight. Jonesy reached down between the seats, then stepped back. He held a revolver gingerly between two fingers.

"Thirty-eight, Smith and Wesson," I said, studying it under the light. "One round fired."

Jonesy was shaking his head.

"You don't think he killed himself," I said.

"Sir, you heard the tape. That sounded like a guy who was going to blow himself away?"

"No. But that's not our call."

"No, sir. But—"

"Go ahead and put the gun back so the cops won't get too excited."

"Want me to check the body? Pat it down?"

I thought, then shook my head. Because of the blood, there was no way to go through Masonis's pockets without leaving signs the body had been disturbed. "We'd better not push it."

I stepped around, shining the light into the passenger seat. Nothing but a Virginia map, folded, showing the area south of Washington, D.C. In the glove compartment, I found the registration and rental agreement. I checked the backseat. A sport jacket hung from a hanger over the right window. On the floor, a crumpled paper bag from McDonald's.

"Jonesy, pop the trunk." I walked to the rear. I heard a click. I lifted the lid.

There were two bags: a rectangular blue one with wheels, and a gym bag.

Jonesy came around. I gave him the light.

I unzipped the blue bag. A spare shirt, change of underwear, socks, toiletries, and a toothbrush. I zipped it up.

Jonesy moved the light over as I opened the gym bag.

"Shit!"

"Damn!" Jonesy said.

"Electric wire, duct tape, latex gloves, D-cell batteries, pliers, screwdriver."

Jonesy grunted. "Wonder if the bomb boys recovered any wire from the boat?"

"I don't know." Something glinted. I reached inside.

"Six-inch blade," Jonesy murmured as I removed a knife. "Bone handle. Looks sharp as hell."

I nodded, returned the knife, then zipped the bag back up. I stood for a moment, shaking my head.

"I know, sir," Jonesy said. "Looks pretty open-and-shut."

"Yeah, but . . ." I slowly closed the trunk.

"It doesn't feel right to me either, sir."

I stared through the rear window at Masonis's darkened form. Jonesy was right. A Masonis suicide was damn convenient. Especially for someone who wanted to keep the story of what happened at Cao Dinh buried.

"I didn't see his briefcase," I said.

"Sir?"

"Or a notebook, or laptop computer, maybe a cassette recorder. Something. And there wasn't any of that stuff in his apartment."

"Maybe he didn't plan on doing any writing, sir."

"Well, we know Masonis tried to question Brady Hanson, possibly about something that happened at Cao Dinh. Unless he intended to memorize Hanson's responses—"

Someone shouted.

We turned. I could see Webster and Talia huddled on a bench by a picnic table near the rest rooms. He had his arm around her. A woman and a man appeared to be trying to talk to them. More cars had pulled in. Maybe a dozen people milled around on the sidewalk, watching us. They couldn't see much, because the van and Jonesy's car blocked their view.

"Colonel!"

Peters and Jurgens were walking toward me with a short, wiry man. The man stumbled, almost fell. Jurgens and Peters steadied him.

"Hey, Colonel! Sir!" Jurgens waved.

I went over to talk to the witness.

33

MR. ROMERO IS ONE OF THE TRUCKERS, SIR," PETERS SAID. "THE GUYS IN THE OTHER RIGS SAY THEY WERE ASLEEP, CLAIM THEY didn't hear anything."

We stood by the van. Jurgens had a hand on Mr. Romero's arm, supporting him. Peters pointed a flashlight at the man's chest. Out of the corner of my eye, I saw Jonesy walk toward the Lexus.

"How about the people in the cars?" I asked.

"They'd only been here a few minutes," Jurgens said. "Didn't hear or see anything until we showed up."

"Figures," I murmured.

"Tell the colonel about the shots, Mr. Romero," Jurgens said. He spoke slowly, as if addressing a child.

Peters raised the light to Romero's face. Romero flinched, tried to turn away, and lost his balance. Jurgens caught him and pulled him to his feet.

"Peters, don't blind the man," I said.

"Sorry, sir." The beam returned to the chest.

"Mr. Romero, I understand you heard the shots."

Mr. Romero tried to focus on me. He had a heavy beard and long hair. The beard opened into a grin as Romero reached a hand under his white

T-shirt and hitched up his jeans. He stood, swaying gently, smelling of alcohol and something else that took me a moment to place.

I said again, "Mr. Romero, you heard shots?"

"*Sí.* Yes. Shoots. *Dos.*" Romero made a pistol with his fingers. "Bang, bang. I hear good."

"*Dos—*"

"He told us he heard two shots, sir," Jurgens said.

"Mr. Romero, are you saying you heard two shots?" I asked.

An emphatic nod. The finger pistol jabbed. "*Sí. Dos.* Bang, bang."

"What time?"

He looked confused.

I pointed to my watch. "What time did you hear the shots?"

A grin. "Ah, time. *Sí.* Maybe . . . eh . . . *trente minutos.* Okay?"

"I think he means thirty minutes, sir," Jurgens said.

"*Sí, sí,*" Romero said. "Tirty, tirty."

"First shot, thirty minutes ago, yes?" I asked.

A nod.

I held up two fingers. "Second shot, how long after first shot?"

Romero just looked at me, smiling.

Christ. "First shot, bang. Then how long time pass before second bang?"

The eyes widened. "*Sí.* Bang. Wait, maybe *uno minuto.* Bang. Okay?"

"Thank you," I said. "*Gracias.*"

Romero grinned broadly, revealing a mouth with more holes than teeth.

I forced a smile. "Make sure he understands the police will want to talk to him," I told Peters and Jurgens. "Maybe clean him up a little. And keep him company. No more booze."

Romero's eyebrows shot up. Now, there was a word he understood. "Booze, no, no. I no drink!"

"C'mon, Mr. Romero," Peters said. He and Jurgens led Romero away.

★★★★

"Rules out suicide if he's right," Jonesy said, coming up beside me. He was stuffing his notepad in his jacket.

"You heard?"

"Most of it." Jonesy gazed across the parking lot. "Captain Webster seems to be enjoying his work." There was a note of disapproval in his voice.

Webster and Talia were still huddled together on the bench. The woman and man they'd been talking to had stepped away, joining the crowd. "Webster's okay. A little smitten, I think."

"Uh-huh," Jonesy said.

"Driver's drunk as a skunk, and he's been smoking dope. You find anything?"

"No, sir." Jonesy nodded to the departing Romero. "Doesn't necessarily affect his ears, sir."

"What?"

"The drinking and toking."

"I suppose." I rubbed a hand over the back of my neck. I could feel my body winding down now that the adrenaline rush from discovering Masonis's body had subsided. "If—and that's a big if—if there actually were two shots."

"That could explain why the driver's window was down."

"The window?" I frowned. Out of the corner of my eye, I saw Talia and Webster coming over. "Maybe Masonis just wanted air."

"Suicide's a funny thing, sir," Jonesy said. "I've seen maybe a couple of dozen over the years. There seems to be one common thread. Always."

"Yeah?"

"Privacy. Alone. A locked room. An empty house. A closed garage. People rarely kill themselves in public."

I'd never really thought about it. "What about jumpers?"

"Most jump without anyone knowing, usually at night. A few get spotted, but not many, considering the number."

"Okay, so what's your point?"

"That is the point, sir. The privacy. The window was down. If he killed himself, the window should have been up. I've investigated five suicides in cars with a gun in twenty-five years. In every case, the windows were up. The raised window is a wall while the person tries to decide to do it."

"Okay . . ."

"But if Masonis was murdered, the killer would have had to have a window down."

"Okay, I'm with you."

"Yes, sir. In this case, the killer might have even had Masonis roll the window down."

"Or the window could already be down, since we're assuming Masonis wasn't in the frame of mind to kill himself."

"Sure, sir. Either way, the important thing is the window is down. Killer waits until the rest area is clear. First shot kills Masonis. Then the killer puts Masonis's hand around the gun butt, fires a second round off into the trees out the window. Gets prints on the gun and ensures a positive paraffin test on Masonis's hand. Nice and tidy."

"And the killer replaces one of the spent cartridges."

Jonesy spread his hands. "A suicide, with no one the wiser."

"A suicide?" said Talia, walking up with Webster. "Then you think Ted killed himself?"

I stared at her for a moment. She still had a slightly stunned look, but her voice was calm. Webster hovered by her shoulder like a dog waiting for a bone.

"Did Ted have a laptop computer?" I asked.

She thought. "No."

"No? You're sure?"

She shook her head. "I've never seen him with one."

"Then how did he write?"

She shrugged. "I don't know."

"Come on. Think."

"He didn't do much writing with me, Colonel," Talia said dryly.

"Touché."

Webster struggled to suppress a grin.

Talia crossed her arms, giving me an expectant look.

"I don't know if he killed himself or not," I said. "Now, if you'll excuse me . . ."

I went to Jonesy's car to call Lieutenant Burton Richards of the Virginia Bureau of Criminal Investigations.

★★★★

Burton was an old drinking buddy. Of course, that was twenty years ago, when we'd been stationed together at Osan Air Base in Korea as OSI rookies. We were young, single, and overseas for the first time. We had a helluva time. Burton and I practically lived in the bar district just off base. During his last three months in Korea, Burton fell hard for a seventeen-year-old hooker named Mih-na. Not that I blamed him. Mih-na had the face of an angel and a body that exuded sex. The problem was Mih-na also had a nasty little heroin habit. Word got back to our boss, Major Fallon, about Burton's living arrangement. Two days later, Burton found himself on an airplane for the States, an Article 15 on his record. He never saw Mih-na again. He separated from the Air Force shortly after returning stateside, joining the Virginia State Police. I'd been the best man at his wedding to Sara a year later.

I punched in the number from memory, got Sara, who passed the phone to Burton.

"Hey, buddy. Little past your bedtime, isn't it?"

"Burt, I've got a problem." I explained.

"You didn't call the highway patrol?"

"No."

"You just went to the meeting on your own?"

"Yes."

"He's dead?"

"He's dead."

"Did you touch anything?"

I'd never lied to Burt, and I wasn't going to start now. "Yes. The gun. And we looked in the trunk."

"Goddammit, Charlie!"

"We put everything back. We wore gloves."

"You crazy, Charlie? What the hell were you thinking? Tampering with evidence!"

"I'm a cop, remember."

"A military cop. With no jurisdiction."

"Burt, I'm tired. Now, are you coming out or should I call this in myself?"

A pause.

"I'm coming, but you stay put, Charlie. You hear me? Don't touch anything else."

"I won't."

"I'm on my way. Thirty minutes."

"Thanks, Burt."

He'd already hung up.

As I climbed out of the car, I saw Jurgens depositing Mr. Romero in the van's front seat.

"Colonel!" Talia called from the Lexus. I went over.

Talia bit her lip. "Colonel, I remembered something. . . ."

34

TALIA AND I WERE LEANING AGAINST THE LEXUS, OUR FACES ILLUMI-
NATED BY THE HEADLIGHTS OF JONESY'S SEDAN, WHICH WAS PARTIALLY
angled in our direction. Jonesy and Webster were standing, facing us.

"Colonel, I've been trying to remember if Ted said anything," Talia
said.

"And?"

"Anything important, unusual. Ted was very closemouthed about
everything. Infuriatingly so, at times. I didn't even know he was still
working with General Watkins since he came back from Vietnam."

"So he didn't tell you anything?"

She shook her head. "But then I remembered walking into the bedroom last Saturday. We were at his place and I'd just come out of the
shower. Ted was on the phone. He didn't see me at first. When he did, he
covered up the receiver, shooed me from the room. He'd never done that
before." She looked down, slowly wrapping her hands over her shoulders,
remembering.

As I watched, the image of Talia, naked, crystallized in my mind.
I couldn't believe any red-blooded male would ever chase her out of
a bedroom. Must have been a helluva phone call. I coughed softly.
"Go on."

She took a deep breath and dropped her hands to her sides. "I think that's why I remember. I was thinking, *What's the big deal about me hearing about a business call?* Even if he did mention a lot of money."

"How much money?"

"Five hundred thousand dollars."

Webster made a sucking sound.

"Do you know who he was talking to?" I asked.

Talia shook her head.

"Can you recall what he said exactly?" Jonesy asked.

She thought. "I wasn't really listening too closely."

"Just tell us what you think you heard," Jonesy urged. "This could be very important."

"I'll try. When I came out, Ted was saying, 'Tell them the price has gone up to five hundred thousand.' I don't think he liked the answer, because he seemed to get angry. 'Five hundred thousand or it's no deal,' he said, or something like that."

"He didn't mention a name, who was on the other end?" I asked.

Talia started to shake her head, then stopped.

"Yes?" I asked.

"Well, there was one thing. But I don't think it will help much. It isn't very specific. He said 'company.' "

"Company? What company?"

"Just 'company.' I told you it wouldn't be much help."

"No name at all?"

"No."

"What was the context, how did he use the word 'company'?"

Talia thought. "I think he said, 'Tell the company the price has gone—' "

"The company," Jonesy interrupted. "You're sure he said it just like that? 'The company'?"

Suddenly, everything started to make sense.

I waved a hand in dismissal, trying to sound casual. "Talia, I'd say Dr. Masonis was working on a business deal of some kind. I don't think it's related to this case."

Jonesy shot me a look of disbelief. He wiped the look from his face almost instantly.

"You don't think there's any significance, then?" Talia asked. I thought she was looking at me funny, but it could have been my imagination.

"No. I don't think so. Webster, why don't you take Talia home now, okay? Your car is at her place?"

Webster looked surprised, then grinned. "Yes, sir. I surely will."

But Talia was shaking her head. "Won't the police want to talk to me?"

I placed a hand gently on her shoulder. "Jonesy and I will handle everything. You've had a shock. You need to rest. Go on home."

I could feel her body tense. She knew I was trying to get rid of her. "Colonel, I don't think that's such a good idea."

"That's an order, Major Swanson. Webster?" I stepped back.

Webster came over, hesitantly taking her arm. Talia shrugged his hand away. "Colonel, I'm not going!"

"Talia!"

The sharpness of my voice caught her off guard. She closed her mouth, her eyes angry.

I softened my tone. "Please, Talia. Just go. I'll explain later. For now, I might suggest you not mention the phone conversation to anyone. You have your keys?"

For a moment, I thought she was going to argue. She slowly reached into her jeans, removed the car keys, extended her hand out, then froze. I could almost see the gears engaging in her brain. She looked up at me, her eyes wide. "The company! My God, you think . . ."

I grabbed the keys and tossed them to Webster. He almost dropped them. "You two better get going."

Talia nodded obediently, allowing Webster to help her into the passenger seat. They drove away.

"You are making a mistake, sir," said Jonesy softly from behind.

I spun around. "What the hell do you suppose Burton will do if he questions Talia and finds out Masonis could be connected to the CIA?"

"Lieutenant Richards will contact the Agency and try to confirm whether Masonis worked for them. The CIA will of course deny it."

"But they'll know we know. Could make things even more difficult for us. Could even put Talia in some jeopardy.

Jonesy shook his head vigorously.

"You don't think so?"

"Only if Masonis really did work for the CIA, sir."

"You're saying you don't believe Talia?"

Jonesy looked over in the direction of Masonis's car. He sounded tired. "Sir, she's already lied to us God knows how many times."

"Doesn't mean she's lying now."

"Maybe not, sir. But I find her statement curious. I mean, we've been busting our rears trying to figure out a motive for the killings, and here she gives us one out of the blue."

"But what she says confirms what Birelli told us, and what you and I both know: the government is up to their eyeballs in this thing. You don't think it's possible for the CIA to have made a deal with Masonis, and taken him out because he knew too much? And a half a million bucks is a lot of money."

"Sir, Masonis made almost that much in a year."

"Then maybe it wasn't just the money. Maybe Masonis was a full-time operative. Maybe Masonis had a personal agenda." *Aw, hell!* I turned away. I was starting to sound like a conspiracy nut.

"Then there's the timing of Major Swanson's statement. Sir, you don't find that just a little suspect? That she suddenly remembers that conversation now, when she's supposed to be overcome with grief? A conversation that implies Masonis killed General Watkins under a contract from the CIA. A conversation that gives us a motive which you know and I know can never be verified, since the accused is conveniently dead and the CIA certainly won't substantiate. A conversation which, when added with all the stuff we found in Masonis's car, means we'd have to be nuts not to say he's the killer."

Jonesy was looking at me, completely devoid of expression. Which is how he showed anger. If he was mildly irritated, which was rare enough, he'd utter an occasional curse, maybe make a snide comment. But when he was really angry, which I'd witnessed only a handful of times over the years, he'd become totally calm, face blank, as if channeling all his rage inside.

"So what are you saying? You think Talia is involved in this thing? Why? What possible reason? And how? You think she could have butchered Watkins? Okay, I'll give you she doesn't have an alibi, but think about it. Do you really see a woman doing something like that? Especially Talia. Be serious. General Watkins was her gift horse, her ticket to the top. The guy had practically adopted her. And how about Masonis? Now, that's a real problem for your hypothesis. Or are you forgetting she was with us when he died, for chrissakes."

"Look, sir, I'm not saying she's the killer!"

"She's part of a conspiracy, then, is that it? Maybe she's working for the CIA?"

Jonesy held up his hands. "Sir, all I'm saying is we should be very careful before we rely on her statement. Not jump to conclusions."

I ran my fingers through my hair. Of course, Jonesy had a point. Before Talia's revelations, my inclination had been that Masonis had probably not been the killer. I nodded at Jonesy and did my best Jack Webb imitation. "Just the facts, eh?" I said with a wry smile.

Jonesy smiled back. "Just the facts, sir."

We stood in silence for a moment.

"Tell me one thing, Jonesy, and I want the truth."

"Okay, sir." There was a note of caution in his voice.

"Something bothers you about Major Swanson, and I want to know what it is."

Jonesy stared into the night and said nothing for a moment. "Little things. Makes me think she knows more than she's telling."

"Like what?"

"That file on the MIAs, for one. I had the feeling she knew the file was missing all along. And remember the way she acted after the exec, Colonel Ryerson, found a copy of the list with the MIA names? She looked like she'd seen a ghost, boss."

I grunted. "Jonesy, that's a bit of an exaggeration. She looked a little surprised. But then, we all were, I think."

"What about the way she seems to be pointing us in Masonis's direction? Not exactly what I'd expect from someone sweet on the guy."

"What do you mean?"

"She gives us the photos from Vietnam that help us ID Masonis. She calls you to tell you he called so we can nail him. Now she practically tells us he might be working for the CIA. I'm telling you, she's been setting the guy up for us all along."

"The conspiracy thing again," I said in a tired voice. "Jonesy, we just went through this."

"I know what my gut tells me, sir. Major Swanson scares the daylights out of me."

I'd never known Jonesy to be afraid of anything, so I said, "Jonesy, you're nuts."

"You notice her eyes, sir?" Jonesy asked.

"They're blue."

"I watched her real close when the tape was played tonight back at the condo. She acted upset, like she was real worried. Almost had me convinced. Except for the eyes. They were cold . . . hard." He turned to me. "Eyes don't lie, sir."

I would have told Jonesy he was nuts again, except for one thing. I now remembered what had struck me as odd when I had watched Talia during the playing of the tape.

The trembling lip, the sagging shoulders, the furtive gestures. A picture of worry and grief, except for her eyes. Jonesy was right.

I checked my watch, then looked out over the parking lot. "Where the hell is Burton?" I growled.

35

URTON ARRIVED FIVE MINUTES LATER. I TOOK HIM TO MASONIS'S TEMPO. GOING OVER THE SCENE AGAIN REINFORCED MY CONVICTION that Masonis hadn't killed himself. A little nagging voice in my head kept saying Masonis didn't fit the profile of a killer. I mentioned my doubts to Burton, which didn't make him too happy.

Burton looked like a cop, a reassuringly big, solid man with intense black eyes that could unnerve a suspect at a glance. In Korea, he'd been an impulsive kid, happily bulling through a case. Over the years he'd matured, become a thinking man's cop. As a field office commander for the Virginia Bureau of Criminal Investigations, he was quickly earning a reputation as a political cop, a guy who never makes a decision until he's considered all angles, and figures out what it's going to cost him.

That worried me.

But Burt was a friend, and ours had become a society driven by politics. Burton liked to say he was just playing the game. But I knew better. He'd become a politician, and our friendship would drag him only so far.

Maybe I would have to lie.

Burton removed a thick cigar from his jacket and bit off the end. He flicked his lighter. A sweet aroma filled the air. We stepped away from the car.

He looked across the parking lot at the growing crowd of onlookers. "No way I can keep you out of it, Charlie. Five seconds after my boys get here, they'll know about you. Pearson will be calling for your head. Dammit, you should have called me." Captain Pearson was Burton's boss, the head of the Virginia Bureau of Criminal Investigations General Investigation Division.

"I'm just asking for time. Before your office files the complaint. I'm in a little hot water with General Holmes."

"I figured. Isn't the stiff the one you went on the tube about, saying he was your chief suspect? Now you're telling me you're not sure. When this gets out, you're gonna be up to your butt in donkey shit, buddy boy."

I nodded. "I may have overreacted. Tippett had just died."

"Look, I know he was a friend of yours, but he was a prick, plain and simple."

"Burt?"

"Yeah. I know. Speaking ill of the dead. I'll go to confession tomorrow, okay?" Burton inhaled deeply, then blew smoke slowly up in the air. "Here's the way we play it so everyone looks good. We go through the drill, take your statements. I'll bury the timing about when you showed in the report. Say you called me, there was a mix-up and you arrived before me. Pearson isn't going to look too close if we get credit for finding the chief suspect in multiple murders. Guy loves seeing his name in the papers."

I was shaking my head. I appreciated what Burt was trying to do, but . . .

"You don't like it! Goddammit, Charlie! The way it looks to me, the stiff blew his brains out because he's guilty as hell and knew he was going down. If you come on board, say yeah, the dead guy was behind the killings, you look good, we look good, get some press, spread out some of the credit to the DCPD. Who's the guy?"

"Lieutenant Harry Lee."

"Yeah, okay. Get him in the press release. Everybody is happy." Burton waved at Jonesy. "Hey, get over here! Talk some sense into your shit-for-brains boss!"

"Not until I'm sure, Burt. I have to check on some things first." I glanced at Jonesy, who had walked up next to me.

Burton grunted. "You buying what Charlie's saying there, Jonesy, that Masonis may not be the perp?" Burton had worked with Jonesy in the past. He knew Jonesy called them as he saw them.

Jonesy gave me what I took as a nod of approval. "Have to agree with Colonel Jensen, Lieutenant Richards. I think it's too soon to tell if Masonis is the perp, and certainly too early to tell if he killed himself."

The cigar glowed bright between Burton's lips in a sudden, almost angry burst. I couldn't see his face well, or the intensity in his eyes. That was just as well.

"You guys are still fucking Boy Scouts," Burton growled. "Now I remember why I got out of the military in the first place."

"So you think Masonis calmly kills a dozen people," I asked, "then when he finds out the cops are onto him, he loses his nerve and pulls in here and kills himself after making a call to his girlfriend?"

"Hey, the guy could be a nutcase. Or maybe he's just a coward. Can't stand the idea of being locked up for the rest of his life."

I felt myself getting angry. Burt had been a good cop. "Look, you initially still have to handle this thing as a homicide."

"That's procedure and you know it."

"Fine. First you take a hard look at the evidence. You convince yourself it's a suicide after that, and maybe I'll come on board. Copy?" I jabbed a thumb at the van. "You might want to talk to Mr. Romero over there. He says he heard two shots."

"Two? No shit?"

I nodded. "But there's a slight problem. He's drunk."

Burton gave a slow shake of his head and laughed. He clapped me on the back. "Deal, you son of a bitch. See ya, Jonesy."

But first he went to his car to make the call.

✯✯✯✯

Jonesy and I stood together while Burton made his call.

"You may have a point about Talia," I said.

Jonesy showed no reaction.

"I guess I just want to believe her."

"It's hard, sir."

"Hard?"

"To be objective, when they're that pretty."

I didn't reply.

A car door slammed.

I watched Burt walk from his car toward the van where Mr. Romero sat.

Jonesy cleared his throat. "If Major Swanson is lying, it's obviously not because she's been pressured by the CIA, since she implicates them. So the question becomes who would want the CIA tagged with Masonis's death?" A pause. "Seems to me it would be whoever killed Masonis, sir."

"Sure. And if we believe Birelli, that leaves either the Vietnamese government, or the unnamed American bastard who paid to have the Cao Dinh POWs murdered, or any one of a number of corporations who stand to lose millions if Vietnamese recognition falls through."

Jonesy shook his head. "Seems a little overwhelming when you put it like that, sir."

Burt was leaning into the van, talking with Romero. I murmured, "Wish I knew if she was telling the truth, Jonesy."

"Me too, sir," Jonesy said softly.

★★★★

A minute later, we heard the first siren.

"I better tell Jurgens and Peters not to mention Captain Webster or Major Swanson," Jonesy said.

I nodded absently. I was picturing Talia's apartment. Expensive tastes, and she was ambitious . . . and she had lied.

★★★★

Forty minutes later, Burt finished taking our statements and told us to leave. No one had mentioned Talia or Webster. I managed to avoid mentioning to Burt anything about Cao Dinh, POWs, Dynatech Transports, or what Birelli had said. I knew there was a chance one of the witnesses would mention to the cops a girl had been with us, but I told myself I'd have everything wrapped up before they tracked her down.

I hoped.

Evading Burt's questions hadn't been particularly difficult. Burt questioned us between calls to his boss, two newspapers, and the governor's office. I had to remind him to have someone notify the D.C. and Falls Church police that Masonis was dead.

Like I said, Burt was a politician.

★★★★

Jurgens and Peters left first. I was just getting into Jonesy's car when a trooper came up.

"Colonel Jensen?"

I nodded.

"A Lieutenant Lee wants you to call him at this number." He handed me a piece of paper.

"Thank you."

Lee answered. I could hear traffic noise in the background.

"Just got the word," Lee said. "Thought you might want to celebrate."

"Not really, no."

"C'mon, Charlie, I'll buy the first round."

"Look, Harry. I'm beat."

"You don't sound very happy for a guy whose prime murder suspect is dead."

I didn't reply.

"Something wrong?"

"Just tired. Say, did the Durham PD search Masonis's home?"

"They checked to see if he was there. That was about it."

"Can you get them to go back?"

A pause. "Why?"

"Check out his computer for any references to POWs. And see if he has a laptop."

"Well, I'll be. You don't think Masonis did it?"

"I'm just not sure."

"You're not holding out on me, are you?"

"Look, I'm just not sure that Masonis is the guy."

"Dammit, Charlie, if you know something, we should talk. Now."

"Okay, Harry, where do you want to meet?"

"The Kimchi Grill in Rosslyn." He gave me directions. "I'll notify the Durham PD," he added. "Maybe they can check out his house."

"Thanks, Harry."

"You can't miss the restaurant. Only red building around. See you in a few minutes."

After I hung up, Jonesy said, "I like him, sir. He's a good cop."

"I know."

We rode in silence for a while. "The killer was lucky tonight, sir," Jonesy said.

I had reclined against the seat and was rubbing my temple. "What do you mean?"

"That we didn't arrive sooner. That we were delayed. You know, the car accident."

"He was lucky, all right."

"I don't much believe in luck," Jonesy said with feeling.

I stopped rubbing and looked over. But Jonesy's eyes were on the road.

36

THE BRIGHT RED PAINT MADE THE KIMCHI GRILL STAND OUT LIKE A BEACON FROM THE TIRED BUILDINGS NEAR THE CORNER OF WILSON and Rhodes. A glowing sign on the roof proclaimed the name in English and Korean. At this late hour, there were only three cars in the restaurant parking lot. One was Lee's.

The sign dangling on the front door said "Closed," but I could see lights on inside. The door opened before I could knock.

"Come on in," Lee said. He had a beer in his hand. A pretty, older Asian woman stood beside him, smiling pleasantly.

As we walked inside, Lee said, "My aunt June. She owns the joint."

"Hello, gentlemen," June said. "Come in and make yourselves comfortable."

Jonesy and I said hello. Like Lee, she had a New England accent, but hers was much more noticeable.

Lee asked, "What do you guys want? Beer?"

"A beer would be fine," I said. Jonesy ordered a diet Coke.

"Coming up," June said, and left.

The dining room was very large, very red, and adorned with Asian artwork and artifacts. There were maybe thirty tables, each with a large grill in the middle. A smell of garlic and broiled meat permeated the room. Two bored-looking busboys stacked glasses on a counter against the back wall. Another young man was mopping the tiled floor.

Lee led us to a table in the corner. "Great having a relative in the restaurant business."

I pulled out a chair. "Why's that?"

Lee grinned. "Eat and drink for free. Hell of a deal, especially for a bachelor who can't cook."

"Your aunt must love you," I said.

"Light of her life," Lee said as June appeared with our drinks.

I reached for my wallet, but she signaled with her hand for me to keep my money. "No, I insist. On the house." She gave Lee a look of affection as she left.

Lee grinned again. "Like I said, hell of a deal."

★★★★

Lee stared into his glass. "When I first heard, I said to myself I could finally wrap this baby up. But I also knew there was nothing solid against Masonis, with that Vietnamese kid dead." He looked at me. "Then there are the questions you brought up when you talked to that MIA guy."

"John Birelli." I set my beer down.

"Yeah, Birelli. Like what the hell is so important about something that happened in a POW camp? And what the hell was Masonis's motive to kill? You implied maybe he wanted to shut people up about something having to do with that camp. But the war's been over for twenty years. I have to tell you, that sounds a little crazy."

I nodded. When I had told Lee about Cao Dinh over the phone earlier, I had been brief, not mentioning Tho, or the arrangement with Watkins and Birelli. I also hadn't told him about the probable interest by the White House or the political considerations for keeping the story quiet. He was smart enough to know there had to be more.

"I'm wondering," Lee said, "just who the hell was in that gray Mustang that followed you? Now, maybe all the answers died with Masonis. And hey, if the Virginia cops confirm Masonis blew his brains out, and with all the stuff they seem to have found in the car, I'll go ahead and file this baby away. But I'm still curious." He paused, staring thoughtfully at me. "I'm still real curious."

I took a large swallow and sat back. Jonesy was also watching me.

"Tell him, Jonesy."

"Everything, sir?"

I nodded.

When Jonesy finished, Lee looked a little stunned. He fished out a cigarette, lit it, and took a deep drag. I killed my beer, watching smoke curl from Lee's mouth.

"Shit," Lee said.

"Yeah," I said.

"So you guys are working on the assumption Masonis didn't kill anybody or himself?"

I gave a slow nod. "For now."

Lee watched me through the smoke. "Everything sounds unbelievable."

"Harry!"

We all looked up.

"Harry!" June said, coming over. She looked horrified. "Harry, I told your mother you quit." She slapped Lee on the back of his head. "You told me you quit."

Lee cupped the cigarette and shoved it under the table as June, arms folded, glared at him. "I've been trying, Auntie."

"You promised, Harry," June said, shaking her head. "Put it out or I'm calling your mother. Now." She looked over to one of the busboys, said something in Korean.

Like a child, Lee produced the cigarette and held it out. The busboy appeared, placing an ashtray in front of Lee. Lee crushed it out.

"The pack." June held out her hand.

Lee reached inside his jacket and handed over an almost empty pack of cigarettes.

June took them, shook her head again, and left.

One of the busboys giggled.

Lee ran both hands back over his head. "Christ, I'm thirty-four years old. You'd think . . ."

"You'll always be a kid to her," I said, smiling at his embarrassment.

"Yeah." He leaned forward, elbows on the table. He looked to Jonesy. "I'd been wondering about the suits. Fits in with what you guys are saying."

"Suits?" Jonesy said.

"After you two left Masonis's apartment, I didn't see them until later. When Puller, the cop playing the security guard, said Masonis had been found. I was just leaving with Annie and Frankie and that kid, Jerry. Man, was Annie upset that Masonis had offed himself. That's when I saw the suits with Lufkin by the entrance."

I frowned. "Suits?"

"Feds," Lee said. "Suits are Feds, the FBI. Man, where you guys been?"

"You wear a suit, Lieutenant," Jonesy said.

Lee rolled his eyes.

"Feds," I murmured. I felt only a mild sense of surprise. I'd expected their eventual involvement.

"Harry," June walked up, carrying a handbag. "The back is locked. You have your key?"

"Yes, Auntie."

"The alarm?"

"One-two-one-seven. Your birthday."

She smiled. "No more cigarettes? Promise me. Your health."

"No more, Auntie."

"Then I am very happy." She reached down and brushed a hand over his hair, then nodded to us. She followed the busboys out. The door swung closed.

"To the Feds," I said sarcastically, and raised my glass in a toast, except the glass was empty.

★★★★

Lee came back with two more beers and another soft drink.

"Your department didn't call the FBI in?" I asked.

"Hell, no. Those guys are a pain in the ass. They waltz in, take over, act like we work for them. Cocky bastards."

"Detective Lufkin know?"

Lee snorted. "Fred looked plenty pissed. I know he didn't expect them to show up. He hates Feds worse than he hates me."

Federal intervention was usually justified only under two conditions. Either a federal crime has been committed, such as a kidnapping or a bank robbery, or the local authorities request help on what is normally a local matter. A third way could be top-down directed authorization. Which is probably what had occurred. A phone call had come from someone in the administration to a high-ranking state official suggesting the Falls Church PD to request federal assistance in the Masonis case.

"Fort Myer is a federal installation, right?" Lee asked. "Could be the Feds worked the authorization because of General Watkins's murder."

"Military institution," I corrected. "Jurisdiction works the same as local. Military has to file a request. We didn't. I would know."

"You sure?"

I hesitated, then shook my head.

"Well, all I know is they're involved," Lee said. "So maybe there is something to what Major Swanson said about the CIA also being in this thing."

"More than likely a move to ensure the investigation is terminated as soon as possible," Jonesy said.

"Why?"

"Because a continuing investigation could lead to Cao Dinh," I explained. "That would be unacceptable."

"So you're talking a cover-up."

"It's been going on for some time."

Lee ran both hands over his face. "Man, what a goat rope. And there's something else that's bothering me."

"Ask away," I said.

"Charlie, did you tell anyone about Masonis's call tonight?"

"Lieutenant Burton Richards."

"I mean before you found Masonis."

"No." I held my beer in both hands, looking at Jonesy.

"A few of our men knew," Jonesy said. "And Major Swanson, of course." He looked at me when he said Talia's name.

"No one else?"

"No."

I knew where Lee was going and started to say something, but Jonesy spoke first. "I know what you're thinking, Lieutenant. If indeed Masonis was murdered, how did the killer know he was going to be at the rest area?"

Lee nodded. "There are only three possibilities."

"And only one that is plausible," I said.

Lee sat back, folded his hands across his stomach. "Either one of your men or Major Swanson told the killer."

"Impossible!" I said.

"Or Major Swanson's apartment is bugged, or her phone is tapped."

"Which is the only real possibility, especially if the Feds are involved. Jonesy, you arrange to have her phone checked and the apartment swept."

"Tomorrow, sir. Webster and I will handle it."

Lee was frowning.

"What?" I asked him.

"I disagree. About the Feds bugging her place. Because they showed tonight at the apartment."

I paused.

"He's right, sir," Jonesy said. "A bug or a phone tap would have told them Masonis was at the rest area."

I nodded, realizing how tired I was. "You're right. They wouldn't have bothered to go to Masonis's apartment."

"So even if her phone is tapped, the Feds aren't responsible," Lee said. "Plus, I gotta tell you, I just don't believe the Feds would kill to keep this thing about Cow Bin quiet—"

"Cao Dinh," Jonesy said.

"Whatever. Christ, you're talking about the murder of a four-star general. Even the CIA or FBI aren't that crazy. Cover things up, sure. Interfere with the investigation, absolutely. But not murder."

Jonesy nodded in agreement.

I thought Lee and even Jonesy were being naive, considering the repercussions of such an enormous scandal. The outrage of the American people over the cover-up of the death of twenty-three POWs would be enormous. If the prisoners had been executed, individuals from both the current and previous administrations might be indicted. Impeachment of the President was a possibility.

I coughed. "Watergate started with only a break-in, if you'll recall."

"Yeah, Charlie," Lee said. "The worst scandal in our history. And no one died. Anyway, if there's no phone tap in Major Swanson's place, and no bugs, that must mean Masonis was followed, right?"

"Extremely unlikely," I said. "Half the police in the area have been looking for Masonis and couldn't find him. How would the killer know where he was, even to begin following him?"

"Maybe someone has been tailing him for the past couple of days," Lee suggested.

"Then why wait until tonight to kill him? Assuming that Masonis knew what General Watkins knew, I would have thought Masonis would have been killed much earlier. That he wasn't has to be because his whereabouts were unknown."

Jonesy was swirling his drink, staring into it. "There is at least one other explanation."

"What?" Lee asked.

"Where did Masonis leave from this afternoon?"

Lee turned to me, but I was looking at Jonesy.

"The Rolling Hills Sanitarium," Jonesy said.

Lee's beeper went off.

He silenced the contraption and went to a phone at the bar.

★★★★

He returned a few minutes later, his face troubled. "Don't hold your breath on finding anything in Masonis's house."

"Why? What happened?"

"Masonis's house just burned to the ground. After this, I'd say his suicide is just a little iffy."

37

WE STEPPED OUT INTO THE NIGHT WELL AFTER MIDNIGHT. JONESY AND I WAITED AS LEE TURNED OUT THE LIGHTS AND LOCKED THE front door, and we walked to the parking lot.

"You know, that Annie's okay," Lee said for no apparent reason.

"Oh, sure," I said.

"I'm serious. We talked a little. She's okay. That hard-ass attitude is an act. You know she was an orphan? Didn't get adopted until she was twelve. That's where the toughness comes from. Always had to fight for stuff."

"You just want to get into her pants, Harry," I said.

He grinned. "There's that, of course. But she really is okay. You'd like her if you gave her a chance."

We reached our cars. "See you guys tomorrow?" Lee asked.

"Yeah. I'll call."

Lee unlocked his door. "Besides, I think she likes me."

"What?"

"Annie, I think she likes me."

He winked, opened the door, and climbed inside.

★★★★

"Sir," Jonesy said as he pulled in next to my car in the Pentagon lot, "remember when Lieutenant Lee said maybe one of us may have called the killer with Masonis's whereabouts."

I had my hand on the door handle. I sat back again. "You mean Talia, of course?"

"She was upstairs, sir. Remember? She has a cellular phone. We know no one else would have called."

"You want to check her cellular phone records?"

"A thought, sir."

"I don't know. We don't have probable cause."

"That won't be a problem, sir."

I shook my head. Jonesy continually amazed me at the number of contacts he had squirreled away in the most unlikely places. "You'll have to dig up Talia's ESN to run a check—" I stopped when I saw Jonesy smile. He already had it. But how?

Then I remembered. When I'd been talking with Mr. Romero, Jonesy had gone over to her Lexus.

"Her purse," I said. "The phone was in her purse in the car."

"Now, sir. Searching her purse would be illegal."

"Uh-huh." I opened the door. "As far as I know, we never had this conversation."

"What conversation, sir?"

I got out. "When will you know?"

"Depends. By tomorrow afternoon probably. I've also sent queries to Air Force Personnel for the names of any nurses at Takli who returned before their tour was up."

I nodded. To be honest, I didn't think this was going to yield much. In light of what had happened, an illegitimate kid just didn't amount to much.

Jonesy paused. "And there's something else."

"What?"

"I'd like to run a routine check on Major Swanson's personnel records. Might turn up something."

"Keep it quiet."

"Yes, sir."

"Good night, Jonesy."

"Good night, sir."

As I watched Jonesy drive away, I found myself hoping he wouldn't find anything.

★★★★

I turned on the car radio. Brahms. Gentle, soothing. My eyes felt heavy. I changed to a jazz station. An up-tempo horn number. Better.

Traffic was light. On I-395, I set the cruise control for sixty-five and sat back.

My thoughts drifted to Tippett. He was dead. That would never change, and I'd miss him. Judging by reactions like Burt's and Birelli's, I could be the only one. I couldn't help but think it sad when one's death wasn't mourned. That was too much like he hadn't existed.

Tippett's had been a heroic and tragic life. He rose from nothing to become a success, then fate turned the tables and he began a slide to the bottom.

I'd often wondered why Tippett and I ever became close friends. We had little in common other than our jobs. Why does someone like someone else? Jean had come up with the answer. She said I just admired the guy. The way he'd come up from nothing, the way he said and did things, not caring what people thought as long as he got results. I shook my head.

I'd always had it easy. My dad was a chemist at DuPont. We had a big house, nice things. My success was preordained. I'd had my pick of colleges, but I'd always wanted to fly, so I went to the Air Force Academy. Of course, that's when I ran into my first—and up to now, my only—true disappointment in life. My eyes went south during my Academy days, and I lost my pilot qualification.

Still, I'd done well. I had a good family. For twenty years, the OSI had provided me with a challenging, rewarding career. I had a shot at full colonel. If I made colonel, I'd hang around a few more years and retire on a good pension. Maybe teach in some college.

I watched the road disappear beneath the headlights. I was risking all of that now, and the realization felt like a weight.

The walls had already begun appearing. They were still subtle maybe, but the harder I poked, the higher and stronger they would become. If someone high up in the government was behind Watkins's murder, I could be risking more than a career. Hell, I was a lieutenant colonel, and someone had already butchered a four-star general.

But as Jonesy said, right is right.

I'd always told myself I had the sense not to keep pushing when I should quit. I wasn't Tippett trying to prove himself. I smiled grimly at the irony. *Jensen, you dumb bastard.*

I pulled into my driveway a few minutes later, and I was surprised to find my hands hurt from gripping the wheel. After killing the motor, I stayed and found myself mouthing a prayer for Tippett.

When I opened my eyes, I was surprised to find them moist.

✸✸✸✸

There were three messages on the machine in my study. The first was from General Tupper requesting me to meet him the next day at his office at nine-thirty. The curious thing was the recording was his voice, not a secretary's or an exec's. Not often a four-star personally calls a lieutenant colonel to arrange a meeting. The second came from Burton. He sounded agitated.

And the third was from Mr. Pinock of Pinock Financial.

I checked my watch. After one, and I was too tired.

I undressed in the dark and crawled into bed. Jean's warmth was reassuring, and I nuzzled close.

"Hi, babe," she said sleepily.

I just kissed the back of her neck. She smelled of soap.

"Did you get your messages?" she murmured.

"Yes."

"Burton called again about thirty minutes ago. He sounds upset."

"He gets excited pretty easy. I'll call him in the morning."

"They find Tippett's body?"

"No." I lay silent for a moment, measuring my response. "They found a leg."

She drew away. I felt her turn, face me.

"Was it his?"

"I don't know. We have to wait for the tests. But from the force of the explosion, I don't think they'll find much else."

"You'll have to tell Dorothy sometime," she said softly.

"I know. Tomorrow."

"It's so sad, it's almost pitiful," Jean said.

"Huh?"

"Even with the divorce, she still loves him. It's sad."

"Yeah. Then why is she marrying someone else?"

"Charlie, I can't believe you'd ask that. After the way Tip neglected her, she deserves a chance at happiness."

"But if she still loves him?"

"She's almost fifty. The kids will be gone. She doesn't want to be alone. And he's nice. An accountant. Rupert Hendricks. Rupert spent most of the day with her. He's stable, kind, and he loves her."

Rupert, I thought. Good name for an accountant. Probably a scrawny runt.

I closed my eyes. The pillow felt soft, welcoming. My mind shifted, sorting through the day's events, searching for a connection. Cao Dinh, Masonis, Brady Hanson, and Talia.

"Night, honey," I murmured.

38

Wednesday

I HEARD THE RINGING AND ROLLED OVER, IRRITATED THAT SOMEONE WOULD PHONE SO LATE AT NIGHT. THEN SOMEONE SHOOK ME.

I opened my eyes and found myself looking at the frowning face of my six-foot-three, rail-thin son, Tony.

"Dad, Lieutenant Richards is on the phone."

I rolled up on an elbow and checked the time. Seven-twelve. "Thanks, Tony." I reached for the phone. Tony stood there, still frowning.

"Something on your mind?"

"Stacy says you're buying her a car," he blurted. He made it sound like a crime.

I nodded, rubbing sleep from my eyes.

Tony looked at his feet, shifting his weight. "I just thought, well, I'm almost fifteen and a half, Dad. I'll get my license pretty soon—"

"In ten months."

He looked up. "That's soon," he insisted. "And if Stacy gets a car now, maybe you won't be able to buy me one next year."

Teenagers. "Tony, can we talk about this—"

"That wouldn't be fair, Dad. For her to have one and not me."

The old fairness trump card. I knew I was beaten. "Okay, okay."

"Awesome, Dad!" His eyes lit up. "I already talked to Marty. His uncle owns a steak house. Marty says he can get me a job bussin' tables."

"Remember, same deal as Stacy. You have to come up with half. No car until you do."

Tony was grinning. "No problem. You're the best, Dad!"

"Tony, bus is here!" Jean called from downstairs.

I smiled. "Scram."

Tony beamed and ran from the room.

I heard Stacy call out, " 'Bye, Dad."

I stared at the phone, thinking I was a lucky man.

★★★★

"Didn't you get my fucking messages, Charlie? Christ. Next time call me back ASAP."

His voice told me he must have found out about Talia and Webster. "Look, Burt, I can explain—"

"I had nothing to do with it. Understand? I was gonna run it like a regular homicide. By the book. Like I said."

Now I was confused. "Burt?"

"But then the fucking Feds roll in. Then Captain Pearson comes to the scene. Drives up from Richmond. Bastard hasn't shown his fat butt at a crime scene in two years. Next thing I know, I'm out, and Pearson puts himself in charge. Won't let me even talk to the reporters. Takes all the credit. Him and the Feds. I ask him what the hell the Feds are doing here. Know what Pearson tells me? The governor called them in. You believe that shit? Then I pick up the *Post* this morning. So you changed your mind, eh? What the hell is going on, Charlie? Never mind. I don't want to know. This thing has too much heat."

"Burt, take a breath, huh? I don't know what you're talking about."

A long pause. "You haven't seen the morning paper?"

"I'm still in bed."

Another pause. "You didn't notify the Feds?"

"Of course not."

"Real curious, then. You better look at the paper. And remember, buddy boy, I had nothing to do with the stuff from the Bureau."

I said, "Okay, Burt."

Burt's voice softened. "Someone big is pulling the strings on this one. You go along quietly, Charlie, you hear what I'm saying? None of the Boy Scout shit."

"Heard Masonis's house burned down last night."

"Prelim word is it was an accident."

"C'mon, Burt!"

"Dammit, Charlie. Listen to me for once and just back the hell off."

I was about to reply when I realized Burt had hung up.

I tracked Pinock down at his office. There was a sense of urgency in his voice, and something else. Not fear exactly, but . . .

"So when can you get here?" he asked.

"I'm not sure. I've got an appointment later this morning. Are you finished with your investigation into Dynatech?"

"Yes."

"You found something?"

Hesitation. "Yes."

"Traced the ownership?"

"Look, I'm in a staff meeting. I'll be in all day. Get here when you can."

★★★★

When I came downstairs, I heard Jean pulling her Prelude out of the driveway, heading for her aerobics class at the YWCA. The two newspapers were lying on the mat just inside the front door, unopened as usual.

I picked them up, went to the kitchen, and poured myself a cup of coffee. On the refrigerator door, a cut-out picture of a car hung from a magnetic flower.

I smiled, noticing the make and model. Not a used Ford Probe, but a brand-new cherry-red Mazda Miata. Stacy had drawn a little smiley face above it.

Not a chance, honey.

I went into the living room, slumped on the couch, and opened up the *Washington Post* first.

The headline blared across the top: MASS MURDERER TAKES OWN LIFE AT VIRGINIA REST STOP.

I set my cup down. The article was accompanied by a photograph of Masonis. Just his face, much younger looking, with a buzz haircut. Military photo, I realized. I wondered how the *Post* had got the photo so quickly.

I read the article:

CAPTAIN TARRON PEARSON OF THE VIRGINIA BU-
REAU OF CRIMINAL INVESTIGATIONS AND SPECIAL AGENT-
IN-CHARGE (SAC) WILLIAM HENDERSON OF THE FBI
RELEASED A JOINT STATEMENT THAT MR. THEODORE
MASONIS, WELL-KNOWN AUTHOR AND VIETNAM SCHOLAR,
TOOK HIS OWN LIFE IN HIS CAR IN A REST AREA NORTH OF
QUANTICO LAST NIGHT. MR. MASONIS HAD BEEN SOUGHT
FOR QUESTIONING BY POLICE AND MILITARY INVESTIGATORS
REGARDING A NUMBER OF RECENT HOMICIDES IN WASH-
INGTON, D.C., AND VIRGINIA, THE MOST NOTABLE BEING
THE DEATH OF GENERAL RAYMOND WATKINS, THE AIR
FORCE CHIEF OF STAFF. SAC HENDERSON SAYS THEY
RECOVERED WHAT HE CALLED "CONCLUSIVE PROOF" FROM
MR. MASONIS'S VEHICLE TYING HIM TO THESE CRIMES.

THE MOTIVE WHICH DROVE MR. MASONIS TO KILL
WAS NOT MADE CLEAR, BUT SAC HENDERSON DID EMPHA-
SIZE THAT MR. MASONIS HAD BEEN A VIETNAM COMBAT
VETERAN AND HAD RECENTLY BEEN KNOWN TO DISPLAY
SIGNS OF IRRATIONALITY. ONLY YESTERDAY, ACCORDING
TO DR. ALPHONSE COLETTA OF THE ROLLING HILLS
SANITARIUM NEAR DANVILLE, VIRGINIA, MR. MASONIS
ATTEMPTED TO COMMIT HIMSELF INTO THE INSTITUTION.
DR. COLETTA SAID MASONIS, AT THE LAST MINUTE,

CHANGED HIS MIND AND LEFT. MASONIS WAS FOUND DEAD
FIVE HOURS LATER.

"I REGRET THAT AT THE TIME I WAS NOT AWARE THAT
MR. MASONIS WAS BEING SOUGHT BY THE POLICE, OR THE
EXTENT OF HIS MENTAL DISTRESS. LIKE SO MANY OTHER
VETERANS, MR. MASONIS IS ANOTHER CASUALTY OF THAT
SENSELESS WAR," DR. COLETTA SAID, IN A STATEMENT
RELEASED LATE LAST NIGHT BY SAC HENDERSON.

THE CHOICE OF VICTIMS SEEMS TO VALIDATE DR.
COLETTA'S CONCLUSION THAT THE CAUSE OF MR.
MASONIS'S KILLING SPREE WAS LINKED TO HIS VIETNAM EX-
PERIENCES. ALL THE VICTIMS, EXCEPT SOME BYSTANDERS
WHO DIED IN THE BOMBING OF A HOUSEBOAT, WERE VIET-
NAMESE NATIONALS OR WAR VETERANS. TWO, GENERAL
WATKINS AND COLONEL WARREN TIPPETT, FALL INTO
THE LATTER CATEGORY.

The article continued on the next page. I flipped to it and found what
Burt had been referring to about halfway through the column.

WHEN QUERIED WHY THE FBI HAD BECOME INVOLVED,
SAC HENDERSON REPORTED THAT LIEUTENANT COLO-
NEL CHARLES JENSEN, WHO HAD TAKEN OVER THE MIL-
ITARY'S INVESTIGATION UPON THE DEATH OF COLONEL
TIPPETT AND HAD GONE ON TELEVISION NAMING MASONIS
AS THE KEY SUSPECT, DETERMINED THAT THE FBI SHOULD
BE CALLED IN. THE REQUEST WAS APPROVED.

I set the paper down. I wasn't angry so much as disappointed and
frustrated. The request must have come out of General Holmes's office.
Probably under pressure from someone in the administration. I took the
use of my name as a message for me to go along. No doubt there was
a carefully crafted paper trail now linking me in the cover-up. Keep
digging, someone was saying, and I'd bury myself.

Smart bastards. They had to know that even if I ignored their threat and protested, I had little credibility. I had gone on TV and named Masonis.

All in all, everything had been accomplished very neatly. All options had been covered. Masonis had been tried and convicted, case closed. Even got this Dr. Coletta to go along, provide a motive. Cao Dinh's secret was safe, presidential reputations preserved, Vietnamese recognition and the billions tied to it protected.

Power was an amazing instrument to behold.

I skimmed through the *Washington Times* write-up. Both stories were virtually identical except for one item of interest. The *Times* write-up mentioned that Dr. Coletta also had a practice in D.C.

I tossed the paper on the coffee table and was about to rise, when I spotted an article on the bottom of the front page. It was headlined DRAFT-GENERAL-HOLMES-FOR-PRESIDENT RALLY TO-DAY.

The short blurb explained that a group of prominent national figures were sponsoring a rally in front of the Vietnam Memorial that morning to encourage General Holmes to enter the presidential race. *Like they'd have to try very hard,* I thought.

I went upstairs and took a hot shower, then dressed quickly, dashed off a note to Jean, and was out of the house by eight. My meeting with General Tupper wasn't until nine-thirty. Which meant I had time to fulfill my obligation.

As I eased out of the garage, I noticed a forest-green sedan half a block away. I'd never seen the car in the neighborhood before, and it was parked in front of the Merkles' house. The Merkles had gone to Hawaii the week before.

I drove past the car. Two men were visible. They wore suits. They pulled in behind me, staying right on my tail. Another message. *We want you to know we're watching to see if you're going to go along,* they were saying.

I was going to need help.

I picked up the cellular and called Jonesy. I caught him en route to the Pentagon. Lee was still in bed. Both calls took less than five minutes. I settled back and drove to Mrs. Dorothy Tippett's, the sedan on my butt.

39

TIPPETT HAD GIVEN DOROTHY THE HOUSE, A WELL-KEPT TWO-STORY IN A QUIET SUBDIVISION IN NORTH SPRINGFIELD. I'D CALLED AHEAD, so Dorothy was expecting me. As I parked in the driveway, the green car drove by, U-turned, and parked against the curb opposite me. They couldn't have been more obvious. I resisted the urge to wave.

Dorothy met me at the door in a simple black dress, eyes puffy, her delicate features drawn. She seemed to have aged five years since I'd seen her a month before. She swept a few strands of her long black hair from her face and gave me a trembling smile. "Oh, Charlie." Dorothy reached up and gave me a hug. I held her, felt her petite frame shiver.

"I'm sorry, Dorothy," I said, stepping away.

"Come in, Charlie."

I continued to hold her hand as she led me into the living room.

"Jean's been such a dear. And Stacy and Tony. The girls have been so upset. And no one will tell us about Tip. If they've found him."

I coughed. I was looking at the man sitting on the couch. A sheaf of papers lay before him on the coffee table. He rose.

"Oh," Dorothy said. "My manners. Rupert, this is Jean's husband, Charlie."

Rupert didn't look like an accountant. Deeply tanned, he had the stocky, heavy build of a running back, a full head of wavy dark hair, and a broad, confident face. He gave me a relaxed grin as we shook. His grip was firm.

"Jean's been a jewel to Dorothy," Rupert said. "We really appreciate it."

I looked fondly at Dorothy. "She's like family, and we love her."

"I do too," Rupert said. He didn't say it defensively, but rather as a statement of fact.

I asked, "How are Abbie and Laurie?"

"As well as can be expected," Dorothy said. "I sent them to school. They didn't want to go, but just sitting . . . Maybe if they stay busy." She dropped my hand. "I really am being a poor hostess. Coffee, Charlie? Maybe a roll?"

I shook my head. "Thanks, but no. I've got a meeting in a few minutes. I just stopped by. . . ." Dorothy tensed as if she could sense what I was about to say. I reached out, taking her hands in mine. "They haven't found his body. I'm sorry." I felt a little guilty, not mentioning the leg. But I didn't think she could handle it, and I didn't want to give her false hope.

Dorothy nodded.

"The explosion?" Rupert said. "Any chance of recovery?"

"Possibly, but . . . I don't think so." I gave Dorothy's hand a squeeze. Rupert came and put a big arm around her. He looked at her with obvious affection.

"The burial," Dorothy said to me. "I . . . we have to have something."

Rupert and I looked at each other. Neither of us spoke. Then Rupert growled, "Well, at least the killer's dead. That's something."

"Yes," I said.

"He was a good man, Charlie," Dorothy said.

"Yes," I said again.

She wiped a tear. "You'll have to excuse me, Charlie."

Rupert and I watched her leave.

"She needs time." I looked at Rupert. "I hope you'll give that to her."

"Absolutely," he said. "I love her, but I know they'd been married a long time. Besides, I kind of wish I'd known him." He must have noticed my surprise, because he added, "Any guy who takes care of his family is okay in my book."

I frowned. "Dorothy will get half his retirement."

But Rupert was shaking his head. "Not that. Look at this."

I followed him to the coffee table. Rupert picked up a stapled sheaf of papers.

"The insurance policy," Rupert said. "For the girls. Dorothy had no idea." He handed the policy to me. "The agent, Mr. Abrams, came over last night. Gave Dorothy and the girls quite a shock. He said once his company receives a death verification from the authorities, he'll make the payment."

I flipped and began skimming.

"You didn't know either, huh? Dorothy thought he might have told you."

I shook my head. Then I saw the figures.

"Yes, sir. Okay in my book. Girls will never have to worry. College, their future. Solves a lot of problems. A million each for the girls. Yes, sir. The man was okay in my book."

★★★★

When I left, the sedan was still there across the street. What the hell. I waved.

No response.

During the drive to the Pentagon, I thought about what Tippett had done.

I wasn't surprised. In his way, Tippett had loved the girls very much.

The sedan followed me to the Pentagon. But no one followed me when I climbed out and started up the walkway. Maybe they didn't need to because they knew I was going to see Tupper. Maybe they had someone inside to trail me around.

Or just maybe they wanted to avoid the mob of reporters and TV types clustered around the entrance, jostling for position with a phalanx of dark-suited security men.

What the hell was going on? At first I thought maybe they were expecting the President or Vice President, or some visiting foreign dignitary. Then I gazed out at the line of limos coming up the drive. The one in front had a placard above the bumper.

I counted the stars. Four. Then Holmes came through the glass doors, leading a large entourage down the steps. The security men fanned out, clearing the way. Reporters began shouting, their questions tumbling over one another.

"General Holmes, is it true you are going to announce your candidacy!"

"General, have you decided on a running mate!"

"General, are you running as a Republican or a Democrat!"

Holmes smiled and waved as he made his way down the walk, occasionally calling out, "No comment." The reporters continued to shout as they scurried to keep up. I stepped back off the sidewalk onto the grass as Holmes approached. His face beamed as he scanned the crowd.

He was maybe six feet away when his eyes stopped on me. For an instant he paused, the smile freezing. A moment later, the smile thawed, and he continued past.

Approaching the limo, Holmes leaned over to an aide and murmured something. Then he turned, majestically waved to the crowd held back by the security men, and climbed into the backseat. Most of the reporters bolted to their cars. Doors slammed as Holmes's entourage climbed into their limos. The aide was making a call on a cellular phone. I shook my head and started up the now-vacated walkway. After maybe a dozen steps, I felt a hand on my shoulder.

"Colonel Jensen?"

I turned. The taller of two men dropped his hand from my shoulder, while his heavyset partner slipped a phone into his jacket. I recognized them as the pair who had been following me.

"You better hope I am, or you boys have been following the wrong man."

The tall man's jaw tightened. Heavyset glared. "The general would like a word," the tall man growled.

I hesitated. I was tempted to tell him to go to hell. But one didn't argue with an order from Holmes.

I nodded, and followed them to the limo.

★★★★

The darkened rear window whirred softly down. I glanced back down the line of gleaming black cars. A few news hounds in the parking lot were giving me curious looks. *Must be damned important to hold up the train,* I thought.

Holmes's regal mane appeared and nodded to the two men. They stepped away. Holmes stared at me for a few seconds, contempt in his eyes.

"Are you in the habit of disobeying orders, Colonel?" he snapped. He kept his voice low, almost as if he were afraid someone would overhear.

"No, sir."

"I thought I ordered you off the case."

I swallowed hard. "Yes, sir."

"Do you deny you've been continuing your investigation?"

"No, sir. But I was ordered by General Tupper to—"

"Behind my back!" Holmes snarled. "God help me, Colonel, you've already shown yourself to be incompetent. Count yourself fortunate I don't bring you up on charges. You are damn lucky the killer was found." He paused, his face suddenly relaxing. "You understand, I'm giving you a break, Jensen."

I nodded dumbly. If I was crazy, I could have argued there were still too many unanswered questions. But crazy I'm not.

A voice from inside the car called out, "General, we need to get going."

Holmes nodded. He looked up at me. "I don't think we'll be talking again, do you, Jensen?" His voice was casual, almost friendly.

I shook my head.

The window whirred.

Nuts, I thought as I watched the convoy slowly drive away.

As I headed up the walkway, I noticed that the two men tailing me had vanished. Then a lanky reporter with a goatee ran over. "Say, aren't you Colonel Jensen, the guy investigating—"

"No comment," I snapped.

As I stepped inside the glass doors, I recalled that Holmes hadn't batted an eye when I mentioned I'd gotten permission from General Tupper, which meant he already knew.

40

FIVE MINUTES! THEY'D BETTER BE UP HERE IN FIVE MINUTES!" THE HAGGARD-LOOKING FEMALE LIEUTENANT COLONEL IN GENERAL TUP-per's anteroom said into the phone. "Ten more boxes and a dolly. Ten. Big ones." She hung up and rubbed her forehead, noticing me for the the first time.

I stepped forward, holding out my badge. "Lieutenant Colonel Jensen, OSI—"

Her phone rang. She picked up. "No, it has to be the big ones. I don't care. Get some." She banged the phone down, then glanced at me, shaking her head. "Unbelievable. I don't think they understand English. And we have to have everything in place by tomorrow. Can you believe it? By 0800. And we just got the word an hour ago."

I nodded sympathetically. In a corner, two sergeants were removing folders from file cabinets and stuffing them into boxes. A civilian female pulled pictures off a wall, stacking them on a desk. Another girl placed them in a big box. A colonel was typing away furiously on a computer, swearing under his breath.

I said, "I have a zero-nine-thirty—"

But the lieutenant colonel looked past me, shouting, "No, Madge, all the shuttle pictures first. Take them over right away so they can be put up, ASAP. The general's an astronaut, for heaven's sakes." She sighed wearily, returning back to me.

"Lieutenant Colonel Jensen, the nine-thirty, right? Just a moment." She scooted down a hallway.

Madge began pulling pictures back out of a box, muttering, "You'd think they'd send some extra bodies to help. He is the Chief of Staff."

"What?" I said. "What did you say?"

Madge glanced at me.

"General Tupper is the new Air Force chief?" I asked.

"You don't know, sir?" Madge said. "General Holmes made the announcement last night. General Tupper is the new Air Force Chief of Staff. Pretty neat, huh? We're all very excited."

"Come on back, Colonel Jensen," the lieutenant colonel called out a moment later. She gave me a little wave from the hallway.

When I walked toward her, I felt a little sick.

★★★★

She ushered me inside and quietly closed the door behind me. General Tupper stood by his desk, hands folded, watching the television. Against a backdrop of the Vietnam Memorial with a podium in front, a commentator was saying something about an upcoming announcement. I'd already guessed that's where Holmes had been headed. The rally to draft him for President. General Tupper pointed me to a chair and killed the sound with a remote.

As I sat, I noticed cardboard boxes scattered around the room, partially filled with plaques and mementos that had obviously been removed from the walls.

Tupper forced a smile and looked around the room. "As you can see, I'm in the process of moving, Colonel." He went to the chair behind his desk. He seemed to be operating at half-speed, as if stalling.

I coughed. "Congratulations on your new appointment, sir."

A plastic smile. "Thank you, Colonel."

"The appointment's rather sudden, isn't it, sir?"

Tupper just looked at me. He leaned over and plucked a folder off the corner of his desk. "Have you seen the copy of the FBI's report into General Watkins's murder, Colonel?"

"I didn't know the FBI was officially investigating, sir." I paused. "Until I read this morning's paper."

"Yes. Well. The evidence is quite overwhelming against Mr. Masonis, isn't it? But then, you are aware of that, aren't you, Colonel?"

I nodded.

He opened the folder. "The knife, bomb paraphernalia . . ."

"I know, sir. I was there."

Tupper shut the folder and tossed it on the desk. "Director Farnsworth advises me the FBI is closing the case."

I said nothing.

"And that the local authorities are doing likewise." Tupper sat forward. "I've advised the Director that the Air Force is also terminating our interest in the matter." He gave me a knowing look.

I kept my face blank, which wasn't hard. After my conversation with Holmes, Tupper's announcement wasn't a surprise.

He slid the folder across the desk. "I'll expect your report on my desk by tomorrow, corroborating the FBI's findings."

My jaw tightened as I glanced down at the report. I made no move to pick it up. Forcing myself to stay calm, I said, "Concerning our discussion, earlier, General. Cao Dinh, the dead POWs?"

"It's over, Colonel."

"There's a chance Masonis didn't do it, sir."

"Goddammit. Don't be a fool, Jensen."

"Someone burned down Masonis's house last night."

Tupper jabbed angrily at the report. "A gas leak!"

"Then consider the men. We abandoned those poor bastards twenty years ago."

"Shut up, Jensen!" Tupper roared. He glared at me for a few seconds, then his face softened. "Look, the deaths are regrettable. Believe me, I'd like to know the truth. But I'm pragmatic enough to know there are things better left unanswered. I've been made aware of certain, uh, information since our discussion yesterday. Any further investigation could cause . . ." He swallowed, searching for just the right word. "Could cause irreparable damage to the country and the military. I want your report tomorrow, along with a recommendation to terminate the investigation. Do you understand?"

I sagged back in my chair. I don't know what I was thinking. Tupper hadn't gotten four stars without being a politician. "Sir, you don't need my report."

"I'm giving you an order, Colonel. You're the investigating officer of record. I want a report on my desk tomorrow by COB."

C-O-B stood for "close of business." I slowly reached over and picked up the report. "Is there anything else, sir?"

Tupper looked me in the eye. "I'm going to be running the Air Force for the next two years, Colonel."

I said nothing.

"I thought you might like to know I looked at your record, Jensen. It's excellent. There's a chance you could get promoted below-the-zone to full colonel on the next board. . . ." He sat back, hands folded, waiting.

It was a not-so-subtle bribe. I wondered if Holmes was behind it. Keep your mouth shut, Jensen, and get your silver eagles. I nodded, not trusting myself to reply. My eyes went to the TV. I sucked in a breath.

"Worth thinking about, Jensen. Hey, looks like it's about to start."

The screen showed General Holmes climbing out of his limo. He slowly made his way to the podium, waving, smiling, resplendent in his uniform. The camera zoomed back. A large crowd, obviously cheering, banners waving. The picture changed to a close-up of a young woman, her face glowing and worshipful, holding an infant. As I read the button on her lapel, General Tupper explained, "He's announcing his resignation as the Chairman of the Joint Chiefs, effective at the end of this week."

"That soon?"

Tupper nodded. "Son of a bitch finally decided he's going to run for president. Now, where is that remote?"

I shook my head. Holmes certainly wasn't wasting any time. I turned to leave, then stopped.

"General?"

"What is it now, Colonel?" Tupper said irritably. He had the remote in his hand.

"You were wrong, sir," I said quietly. "Four-stars can get promoted."

As I walked out, Holmes's voice boomed out from the TV.

★★★★

In the anteroom outside, the bustle continued, but someone had turned on a television. People were watching as they packed and sorted. I stayed and listened to the speech. General Holmes had the gift of oratory. The speech was stirring, a skillful mixture of patriotism, compassion, and promise, reinforcing a number of populist and popular themes. Less government, less taxes, more police, more jobs. The list seemed endless.

The Medal of Honor on his chest was like a beacon, proclaiming Holmes's courage and valor, and ringing up votes. Upon closing, Holmes stood, arms outstretched, basking in the cheers of the crowd.

A helluva speech. I knew I was looking at the next President of the United States.

Afterward, the commentator appeared with a well-known political pundit. The pundit spoke of the general's recent approval rating. "Almost eighty percent, Tim. Unbelievable. They ought to call the election now and swear him in."

"Seems that way, Jake. We all knew he was going to run, but the suddenness of the announcement has me curious. A tactical maneuver?"

"A political blitzkrieg, Tim. An announcement wasn't expected for a couple of months, when General Holmes's term as the Chairman of the Joint Chiefs ended. But as a military man, the general knows the value of shock and surprise. And this rally was the perfect setting. Surrounded by supporters, with the Vietnam Memorial as a backdrop. Wouldn't surprise me if this was Holmes's plan all along. The other candidates must be reeling, trying to come up with a strategy to combat Holmes's entrance into the race."

"Say, Jake," the commentator said, "how about verifying a rumor that Holmes plans on spending fifty million dollars from his personal fortune on his campaign?"

"Wouldn't doubt it. But something tells me he's not gonna need it."

"Not much doubt who you think is going to win, " the commentator said. "Now I think Marsha has the Holmes campaign chairman, Roger Walsh, standing by. Marsha . . ."

The screen changed to a pretty woman standing with a surprisingly young man who was grinning from ear to ear. I recognized him as the man who'd engineered the current President's successful campaign. Obviously, loyalty wasn't one of Roger Walsh's more enduring traits. But Holmes had about half a billion dollars more than the President.

I felt very tired. I glanced over at the lieutenant colonel who had just returned to her desk. "I'm curious. About the announcement for President. When did you find out?"

"This morning. But I think General Tupper received a call last night."

"Who's going to be General Holmes's replacement as Chairman of the Joint Chiefs?" I asked no one in particular.

"Admiral Williams," the colonel answered.

Holmes's pawn. No surprise there. I nodded, looking at the TV. The camera panned over the crowd, but I wasn't looking at the people.

I saw only the black granite wall in the background. I thought of the twenty-three names carved in that black stone.

I walked out before I said something I would regret.

★★★★

I figured I had until 1700 hours tomorrow afternoon until I was relieved. Maybe thirty hours, if I didn't sleep.

I stopped at a pay phone on the lower Pentagon concourse, across from the escalators leading down to the Metro. I watched the pedestrians stroll by, ignoring those in uniform. Anyone following me probably would be wearing civilian clothes. But there were still too many people, and none appeared to be paying me particular interest.

I found Dr. Alphonse Coletta in the D.C. white pages. His secretary said he was in but would be booked all day with patients. Perhaps next week. I told her I was a Washington, D.C., homicide detective, and just needed to ask a few questions. I gave her Lee's name, figuring a local cop had more weight. She put me on hold.

"The doctor can give you a few minutes around eleven," she said when she came back.

I checked my watch. *Less than an hour from now.* I'd have to go there first.

I reached Lee at his precinct, where he was waiting for my call. A familiar face walked by but didn't even glance in my direction.

A minute later I stepped on the down escalator.

★★★★

At the Metro fare-card machine, I took my time, contemplating what amount to purchase, fumbling for change. After retrieving my card, I studied the Metro system map. But I didn't look around. At the rumble of the approaching blue line, I headed for the turnstiles.

As usual, the midmorning crowd was sparse, maybe thirty people, about half in uniform. The turnstile sucked in my ticket and I passed through. The Metro train appeared, slowed. I paused, unsure. The bells chimed. Last call.

I darted for a door.

I heard the sound of a commotion behind me. Voices, loud, jumbled.

"Hey! Mister! My wallet. You took my wallet. Hey!"

"Let me go. I didn't! Dammit! Let me go!"

"Hold it! Police! Coming through!"

"You're crazy! Get your hands off me. You don't know what you're doing. I didn't take your wallet."

I stepped inside the almost-empty car.

The doors hissed closed. I took a seat. A Navy commander a seat over said, "Wonder what's going on?"

A woman murmured, "Something about a wallet."

"Guy sure looks upset," the commander said.

"Doesn't look like a thief," the woman said. "Dresses too nice."

"Never know," the commander said.

The subway began to move.

I turned and looked. A blond man and a black man were holding on to a well-dressed man who seemed to be screaming at them. As we pulled away, the well-dressed man spun around. He seemed to look right at me.

I settled back and closed my eyes.

41

McPHERSON SQUARE WAS THE FIFTH STOP. I WALKED OUT INTO THE NOISE, THE LIGHT, THE HEAT, AND THE SMOG. I TURNED NORTH. After a block, someone honked. "Charlie! Hey, Charlie!" A car pulled alongside and stopped.

I went over and climbed into the passenger seat.

"No one followed?" Lee asked.

"One. Webster and Jonesy managed to distract him until I got away." I smiled. "By now I'm sure he is quite busy explaining to his superiors how he lost me."

"FBI?"

"I'm certain."

"Good. Hate those cologne-wearing prima donnas." Lee looked over his shoulder, then cut in front of a cab. A horn blew. Lee flipped the cabbie off. He reached into his jacket, removed a notepad, and handed it to me. "Address and number you want are on the last page."

I copied it.

"You called it, Charlie. My captain showed as I was leaving. I tell him I want to keep the case open for a while. Give him the usual spiel about needing to tie up a few loose ends. Mentioned the fire at Masonis's place." Lee shook his head, making a face. "Bad idea. Fitch jerks me into the office, slams the door, and reads me the riot act. Makes it very clear that if I don't want my ass humping the midnight-to-eight beat, I'll close the case ASAP. Man, he was really hopping mad, which is strange. Captain Fitch is usually cool."

"Did he say who's pushing him?"

"Hell, no, and I wasn't about to ask. Just got my ass out of there."

"No matter. He probably doesn't know."

The cabbie suddenly darted by, his horn blaring. Lee ignored him.

"If we keep asking questions, it's gonna come back at us."

"I know."

"We could be screwing ourselves."

"Yes." I shifted so I could face him. "Harry?"

"What?"

"You can always bow out."

Lee shrugged. "Could, I suppose. Except for one slight problem."

"Which is?"

"I'm Korean." He saw I didn't understand. "You know, the obligation thing with Colonel Tippett. Just my luck the guy picks my ass to save. Remember, I could have been on that boat."

I shook my head. There was a lot more to Lee than his cavalier image.

★★★★

We pulled into a parking lot in front of a large two-story pink and yellow stucco building. Anywhere else in the city, the avant-garde decor would have stood out. Not here. Dupont Circle was known as a haven for free spirits, sixties holdovers, and homosexuals. A placard by the entrance's square pillar read "Dupont Circle Psychiatric Center." Dr. Coletta's name was listed along with a half-dozen others.

As we walked inside the frosted-glass doors, Lee grunted, "Kinda expect Don Johnson to come storming in after a drug dealer."

We passed through a plant-filled lobby with pale-pink walls decorated with seascapes.

"Damn, this is ugly," Lee said.

"Pink is supposed to be soothing," I said. "Office should be down the hallway ahead."

★★★★

"Hold it." The receptionist, an Amazonian brunette with a pageboy haircut, rose from behind her desk, peering at us through wire-rimmed glasses. "Hold it right there."

We stopped in the middle of a plush and surprisingly subdued waiting room. No Art Deco here, just dark paneling, thick navy-blue carpeting, and fine furnishings. A heavy mahogany door inscribed in gold with Dr. Coletta's name stood off to the left.

The receptionist demanded, "You reporters? If you are, I'm calling security."

"Take it easy, miss," Lee said, reaching for his wallet. "We're the police."

"We called earlier," I said.

The receptionist relaxed. "Oh, sure. Lieutenant Lee." She stared at his badge and ID as if she knew what she was looking at, then gave him a bright smile. She barely glanced at my badge. "Sorry about that, Lieutenant. But if you knew the calls we've been getting . . . and a couple of reporters came over earlier. I had to practically throw them out. All that business with that killer. Did he really kill all those people?"

"So they say. How much longer?"

"Oh, just a few minutes. Have a seat." She gave Lee a dazzling smile. As she went back to her desk, she said, "I can tell you Doctor Coletta feels terrible. I think he feels like he should have stopped that guy from killing." She picked up a folder and went to one of three polished-wood file cabinets.

"The doctor treats a lot of Vietnam vets," she said, returning to her desk. "They're kind of a specialty with Dr. Coletta. There's quite a few up on the hill."

"The hill?" I asked

She smiled. "Rolling Hills."

"Is Rolling Hills affiliated with veterans' hospitals, then?"

"Oh, no. Strictly private." She turned back to Lee. "Aren't you kind of young to be a lieutenant?"

"Uh, not really." Lee shifted in the chair.

"My name's Jenny. Jenny McGerry."

"Uh, mine's Harry," Lee said.

When the office door opened, Lee almost jumped to his feet.

★★★★

Dr. Alphonse Coletta looked like a psychiatrist. Fifty, graying, with a thin, intelligent face and a goatee. All he needed was glasses. He walked by, talking softly to a timid little man in a thousand-dollar suit. Then he stopped, eyeing us with a frown.

"Doctor," Jenny said. "This is Lieutenant Lee and . . ." She gave me a blank look.

"Lieutenant Colonel Jensen," I said. "Air Force Office of Special Investigation."

A thin smile. "You're the military investigator mentioned in the paper."

I nodded.

To the timid man, Coletta said, "Next week, Mr. Steen."

Mr. Steen smiled, bobbed his head, and hurried out.

"This will have to be quick, gentlemen," the doctor said.

He led us into the office.

★★★★

Coletta had a couch, but we sat on chairs in front of a desk the size of a pool table.

"I told everything to the FBI," he said. "I'm not sure there is anything more to discuss. Why are you here? I thought the case was closed."

"Just a few routine questions to wrap things up, Doctor." Lee had his notepad out. "Yesterday afternoon, a Nurse Jacobs called my precinct and told us about Mr. Masonis."

A nod. "Sally."

288 Patrick A. Davis

"She said Masonis had sought an interview with one of your patients, a Mr. Hanson. But in the paper you mentioned Masonis wanted to commit himself."

"Ah, I see the source of your confusion." Coletta sat back, stroking his goatee. "I must apologize. Had I known Sally's exact words, I would have had her call you back and clear up the misunderstanding. In her excitement upon seeing the television report, Sally confused Mr. Masonis with another individual who arrived at approximately the same time. Quite understandable under the circumstances."

I leaned forward. "Doctor, are you saying Mr. Masonis never wanted to see Mr. Hanson?"

"Correct." He smiled through perfect teeth.

"So, Doctor," Lee said, "who, then, was this other guy? The one Nurse Jacobs got confused with Masonis?"

Coletta flexed his hands outward. "One of our many patrons. A very wealthy and very noble man who personally funds much of the care of our patients. But a man who insists on discretion. A man who doesn't want his good deeds publicized."

"Uh-huh," Lee said dryly. "Say, Doc, do you know we have Nurse Jacobs's call on tape?"

"I would think you remiss if your department did not, Lieutenant."

"Then you should know Nurse Jacobs specifically says she turned Masonis away."

"It wasn't Mr. Masonis, Lieutenant." He said it easily, with a smile.

Lee's jaw clenched for a moment, then he let out a slow breath. "On the tape, Doctor, Nurse Jacobs says she turned a man she says is Masonis away from seeing Hanson because he had no authorization from Hanson's mother."

"Odd." Coletta tented his hands together, managing to look confused. "I'm not sure why Sally would say such a thing. Our patron was of course allowed to see Mr. Hanson, and a number of our other patients whom he supports." He shook his head. "Sally is young, excitable and does tend to get things muddled. But I was present when both our patron and Mr. Masonis arrived. I can assure you Mr. Masonis was deeply troubled. He inquired only about the services of our institution." He looked at us, his face open, sincere.

I knew he was lying, so did Lee, and Coletta knew we knew he was lying. But Coletta obviously knew we couldn't prove it. I could guess why, but I asked anyway.

"Doctor, perhaps if you could provide us with Nurse Jacobs's phone number and address." Coletta was shaking his head. "There's a problem?"

"I can give you the information," he said. "But it won't be much help. Sally requested a leave of absence. She caught a flight out this morning, I believe."

"Did she say why or where she was going?"

A head shake. "Umm, not that I recall, no."

"I'll bet," Lee muttered.

Coletta had a plastic smile fixed on his face and appeared not to hear. "When will she be back?" I asked.

"She didn't say." Coletta checked his watch. "Look, gentlemen, I went over all this with the FBI. Perhaps you should contact them. I do have other patients."

"Just a few more questions," I said.

"Now, I think I've been more than patient."

"Brady Hanson. What's wrong with him?"

Coletta gave me a long look. I thought he was going to avoid answering the question by claiming patient-doctor privilege. But instead he shrugged and said, "Severe cerebral lesions as a result of petechial hemorrhaging. The destruction is general, though the most severe lesions are in the frontal lobe. As a result, Mr. Hanson suffers from a number of chronic disorders, including amnetic syndrome and hallucinosis, with a marked reduction in general intellectual function."

"C'mon, Doc," Lee said sarcastically. "Spill it in English."

Coletta gave Lee a cold look. "In layman's terms, Lieutenant, Mr. Hanson suffered severe and prolonged head beatings which irreparably damaged his brain. You're probably familiar with the term 'punch-drunk' for boxers?"

"Yeah, sure. Like Muhammad Ali."

"This is an extreme case." He looked at his watch again.

"You said Hanson has amnetic syndrome," I said. "Is that like amnesia?"

An irritated sigh. "Yes, Colonel. It's typical in cases of severe cerebral pathology like Mr. Hanson's. He can only recall events prior to his injuries, or remember events in the present for a few minutes. Anything in between is gone."

I frowned. "So you're saying he can't recall anything from his beatings until now, but can recall stuff before—say, when he was a kid?"

"Correct."

"When did he receive his injuries? Do you know?"

"Apparently shortly after he was shot down. He was beaten terribly by the villagers and soldiers who found him. That's when his memory ends, so it's logical that is when the damage occurred."

Lee cleared his throat. "Just how long was Mr. Masonis actually at Rolling Hills?"

Coletta shrugged. "Not long. We talked for ten minutes or so. He arrived a few minutes before that." He rose. "Now, really, you must go."

We stood. Coletta stepped around quickly and opened the door.

I paused at the doorway. "Doctor?"

"What now?"

"I'm curious. If I understand you, then Mr. Hanson can't recall anything about his incarceration or his subsequent escape."

Coletta's hand automatically stroked his goatee. "Correct." Then he stepped quickly into the reception room.

As I followed, I wondered if the good doctor had just lied again.

★★★★

Lee unlocked the car. I leaned against the door, my finger tapping the roof, thinking about that long-ago movie of Holmes's escape. I was certain Hanson had not been portrayed as being mentally ill. Lee looked across the roof at me, noticing my frown.

"What's up, Charlie?"

"Tell me, Harry, if you were about to escape from a prison camp in the middle of Vietnam, would you go with a man with mental problems?"

He blinked. "Hell, no. That would be nuts. No pun intended."

"And we know General Holmes isn't crazy."

"Yeah. Must have had a reason, I suppose . . ." Lee shook his head. "Can't for the life of me see one, though."

I checked my watch. "Almost lunchtime."

"Okay."

I gave him a meaningful look. "Jenny is probably free."

"Now, hold on, Charlie."

"You notice the file cabinets behind Jenny's desk?"

"Yeah."

"Here's what I want you to do."

42

LEE DIDN'T LOOK TOO HAPPY WHEN HE CAME OUT A MINUTE LATER. FROM HIS EXPRESSION I KNEW JENNY HAD ACCEPTED.

"I'll meet you at Pinock's when I'm finished," he said. "But you're paying for lunch, Charlie."

"Fine."

"And the cab fare. And tips."

I readily agreed and drove away.

Pinock's office was in Fairfax. But the Watergate was a straight shot down New Hampshire Avenue, maybe ten minutes away. I called the number Lee had given me. A woman answered. I told her who I was. She seemed puzzled but said to come on over. Then I called Jonesy at Talia's. Talia answered.

"Colonel, I want your men out of my house," she began at once. "I'm tired. I need some time. I want them to leave. Now."

"Sure, Talia, but we need to check out your place for bugs—"

"Ted's dead, Colonel. It's over. The FBI says he killed himself. Maybe he really did. Who knows? All I know is I'm tired. And I want you and your men to leave me alone. Please."

"Okay, Talia. Put Jonesy on."

She yelled for Jonesy. "You will tell them to leave," she said to me.

Before I could reply, Jonesy picked up an extension. "Hello, sir."

A click as Talia hung up.

"What's with her, Jonesy?"

Jonesy hesitated.

"Can't talk?"

"No."

"Your car. Three minutes." I hung up.

★★★★

I stopped at a red light, punched in the number. Jonesy answered immediately.

"What's with her?"

"I'm not sure," Jonesy said. "She wasn't expecting us. Seemed pretty upset when we showed. Didn't want to let us in. Said we'll have to come back some other time. I threatened to call Colonel Jowers and she backed off. But she's acting funny . . . real agitated, nervous. Like she's hiding something."

"Hiding something?"

"Just a feeling. But she was out when we arrived. We waited for about ten minutes. You should have seen her face when she saw Webster and me get out of the car. Like we were the last things in the world she wanted to see. Driving over, I'd tried to call a couple times, let her know we were coming. No answer."

"Did she say where she was?"

"No, sir. But she received a phone call a few minutes after we arrived. Seemed to upset her."

"Did you hear who it was?"

"No. The call was brief. She said no a few times and hung up."

"Maybe she's just in shock over Masonis's death?"

"Not a chance." He said it matter-of-factly.

"You almost finished?"

"Few more minutes."

"And?"

"Nothing yet. And I'll bet a month's pay we won't find anything."

It wasn't the answer I hoped for. "No problems with the FBI guy this morning?"

"He was plenty mad. We'll hear about it. And, sir, I stopped by Air Force personnel at the Pentagon and picked up an RIP on Major Swanson."

His voice told me he'd found something. I pressed the phone to my ear.

"She's been General Watkins's aide for almost two years."

"We know that."

"But before. For eighteen months, she was also an aide for another four-star."

"Who?"

"General Holmes."

I sat back, listening to the hiss on the cellular. Talia and Holmes.

A connection where there shouldn't be one.

A horn blared behind me. The light had turned green.

★★★★

I went through the intersection in a daze. The phone hissed in my ear.

"Sir?"

"I'm here, Jonesy."

"General Holmes's name sure comes up a lot. . . ." He lapsed into a suggestive silence, then cleared his throat. "I finally ran down that nurse from Takli, the one Holmes was supposed to have had the affair with. Nothing. Her name was Gail Colson. She retired as a lieutenant colonel. Passed away a couple of years back from cancer. Married but no children."

I sighed. So that was a rumor after all. Not that it mattered anymore. Holmes and Talia. I shook my head.

"Did you get a list of Talia's cellular calls yet?"

"I'm supposed to stop by and pick it up."

"Get it. Then meet me at the Watergate." I gave him the apartment number. "Tell Webster to stay and keep Talia under surveillance. Does he have a camera?"

"I can give him mine, but . . ." He coughed. "About Webster. I'm not sure he's the man to—"

"He may want to fuck her, Jonesy. But he's still a big enough boy to handle a surveillance."

"But if she leaves. Single car. Midday traffic. She'll spot him for sure if he doesn't lose her first."

"Okay, okay. Have Webster stall in the apartment as long as he can. Call out Jurgens and Peters for backup. Tell them to keep it discreet on the tail. But tell them if they lose her, I'll have their asses. I'll want to talk to her later, and I want to know where she is."

"Give me forty-five minutes, sir." He hung up.

★★★★

I knew what the cellular call sheet was going to show. Coletta said Masonis had been at Rolling Hills for just a few minutes. So unless the killer just happened to be there, which was unlikely, there wasn't enough time for someone to have summoned the killer to come there, follow Masonis, and kill him during the trip home.

Unless maybe Coletta did it himself.

But the thought that Coletta would soil his manicured hands on a dirty little murder struck me as ludicrous. Besides, the killer had been a pro.

So if there were no listening devices in Talia's apartment . . .

I wondered if the person Talia had called the night before was the same one who killed Watkins . . . and Tippett.

What a waste, I thought bitterly. Beautiful, smart—Talia had it all. Why? Then I thought about Holmes. Talia had been his aide.

A picture began to form.

I took a right on Virginia, then made a quick left into the Watergate complex.

★★★★

I drove into the underground garage for the Watergate Hotel, showed the attendant my badge, and parked in a designated visitor's slot. Taking the stairs up a flight, I walked past ground-floor boutiques with expensive-sounding foreign names to the building next door.

As I rode the elevator up to the seventh-floor apartment, I thought about Talia's ambition and her love of expensive things. *I should have seen it sooner,* I told myself.

The apartment door was opened by a woman in her early forties wearing a lavender suit. She had the confident look of someone who's used to being in charge.

"I'm Colonel Jensen, looking for Ms. Hanson."

"I'm Ms. Hanson, Colonel."

I frowned. "But . . . ?"

She smiled. "You must be looking for my mother. I should have said something on the phone. She's not in, but please, come in. She should be back soon. We're supposed to meet for lunch."

I stepped into the largest, most elegant apartment I'd ever seen. I knew they went for well over a million dollars apiece. Ms. Hanson led me to an ash-white living room that commanded a view of the river and Theodore Roosevelt Island.

As I sat on a couch, she asked, "Something to drink?"

"No. I just have a few questions."

She folded her skirt around her legs and sat. Her features were a little too sharp to be called beautiful, but she was an attractive woman. Her face became serious. "You said this is about my brother. Does this have something to do with that man who tried to see him, that killer? My mother mentioned the police thought he might have been coming here."

I nodded. "He may have thought your brother knew something."

"Like what?"

"I'm not sure. I'm hoping you or your mother can help. I've been by to see Dr. Coletta . . ."

"That pompous quack." Her face turned ugly. "Don't believe a word that charlatan says."

"I thought he was one of the best in his field."

"That's his reputation, but don't believe it. I've been trying to convince my mother to remove Brady for years. But she's completely smitten by Dr. Coletta. She thinks Brady is getting the best care possible."

"And you don't?"

She gave me a grim smile. "How much time do you have, Colonel?"

I sat back, stretching my arms over the back of the couch. "All the time in the world."

She removed a cigarette from a silver case on the coffee table, offering me one, which I declined. She lit her own from a lighter shaped like an eagle. She took a deep drag, then waved her hand around the room. "How do you like this place?"

"Very nice."

"It's not mother's."

"No?"

"Neither are the furnishings."

"I see."

"Or the Mercedes my mother drives."

"Uh-huh."

"She also gets all her utilities paid, a generous monthly allowance, medical, dental, everything. Including care for Brady under the esteemed Dr. Coletta." She flicked an ash angrily into an ashtray. "Want to know why?"

I nodded.

"Because of General Holmes." She gave me a long look. "You must think I sound pretty ungrateful."

"You must have your reasons."

"Only one."

"Your brother?"

"My brother. They're destroying him at that place."

"Rolling Hills."

A nod. Another deep drag. "When Brady first went there, at the insistence of General Holmes—Major Holmes back then—mother and I were ecstatic. We thought Brady might have a real chance to get well. Then came General Holmes's offer to take care of my mother until she dies. Well, we were really appreciative. For the first few years, Brady's condition seemed to improve. Then, about fifteen years ago, he abruptly declined. Almost overnight. I began to ask questions. I mean, Brady used to be able to converse. Not well, but he could talk with some semblance of coherence, as well as dress and feed himself." She crushed the cigarette. "You should see him now. He can barely talk. He has trouble recognizing my mother and me. Before, he liked to go for walks, watch TV. Now he sits in a corner in a rocking chair and stares at the walls."

"You said the change happened overnight?"

"I saw him during Thanksgiving 1980. He was fine. I was attending Penn State at the time. When I came home for Christmas, he'd undergone a dramatic regression. I was shocked. Brady almost didn't recognize me."

"Maybe he just regressed because of his injuries, and Coletta could do nothing about it."

"That's what Dr. Coletta says. But ten years ago, I took Brady's medical records to a number of prominent psychiatrists. Most said there shouldn't be regression. That with therapy, he should be improving. They were puzzled. I tried to get Coletta to allow Brady to be examined by other doctors. You can imagine what happened. He contacted mother, said I obviously didn't trust his opinion. Then Holmes got into the act. He convinced mother I was overreacting. Mother thinks General Holmes is the next thing to a living saint. Without him, Brady would be dead in Vietnam. She worried that General Holmes would think her ungrateful, so she kept Brady in Dr. Coletta's care. She gets mad if I even bring the issue up."

I leaned forward. "Has your brother ever talked about his POW experience?"

She thought about that for a moment. "A lot of years ago. When he was coherent, he wouldn't remember anything. He has memory problems. But when he hallucinated, he said all sorts of crazy things. Dr. Coletta said they didn't mean anything."

"Like what? Please. If you can recall specifics."

She shivered. "Most you couldn't understand. Babbling nonsensically, or whimpering. But he had one hallucination that recurred." Her voice wavered. "He was being beaten. He'd scream out names. Vietnamese names. They must have been his guards or tormentors. It . . . it was horrible." She ran her hands over both shoulders.

"That's all?" I said gently. "He didn't say anything you really recognized. Maybe names of other prisoners?"

A tentative nod. "There was one time."

"Yes?"

She took a deep breath. "During one of those recurring hallucinations, Brady usually called out names or words I couldn't understand. But not this time." She closed her eyes. Her voice trembled. "He sounded like he was in such pain. Such . . . pain." Her eyes flickered open, settling on me. "He kept yelling one name, over and over. The only American name I ever heard him say."

"Whose name?"

"Holmes," she said. "He screamed Holmes."

43

SOMEWHERE IN THE APARTMENT A CLOCK CHIMED. THE HAND HOLDING MS. HANSON'S CIGARETTE VISIBLY SHOOK.

"When did this hallucination occur?"

"Fifteen years ago."

"You're certain your brother screamed out General Holmes's name?"

"Yes."

"And he did that only once?"

A nod. A long tendril of smoke climbed its way from her cigarette toward the ceiling.

I stared at her. "When exactly? The date, if you can remember?"

She tapped the cigarette on the ashtray, ridges deepening on her forehead. She looked up, surprised. "That Thanksgiving. In 1980. Yes, I'm sure."

"The time when your brother underwent his sudden regression?"

Another nod. "Such a shame. Brady had been doing so well."

"Did you tell anyone? Coletta? Holmes?"

She shook her head. "Not Holmes. But Dr. Coletta was there. He had Brady sedated immediately."

I sat back, my stomach tightening.

The doorbell rang.

★★★★

One look at Jonesy's face told me something was wrong. I thanked Ms. Hanson, gave her my number, and told her to call me if she thought of anything else important, or if her mother had anything to add. Her look told me her mother wouldn't be calling.

As Jonesy and I walked to the elevator, he said, "You better call the office, sir. Lieutenant Martel's been trying to reach you, and she sounds pretty upset."

I pushed the elevator button. "Why?"

He swallowed, looking uncomfortable. The elevator doors slid open. As we stepped inside, I said, "C'mon, Jonesy. Spit it out."

"Uh, maybe you should talk to Lieutenant Martel, sir."

I gave him a look of annoyance.

"You've been relieved as the P-Directorate commander, sir," he said softly.

★★★★

Lieutenant Linda Martel sounded as if she was about to cry when I called her from Jonesy's car in the parking garage, a couple of spots from where I'd parked Lee's car.

"General Tupper was really mad, sir. Yelling. Wanted to know what you were doing talking to a Dr. Coletta. Said to tell you that you will cease any further inquiries. Said . . . said to find you, tell you you're relieved."

"Take it easy, Linda. Relax, okay?" I could hear her take a few ragged breaths. "Better?"

"Sir, you better call the general. He was real mad, sir. Real mad."

"Thank you, Linda. If he calls again, you make sure and let him know you told me, okay? Now, if there's nothing else?"

"A message. From a Mrs. Moffitt. Wants you to call."

"General Watkins's secretary?"

"Yes, sir. She seemed pretty excited."

"I have the number. That it?"

"And your wife has been calling, sir. Says it's urgent. That's all."

I frowned. I wondered why Jean would call. "Thank you, Linda. You take care." I tried Jean first and got a busy signal. I hung up, then called Mrs. Moffitt at General Watkins's office. Colonel Jowers answered. Mrs. Moffitt was at lunch. I left a message. Then I tried Jean again. She answered on the second ring.

"What's up, honey?" I asked.

"Thank goodness! Charlie, what's going on? Are you in some kind of trouble?"

I hesitated. "Why?"

"General Tupper has called twice. Said you are to contact him immediately. He sounded very angry. Charlie, what did you do?"

"Jean, look, I can't really say. But I know what I'm doing. Don't worry, okay?"

"Charlie?"

"I can't talk now. Please. I've got to go. But try not to worry."

There was a long silence. "Then tell me who's in the van."

"Van? What van?"

"There's a van parked across the street. A few times, I've glimpsed someone through the window, but no one comes out. I think he's watching the house."

"Don't worry about them. They're looking for me."

"You *are* in trouble."

"No. Look, Jean, please. Everything will be fine. I love you."

"Take care of yourself, Charlie," she said softly.

I hung up, hating myself for causing Jean to worry. But there was nothing I could do about it now. "FBI is back at my house waiting to pick me up," I told Jonesy. Then I sat back and gazed out the window at the concrete wall of the garage.

Jonesy looked over in disbelief when he realized I wasn't going to pick up the phone again.

"You're not going to call General Tupper?"

"What's the point? He'll just order me to back off. Reprimand me. Or worse."

"Yes, sir, but . . ."

"I've been relieved, Jonesy."

Jonesy said nothing.

"I just didn't expect it quite so soon." I checked my watch. "Less than an hour."

"An hour?"

"For my visit to Coletta to reach Tupper and for the FBI to get back into the act." I gave him a grim smile. "I'd say Dr. Coletta is rather well connected. Now, you get that cellular phone list?"

A nod.

A car came down the parking ramp and squealed into a spot. A teen-aged kid with spiked hair and baggy jeans climbed out, glanced at us just sitting there in Jonesy's car. The kid shrugged and headed for the stairwell. "Talia called, didn't she?" I murmured.

Another nod.

"You have the number she called?"

"Another cellular." He indicated a folder on the backseat. I reached around and grabbed it. One page inside. Jonesy had underlined the call. Eight-forty the previous night. Within minutes of when Masonis had called Talia. Even though I'd known what was coming, I felt an overwhelming sense of disappointment.

"You ask your friend to check whose number Talia called?"

"She can't. Not a local cellular carrier."

"We'll have Lee run it." I removed the page, folded it, and stuck it in my jacket.

"Sure as hell wish I knew why she did it, sir."

I said nothing.

"Knowing her, it's either money or power."

"Or Holmes."

Jonesy sat back slowly. "I'm listening."

★★★★

After I had explained, Jonesy stared out the window for a full minute, saying nothing. Then he shook his head. "Sir, he's gonna be president."

"Maybe."

"You really think he had Coletta do something to this guy Hanson's head?"

I nodded. "Or maybe Coletta took it upon himself. At any rate, Coletta acted because Hanson was improving, getting better, regaining his memory. Remembered something about Holmes."

"But you said Hanson was hallucinating."

"Yes, but I'm betting there's some truth behind his hallucinations. Or maybe Coletta didn't want to take any chances. Probably he just did what Holmes told him to. At any rate, the bastard definitely did something. How else do you explain Hanson's dramatic regression shortly after the incident?" I felt myself getting angry. "Man, what a son of a bitch."

"What'd he do, sir? A lobotomy?"

I thought. "That's illegal. He wouldn't do something so obvious which could be detected in an examination. I'd guess drugs."

"So I guess interviewing Hanson will be a waste."

I nodded. "If it wasn't, Hanson would be long dead by now."

"But what could Hanson know, sir? I mean, they were both POWs. Holmes risked his life to bring him out. He's a hero."

I swore viciously.

Jonesy frowned. "Sir?"

I closed my eyes. The picture formed again. Fuzzy. An image, clearer. "Hero," I said suddenly, opening my eyes again.

"What?"

I spoke fast. "You said Holmes is a hero, right? But what if he wasn't? What if Holmes wasn't a goddamn hero?"

Jonesy looked at me as if I were crazy.

"What if Holmes was a collaborator? A traitor? Damn! If he was . . ." I punched the dash. "Son of a bitch. That's why he chose Hanson."

"Sir?"

"Hanson, Jonesy. That's the key." I grinned at him, my body trembling. It was like someone had flipped a flood lamp on in my head. "You follow?"

"I'm trying."

"Think. What was unique about Hanson? Made him different from the other prisoners."

"Well, he had no memory."

"Exactly. So when Holmes was released, he chose him. The one prisoner who couldn't say Holmes was a traitor because he couldn't fucking remember."

"Released? Are you saying the North Vietnamese let Holmes and Hanson go?"

"Had to be. The more I think about it, the more preposterous I find the notion that someone in Hanson's mental condition actually escaped successfully. You don't really think Holmes would have jeopardized his own safety by taking him on a real escape?"

A slow nod. "No, I guess not. But the idea that the North Vietnamese just let them go . . ." He paused. "Money?"

"Why not? Holmes is worth millions. The North Vietnamese must have known that. Remember what Birelli said. Someone dished out fifteen million bucks to the North Vietnamese. My guess is Holmes worked out a deal to have his family pay for his freedom. But there was a slight problem. Holmes can't be released outright. He'd really be crucified by the public, the press. Rich guy buys his way out while his poor buddies rot. And if he's been a collaborator to boot, Holmes has an even bigger problem. As soon as the other prisoners get released, Holmes knows he is going to be found out. Which means the end to his career, any future aspirations."

Jonesy's jaw clenched. "Sir, if you're right, that means . . ." He shook his head. "That murdering son of a bitch. So part of the deal is the rest of the POWs get taken out."

"Holmes can't have it any other way."

Jonesy looked disgusted.

"So the North Vietnamese arrange to allow Holmes to escape. Hanson goes along, probably to enhance Holmes's story, give him a little credibility. Holmes probably suggested it. Then makes up the story about carrying Hanson on his back to make himself look like a hero. It works. Holmes comes out smelling like a rose, gets the Medal of Honor, goes on to become one of the most admired soldiers in the country. His secret remains safe because the North Vietnamese make the Americans think we killed our boys, which keeps us from digging into what really happened."

Jonesy murmured, "Which is why the Feds, the White House, everyone is helping with the cover-up. Sweet. All these years, Holmes must have been laughing himself silly, knowing Uncle Sam was keeping his secret safe."

"Until General Watkins comes along. Watkins finds out about Holmes from Tho. Tells Masonis. They had to be killed."

"But someone had to tell Holmes what General Watkins and Masonis found out."

"Yes."

"If it wasn't Masonis . . ." He didn't say the obvious. He didn't need to.

We both knew Watkins told someone else, someone close to him, someone he trusted, someone he thought of as a daughter.

Talia.

I slumped back against the seat and took deep breaths in an effort to calm myself.

"Man, what a cold bitch." Jonesy looked angrier than I'd ever seen him.

I said nothing.

He looked at me. "Now what?"

Realistically, we still had nothing to make a case. Everything was innuendo, suggestion, anything concrete long destroyed. I shook my head. "I'm not sure. We've got no real proof."

"But we have Major Swanson."

"If she'll talk." I checked my watch. "C'mon. You follow me. Let's see if Pinock has something we can use first."

44

PINOCK FINANCIAL TOOK UP MOST OF THE SECOND FLOOR OF A FIVE-STORY OFFICE BUILDING IN FAIRFAX, JUST DOWN THE STREET FROM Fairfax City Hall. We passed through a maze of desks partially hidden behind modular partitions, where studious faces stared at rows of figures on glowing computer screens. Printers clicked incessantly in the background.

We stepped through a door marked "President," into a glass-enclosed reception room. Lee sat in a chair, reading a magazine on fishing. He looked up, started to say something, and noticed my serious expression.

Two secretaries sat at circular desks in the middle of the room. The older one clicked away at her keyboard, ignoring us. The younger one, a cute brunette, gave me a smile. I walked up. "Lieutenant Colonel Jensen. Is Mr. Pinock in?"

She practically leapt to her feet. "Yes, Colonel Jensen. Mr. Pinock was wondering when you'd arrive. He's quite anxious. I'll let him know you're here." She went toward the back, to a set of double doors, and knocked softly.

Lee rose, tossing the magazine on a table.

"What'd you find out?" I asked.

He lowered his voice. "Dr. Coletta keeps duplicate files of his patients in the office."

"You get a look at Hanson's?"

"Not there. But every other patient's file is."

"But Hanson's is missing?"

"Not missing. His file has never been kept with the others in the office."

"Dr. Coletta is a careful man."

"So it would seem. And one other thing. A body just washed up a couple of miles from the marina. A salesman from Albuquerque." He paused. "A leg was missing."

I sucked in a breath and nodded.

The door opened.

"You can go in, gentlemen," the secretary said.

★★★★

"We've met," Lee said, with a nod at Pinock.

I introduced Jonesy. We all shook, and took seats around an oval conference table in a corner of the large office.

Pinock was a short, intense-looking man in his sixties with a firm jaw and a firmer grip. From the mementos on display, he worshiped two things: golf and the Air Force. Trophies topped with silver golfers in midstroke filled two bookcases. Pictures of a younger Pinock in a flight suit standing next to a variety of fighter aircraft adorned the walls. A glass shadow-box displaying his medals and decorations on a background of blue felt sat on a pedestal in a corner.

Pinock opened up an inch-thick file, removed a computer sheet, and spread it on the table. I could see boxes and lines, arrayed similar to one of those corporate organizational diagrams.

"I finished last night," Pinock said. "Cost me a fortune in overtime. I had six people working full-time for three days. Now, I'm sure we missed some links. Probably a few subsidiaries we just don't have the ability to find. All we had to work with is what's in the public domain: corporate reports, filings with the FTC. But all in all, I think we've got a general idea of the setup."

I leaned forward to see the diagram better. There were about a dozen colored boxes, names printed inside each. Companies, I realized.

"Now, Six-Pack—uh, General Watkins—wanted to know about Dynatech Transports, which is here," Pinock said. He pointed to a box at the bottom, highlighted in yellow. "Now, I can give you the hundred-dollar brief, which will bore the hell out of you, or I can give you the nickel tour."

"The nickel tour will be fine," I said.

"Good. Otherwise I'd have to call in Julie Priestly to give it." He sat back, tapping a pen on the table, looking at me. "You know, Six-Pack wouldn't tell me why he wanted me to check out Dynatech Transports. I don't suppose you'd like to tell me why my people busted their ass?"

"I can't comment. Sorry."

"This have anything to do with Six-Pack's murder?"

"I really can't say."

Pinock stared at me. "Curious. Paper says you already have the killer and . . ."

"Just tying up some loose ends. Beyond that, I really can't comment."

Pinock shrugged and pointed to the computer sheet again. "Dynatech Transports is an international R and D company, specializing in the development of high-speed rail technology. At least, it's supposed to be."

Lee said, "Supposed to be?"

"Yes. But as far as I can tell, the company hasn't turned out anything in twenty-plus years of existence. Hasn't developed shit. Not one patent, not one prototype, nothing. All the company manages to do is spend money to the tune of about five million dollars a year, give or take."

I frowned. "How does it manage to stay solvent?"

"See those other companies on the chart there?" he said. "Each one annually contracts with Dynatech to perform R and D, paying up to a million dollars a pop for services rendered. All very legal and proper."

"For what kind of services?" I asked. "You said Dynatech hasn't produced anything."

"They haven't. Sounds crazy, I know. But to be honest, R and D production is essentially information. Hard to measure. All I can say is Bradley Reasor must have his reasons."

Jonesy said, "Bradley Reasor?"

Pinock nodded. "CEO of Global Petroleum." He leaned over and tapped the box at the top of the chart. "Like Dynatech, all these companies are subsidiaries of Global. Unlike Dynatech, they're moneymakers. That's why it doesn't make much sense. Bradley's tough, smart, so tight his ass squeaks when he walks. Don't see him just throwing money in a losing venture like Dynatech."

But I wasn't listening. Not since Pinock had said "petroleum." Which meant oil.

Pinock stopped talking. He was looking at me. "Something wrong, Colonel?"

My mouth felt dry. "Global Petroleum. Who owns it?"

"It's a public corporation."

"The principal stockholder, then."

"That would be Bradley Reasor's half brother," Pinock said. "General Holmes. You sure you're okay?"

I sat there, staring at Pinock, my heart pounding.

He frowned. "Say, is Holmes somehow involved?"

"You said Dynatech is an international company?"

"Yes, headquartered in New York and the Far East someplace. . . . I've got it here." He opened the file, flipped a few pages. "Here it is. Now, that is a damn strange place to do high-speed rail development. Hell, I've been there enough to know. They aren't close to having the infrastructure for a rail line that can support trains going fifty miles an hour, much less two hundred."

"And where is this?" I asked.

"Thailand. Bangkok, Thailand."

I edged forward in the chair. "When was the company formed?"

He glanced down. "Says here in 1971."

"And it's lost money every year?" Jonesy asked.

"From what we've got, yeah. By our calculations, losses exceed well over a hundred million dollars during that period."

Lee whistled softly.

Pinock shook his head. "Just don't understand how Global continues to allow Dynatech to stay in business. I must be mistaken. Dynatech has to be producing something. But damned if I know what." He shut the file and looked at me. "You sure you're okay?"

"I'm fine, just fine."

I gave him a smile to prove it.

★★★★

Pinock walked us to the door. Jonesy carried the file on Dynatech, which Pinock told us to keep.

"I really appreciate your help," I told Pinock.

"Just come by when you get things tied up. Like to know what the real story is. By the way, he was in my squadron during my first tour in 'Nam, you know. He flew like shit."

"Who?"

"Holmes. Hands like Hormel. A real prick to boot. If Six-Pack was checking him out, there had to be a reason." Then he gave me a meaningful look, opened the door, and stepped aside.

"Hands like Hormel," Lee murmured as we walked out.

"Ham hands," I explained.

"Oh? Hey, that's good."

★★★★

Jonesy and I waited in the anteroom while Lee placed a call using the younger secretary's phone.

It was difficult not to listen in. Lee spoke loudly, obviously engaged in an argument.

"Just run it, for pete's sakes, Wally. No. I swear. This is tied to the

Barnes homicide. Goddamn—" He stopped, realizing both secretaries were staring at him. He gave them a sheepish smile and lowered his voice. "Look, Wally, be a sport and run it. Then tell the captain I'm on the way back. But after, okay? This is hot. Thank you." He cupped the phone, rolling his eyes at Jonesy and me.

"A hundred million dollars," Jonesy said. "A lot of money."

"Yes," I said.

Lee hung up a few minutes later. His face told me he had news. I opened the door to the clatter of the main floor, and we walked out.

Lee fell into step beside me. "Captain Fitch is blowing a gasket. Seems he got a call that I'm still working the case. Wants my ass back ASAP so he can rip me a new one."

"But you checked out the number Talia called?"

"Yeah." He paused. "Corporate account."

I stopped so suddenly in the narrow aisleway, Jonesy bumped into me. "Dynatech Transports?"

"No. The other one. Global Petroleum." Then he grinned.

"I'll be damned," I said, and walked at a much faster pace.

★★★★

When we stepped from the elevator into the lobby, Jonesy had filled Lee in on what we had figured out.

Lee's face had darkened as he listened, his jaw muscles flexing into taut ropes.

We walked out into the brightness of the midday sun. The heat radiating off the asphalt parking lot felt like a sauna.

Jonesy finished explaining.

"Shit!" Lee said, letting out a slow, deep breath.

"I'd say that about sums it up," Jonesy said.

"No wonder we're getting all the pressure," Lee said. "And you guys think that's where the money is going? That Holmes is still paying North Vietnam millions each year? To buy silence?"

"Looks that way," Jonesy said.

"That murdering son of a bitch." Lee frowned. "You think we got enough for a case?"

"No," I said.

"Even with what Pinock gave us?"

"Never hold up in court. A company loses money, big deal. Same thing with the phone call. We can show Talia made it. We can show it went to Global Petroleum. But we can't prove what was actually said or even who she talked to."

"But we can confront her with the call, frighten her," Jonesy said. "And I don't think she can explain it. And she won't go down alone."

I didn't like it. We would be tipping our hand. Talia could deny the call had anything to do with Masonis. If she was smart, she would clam up, get a lawyer. . . .

I ran a hand over the back of my neck. But it wasn't as if we had any other options. I told Jonesy, "Let's go talk to Talia."

Jonesy smiled grimly.

"What's her address?" Lee asked.

"I thought you had to get back to the precinct," Jonesy said.

"Screw Captain Fitch. What's her address in case I lose you guys?" Lee copied the address. "That's less than fifteen minutes from here."

True, except for the detour we took because of Mrs. Moffitt's call.

45

I WAS JUST STRAPPING ON MY SEATBELT WHEN THE PHONE RANG.

AN ANXIOUS VOICE SAID, "HELLO? COLONEL JENSEN?"

"Mrs. Moffitt?"

"I just thought you should know about a call I took this morning. The office has been so hectic, with General Tupper moving in. I didn't think much of it at the time, but . . . then I began thinking it might be important when I realized it was the same day, you see."

"Mrs. Moffitt, I'm not sure I follow."

"The day the general died. The same day. Monday. That's why I'm telling you about the call."

"What call?"

"To pick up the order. Today. A Mr. Joseph Risser."

"And he is?"

"From Sunset Photography."

"I see."

"He said the pictures were ready."

My hand tightened on the phone. "Pictures. What pictures?"

"Why, the pictures the general dropped off on Monday. To get prints made."

But I wasn't really listening. I was thinking pictures, and I was remembering what Birelli had said.

"Tho says he has pictures, Charlie."

"Colonel? Colonel Jensen?" Mrs. Moffitt said.

Jonesy was about to pull out into the street. I cupped the phone. "Wait," I ordered him.

He shrugged, shifting to park.

"I'm still here, Mrs. Moffitt. An address?" I read it back, thanked her enthusiastically, and hung up.

Jonesy was looking at me with interest. "What's up, sir?"

I gave him a slow smile. "A break, I think."

I got out to tell Lee we had a change in plans.

★★★★

"Last name?" said the girl behind the counter. She had pretty green eyes. Her name tag said Trisha. I gave her Watkins's name and waited as she typed it into a computer.

We were in the film section of Sunset Photography, a large camera and video superstore. Through a glass partition, I could see rows of cameras and VCR camcorders. To my right, a makeshift studio, sample portraits covering a wall, a tall bearded man fretting over a young couple about to have their picture taken. Elevator music played softly in the background.

Trisha punched a button on the keyboard. Her eyebrows knitted. "Watkins, Raymond?"

I nodded.

She glanced back down. "And the film was dropped off here, sir?"

I dug out my notepad. "A Mr. Risser called."

She brightened. "Oh, that explains it. Mr. Watkins must have had a picture taken."

I frowned.

"Joe Risser runs our studio department." She nodded toward the bearded man. "That's him over there."

✯✯✯✯

"Something I can help you with, gentlemen?" Risser asked.

I told him about his call to Mrs. Moffitt.

He set his pen down and tossed an envelope into a tray. "Sure. I remember. I was sure surprised when she told me that the guy was the general who was killed. Never made the connection. Didn't even know he was a general. But when he came in here, he wasn't wearing a uniform or anything."

"Well, we'd like to pick up the pictures."

"Can't help you. They're gone."

I stared at him, incredulous. "Gone?"

"Picked up. Look, did one of you call earlier? Like I said before, I was only going to give you the pictures if you had a receipt."

"Someone called earlier?" Lee asked "Who?"

Joe let out a sigh of exasperation. "I dunno. A guy calls saying he's been told to pick up the pictures Watkins left here. I say okay, if he has a receipt. Guy says okay. Wants to know how many pictures we're talking about. How much is the bill? That sort of thing. I tell him. Then I say that the girl is coming out to pick them up anyway."

"Girl? What girl?"

"When I was told this guy, Watkins, was dead, I called the other name in the computer right away. I remember when Watkins came in, he was very specific that if I didn't reach him to call this lady. So I did."

My knees felt weak. "Her name?"

He thought. "Pretty thing . . . oh yeah." He grinned. "Talia."

"What time did she stop by?" Lee demanded viciously.

Joe looked flustered. "Uh . . . this morning. Maybe ten or so. Something wrong?"

"And you gave the pictures to her without a receipt?" Lee asked.

"She was on the work order. I checked her ID."

"What can you tell me about the pictures?" I asked.

But Joe was shaking his head. "The lady's name was on the ticket, okay? So if there's a problem—"

Lee plopped his badge on the counter. "Now, tell me about the pictures."

"Sure, Lieutenant." Joe ran a tongue over his lips. His hands went to the computer, began typing. "First, it was only one picture. I remember he had more, but most of them were pretty bad . . . cracked and faded."

"How many?"

"I don't know. Maybe a dozen."

"No negatives?" Lee said.

"No. That was the problem. Pictures were real old. Hard to make out. Told him they wouldn't photograph well, said maybe it'd be better if I scanned them into the computer so I could alter them, enhance the clarity. He shot that down quick." He stopped typing, eyes reading the screen. "Yeah, one original. Made him ten prints, five five-by-sevens and five eight-by-tens. And the negative."

"He say why he didn't want you to scan the pictures?" I asked.

Joe shook his head. "Nope. Just said he wanted it photographed only. No computer stuff."

"What were the pictures of?" Lee asked.

Joe ran a hand over his beard. "I really only remember the one I worked on. Pretty gruesome. Showed a guy holding a gun up to another guy's head, shooting him. And you could tell he was really shooting him because . . . well, of the stuff, you know, that was coming out of the head. Like I said. Gruesome." He swallowed nervously. "Makes sense now when I think about it. That Watkins was a general. He mentioned they were old pictures from the Vietnam War."

I asked, "The setting, background. What could you see?"

"Let's see, a jungle background. Guy who was shot was kneeling. Other guy was over him. Oh, and wearing ratty clothes, dark, like you always see people wearing in those Vietnam War flicks."

"Black pajamas?" I asked.

He nodded. "Yeah. Both of them. I remember thinking it looked funny, white guys wearing that stuff."

"Were there others in the picture?" Lee asked.

Joe looked confused. "No. Only two."

"Are you saying the shooter was a white man too?" I asked.

"Yeah, that's what I said."

Lee seemed surprised, but I wasn't.

"You have any copies of the picture?" I asked.

"Just made the ten."

"And you returned the negative you shot?"

"Yeah. Along with the original picture." He was shifting his eyes between Lee and me. "Look, I was just doing what the man told me."

"Take it easy, okay?" Lee said. "Now, you have the receipt showing Talia Swanson picked up the pictures?"

"Yeah, Lieutenant. Sure. I can make you a copy if you want."

"Please."

Joe reached below the counter.

As Lee and I were leaving the counter, I was thinking who the man could be who had called about the pictures. Did Mrs. Moffitt notify someone else? Then I spotted Jonesy in the camera section walking very fast in our direction, his eyes fixed on us. He began motioning.

"Now what?" Lee said.

★★★★

"Jurgens and Peters never arrived for the surveillance," Jonesy said. "Linda says General Tupper sent out a one-star to take over the P-Directorate. Guy's name is General Sanders. Sanders had Linda order everyone off the surveillance at Major Swanson's. She contacted Jurgens and Peters en route a few minutes ago."

I swore.

We continued toward the door.

Jonesy said, "General Sanders gets on the horn while I'm talking to Linda, reads me the riot act, says to get my ass back there." He paused. "You too, sir. Especially you."

I gritted my teeth hard. "That stupid, meddling son of a bitch. You mean no one is watching Talia?"

Jonesy pushed open the door and we walked through. "I'm not sure. Webster could be."

I stopped on the sidewalk. "What do you mean?"

Jonesy shrugged. "Linda says Webster checked in about an hour ago from the car. Says Major Swanson ordered him out of the apartment. Linda tried to contact him a couple of minutes ago to recall him, couldn't get a response. Not on the beeper or the phone." I caught an inference in his tone.

"You think he might have gone back inside Talia's apartment?"

"I'm not saying that, sir."

"He's not that stupid. Besides, he should still have answered his beeper."

Jonesy said nothing for a moment, then asked, "What about the pictures?"

"We'll have to ask Talia. Now, let's get going. We're wasting time. Let's hope to hell she's still there."

✯✯✯✯

We were only a few miles away from Talia's house, and this time we followed Lee and his flashing lights. I tried Webster's cellular and beeper. I gave him a minute to call back before trying his car phone again. There was no answer.

"Where the hell is he?" I asked.

Jonesy didn't bother to answer.

46

LOOKS LIKE MAJOR SWANSON'S STILL HERE," JONESY SAID AS HE SET THE PARKING BRAKE. "DON'T SEE WEBSTER, THOUGH."

We were parked next to Lee, in spaces across from Talia's gleaming red Lexus and a brown utility van with a ladder strapped to the roof.

"Where was he parked earlier?"

"Couple spaces to the left," Jonesy said. "But he would have moved it out of sight."

I ran my eyes over the almost-empty lot. No Webster.

We climbed out. Lee joined us in scanning the area. A convenience store and a fast-food restaurant at the corner, an apartment building directly across the street, a church next door . . .

"There." Jonesy was pointing to the church. I squinted against the bright sunlight. Maybe a dozen cars out front. Webster's tan sedan was in the shade of a large tree.

"Damn," I murmured. Even from that distance, I could see there was no one inside.

We crossed the street.

The car's front windows were open and both doors were unlocked. A paper sack sat on the passenger seat, sunglasses next to the bag. A soft-drink cup, still almost full, rested in a cup holder. Jonesy opened the passenger's door and picked up the sack. "Half-eaten burger." He looked at the cup. "Still got ice in it."

"Then he hasn't been gone long," I said. I was standing on the driver's side. I opened the door and saw Jonesy's camera, lying on the floorboard on the passenger side.

A sinking feeling tugged at my gut.

"Pretty stupid," Lee said behind me. "Leaving the car unlocked. Lucky the camera wasn't stolen."

Jonesy retrieved the camera. "Took two pictures," he said. "Used the zoom." He looked at me.

I swallowed, the sinking feeling growing.

"Two pictures?" I asked Jonesy.

A nod. He wrapped the strap around the camera and jammed it in his jacket pocket. "Looks like Captain Webster left in a hurry."

"Yes."

"He'd never have left the car unlocked."

"I know."

"What the hell are you guys talking about?" Lee said.

"I think Webster saw something, Harry."

I turned and walked toward Talia's condo.

★★★★

We tried the bell, pounded on the door. No answer. I tried the handle. Locked. Jonesy called on the car phone. We could hear ringing inside. Jonesy hung up when Talia's tape machine answered.

The sense of foreboding was growing. Jonesy felt it too. I could see it in his eyes. Something was wrong.

Then a dog's barking began, an urgent, insistent barking.

"Coming from out back," Jonesy said.

We went around the side.

The barking intensified.

★★★★

The gate for the white picket fence that surrounded Talia's tiny, landscaped yard stood open. A golden retriever and a German shepherd next door were pressed against a steel-mesh fence, barking intently at a clump of trees that ran down into a ravine. Lee hollered something and took off down the hill, his pistol in his hand. The dogs turned and ran over to our side of the fence, barking with renewed energy.

I stepped up on the wooden deck and tried the sliding glass door. Locked. Cupping my hands, I peered inside. The drapes were almost closed, but I could see through a three-inch slit. My eyes slowly adjusted to the gloom.

I was looking into the living room. Part of a black couch, end of a glass coffee table. Then something else. On the white carpet. Something long, partially hidden by a chair. My eyes adjusted, sharpening.

I stepped back suddenly.

"What?" Jonesy asked. "See something?"

"An arm, Jonesy."

✯✯✯✯

Jonesy used a landscaping brick from a flower bed to shatter a hole in the door. He reached through, flipped up the latch, and slid the door open.

Weapons drawn, we stepped inside.

Webster lay behind the chair, faceup, staring with unseeing eyes. His throat had been cut.

Jonesy went to a wall. Lights came on. He peered into the dining room and kitchen.

I stared down at Webster. A clock ticked, the air conditioner hummed. Then a thought hit me. Webster had a gun. How could someone have come up to him and killed him with a knife? I looked around. No weapon. Then I leaned down and opened his jacket. His gun was still in his holster.

"Sir?" Jonesy said softly. He gestured with his pistol toward the stairs.

I looked over, nodded.

We went up and made a quick search of the two bedrooms on the second floor. I was peeking into the bathroom when I heard faint thumps, staggered, muffled, moving slowly across the ceiling.

"Footsteps," Jonesy said.

We headed for the stairs.

We climbed slowly, carefully, guns pointed.

The footsteps stopped, replaced by sounds of objects dropping on the floor.

We reached the landing. Facing us, an open door, another bedroom, the master. A trail of red splotches trailed across the white carpet, down a hallway, and disappeared into another room—where the sounds were coming from.

Jonesy mouthed, *Cover me.* I pointed my pistol down the hallway. A drop of sweat stung my eye. Jonesy took a step. Something heavy crashed to the floor. Jonesy dropped to a crouch.

I blinked, staring, my finger tense on the trigger.

A soft, wheezing sound. Then silence.

We waited.

Finally, Jonesy moved forward, I followed, and we found her.

★★★★

The room was furnished as a study, with black laminated bookcases and a glass desk and a white linoleum floor. Talia lay in a heap on her side, in the middle of the room, a growing stain darkening the front of her silk blouse. Jonesy bent down. He didn't even bother to check her pulse.

"At least two stab wounds in the chest," he said. "Got her in the lungs, I think."

I stared at Talia. She didn't look so beautiful now. Her face was locked in a frozen grimace, her nose and mouth covered with a red froth, a grim testament of her hopeless battle to breathe as her perforated lungs filled with blood.

Jonesy rose. "Wonder what she wanted in here that was so damned important she had to get to it before she died?"

The blood trail led to a bookcase in the corner. I walked over. Books were strewn on the floor. "Maybe one of these."

"A book, huh?" Jonesy said. "That doesn't make much sense."

"No."

"I'll check out the master," Jonesy said.

"Killer's long gone," I said.

"I know." He went anyway.

I looked down at Talia on my way to join Jonesy, when I noticed both hands were under her body. Odd. I knelt down and slowly rolled her over. A few deep gashes on her forearms—defensive marks, against the knife. The hands were holding something. Something black. A book. I reached down, pulled. Her hands gave way.

Blood covered much of the title. But I knew what it was anyway and shook my head in wonderment.

I left, carrying the book between two fingers.

Jonesy was coming out of the bedroom. "Knifed her in there," he said. "Some stuff knocked down. Looks like there was a fight. What have you got there, sir?"

Before I could answer, a voice called out, "Charlie! Jonesy! Where the hell are you guys?"

I held up the book to Jonesy.

"You've got to be kidding," Jonesy said after a moment.

"Charlie! Jonesy!"

We went downstairs to talk to Lee.

★★★★

"So you didn't see anybody?" I asked Lee. We were in the kitchen. I set the book on the counter, then turned on the tap in the sink, glancing at Lee as I washed Talia's blood off my hands.

Perspiration flowed in tiny rivers down Lee's face. He ran the back of his hand over his brow, wiping the sweat off on his trousers. "Fuck no. I heard someone, but the damn trees were too thick. Got to the bottom of the ravine. There's one of those bike paths. I ran up and down. Didn't see anybody. Hill was a bitch to climb back up." He shook his head. "So how long after Talia was stabbed you figure she died?"

"Not more than a few minutes," Jonesy said. "Probably did her when we were at the door. In the lungs so she couldn't cry out. Old combat trick."

"Dammit," Lee said. "Then the guy I heard had to be the killer. Son of a bitch."

"Not your fault," I said.

"Yeah. Maybe." Lee looked over his shoulder at Webster's body and shook his head. "Why didn't your man draw his weapon?"

"I don't know," I said.

"He must not have felt threatened," Jonesy said.

Lee frowned. "Then why did he come barging in, then?"

I turned off the water. "I don't know, Harry."

Lee took a deep breath. "At least we know one thing."

"What's that?" Jonesy said.

"The Feds," Lee said dryly. "Like to see how those assholes are going to try and pin this thing on Masonis now." He took a step toward me. "Charlie, what are you doing?"

I had removed a paper towel from a dispenser and was wiping blood off the front of the book. The title was now visible.

Lee and Jonesy clustered around.

"What the—" Lee grunted. "That's a Bible."

"Yeah," I said.

I opened the leather cover. Unable to speak, I just looked.

Jonesy sucked in a breath.

"How about that?" Lee said.

47

THE BLACK-AND-WHITE PICTURE WAS GRAINY AND FADED, BUT THAT DIDN'T LESSEN THE IMPACT OF THE IMAGE OR DAMPEN THE HORROR. I continued to stare, mesmerized and sickened.

Joe Risser had been accurate in his description. The photo showed two emaciated Americans in black pajamas, one kneeling, the other standing behind, a pistol in his hand. Obviously POWs.

The picture had been taken from the right oblique of the two men, so the faces were clearly visible. Which, of course, had been the intention. The photographer wanted there to be little doubt as to the identity of the men, especially the one doing the shooting. The man kneeling had closed his eyes as the bullet sprayed his brain tissue into a mist. I wondered who he was. Did he know why he or the others had to die? I locked in on the man with the pistol. His gaunt face appeared calm, stoic, eyes open, looking down on the victim. He looked freshly shaven, dark hair combed neatly back.

"Bastard!" I murmured, too angry to shout my rage.

"Is it Holmes? Can you tell?" Lee asked.

"Hard to say," Jonesy said slowly. "Must be a hundred pounds difference in weight. And it's been almost twenty-five years. To be sure, have to compare it to a photo of Holmes when he was released."

"Same jaw," I said. "Same nose. It's him."

"Yes, sir," Jonesy said.

Lee said, "So where are the other nine prints? And the original?"

I shrugged. "Talia might have hidden them."

"Or the killer may have them," Jonesy said.

"I'll get the Falls Church PD to tear this place apart," Lee said.

"That doesn't really matter," I said. "We have this one. That's all we need."

"Let me get this straight," Lee said. "The North Vietnamese photographed Holmes killing a prisoner before they released him. Then, for the last twenty-plus years, they've been essentially blackmailing him for millions."

"Something like that," I said. "But it's not just money anymore. They're seeing influence and power beyond their wildest expectations if Holmes gets elected president."

"Well, I'd say the Holmes candidacy is about to turn into a bucket of shit," Lee growled.

I nodded and carefully removed the photo from where it was taped inside the Bible's cover.

"Doesn't look like much, does it?" Jonesy murmured.

I slipped the photo inside my jacket, giving Jonesy a questioning look.

"To be worth a hundred million dollars," Jonesy said softly. "Or to be worth so many lives."

No one said anything for a moment.

Lee said, "Guess I better call this thing in." He stopped. A phone in the living room was ringing.

I walked over, trying not to look at Webster, and picked up.

The voice was heavily muffled, deep. "Colonel Jensen?"

I blinked in surprise. Who could know I was here? "Speaking. Who is this?"

"Call your wife. Then we'll talk."

"What?"

But the phone went dead.

I punched in my home number. Lee came over. "What is it? What's wrong, Charlie?"

The phone was ringing.

"Hello."

"Jean! Are you okay?"

She sounded terrified. "Charlie, what's going on, Charlie? Who are these men?"

My stomach tightened. "Men? Honey . . ." I heard the sound of a commotion. "Jean!"

A male voice came on. A thick Asian accent. "Do what we say or wife die." He hung up.

I stared dumbly at the phone as the horror sank in. The men hadn't been FBI. They were Holmes's men. I cradled the phone. I could see Webster's vacant eyes. My hand shook. "Oh, sweet Jesus!"

Lee and Jonesy were staring at me. "What is it?" Lee asked. "What's going on?"

"They've got Jean."

"My God," Jonesy said.

The phone rang. I snared it. Jonesy bolted up the stairs.

A muffled voice said, "Colonel Jensen?"

"What do you want, you son of a bitch?" I could hear a soft click as Jonesy picked up the extension.

"You called. Good. Then you know how things stand. We don't want to hurt her, or your children."

"You've got my kids?"

"No. Stacy and Tony are fine. At school. Then Tony has football practice, and Stacy will be at ballet."

Christ. He knew their names, their schedules. I tried to swallow, and coughed instead.

"I'll do what you want."

"I thought you would. We are missing a picture. It is still in Major Swanson's residence. We want it."

"I don't know what you're talking about."

The voice hardened. "Don't be a fool. Major Swanson kept back a print. It's in the house. You have thirty minutes. I suggest you start looking."

Dammit! They must have been watching Talia. They were probably outside watching now. "What if I can't find it?"

The voice became savage. "Goddammit, Charlie. You've got thirty minutes. Don't fuck this up."

"No! Don't hang up. I have . . ."

But he was gone.

I was suddenly confused. The tone of the last statement. Something about it struck me. The way he called me Charlie. Like he knew me.

I felt panicky as I called information, got the number for the school. Stacy came to the phone first.

"Dad?" There was concern in her voice.

I tried to sound calm. "Hi, honey. Tony there?"

"He's in gym class. They're getting him. Dad, what's wrong?"

"Nothing to worry about. Just something came up. I want you and Tony to stay at school until I can pick you up, okay? Don't go to ballet, and tell Tony not to go to football practice. Wait in the office."

"Dad. What is it? Is it Mom?"

"Everything's fine," I lied. "When Tony comes, you tell him. Wait for me. No one else."

"Dad, if something is—"

"I've got to go. Now, don't worry. I'll see you soon. I love you."

A long pause. "I love you too, Dad."

★★★★

"Charlie."

Lee was staring at me, the same dead look in his eyes I'd seen back in Masonis's apartment when he got into it with that fat cop. "Those bastards want the picture in exchange for your wife?"

I nodded, cradling the phone.

"What are you going to do?"

"Give it to them," Jonesy said, appearing suddenly from the stairwell, clutching a portable phone. "You give it to them, sir."

"Then Holmes walks," Lee said.

"Maybe not," Jonesy said. There was a glint in his eyes.

He reached into his jacket pocket and removed the camera he'd lent Webster. "See this?" he said.

★★★★

Jonesy placed the photograph on the coffee table, then stood directly over it, shooting straight down. Lee stood just off to his side, looking a little silly holding a lamp.

Jonesy clicked off a series. "A little to the left," he told Lee. "Good." He clicked some more.

I watched, my mind drifting. I thought of Jean. I closed my eyes. I could see her face, eyes wide, terrified, calling to me.

"That's it. That finishes the roll," Jonesy said.

I opened my eyes. A drop of sweat ran down my neck. I wiped at it, and followed Jonesy and Lee into the kitchen.

"Think the pictures will come out?" Lee asked as Jonesy set the camera down on the kitchen counter.

"Glare could be a problem," Jonesy said. He handed me the photo. I slipped it in my jacket. "But I think we'll be okay."

"You guys do know that photographs aren't always admissible as evidence?" Lee said.

"Yes," I said. Lee was referring to the fact that with today's computers, photographs could be scanned in and altered so perfectly that detection was almost impossible. Which is probably why Watkins had not agreed to allow the picture to be reproduced by computer. He didn't want to leave himself open to a charge of having doctored it. "But as long as you can verify the authenticity . . ."

"But we can't, can we?" Lee asked.

I knew what Lee was getting at. Tho was the only one who could have certified the photo as to when and where it was taken, and he was dead. "A judge might allow it in light of the other evidence."

"Good luck," Lee said dryly.

"I'm referring to a military judge, Harry."

"If it even gets that far," Lee said, sounding bitter. "Seems to me the government has an even bigger stake in keeping this thing hushed up now. I mean, they covered up for a mass murderer and built him into a hero. They're sure not going to want that to get out."

"He's right, sir," Jonesy said.

"I know," I said softly.

Lee blinked. "You agree?"

I nodded.

"And you're still going to turn over everything, hoping Holmes will be prosecuted."

"In a manner of speaking."

Lee shook his head. "You're dreaming, Charlie. They can't afford to bring Holmes to trial. He's going to walk."

"No, you're wrong. There is a way."

Now Harry was looking really confused. Jonesy too.

I explained.

★★★★

Afterward, I sat on one of the wrought-iron stools at the kitchen island, blank eyes fixed on the portable phone I'd carefully placed on the counter. My stomach churned.

Jonesy and Lee watched the front from the kitchen windows. Lee had offered to call out a SWAT team to help Jean. One look from me shut him up. We would make no calls, make no moves. Jean's only chance was for me to do exactly what they said.

I'd known Jean most of my life, since the fourth grade, though we didn't date until my junior year in high school. When I went to the Air Force Academy, Jean moved out to Colorado Springs, waiting tables for a couple of years. Everyone back home knew we were going to get married when I graduated. Then, during my senior year, Jean told me she was leaving. She felt frustrated, trapped, worried she'd come to define her life through me. She was going off to find herself, make something of herself. I was devastated. We stayed in touch. Jean moved to L.A., became a set designer in films. Three years later, right after I returned from Korea, she called. She'd become successful, worked on a few big films, had some money and a name. That was enough. She knew she could make it on her own.

"I still love you," she said.

We were married three days later. That was eighteen years ago.

"Can't see shit," Lee said.

"They're out there," Jonesy said.

Another minute passed. I looked at the phone.

Lee said, "So Talia Swanson was really working for Holmes all this time?"

I nodded. "She had to be the one who told Holmes General Watkins was looking into Cao Dinh. She sabotaged the computers and seduced Masonis to find out what he knew."

"Sounds like a very busy girl," Lee said. "And she knew Holmes was going to have Watkins killed all along, eh?"

"She had to know," Jonesy said. "And she had to know that calling Holmes about Masonis was going to get Masonis killed."

Lee grunted. "Sleeps with a guy, then has him killed. She was a piece of work. So how do you guys figure it? Holmes finds out she kept one of the prints, knew she was going to blackmail him, and took her out?"

Jonesy was frowning. "That's probably pretty close. But what I can't figure out is how Holmes found out she kept a print?"

"The phone call," I said. "The one Joe Risser received at Sunset Photography."

"Phone call?" Jonesy asked. "What phone call?"

Then I remembered Jonesy had been outside in the car when Joe had mentioned it. I explained.

"Then it was Holmes's man that called?"

"Had to be," I said. "Only way that they could have known there were ten prints. But I can't figure out how Holmes's people even knew the pictures existed in the first place."

Jonesy said nothing for a moment, deep in thought. He stepped away from the window and began to pace slowly on the kitchen floor. He stopped. "Talia told them, sir."

"No way," Lee said, spinning away from the window. "That would be damn stupid if she was going to use them for blackmail, Jonesy."

I agreed with Lee.

"Try this for size," Jonesy said. "Risser called Major Swanson and told her Watkins's prints were ready. She put two and two together and knew they must be the ones implicating Holmes. She must have called Holmes or one of his men and told them about the pictures then."

Lee was shaking his head. "Doesn't make sense."

Jonesy's hand went up. "She wasn't thinking blackmail at the time she called, Harry. Remember, up to then she was doing everything to help Holmes. I'm betting once she saw how incriminating the picture was, she realized just what an opportunity she had to blackmail Holmes. And she couldn't resist."

"That's nuts, Jonesy," Lee said. "Holmes knew she had the pictures."

"So what? She only needs one print. She reasons Holmes won't know how many were made. Which we now know was her mistake. She picks up the pictures, delivers the packet to a prearranged drop site, minus the one picture, and comes back here to find Webster and me waiting. Which I guarantee was the last thing she wanted to see at that moment. Explains why she was so nervous."

Lee gave a grudging nod. "And Holmes's people check the packet. They see a print is missing."

"And send someone over here to have a little talk with Talia," I said.

Jonesy nodded. "And remember, sir, the guy on the phone made it sound like they must have been outside keeping her under surveillance for quite a while, probably waiting for us to leave. So they must have seen Webster set up."

"Now they know they have a real problem," Lee said. "Talia Swanson is obviously a suspect now. They know eventually we'll be pressuring her. They have to move fast to get the picture and shut her up. Which means they have to take out Webster too."

"Why?" I asked. "They could have come in the back way. The

back door opens into the laundry room. Webster never would have seen them."

Jonesy shook his head. "Too risky. Major Swanson would have heard the dogs barking. She'd have been alarmed if she saw them crawling around her yard. At any rate, we know they came in the front door, sir." He must have noticed my confused look, because he said, "Remember the two pictures Webster took."

"So what are you saying?" I said. "That they just rang the doorbell? With Webster watching?"

Jonesy nodded. "That's just what they did."

"I don't buy it, Jonesy."

He pointed to the window. "Take a look out there, sir."

I frowned, then eased off the stool and shuffled over. "What am I looking for?"

"The van, sir," Jonesy said. "The one with the ladder. Remember?"

I looked. There was no van. I was about to tell Jonesy so, when it dawned on me.

Son of a bitch.

I spun around. The van would have been the perfect cover not to arouse Webster's suspicion. "They were dressed like workmen."

Jonesy nodded. "One must have stayed in the van as a lookout."

"Damn," Lee said. "Any of you guys see it leave?" He swore again when we shook our heads.

"But if Webster saw workmen, why would he leave his car?" I asked.

"Maybe he'll still tell us, sir," Jonesy said quietly.

He picked up the camera from the counter and looked down at Webster.

No one spoke. The icemaker rattled as it dumped a tray. I checked my watch. Almost time.

The phone rang. I snatched it up.

"Lieutenant Colonel Jensen speaking."

48

THE INSTRUCTIONS WERE SIMPLE.

I DROVE WEBSTER'S CAR TO THE PHONE BOOTH BY A 7-ELEVEN near Baileys Crossroads, and waited. I knew I had been followed, but I hadn't been able to spot the tail. Two minutes later, the phone rang and I was given new instructions. Another pay phone at a 7-Eleven in Annandale. It took me fifteen minutes to get there. Then another call. Another phone booth, a gas station in Falls Church. They were being careful. Wanted to be sure I was a good boy and didn't have police following. At the gas station, I was told to drive to a strip mall four miles away, leave the car, and walk around the block.

After parking, I slipped the photo out of my jacket and left it facedown on the passenger seat. Then I climbed out, leaving the doors unlocked. Without looking around, I began walking.

The walk around the block took me a quarter of an hour. I thought of Jean the entire time, feeling totally helpless. Still, I had no choice but to cling to the hope that once they had the photo, they would know they'd won. That there was no reason to harm Jean.

I was soaked with perspiration when I returned. Opening the car door, I looked down on the seat. The photograph was gone.

A quick scan of the parking lot didn't show anything unusual: a few women with grocery carts, a couple buckling a crying baby into a car seat, a little boy whining to his father that he was tired. Then, no more than twenty yards away, I saw a man in a suit coming toward me. He was young, clean-cut, and Asian.

He smiled at me.

My hand dropped to my waist.

The man held out a cigarette, making the motion for a match.

Alarm bells sounded in my head. I shook my head no.

He shrugged, kept coming.

I reached inside my jacket and unsnapped the leather guard on my holster.

He grinned.

I blinked sweat from my eyes.

He stopped, maybe five yards away, and began to laugh. His eyes flickered for an instant to my right.

I knew it was a trick.

I spun around.

A second Asian man was behind me, maybe thirty feet away. He threw open his jacket. Sunlight glinted off the barrel as he raised the sawed-off shotgun. My pistol came free. Too late. He was already leveling his weapon.

The man grunted suddenly, his face surprised. He looked down. A red stain appeared magically on his chest. He took a step, teetered, and fell forward, his weapon clattering to the pavement.

For an instant, I froze, confused. Then, in one motion, I dropped and turned, gun in my hand.

But the first Asian had disappeared.

The sounds of footsteps running. Moments later, tires squealed. Rising, I saw a car roar out of the parking lot, two occupants visible.

Behind me, a tentative voice called, "Hey, mister, you okay? Mister . . ." I looked. A young man was tentatively approaching the body. I was partially shielded by a large truck, and the man didn't appear to notice me. I holstered my gun.

The young man suddenly shouted, calling for help. People began running over. An older man jogged up to me. "What the hell happened?"

I waved to the body. "I don't know. He just fell over."

People were bending over the body, firing questions.

"Is he dead?"

"God, I think he's been shot!"

"Shot? I didn't hear anything."

"Get an ambulance."

"Jesus almighty, would you look at that gun he was carrying!"

"Better call 911," I told the older man before he ran off.

I looked around. No one was giving me a second look. I climbed into my car and drove away.

☆☆☆☆

After my answering machine at home picked up, I disconnected, trying to keep calm. Maybe there was a reason Jean wasn't answering. Maybe she'd been tied up. Maybe she was unconscious. Maybe . . .

I called the Burke police and told them to get someone over to my house. The dispatcher tried to ask me the usual assortment of questions. I snarled that I was Lieutenant Colonel Jensen and that I would explain everything to the cops on the scene. Then another voice cut in.

"Uh, Colonel Jensen, be advised we already have units responding to your residence."

"What?"

"Yes, sir. A report came in a few minutes ago. From your neighbor, a Ms. Marjorie Claussen, notifying us your wife is incapacitated. EMTs are en route."

"How is she?"

"We don't know."

"Is she alive?"

"Yes. But we won't know specifics on her condition until the EMTs arrive."

I thanked him. Hanging up, I drove like a maniac, riding the horn and darting in and out of traffic.

When I roared onto my street, I could see police cars and an ambulance in front of my house. The front door was open. A man and a woman in uniform were walking out. The EMTs.

They were wheeling a stretcher.

****

The tires squealed as I stopped against the curb. I grabbed the male EMT by the shoulder, halting his progress. Jean lay on the stretcher, eyes closed, a sheet up to her neck.

"Hey!" the man grunted, head pivoting around in annoyance.

"I'm her husband."

His face relaxed.

"You Lieutenant Colonel Jensen?" a cop asked.

I nodded. My hand shook as I touched Jean's face. "Jean, it's Charlie." No response. "Jean . . . ?"

The other EMT, a wiry young woman, said reassuringly, "She's not in any immediate danger, sir."

I swallowed hard. "You're sure?"

The woman nodded. "Her breathing is regular, vital signs low, but stable."

"Then what's wrong with her?" I asked. "Why isn't she awake?"

"Not really sure. There's a bruise on her arm with a puncture mark. My guess, she's been drugged." She paused, then asked, "Sir, does your wife have a history of drug use?"

I glared at her, furious. "Jean? Drugs? Absolutely not!" I stopped, realizing the woman had to ask the question.

She just looked at me, her face showing no reaction.

"I'm sorry, miss."

"No sweat, sir. But if you had any idea what the drug might be, it would really help us out."

"I don't."

"Sir, we really need to get her to the hospital," the male EMT said. "If you'll let us pass . . ."

I caressed Jean's face and stepped aside. As the EMTs passed, the woman said, "We're taking her to Commonwealth Doctors Hospital, sir."

I watched them load Jean into the ambulance.

"Colonel, you have any idea what happened here?" the cop asked.

"I . . . I was talking to my wife on the phone. She said a couple of men had broken in. The line went dead. When I tried to call back, there was no answer."

The cop was nodding. "That matches the story one of your neighbors told us. Two Asian males were seen leaving about thirty-five minutes ago. You have any idea who they were?"

I shook my head.

"Any idea why they attacked your wife?"

I gave him a long look, then again shook my head.

The cop frowned. "No idea, huh? None at all?"

"I don't know anything, Officer."

"This is a funny one," he said. "No signs of forced entry or a struggle. Nothing appears to be stolen that we can tell. You better take a look."

"Maybe they were frightened off before they could take anything," I said.

A second cop walked out of the house. I watched him go over to my next-door neighbors, Janine and Brad. They were a retired couple. Brad waved to me, hollering, "Anything we can do, Charlie?"

I shook my head. "Thanks, Brad."

The EMTs were closing the ambulance's rear doors.

"Look, Officer," I said. "I'd like to go to the hospital."

The cop hesitated. "Yeah. Okay. But we'll need a statement later."

I was already walking to the car. Explaining everything to the cop would be a waste of time. Because now I knew exactly what I had to do to finish this thing once and for all.

Marjorie, across the street, was looking sad and worried. I ran over.

"You called the cops, Marge?"

She nodded. "Jean and I were supposed to go shopping over at Ballston. I went over earlier and rang the bell, but there was no answer. A few minutes later, I saw those men leave, so I went back over."

"You got a good look at them?"

"Sure. Two Orientals. Young. They drove away in a van. God, I hope Jean's going to be okay."

"Thanks," I said. I patted her hand and then ran to my car to follow the ambulance.

Jean was still alive. I thanked God for that.

★★★★

An hour later, I was talking to a doctor in a second-floor waiting room. He said Jean had indeed been drugged, but would recover. He would keep her for observation for a couple of days. I thanked him.

Two detectives showed up and questioned me for a few minutes. I repeated what I had told the cop earlier. No, I didn't know anything.

I hated leaving Jean, but I had to pick up the kids, and I had to get Holmes.

★★★★

"But if Mom is sick, why can't we go to the hospital to see her?" Stacy asked. She shifted in the passenger seat, facing me, worry in her beautiful green eyes.

I looked over. "She's sleeping now. We'll go by tomorrow."

"I don't get why I can't go to football practice, then," Tony said.

Stacy whirled around and glared at her brother in the backseat. "Is that all you can think about? Mom's in the hospital."

"Dad said she's going to be okay."

"So?"

"Sis, we're not even going to see her." Tony slumped back against the seat. "And I don't see why we have to stay with Mrs. Tippett. We can take care of ourselves."

I spun around, giving him a hard look. "Because I said so, Tony."

He folded his arms and looked away.

"Now, I told you I'll have to work late," I said. "You'll only be staying for one night."

"But, Dad, we don't have any clothes."

"There's a suitcase in the trunk. I stopped by the house and picked up a change. Toothbrushes too."

Tony glowered, saying nothing.

"You are such a jerk," Stacy told him.

"Creep," Tony muttered.

"Quiet! Both of you."

A few minutes later, I parked in Dorothy's driveway. The kids were still glaring at each other, but managed to stay quiet.

I was happy to see Rupert answer the door.

A minute later, I was back on the road. I called Lee's cellular.

"Yeah, I got the pictures," Lee said.

"Did they come out?" I asked.

"Yeah. Lab did a good job. Your wife's going to be Okay?"

I'd called him earlier from the hospital. "Yeah. They're going to keep her for a couple of days for observation."

"That's really great, Charlie. Jeez, we were worried." Jonesy must have been nearby, because Lee called out, "His wife is going to be fine."

"How'd it go with the Falls Church cops at the apartment?" I asked.

"Okay," Lee said. "Detective running the case is a buddy of mine. Sergeant Brandt. Jonesy and I filled him in on what we could without saying too much."

"You check on the stiff in the parking lot?"

"Sounds like he could be a pro. Wore gloves. Wasn't carrying ID. Gun was a sawed-off twelve gauge with the serial number filed off. Son of a bitch wasn't going to take a chance on missing. You were damn lucky."

My mind went back. I could see the barrel coming up. Another split second . . .

Lee said, "And you never heard the shot?"

"Whoever took him out used a silencer."

"And you didn't see the shooter?"

342 Patrick A. Davis

"Maybe the other Asian, but I don't think so. He didn't have time. My guess is it was the guy driving the car."

"You get a good luck at the driver?"

"Just a glimpse. Another Asian, I think."

A pause. "I don't get it. Sounds like they were all working together. Why kill their own man?"

"I don't know, Harry. Anyone get a license number?"

"No, no one saw anything."

"Figures."

"Jonesy thinks the goons who're after you and your wife could be Vietnamese agents. You know, working for Holmes to protect their investment."

As usual, Jonesy was probably right. I accelerated onto the ramp for I-395 northbound. "So where are you guys now?"

49

I DROVE AROUND ROSSLYN FOR TEN MINUTES, MAKING SURE I HADN'T BEEN TAILED.

The parking lot for the Kimchi Grill was almost empty, since it didn't open for dinner for another hour. I rapped on the door. Lee's aunt opened it, then directed me up the stairs to one of the private dining rooms. Lee and Jonesy were sitting around an ornately carved round table. The place settings had been piled on the lazy Susan to make room for the scattered stacks of papers and photos.

Lee sat back and gave me a tired grin. "Glad to see you, Charlie. You want something to drink?"

"No, thanks, Harry." I took a seat.

Jonesy gestured to a stack of photos. "You might want to take a look at those, sir."

"The ones you took?"

Jonesy nodded.

I picked one up. There was very little degradation from the original. Jonesy had done well.

Lee plucked out a picture and gave it to me. "I had the lab boys blow the best ones up, Charlie. Now compare that to this one, which I managed to get from a friend over at the *Post*. He slid over another picture.

Lee's picture showed a young man in a hospital bed, smiling broadly, giving a thumbs-up. I looked at the photo he'd first handed me. The two faces were the same.

"They match," I said.

"Yeah," Lee said. "The hospital picture was taken in 1971, of then-Major Clayton Holmes shortly after his escape."

Glancing over the rest of the photographs, I asked, "Where are the surveillance shots? The ones Webster took?"

Jonesy wordlessly passed me a manila folder.

I opened it, drawing out two photographs. The first was shot from behind and to the right of a man in blue coveralls wearing a baseball cap and dark glasses, walking up to Talia's door. In his left hand, he carried a small tool chest. His face was hidden by the angle of the shot. I flipped to the second photo. The same man was standing at the door, head turned slightly to the right, hand raised, ringing the doorbell.

I grimaced. I could make out he was a stocky white guy, but nothing else. "That's it?" I asked Jonesy.

"Afraid so, sir. Looks like it was just one guy."

"Had blowups made of his face," Lee said. "Still can't tell much from the angle."

"In here?" I flipped through a few more photos in the file.

"Yeah. The last couple."

I found them. I shook my head. I couldn't tell much. "Wish I knew who this son of a bitch was," I said, laying the pictures down.

"Probably just contract types hired by Holmes," Lee said. "Maybe working with the Vietnamese."

I nodded. Jonesy coughed. "Something on your mind?"

Jonesy gave me a sheet. "Found this when I was going through Masonis's personnel file, sir. Missed it the first time." There was an odd note in his voice.

The sheet was one of Masonis's performance evaluations. From 1970 to 1971. When he was a sergeant in Vietnam. "Yeah, so?"

"Look at the rating officer's block, sir."

I saw what Jonesy was getting at. I even recognized the signature. I looked up, confused.

"I know, sir. Colonel Tippett never mentioned he knew Masonis, did he?"

I shook my head.

"And we know Masonis's files were sealed to hide something."

"Hang on," I said. "You think this is what Holmes was trying to prevent us from seeing?"

"I've been through the file three times, sir. I've read every line. That's the only thing I've found that doesn't make sense. Colonel Tippett should have said something."

"Maybe he just forgot," Lee said.

I said nothing. But I knew he wouldn't have forgotten. I set the sheet down next to one of the photos Webster had taken. No, Tippett wouldn't have forgotten to mention he knew Masonis. He had suspected Masonis was the killer. We all did. Why didn't he say something? I shook my head, my eyes drifting to the photo.

"Doesn't seem that big a deal to me," Lee said. "Hell, we got Holmes, right, Charlie?"

I frowned, picking up a picture, one of the blowups, showing the man's face turned slightly. Something about the face . . . I swallowed, drawing the picture closer. The cheek. My hand darted out, picking up another photo.

"Sir?" Jonesy said.

There it was again. A bump. My eyes shifted between the pictures.

"Charlie, what is it?" Jonesy asked.

My mind raced, eyes focusing on the back of the man's head. Even with the baseball cap, I could tell.

The man was bald. A short, stocky, bald man.

A tap on my arm. "Colonel Jensen."

I looked up, the photos trembling in my hands. Jonesy was giving me a concerned look. So was Lee.

Jonesy said, "What is it, sir? What's wrong?"

"Damn, Charlie," Lee said. "You look like you've seen a ghost."

★★★★

I stared into space as Jonesy and Lee studied the pictures. I felt numb, dazed.

Impossible. Yet . . .

I slipped back to the moment when I walked into General Watkins's study and saw his body. Then I slowly flashed forward, thinking about everything I'd seen and heard. So many things that hadn't made sense before slowly came into focus.

The unexplained absences, the fear in the Vietnamese boy's eyes when we walked into the kitchen, the boy lying, describing Masonis as the killer, how the killer knew the boy had seen him, the police description of the man seen leaving the Vietnamese girl's apartment after she was murdered, how the killer gained access to the computer virus and how he knew my kids' names, that Tony played football and Stacy took ballet.

Suddenly, everything made sense.

I could hear the muffled voice on the phone. The way he said it. Not Colonel Jensen, not Charles, but Charlie.

As if he knew me.

"Don't see much here, Charlie," Lee said.

"Look at his cheek."

"Looks like he's holding a big wad of gum."

"No," Jonesy said softly. "It's not gum." He was looking at me when he said it.

"Tobacco," I said. "A wad of tobacco."

Lee frowned. "How do you know?" He stopped, seeing Jonesy's face. "All right. Who the hell is he?"

Jonesy told him.

"You guys are crazy."

"No," I said. "That's Tippett."

★★★★

We finished past midnight, and Jonesy and I gathered up the papers and photos from the table. Lee left to take the empty plates down to the kitchen. His aunt had whipped up a stir-fry before she'd gone home.

Jonesy and I went downstairs and sat in semidarkness at the bar. Everyone had left an hour earlier. We could hear Lee whistling in the kitchen.

I closed my eyes. My tired mind turned to Webster. I saw him sitting in the car, hot, bored, eating a burger. The van pulls up. A man gets out. Just some handyman, Webster thinks. But he follows orders, raises the camera. He looks through the viewfinder. Punches the zoom.

The man grows. Webster clicks another picture. Now the door is opening.

Talia is there in the doorway. He sees her face. Sees her fear. She tries to shut the door.

But the man moves fast, shoving past Talia. The door closes.

Webster is out of the car.

He pounds on Talia's door. He has his gun out.

The door opens.

And Webster gets the shock of his life.

Webster goes inside slowly, confused. Tippett is telling him to put the gun away. Webster is a soldier. He obeys.

And dies.

That was the way it happened. Maybe not exactly, but close.

"Let's go," Lee called.

★★★★

The night was cool and quiet, the only sound our footsteps on the sidewalk as we headed toward the restaurant's parking lot.

"Maybe you should stay at my place for the night, Charlie. Be safer," Lee said.

"Thanks, Harry. I'll be okay."

"Suit yourself. But if I were you . . . What the hell?"

We'd just entered the parking lot which was partially lit from a streetlamp. Our three vehicles were near the front. I spotted what Lee was looking at. In deep shadows toward the back, maybe fifteen yards away. A sedan.

And the form of a man leaning against it.

We stopped.

The man pushed away from the car.

My muscles tensed.

Lee called out, "Who are you?"

The man stood there, saying nothing. Then he began walking toward us.

Lee took out his gun. Jonesy and I did the same. "Police! Identify yourself!" Lee called.

No response.

I scanned the lot. To the left, our cars. Behind us, a large Dumpster. And beyond, just darkness and shadow.

"Hold it right there!" Lee yelled.

The man kept coming.

My finger tightened on the trigger.

The man stopped. "Hello, Charlie."

I recognized the voice. "You son of a bitch," I said.

Tippett stepped out into the light.

50

IS FACE WAS CALM, RELAXED. "IS THAT ANY WAY TO GREET AN OLD FRIEND, CHARLIE?"

I felt like shooting him right then and there. "You killed Watkins, you bastard! You killed Webster!" I stopped. Tippett was smiling.

"You're beautiful, Charlie. I wondered how long it would take you to figure things out. I knew you would, but congratulations anyway. Hello, Jonesy. Harry."

Jonesy said nothing. His face was absolutely cold.

"Go to hell," Lee said.

Tippett spit tobacco juice on the ground. His eyes went to Jonesy's briefcase. "Pictures in there, I take it?"

Jonesy blinked, surprised.

"How the fuck do you know about the pictures?" Harry asked.

I was wondering the same thing. He couldn't know unless . . . I stepped forward. "You bastard, you bugged my car!"

Tippett laughed. "You really had no clue, did you, Charlie. I've been tracking you for two days."

Tippett was too confident, too sure of himself. Jonesy and Lee had picked up on it. Their faces were taut, eyes darting around. I scanned the area but saw no one.

"Let's take this inside," Lee said. He sounded worried.

I motioned to Tippett with my gun. "Let's go, Tip."

Tippett slowly turned his head and spit. He gave me an arrogant grin. Then he barked out something. I didn't understand it, but then, I wasn't meant to.

But I could tell it was some kind of a command.

In Vietnamese.

Footsteps.

I swore.

"A trap!" Jonesy called out.

I was already turning. Something moved by the Dumpster. I aimed, tried to follow a target.

Then the sound of a round being chambered into a shotgun froze me for an instant.

"Don't fucking move!" Tippett said.

I spun back around, half expecting the impact of a shotgun blast. An Asian man had materialized from behind my car, a shotgun pointed at my chest. Jonesy grunted in pain as something clattered noisily across the asphalt. Lee tried to shout but was cut off. I slowly faced Tippett, my pistol pointed at him. The man with the shotgun grunted something. Tippett snapped off a reply.

"Better put it down, Charlie," Tippett said.

"I could get off a shot."

"Maybe. But then you'll all die for sure."

I looked at Jonesy. He was rubbing his wrist, grimacing. Lee was standing next to him, hands raised. Two Asian men had pistols pressed against the backs of their heads. Bastards must have been hiding behind the Dumpster the whole time.

"Put it down, Charlie," Tippett said.

I didn't move.

I thought I saw a look of regret in Tippett's eyes. "Don't be stupid, Charlie," he said softly.

I looked at the shotgun.

My hand slowly dropped.

One of the men came over and took my pistol. He stood there for a moment, giving me a malevolent stare. He looked familiar. Sure. Earlier today. The man with the cigarette.

"Lieutenant Pham doesn't like you, Charlie," Tippett said. "He blames you for the death of his friend today."

"I didn't kill him."

"No?" Tippett shrugged, unconcerned.

Pham still looked at me with hate.

"Are all these men Vietnamese Army?" I asked.

"Special Forces, actually." Tippett strolled over and picked up the briefcase beside Jonesy. "You almost outsmarted us today. When you handed us that picture, we thought we had them all. We never guessed you made dupes." Tippett knelt down, clicked open the locks, and checked the contents with a small flashlight, humming to himself.

I shook my head. "Christ, Tip. Why? Money?"

Tippett appeared not to hear. He carefully shut the briefcase and rose. Then he looked at me. "You think I did this for money, Charlie?" He sounded disappointed.

We stared at each other in silence.

I slowly nodded. No, not for money. It never had been for money with Tip.

Tippett said something in Vietnamese. Major Pham stepped over to me. "He wants your car keys, Charlie."

"Why?" I asked.

Tippett casually walked behind me. "You're all going on a little trip in your car."

"You'll never get away with killing us," Lee said. "There will be an investigation. . . ."

"That will lead nowhere," Tippett said. "Charlie, your keys."

Pham held out his hand. I didn't move. He raised the pistol to my head.

A bullet now or a fatal car accident later. Did it really matter?

I reached into my pocket.

It happened fast. One moment Pham was standing in front of me. The next, something whined by my ear and Pham's head snapped backward, a bloody hole where an eye had been. He toppled to the asphalt.

Something moved to my left. An instant later, I heard a dull thump.

"The bastard's hit!" Lee yelled as the second Asian fell to his knees, blood spurting from his throat.

"Get the fuck down, Charlie!" a voice yelled.

I dropped flat.

Something nearby coughed twice.

The Asian with the shotgun staggered, sagged . . .

Footsteps sprinted by.

I lunged forward, grabbing at Pham's gun. Tippett was running toward the car. I picked up the gun, rolled up on an elbow, and aimed.

Tippett was in my sights.

I tracked him. His heavy frame swayed like a duck, arms and legs flailing side to side.

I squeezed.

And then I noticed he didn't have the briefcase, only a gun.

I hesitated.

Tippett disappeared into the shadows.

I scrambled to my feet and took off after him.

An engine started. I heard the squeal of tires as the car spun around and came toward me. Jonesy screamed out a warning. I threw myself to the side as the car roared by and tore onto the street.

I lay facedown on the ground for a few seconds, dazed, trying to catch my breath.

Someone was over me.

Jonesy's voice. "You okay, sir?"

"I'll live." I rolled over. Jonesy helped me up.

Lee ran over. "I thought you had him, Charlie. What the hell happened?"

"I don't know what you're talking about, Harry."

Lee looked incredulous. "Dammit, I saw you. You had him. But you let him go. Now we have nothing. Tippett's got the photos, everything."

"No," I said. "No. We're okay. He wasn't carrying the briefcase."

"There," Jonesy said, staring at something behind us.

Lee and I turned.

The briefcase was on the asphalt where Tippett had been standing when the shots were fired.

"I'll be damned," Lee said.

★★★★

"Man, what a mess. How are we going to explain three fucking stiffs?" Lee asked.

We were standing beside my car. Harry was puffing on a cigarette.

"We don't," I said.

Lee's eyebrows shot up. "You mean we just leave?"

"I don't think we have much choice."

"I dunno, Charlie. We should at least call this thing in." He looked to Jonesy as if for support.

Jonesy stayed silent.

"I'll take care of it, Harry," I said.

Lee let out a lungful of smoke and shook his head. "I sure hope you know what you're doing."

"Me, too," I said softly.

I climbed into my car.

★★★★

Five minutes later, I pulled into a service station. Jonesy parked behind me. The place was closed, but I found a phone booth. The call took less than a minute. I hung up when the 911 operator asked me to identify myself.

When I came out, I drove to the Pentagon. Jonesy followed. After parking, I got into Jonesy's car. Maybe Holmes's men wouldn't try anything else tonight, but I wasn't taking any chances. And searching for the bug would take too long.

We drove away.

★★★★

Standing in the semidarkness of the hospital room, I watched Jean, listening to her slow, even breathing. She looked beautiful and peaceful. I leaned over and removed a few strands of hair from her face, leaving my finger on her cheek for a moment. I felt relief, anger, and a profound sadness. I felt I now knew why Jean hadn't been killed.

Tippett had always liked Jean. Liked her a lot.

That accounted for something, I suppose.

The door opened. A silhouetted figure stood in the light of the hallway.

"Thought you could use these, Colonel," the nurse said. She gave me a pillow and blanket.

I thanked her. The door closed.

I drew two chairs together, placing them next to Jean's bed, and settled in.

And then I remembered I'd forgotten to call Dorothy and the kids.

I would have to tell Dorothy sometime, but Lord help me, I didn't know how.

51

Thursday

T|HAT'S ABOUT IT, SIR," I TOLD SECRETARY BAINES. I LEANED BACK IN MY CHAIR AND RUBBED MY EYES, WHICH ACHED FROM LACK OF SLEEP. Jonesy had picked me up promptly at seven. We'd spent most of the morning going over the facts again to make sure we had everything straight.

Secretary of Defense Baines sat slumped in his chair, chin to his chest. He looked up and ran both hands over his thinning hair, peering at me over his desk. "So Tippett killed the Vietnamese and left you the briefcase?"

I nodded. "He also shot the man who tried to kill me after I dropped off the photograph."

Baines shook his head. He picked up the photo showing Tippett at Talia's condo. When he'd been the head of the OSI, he'd worked closely with Tippett.

"Tippett got involved because of his relationship with Masonis. He was Masonis's commander in Vietnam. Masonis contacted Tippett, seeking his help in the investigation of General Holmes. As CID chief, Tippett had access to a lot of information which would be helpful to Masonis."

Baines set the photo down. He frowned. "Seems to me you're saying Masonis was investigating Holmes prior to Monday, the day Watkins was killed. Wasn't that before Tho told Watkins of Holmes's role in the POW killings?"

"That's according to Birelli. But remember Tho asked for another two hundred grand last week. He dropped Holmes's name to convince Watkins he was worth the extra money."

"And Masonis told Tippett."

I nodded. "But probably not everything, because that would have been foolish, considering the import. Even Birelli was kept in the dark. But Tippett learned enough to figure out Holmes could be in big trouble. Tippett saw his chance. He contacted Holmes, who by now already knows about the investigation into Cao Dinh through Major Swanson and is desperate to stop Masonis and General Watkins. They worked out the plan to kill Watkins and frame Masonis. With Tippett running the investigation, success seemed inevitable."

"Why didn't they just go after Tho, get the photographs? Without them, Watkins had nothing."

"Obviously because they didn't know where to find him. Might not even have known his name. Like I said, Masonis didn't tell Tippett everything. I'm sure Major Swanson also tried to find out about Tho from Masonis, but apparently without success."

Baines thought for a moment. "You said Tippett wasn't after money?"

"No. Though Holmes probably paid him a substantial amount."

"What, then?"

I took a deep breath. "He knew Holmes could get him a star."

Baines slowly sank back in his chair. "General Tippett," he said bitterly. He shook his head. "And Tippett killed Watkins?"

I nodded. "He knew the . . . technique. I'm certain he used it in Vietnam. We were damn lucky General Watkins died before he told Tippett about the prints he had made."

"You don't think the Vietnamese could have . . ."

"No. Too chancy for them to have gained access to Fort Myer and General Watkins's quarters without someone noticing."

"Who knocked off Tho?"

"At first I wasn't sure. I figured Tippett couldn't have killed him because, at the time Tho was killed, Tippett was overseeing the crime-scene investigation at Watkins's residence. But then I remembered I'd tried to call Tippett that night and he wasn't around. I'll bet if we check, no one will remember seeing Tippett for at least an hour and a half."

"Pretty risky him taking off like that to kill Tho."

"Tippett had no choice. Watkins told him where to find Tho. But before Tippett could act, Watkins's body was discovered much sooner than he anticipated by the maid. Tippett knew I'd want to check out why Watkins's last call was to a Vietnamese restaurant. He sent me off with Major Swanson to buy time. The Fort Myer gate guards should be able to verify seeing Tippett leave and return that night."

Secretary Baines abruptly pushed back from his desk, looking decidedly unhappy. He picked up his glass and pointed to mine. I shook my head; he went to the bar.

"The phone call on the answering machine was Tippett's first mistake," I said. "That phone call led us to Mr. Tho. His second was letting the Vietnamese kid see him leaving Tho's place."

Baines was pouring scotch into his glass. He glanced over. "That's why the kid was so scared when you guys walked in?"

"Yes, sir. He must have been terrified to see Tippett. And of course Tippett figured out immediately the kid had seen him. Played to the kid's preconceived fears of the police back home. Probably told the kid if he said anything to anybody, he was dead. Maybe even told him he'd kill his sister. Who knows?"

Baines came back, his face tight. "And Tippett used the opportunity to fabricate a description of the killer to match Masonis. Damn clever."

I nodded. "Anyway, the kid bolts. Tippett goes to the apartment where the kid lives with his sister, kills her after getting her to talk—"

"That son of a bitch."

"Then he kills the kid and rigs the boat to blow up."

"That still bothers me. Why the hell did he blow up the boat?"

I shrugged. "Hard to say. I don't think Tippett's been thinking rationally for a long time. The date on that insurance policy for his children suggests he may have been planning to fake his death all along. Maybe the boat was just a convenient opportunity."

"When was the policy taken out?"

"Two weeks ago." I closed my eyes for a moment and massaged my scalp. "I suppose I forced his hand. Tippett knew I was going to recommend that he be pulled from the case."

"For the boozing?"

I nodded. "Tippett is a very proud man, fanatically so. Faking his death saved him the humiliation of being relieved. In fact, he became a hero of sorts. He must have loved that. I think he was worried his involvement in the murders might come to light. His 'death' insured he wouldn't be considered a suspect. He could just disappear. That's important."

"Why?"

"A way of erasing the past, ridding himself of a life that he saw as a failure. At any rate, Tippett must have had scuba gear on the boat. He simply slipped over the side while we were watching and swam away."

Baines was looking at the photo of Tippett at Talia's again. "And he obviously killed Webster and Swanson."

I nodded.

"How about Masonis?"

"Tippett probably arranged the killing after getting the call from Major Swanson. That car accident to slow us up is something Tippett would think of. He wouldn't leave anything to chance if he could help it. But as to pulling the trigger, who knows. Could have been one of the Vietnamese."

Baines sat back. "You know I personally worked with Tippett on a number of cases."

"Yes, sir."

"He was a good man."

"Yes, sir." I took a long pause. "He was."

Baines sipped his drink. "Strange, don't you think. He kills so easily, yet he saved you twice."

"Yes."

"Left the briefcase."

"Yes."

"Damn curious."

I ran a hand over my head. "I don't know. Tippett knew he'd gambled and lost. He wasn't going to be a general. Maybe he finally decided the price was just too high and it was time to get out."

Baines gestured to the photos on his desk. "What else do you have to back up what you've told me besides this?"

I opened my briefcase and handed him a thick sheaf of papers.

"This is everything?" Baines asked.

"Copies."

He frowned. "Copies? Where's the original file?"

I shifted in my seat. "I've arranged for it to be sent to the media unless you take action, sir."

Baines looked at me in disbelief. He shot forward in his chair and slammed down his glass. "Goddammit, Charlie. You trying to tell me what the hell I'm supposed to do?"

I kept my face blank.

"Well, that's not going to happen. Now, I want everything turned over immediately. You got that?"

"I can't do that, sir."

"I could have you arrested for disobeying a direct order," Baines said.

"The media will still get the files, sir."

He glared at me. I looked back calmly.

The anger slowly ebbed from Baines's face. "You have any idea what will happen if this gets out?"

"I know," I said.

Baines was shaking his head. "My God, this will be catastrophic for the administration, for the military. For the country."

"I want Holmes, sir. And I want Tippett."

"You'll have your pound of flesh? Is that it?"

I leaned forward, fighting off a growing sense of disgust. How could I be so wrong about Baines? "Maybe you're forgetting the twenty-three names on the wall that never came back, sir. Or General Watkins. Or Masonis. Or Webster. Or that poor, mindless bastard Brady Hanson. Or—" I stopped, breathing hard.

"You through? Got it out of your system?"

I nodded.

"You must really think I'm a horse's ass."

I didn't respond.

Baines sighed. "Maybe you're right." He picked up his glass and swirled it. "Look, Charlie, nothing would give me more pleasure than to have Holmes and Tippett brought to trial and fucking shot, along with that sadistic quack Dr. Coletta. Hell, I'd like nothing better than to pull the trigger myself. But the country couldn't handle what would come out in a trial. The cover-up of Cao Dinh, the murder of the POWs, the government's involvement. Then there is the pain of the families to consider. You'd just reopen old wounds. Think about what you're doing, Charlie. What possible good could come out of bringing all that out now?" He sipped his scotch, his eyes never leaving me.

"I don't think I said anything about a trial, sir," I said.

Baines's eyebrows inched up.

"As long as there is justice . . ." I left the statement hanging.

Baines gave me a thoughtful look. He shook his head. "You know the government doesn't do that kind of thing anymore," he said quietly.

"No?" I started to rise.

Baines motioned with his hand. "Sit down, Charlie," he said, a tone of resignation in his voice.

I eased back into the chair.

He gave me a long look. "Maybe something could be . . . arranged."

"Fine, sir."

"And the original files . . ."

"I will turn them over to you. And regarding the shootings last night. There will be questions."

"I'll handle it."

"One other point."

"Yes?"

"Concerning the investigation. I'd like to stay . . . involved."

"Don't trust me, eh, Charlie?"

I said nothing.

Baines reached for the phone. "Have a seat outside. This will take a while."

I didn't move.

"You don't really want to hear this, Charlie."

He was right. I didn't.

I walked out into the anteroom.

52

I WAS DOZING ON THE COUCH WHEN BAINES'S SECRETARY SHOOK ME. MY WATCH SAID ALMOST THREE HOURS HAD PASSED. I WENT BACK INTO the office. Baines didn't say anything specific other than a Mr. Smith would be contacting me soon. He didn't say who Mr. Smith was, and I didn't ask. He also suggested I might want to drive out to Andrews Air Force Base. He mentioned a time.

As I walked out, he said, "We never had this meeting, Charlie."

I kept walking. I went down to the computer center. Jonesy had called me from there about an hour before, saying he swept my car and found both a bug and a tracking device. Maria said something about cruel and unusual punishment as she led me back to her office.

"What do you mean?" I asked.

"The poor guy was absolutely exhausted when he came in." Maria opened her door. "Come to think of it, you don't look too good yourself."

"Thanks a lot."

"You going to tell me what's going on?"

"I will someday."

"Uh-huh."

I followed her inside.

Jonesy was sitting in a chair, legs stretched out, head tilted back. He was snoring.

★★★★

The massive C-5 cargo plane came out of the late-afternoon sun and turned a lazy final as it came in to land at Andrews Air Force Base. Just before touchdown, the high-pitched whine of its engines went quiet as the pilot brought them to idle. The plane touched down smoothly.

"Nice landing," I said.

Jonesy nodded.

We were listening to a soft jazz station on the radio, driving along the flight line past blue and white Air Force Boeing 707s and Learjets used for high-level government travel. In the distance were the enormous hangars that housed the two presidential Boeing 747s.

"Base operations coming up," Jonesy said.

I nodded absently. The music ended. A voice said the five o'clock news was coming up. A moment later, the newscaster came on, saying something about a couple of shootings: one in a Falls Church parking lot and another near the Kimchi Grill in Rosslyn. I turned up the volume.

We headed down a drive toward a C-140 Jetstar mounted on a pedestal. Behind it was the red-brick building that doubled as the air terminal and base operations. We turned into an area with a sign that said, "For General Officer and Equivalents Only."

The news report was saying the killings were probably gang related. Jonesy pulled into a parking spot. The newscaster switched topics, talking about a fatal car crash. Jonesy reached up to kill the ignition, when his hand froze. His eyes went to the radio.

". . . Coletta, chief psychiatrist of the Rolling Hills Sanitarium, died when his car struck a concrete median at a high rate of speed. Recently, Dr. Coletta had been in the news as the individual who had talked to the alleged murderer, Theodore Masonis, the man implicated in the—"

I clicked the radio off.

Jonesy looked at me. "They don't waste much time, do they?"

"No." I reached for the door.

★★★★

Maybe a hundred people, almost all military, milled around inside base operations. I counted seven general officers. I checked my watch and went to the operations counter where a pretty airman stood.

"Oh, miss."

She looked up, smiling.

"When is General Holmes supposed to take off?"

She frowned. "Gosh, sir, in just a few minutes. They're running a little late."

"Oh? Why?"

"Some kind of airplane problem. Ejection seat, I think. Maintenance just finished working on it. Boy, was the general mad."

"How long is he supposed to fly?"

"Flight plan says thirty minutes."

"Thank you." Jonesy and I went outside and stood by the flagpoles. Before us was the enormous tarmac where Air Force One always drops off the President. There was a sleek, twin-engine F-15 fighter there now, a lean pilot in a green flight suit standing next to it. He was talking to a man in fatigues, probably the maintenance supervisor. An honor guard stood at parade rest on the walkway. Nearby, perhaps another fifty or so people were clustered about on the manicured lawn. Three photographers strolled among them, taking pictures of some of the dignitaries. I recognized a handful of congressmen among the uniforms. But I didn't see Holmes. Probably inside, in the distinguished visitors' lounge, I thought.

"So this is General Holmes's fini-flight," Jonesy murmured.

I nodded. Fini-flights were special events for military pilots, their last official flight in an airplane. According to Secretary Baines, Holmes had arranged to have his in the F-15. The plane and instructor pilot had flown up this morning from Langley Air Force Base in Virginia.

Two young female captains were coming toward us. One said, "What do you mean you forgot the camera? I can't believe it."

"I'm sorry, Julie. But I was in such a hurry. The kids were running late this morning. I thought I had the camera in my gym bag."

"You live on base," Julie said. "Go get it. How many chances do you get to be this close to a president?"

"He's not the President yet."

"He will be. Go on."

An irritated sigh. "There's not enough time. Hey, there's Major Sorenson. He's got a camera. Come on."

As the two captains hurried over to a stocky major, I shook my head.

No, he won't.

Then came a voice from behind, an angry voice. I turned.

General Holmes wore an immaculately tailored flight suit.

"What the hell are you doing here, Jensen?" Holmes's face was locked in a snarl. General Tupper stood next to him, looking at me with pure malevolence.

"Official business, sir."

"General Tupper relieved you. He's ordered a court-martial to be initiated." Holmes glanced at Tupper, who was nodding vigorously. "You're in a lot of trouble, Jensen."

I gave Holmes a thin smile. "I've been reinstated, sir."

Holmes's face reddened. "Impossible. Now, get the hell out of here!"

"I suggest you talk to Secretary Baines, sir," I said quickly.

The mention of Baines stopped him. His mouth worked, but no sound came out. He blinked furiously as he tried to figure out how to play the situation. I became aware that people were staring. Holmes must have noticed them, too, because he lowered his voice. "What the hell is going on, Jensen?"

"I suggest you ask Secretary Baines, sir," I repeated.

"Dammit, Jensen!"

"They're ready, General," Tupper interrupted. He indicated the pilot by the jet. The pilot flashed a thumbs-up.

Holmes glared at me. "You be here when I get back."

"Yes, sir," I said calmly.

As Holmes started to turn away, I stepped forward. I probably shouldn't have done it, but I was mad. I wanted to see the bastard sweat. I spoke in his ear, my voice just above a whisper.

Holmes froze. The blood drained from his face and his mouth twitched. He acted as if he wanted to say something. But all eyes were on him and the band started playing. He abruptly turned away and headed down the walkway, the honor guard raising the rifles in a salute as he passed. Shouts of encouragement followed him as the photographers clicked away.

Tupper grabbed my elbow hard. His voice was low, but there was no mistaking the rage.

"What did you say to him, Jensen?"

I glared at him until he released my arm.

"Damn you, Jensen!"

I shrugged. "I told him I have the picture."

Tupper blinked, confusion in his eyes. "What picture?"

"This!" I thrust the photo in front of his face.

"What the—" Tupper took the photo and stared at it. I told him what it was. His face turned pale. He looked up. "My God," he said weakly.

Holmes was at the jet now, climbing up the ladder into the backseat. A crew chief helped him strap in. A few people were watching Tupper and me, giving us curious looks.

"I told you Masonis wasn't the guy, sir," I said softly.

Tupper nodded dumbly, then handed the picture back. His hand shook. "You're going to arrest him when he lands?"

"No, sir," I said.

Tupper looked surprised.

"No," I said again. "I'm not here to arrest him."

Then came a roar from the ramp as the first engine was started. The crowd surged forward against the short metal fence. The photographers scurried out onto the tarmac. The second engine roared to life. Holmes, in the backseat, waved. He was wearing his flight helmet, dark visor down. Still, I think he was looking at me.

As the jet began to taxi, Jonesy and I moved through the crowd onto the edge of the ramp. Once on the parallel, the fighter picked up speed, the shrill whine of the engines slowly fading as it moved away. The cockpit's Plexiglas canopy was still open, but Holmes had stopped waving. The fighter was maybe half a mile away.

We heard no sound when it happened. The rear ejection seat flew straight up into the air, propelled by the plume of a rocket; the frantic gestures of the man still strapped to it were clearly visible. At the apex, the seat hung, then began a slow, tumbling fall to the concrete below.

The crowd was stunned into silence.

The seat bounced once as it struck the concrete taxiway. The crowd became still, all eyes focused on the still form of the man who would have been president.

Then the crowd erupted, some just screaming, others shouting for an ambulance. A few began running out onto the tarmac. The F-15 stopped; the pilot in the front seat looked frantically behind him. I heard the faint sound of a siren.

A hand touched my arm.

"You knew," General Tupper said softly.

"Let's go," I told Jonesy.

As we climbed into the car, Jonesy asked, "Where to now?"

"I want to go home," I told him.

53

THE KIDS AND I HAD JUST COME HOME FROM THE HOSPITAL. THE DOCTOR HAD OKAYED JEAN TO JOIN US FOR DINNER IN THE HOSPITAL CAFETERIA. The food was terrible, but none of us cared. We were just happy being together as a family. Tony and Stacy had been on their best behavior.

I hung up the car keys on the hook by the front door. "Tomorrow's garbage day," I told Tony. "Better put it out."

Tony nodded. "Sure, Dad. Mom looked good, huh?"

"She did."

Jean and I had told the kids that she had an allergic reaction to medication.

A squeal of delight. Stacy looked up from the stack of mail on the kitchen table. "Dad, a letter."

"Yes?"

"From Juilliard."

I grinned. "Open it."

"I . . . I can't."

I came over. "Go on. Open it."

Stacy gave me the letter. "You do it."

"Jeez, Stacy," Tony said. He began removing the garbage pail beneath the kitchen sink.

Stacy bit her lip as I carefully pried open the envelope flap.

"What's it say?"

I looked up, fighting to suppress a smile.

"Dad!"

I thrust out the letter. "You're accepted, sweetheart."

Stacy grabbed the letter from my hand. When she finished reading, she had a dazed look. "I'm . . . I'm going to be a dancer," she said.

I hugged her. "I'm proud of you, sweetheart."

"Hey, that's great, sis," Tony said. He was even grinning.

Then the phone rang. Tony grabbed it. "A Mr. Smith, Dad," he said.

★★★★

I took the call in my study.

"Mr. Smith" gave no identification other than his name. He spoke quickly in a flat monotone. "We found a motel in Alexandria where Colonel Tippett apparently was staying. There were two bodies inside. Asian males. Both had been shot once." He gave me a description. They sounded like the men who had attacked Jean. I told him so.

"Any leads on Colonel Tippett?"

"We found his car, a Ford Mustang, parked at Dulles."

I swallowed. "Was it gray?"

A pause. "Yes. I understand you know Colonel Tippett well?"

"I used to think so."

"Do you have any idea where he might have gone?"

I thought. "No."

"Did he ever mention any special place?"

"Wait. There is one place he talked about. Said he'd like to retire there someday."

"Where?"

"He might have just been talking."

"We'll check it out."

I swallowed, then told him about the place on the beach. After answering a few more questions, I was about to hang up when Mr. Smith said, "Oh, Colonel, have you heard about Dr. Coletta?"

"Yes."

"Fine. Good-bye." The connection went dead.

I stared at the phone for a long time.

Holmes was gone.

Coletta was gone.

Only Tippett remained.

Even after all he'd done, the thought that Tippett had been my friend tugged at me.

A shout from downstairs. "Dad! Are you off the phone? I want to call Brittany. She's going to be so-o-o jealous."

"I'm finished, honey," I said.

I went downstairs and made myself a drink.

★★★★

On Saturday morning Jean and I were sitting on the back porch enjoying a cup of coffee after a late breakfast. Jean had been home a day. She was quiet, almost sad, but not from any lingering effect of the drugs or her ordeal. The night before, I had told her everything about Holmes. Then I told her about Tippett.

She reacted with understandable disbelief and shock. I don't think she fully accepted Tippett's involvement.

I picked up the paper. The headline announced Holmes's funeral was that day at Arlington National Cemetery. I read through the article. A quick rehash of the accident, and a status report on the ongoing investigation into the cause. A short circuit that had initiated the ejection seat was being blamed. Fourth inadvertent ejection-seat firing in ten years. The Air Force was saying there was a design flaw. The manufacturer charged the Air Force with shoddy maintenance. The article finished with particulars on Holmes's career, calling him a genuine American hero. The President was going to give the eulogy. I shook my head and put the paper back on the table.

Jean was staring out over the garden, absently sipping her coffee. We could hear clinking from the kitchen as Stacy and Tony finished doing the dishes. They'd been a big help these past few days.

"You think they'll find him?" Jean murmured.

"Eventually."

"I don't think Dorothy could handle a trial."

I should have let the comment go. But I said, "I don't think that will be a problem."

Jean turned. "How can you be so sure?"

I looked into her eyes. "I just know."

She bit her lip. Her eyes fell on the paper. "You're really bothered that everyone thinks General Holmes was a hero."

"Doesn't it bother you?"

She hesitated. "Yes, but I can live with it. Can you?"

I didn't say anything.

"I can tell what you're thinking, Charlie."

A bird cawed. I avoided Jean's eyes.

Jean sighed. "Oh, Charlie, Charlie . . ." She shook her head.

I took a deep breath and exhaled slowly. "If I had been murdered by Holmes in the war, would you want to know?"

A long pause. Then a nod. She reached out and took my hand. "But if Dorothy ever finds out what Tippett did, it would kill her," she said softly.

"She's a strong woman. She's got Rupert. She'll be okay."

I thought Jean was going to say something else, but thankfully she resumed looking at the garden.

A few minutes later, she murmured, "You'll make a good teacher, Charlie."

I read the headline again.

"I know, honey."

★★★★

I was washing the car later when Jean came running out of the house. Her eyes were wide and she had a look somewhere between fear and shock. She stumbled over her words. "Charlie! Come quick! The phone. God . . . !"

"Jean, calm down. You're not making any sense."

She stopped, sucking down deep breaths. "I . . . he sounds drunk—"

"Who?"

"Tippett!"

I dropped the hose and ran inside.

Jean was right. He sounded drunk. Very drunk, laughing as he talked. "Wish I could see your face, Charlie. You must be shitting in your pants. Am I right? Sorry I had to scare Jean."

"What do you want, Tip?"

"You don't sound very friendly, Charlie. What's the matter? Don't like hearing from the dead?" He laughed again.

"Where are you, Tip?"

The laughter died away. "Hell, you know where I am. You told them, right? Only way they could have known."

I frowned. "What are you talking about?"

"Those bastards outside. I counted four. Could be more. You should see this place I got, Charlie. Right on the beach. Real pretty. You oughta see the sunsets. I was right about Costa Rica."

"Who's outside, Tip?"

"You tell me." He coughed. "The way they shoot, got to be chicken-shit CIA types."

"They're shooting at you?"

He coughed again. "Don't act so goddamn surprised. Tried to take me out on the beach with a fucking rifle. Now they're moving in for the kill."

I heard the sound of gunfire.

"Tip!"

"Just scared them a little, Charlie. We got some time now. Heard about Holmes. Good. Guy was a cocksucker. Even if he did pay well." Another laugh.

I could feel my heart pounding.

The laughter ebbed. Tip's voice became quiet. "Tell Jean I never was going to let them hurt her. Not in a million years."

"I know."

"Or you, Charlie."

I didn't reply.

"Couldn't have anyone mess with my buddy, right?"

Something caught in my throat. "Jesus, Tip. How could you get yourself in this mess?"

A long silence. Then his voice, harsh, bitter. "Two tours in 'Nam. Wounded twice. You know how many people I killed for good ole Uncle Sam? You have any idea? Twenty-seven years I was in. Twenty-seven long years of busting my hump. I gave them everything. For what? Dorothy left me. Army passed over my ass. I was damn near broke. I did what I had to do."

"You killed people. Innocent people."

A deep, wild laugh. "You sanctimonious bastard. You didn't say that when I was killing for Uncle Sam. That killing was okay, huh? But if I kill for ole Tip, that makes me an animal. Go to hell, Charlie. Killing is killing. Let me tell you a little secret." He lowered his voice. "I'm good at it, Charlie."

There was a long, uncomfortable silence. I wondered if Tippett was going to hang up.

"Charlie?"

"I'm still here."

Then, so soft I almost didn't hear, "I could've been a fucking general."

"I know."

Another long pause. "Maybe they were right, after all."

"Who?"

"Maybe . . . maybe I am just a goddamn pig fucker."

"Tip . . ."

"Dammit. The boys are moving again. Gotta run."

A shot. A clatter as the phone struck something hard.

"Tip!"

A groan. The sound of breaking glass.

"You fuckers . . . !"

Flat cracks, rapid-fire.

Silence.

Footsteps.

Voices in Spanish.

The phone went dead.

EPILOGUE

Sunday

THE SUN WAS DIRECTLY OVERHEAD, TURNING THE DAY INTO A SCORCHER. PER-
SPIRATION RAN DOWN MY FACE. MY SHIRT CLUNG TO ME, BUT I WAS ALMOST
finished.

I rubbed the pencil over the paper. The last name appeared almost magically. I handed the paper to Jonesy, who placed it with the others.

"That's twenty-three," Jonesy said. He handed me the stack, which I folded and tucked in my jacket.

I stepped back a few paces and stared at the black granite of the Vietnam Memorial with a sense of profound sadness. All those names, all those men. The usual assortment of mementos: flowers, old war medals, letters, photos, and tiny American flags reverently lining the base.

"Makes you wonder if the war was worth it." Jonesy murmured, a rhetorical question that needed no answer.

"They're here," Jonesy said a few moments later. He was looking down the sidewalk. He picked up the briefcase.

I turned. Two figures came toward us.

Jonesy said softly, "You sure you want to go through with this, sir? Your career will be over. Secretary Baines will crucify you."

I gave him a tired smile. "In a way you're responsible, Jonesy."

"Sir?"

"Right is right. Isn't that what you always say?"

Jonesy didn't reply. But I could see approval in his eyes.

"Charlie!"

Lee and Annie were waving. Annie looked as stunning as ever in a tight-fitting red dress that was far too short to wear on the air.

"Hello, Annie."

"Hello, Charlie. Harry says you have something for me about General Holmes being connected to the murder of General Watkins?"

I nodded to Jonesy. He gave her the briefcase. "Everything's in there, Annie," I said.

"Everything?"

"Yes."

"Why are you doing this?"

I handed her the papers with the twenty-three names. Then I added one more: Brady Hanson.

"What are these for?" Annie asked.

"You'll figure it out," I said.

★★★★

Still so much to do. I had to call Secretary Baines, of course. I owed him that much. Then tonight I would fill out the paperwork to retire from the Air Force.

But now I had to talk to Dorothy. I called her from the car and said I was coming over.

As I parked in the driveway, she came from the house. "Hello, Charlie!" she called.

I slowly climbed from the car.